TO REIGN IN HEAVEN

BY
MELINDA M. SNODGRASS

Credits
Cover Design: by Fakel Barros

When you're Paladins, there's never a day off.

On the eve of his ward's graduation from M.I.T., instead of celebrating, Paladin and warrior Richard Oort finds himself rescuing a young scientist from attack by horrific monsters from an alternate dimension. His ward, Mosi, Paladin-in-training, helps to save the physicist, Fox Erskine. They soon discover why Richard's ancient enemies, the Old Ones, targeted Fox: the Brit is on the verge of developing faster-than-light-speed travel.

Because nothing goes smoothly for Richard, his husband Damon, and Mosi, more mysterious enemies attack the graduation ceremony leaving dozens dead.

The coincidence is too great, and it seems the twin attacks may be intended to stop humans from escaping the confines of Earth. When a rocket carrying a critical component is destroyed on the launch pad, and there are attempts to kidnap Richard and Mosi, it seems certain.

While Richard, Mosi and Damon are dealing with multiple crises, Fox discovers that his efforts to develop a workable model for faster than light travel has birthed fully sentient A.I.. With the A.I.'s assistance, what was merely theory becomes reality.

But Fox's breakthrough represents a profound danger to the other multiverses, and an Old One arrives, not to kill Richard, but to beg for his help. Promised the stars, humans will only trigger devastating genocide.

Faced with a terrible choice that could cost humanity their future among the stars, Richard considers a desperate step which may well forever trap humanity on Earth—and that will require that Richard make the ultimate sacrifice.

But Damon and Mosi may not be willing to let him pay that price.

THE CAROLINGIAN BOOK 4

TO REIGN IN HEAVEN

NEW YORK TIMES BESTSELLING AUTHOR
MELINDA M. SNODGRASS

CHAPTER ONE

IN THE NICK OF TIME

FOX ERSKINE SQUINTED, realizing he was having trouble reading the calculations he was scribbling on his legal pad. He pushed his glasses back up his nose and frowned at the fluorescent lights inside the MIT computer lab. They were slowly dimming. He scratched his head, making his unruly red hair even more unkempt, and reflected again that he needed to stop using paper and scribbling notes by hand. He should really start using a tablet. An iPad Pro would have its own illumination.

The whisper of air conditioning stopped and then the lights went out. The only illumination remaining was provided by the Sofia computer that stood like a massive ice crystal in the center of the room. Whatever was affecting the power in the rest of the building, the quantum computer built by the *Leukós* division of Lumina Enterprises was proving to be resistant. Perhaps, Fox thought, because the computer was linked in network with other Sofias worldwide.

After fruitlessly searching his pockets, Fox finally located his cell phone beneath some loose pages that he had torn from the legal pad in frustration. It too was dead. He glanced down at his Apple watch. Dead. A power outage no longer seemed a logical explanation. Leaving the desk, the young scientist went to the door of the lab, opened it, and peered out. There was a turgid red glow at the far end of the hallway.

Fox started moving cautiously down the hall. The walls on either side seemed to be pulsing like a beating heart. *I'm either having a hallucination or a stroke*, he thought. Neither one seemed like an attractive option. He hesitantly reached out to touch one wall, then snatched his hand back before it connected. Because what if that wall really *was* pulsing? The red light was emanating from what looked like a tear in wall at the end of the hall.

Advance and investigate? The very thought had his breath coming in shallow pants. Fox began backing toward the door of the lab, then yelled in terror as a *thing* came boiling through the jagged opening in the wall. It was like an undulating snake of darkness, and once it spotted Fox, long arms suddenly sprouted from the tubular body.

Fox whirled and ran.

✧   ✧   ✧

"THIS IS *NOT* how I envisioned spending the night before your graduation," her guardian, Richard Oort, groused as they ran across the grassy area between buildings on the MIT campus.

"Yeah, ravening monsters from an alternate dimension just ain't got no manners or sense of decorum," retorted the tall man loping along at Richard's side.

Mosi Tsosie, running on Richard's left, laughed, and her guardian transferred his glare from the taller man on his right to her. Richard wore an impeccably-tailored bespoke suit, while Cross looked like a bum in dirty blue jeans and a tee shirt so faded, that the Milky Way galaxy looked more like a bleach stain, and the arrow and words *You Are Here* could barely be discerned. Although their attire and height weren't the only differences between the men.

There was also the fact that Cross wasn't actually human.

"This is not supposed to be happening," Richard panted as he struggled to keep pace with his taller companions. "We sent you here because this amount of science and tech was supposed to keep Old Ones away," he huffed unhappily.

"And it did for four years," Mosi soothed.

"Which means it's something pretty damn compelling that has drawn them here now," Cross added.

"Where are you leading us?" Richard demanded of Cross. "Where are you sensing the incursion?"

"Don't know for certain. Just know *the magic*"—Cross gave a derisive snort—"is happenin' there." Cross pointed at a building.

"Computer lab," Mosi said. "There's a Sofia in there. That should help slow them down until we arrive."

"Do you sense what the Old One is after?" Richard asked Cross.

"Nope."

"Well, what *do* you know?" Richard snapped.

"That a tear has appeared in the fabric of your reality and some of my kind are coming through. So, we better fucking hurry." Cross abruptly stopped—causing the others to rush past him—and cocked his head to the side in a bird-like gesture. "Oh, and there's a human in there." He smacked his lips. "Tasty one too. Working up from panic to full-on hysterics."

"Stop that," Richard ordered Cross, then said in an aggrieved tone to Mosi, "It's two in the morning. Why on Earth would someone be—"

She ticked off the reasons on her fingers. "College campus. End-of-semester crunch time. Science nerds. Lots of people under thirty. What did you expect?"

"I trust you're not going to tell me that *you've* pulled all-nighters," Richard said as he kicked into a run again.

"Oh no. Of course not. Never. Wouldn't dream of it." She called after his retreating back and watched as his shoulders tensed at her droll tone, then realized he was chuckling.

"Maybe more rescuing and less talking?" Richard called. Mosi and Cross exchanged glances, then soon caught up with Richard.

"Wish the damn things had attacked a graduation bash at one of the frat houses. At least we could have gotten a drink after this was all over," Cross grumbled.

✧ ✧ ✧

FOX SLAMMED THE door, threw the lock, and pressed his back against the metal and glass. Breathing hard, he groped in a pocket for his inhaler and took a hit. Then yelled in terror as the window in the door shattered and an appendage dripping a foul-smelling ichor thrust through. There was now a mass of stubby fingers on the end of a club-like hand. As Fox watched in horror, they began to lengthen, narrow, wriggle, and grope. Electricity seemed to dance on the tips.

And they were reaching for him.

With a sob of fear, he threw himself down on the floor. His glasses went flying and the objects in the room became blurry. Cursing, he belly-crawled toward the Sofia while sweeping his hands all around as he searched for his lost glasses. *So you can see the thing that's going to kill you better? What the fuck!* He found the glasses and jammed them back on.

He was at the base of the computer now and rolled over in time to see the thing come oozing through the shattered window. The shards of glass embedded in the frame scored its tubular body and more ichor ran down the inside of the door from the cuts. Fox's head was snapping from side to side as he looked for anything he could use as a weapon. The smooth concrete floor offered nothing. The chair in which he had been seated was too far away.

The thing was fully in the room now. There was a loud bang as something crashed against the door. The monster paused in its undulating advance on Fox, and the strange flattened face turned away from him and back toward the door. Another blow and the door flew open—shards of wood from the door frame flying into the room. The door crashed against the wall, and a dark-haired woman and a blond man charged through. The woman was far taller than the man and her longer strides had her rapidly closing in on the thing.

The man shouted a warning. "Look out!"

The creature had extruded four more arms and reached for the girl. Her long black hair flying like a pennant, she dropped to her knees, bending backward until the back of her head was nearly touching the floor, and she went sliding beneath the flailing arms.

"Mosi," the small man called, and he threw an intricately-twisted grey glass object to her.

She caught it out of the air, leaped to her feet, placed her hand against the base of the object and pulled. A space-black blade filled with swirling points of light like stars appeared as if from the palm of her hand, and there was a basso sound like the largest cosmic organ had just played a single shivering note.

The swirling lights seemed to rise up from the blade, twining themselves about her body until she was wrapped in a nimbus of stars. With a grace worthy of a dancer, she spun on one foot and the blade cut completely through the body of the monster. The two parts fell apart and were reduced to bubbling, stinking sludge.

Fox threw up.

"More comin' through," called another man who was standing in the hallway. In his torn, food-stained jeans and tee shirt, he looked like one of the homeless men who shuffled into the shelter over on Albany Street.

The girl threw the sword to the small blond man and as soon as it left her hand the blade vanished. The blond caught it with his left hand, and repeated the gesture the girl used with his right hand. The blade reappeared along with the bone-shaking musical note.

"See to him," the man ordered with a jerk of his head toward Fox, and trailed by that nimbus of stars, he plunged into the hall. The homeless guy had vanished, then a strange and horrifying screaming and keening began.

Fox climbed to his feet and staggered toward the door.

The girl put a slim hand against his chest and held him back. "You probably don't want to go out there."

"Yes! I, by God, do! What the fucking hell is going on?"

"Well, aliens from a nearby multiverse seem to want to kill you. We'll figure out why after we deal with the rest of them." Her tone was as matter-of-fact as if she were discussing the weather or the prospects for a sports team.

He goggled at her then mumbled, "I'm rather sorry I asked. On the other hand, I'm now bloody well determined to see what's happening."

She shrugged. "Okay," and she stepped aside to allow him to enter the hallway.

The ungodly sounds were emanating from the homeless man, echoed by equally frightful shrieks from another creature like the one the girl had just dispatched. The space-black blade of the sword was weaving an intricate pattern in front of the monster as its multiple arms swiped at the small blond man. The bright bolts of electricity arcing in the darkness had Fox's eyes watering as the monster tried desperately to electrocute the sword wielder. Electricity was sparking against the walls as it swung its arms wildly.

The angry red light poured through a jagged tear in the wall, and through that opening Fox could see strange trees like black broccoli, buildings that seemed to be floating and a bloated red sun low on the horizon. He stood transfixed.

The swordsman fell back as if defeated. The creature leaped, arms and legs coiling like a horrifying jumping spider, but before it bore the man to the ground, the blade was there, driving up through the creature's chin to emerge from the top of its head. The man rolled out of the way as this monster also collapsed into bubbling sludge. He climbed to his feet, rested the point of the sword on the floor and leaned on it, panting for a moment.

"Fucking close the tear already or we'll be up to our asses in motherfuckin' monsters!" the homeless man yelled.

The blond man lifted the sword and the point wove back and forth like a tailor stitching a tear in cloth. The opening vanished, leaving strange grey striations in the drywall, like the shadowed imprint of a spider web. The only other evidence of what had just occurred was the green and black ichor bubbling and pooling on the linoleum, and the burned places on the walls and floor from the electricity the creature had been throwing about.

The man drew his hand down the length of the blade and it seemed to sink into the hilt. Which, upon closer inspection, Fox realized was in the shape of a Klein bottle. A twitch of his suit coat and the hilt was placed in a holster at the small of the man's back. In that moment Fox saw that he also wore a shoulder holster and the butt of a pistol was terrifyingly evident. *God, these Americans and their bloody guns,* Fox thought.

Hand outstretched, the man walked toward him. His panic subsiding, Fox was able to truly study his three rescuers. The blond man looked to be somewhere in his early forties with a few threads of almost undetectable silver in his platinum blond hair, but what really stood out were his preternatural good looks and the fact he was very short.

The girl was equally stunning with long black hair that hung almost to her hips, winged brows over dark, expressive eyes, and tawny skin. She also looked vaguely familiar to him. The bum had brown hair that brushed his shoulders, and a beard and mustache. It suddenly occurred to Fox that he looked like one of the more insipid paintings of Jesus Christ ... if the Son of God had mustard stains on his shirt and had a tendency to curse like a drunken sailor.

"Hello. Allow me to introduce myself. I'm Richard Oort." Fox tried to process that and failed. "This is my ward, Mosi Tsosie."

She raised a slim, tan hand, "Hi."

"And this is Cross."

The bum put two fingers to his forehead in a sloppy salute. "Yo."

Fox didn't accept Oort's proffered hand. He tried to speak and a sound emerged that was more like a squeak than an actual word.

"And you are?" Oort prompted. The man's cultured East Coast accent combined with the commonplace pleasantries seemed surreally out of place in a hallway filled with stinking, bubbling monster goo.

Fox cleared his throat and tried again, "Pardon me, but I think I need to have a bout of very strong hysterics before ... before ..."

"Quite all right. Take your time," Oort said.

The older man turned away to speak to the homeless man while Fox tried again to process that Richard fucking Oort, CEO of Lumina Enterprises, and one of the wealthiest men in the world, had just made like some kind of ninja super hero—along with a stunningly beautiful girl who could double as Black Widow or Wonder Woman or Captain Marvel—and they had saved him with a sword that magically appeared and disappeared into a Klein bottle, and killed monsters leaving only—

"Best not leave this mess for the janitorial staff," the aforementioned superhero was saying to the guy called Cross, as he gestured at the remains of the monsters Fox had just been contemplating.

"So, *I* get to clean up stinky Old One ooze? Gee thanks, boss." Cross said.

The beautiful girl, Mosi, walked over. "If you're done with your rather demure bout of hysterics, I think it would be best if you come back to the hotel with us."

"Yeah, buy the poor sap a drink. He looks like he could use one," Cross called, as he returned with a rolling bucket and mop from the janitor's closet. The rattle of the plastic wheels across the linoleum seemed to echo Fox's suddenly chattering teeth.

"Thank you, but I think I'd rather just go home. Have a cup of tea," Fox stuttered.

Mosi rolled her eyes. "Oh god, you're a cliché." Her smile removed any sting. "And could we learn your name?"

"Um ... Fox ... Erskine ... Fox Erskine, and don't we need to call ... the authorities?" Fox asked haltingly.

"Who ya gonna call?" Cross sang out as he dunked the mop into the soapy water in an imitation of the theme song to *Ghostbusters*. "Seriously, the fuckin' ghost busters just showed up and saved your skinny ass. You think there's somebody *better* qualified to deal with this shit?"

Oort ignored both the girl and the bum. His gaze was firm, almost cold as he fixed his stare on Fox and said, "I'm afraid that wasn't actually a request, however graciously Mosi might have phrased it. We need to find out why the Old Ones want you dead."

Fox felt his lungs squeezing down. "I-I need my ... inhaler. Dropped it when ... when—"

"A monster tried to kill you?" Cross suggested cheerfully, as he started to mop at the ichor. It stirred up the reek once more.

Fox threw up again.

"Dude! Seriously?" Cross yelped.

CHAPTER TWO

THE SECRET BEHIND THE WORLD

"**I** CAN'T BELIEVE I'm sitting in a hotel suite with *the* Richard Oort. The man who owns Lumina Enterprises. Who holds the patent on the Sofia quantum computer. Who built a private space launch program and an orbital construction platform. And you have a private security force like a freaking Bond villain—" Fox broke off with a gasp, unable to process that he'd just allowed his misfiring thoughts to emerge from his traitorous mouth. Also, he'd run out of breath. He took another hit on his inhaler.

His arrival at the Four Seasons Hotel had been surreal. Despite it being three in the morning, there had been a man and woman overtly loitering in the lobby, positioned so they could watch both the front doors and the bank of elevators. They had exchanged small nods with Richard.

Once they reached the top floor that held the presidential suite, there had been two men waiting. One at the elevators, and one at the end of the hallway, posted by the door into the Presidential suite. They too had exchanged small nods with Richard, and Fox had realized with shock that they were *all* private security.

It felt like a world torn from the pages of some of his favorite novels or a James Bond movie which was why he had just said the quiet part out loud in front of *everyone*.

"But of course I don't mean you're anything at *all* like a Bond villain. I mean you're doing God's work ... with the environment ... but with science ... lots and lots of ... *science* ..." His voice dwindled away like water in desert sands.

An older man, Damon Weber, who had been introduced as Oort's husband, gave a snort of laughter that caused the tea he was offering to Fox to slosh over the rim of the cup, and said, "Easy there, junior. Maybe slow your roll." Fox noticed how Weber's suit jacket hung on his frame, and he wondered if the man had been or was currently ill.

Fox rolled a frantic eye toward Mosi. His faux pas had stopped her in the process of exploring the offerings in the room service fridge, and Fox couldn't help but notice how her tight jeans defined her buttocks as she bent over, or that when she cast back her waist length hair, it caused her back to arch and her breasts to press against the material of her crisp white shirt.

She was smirking at Oort who was leaning casually against the credenza that held an array of liquor bottles and tools appropriate for mixology, but the man's ice-blue gaze wasn't on the girl. It was laser-focused on *him*, and Fox had a dreadful feeling his reaction to Mosi had *not* gone unnoticed.

Oort had loosened his tie and discarded the suit coat, which made the leather shoulder holster and pistol all the more obvious. Fox found himself staring at the weapon. Oort's gaze on him didn't waver.

✧ ✧ ✧

DAMON CAUGHT THE byplay and found it oddly endearing. Richard prided himself on his emotional control—a thing Damon did not consider to be an actual asset—but it was the legacy of his emotionally repressed family and rigid upbringing. To see his spouse acting like a typical father when he realizes that his little girl isn't such a little girl any longer, amused him.

Damon crossed to Richard, slipped an arm around his waist, and gave him a kiss on the cheek. He said softly into his ear, "Honey, don't terrify the kid by acting like a cliché. He's had a rough night. And as you well know, nearly dying is one hell of an aphrodisiac."

Blue eyes looked up to his. They held a jumble of emotions, and Richard's expression was regretful and wistful. Damon hugged Richard closer to his side.

There was a sharp rap on the door. Mosi went to answer, revealing Estevan, Lumina's head of security, along with Cross, who carried a large box from the all-night pizza joint near campus. The smell of grease, pepperoni, and jalapeño entered the room along with the pair. Cross settled at the table, popped open the box, and began gulping down a slice of pizza. Damon swallowed hard, forcing down the sudden rise of nausea. Richard gave him a concerned glance, but Damon just shook his head, indicating he was okay. At least for the moment.

Richard stepped away from him and made introductions. "Dr. Erskine, my head of security, Estevan Gallegos. Estevan, Dr. Erskine. Dr. Erskine is to be treated as essential personnel," Richard ordered. Damon watched to see how that landed. The boy blanched a bit, clearly understanding the implication.

"Got it, sir," the security chief said.

"Um," Fox began and the boy shrank down when he realized he was the center of attention. "Uh, in the interest of full disclosure, I'm not a doctor yet. I'm finishing up my PhD. Hoping to defend in the fall."

"All right, *Mr.* Erskine," Richard corrected. So, tell us what you are working on."

"And more to the point, why is it so interesting to my kind?" Cross mumbled around a huge bite of pizza.

"Your ... what? Wait."

"Aliens, kid. But we don't come in peace for all mankind," Cross said and gave a loud belch.

Exasperated, Richard asked, "Must you add to the general confusion right now?"

"So what were you gonna tell him? Monsters? That would be better how?" Cross asked.

Fox cleared his throat, pushed his glasses back up his nose, and ran a hand through his hair. Damon would have loved to know what the kid was thinking as he watched what seemed to be a bum and the man he knew to be a billionaire exchanging glares. Damon gave a soft snort. Kid must think he fell through the looking glass. That sure as hell was how Damon had felt all those years ago when he had been brought in as a soldier in this secret war.

"So, you're saying those things ... those things in the computer lab ... they were ... aliens?" the boy squeaked.

"Yep," Cross said.

"And they were there because ..." Fox's voice trailed away. Damon had spent nearly two decades as a cop and it was pretty clear the boy wasn't at all sure he wanted to hear the answer.

"Like I said before, they were there to kill you," Mosi casually said, as she sat down next to the white-faced young man.

The ease with which this almost-daughter said those words made Damon sad. He knew it had been necessary for Richard to bring her into their strange and secret world. It was the only way to keep her safe. And the fact that she's a Paladin—like her guardian—meant that she is intimately familiar with death and battle, and had been since the age of nine.

Fox paled and Damon quickly crossed to him. "Sure you don't want a splash of something stronger in that tea?"

Damon watched the boy's Adam's apple bob as he swallowed hard. "I'm rather afraid I'd go off into loud hysterics if I did, sir."

"Don't believe him," Mosi said. "He said that before and then didn't."

"He just puked," Cross added helpfully. "Twice."

"Ignore these reprobates," Damon said, as he jerked a thumb toward Cross and his chin toward Mosi. "And please call me Damon."

"Damon," Fox repeated. "Well, perhaps a touch of whiskey."

"Good man." Damon clapped him on the shoulder and went back to the credenza.

"I mean seriously, if that was hysterics, it was pretty

tame," Mosi said. Damon kept a discreet eye on them as he located the whiskey and watched Mosi nudge Fox with her shoulder.

"I *am* British," Fox said.

Damon returned with the bottle and Fox rather desperately shoved his cup at him. Alcohol gurgled from the bottle, and Fox took a large sip and coughed. Damon *had* poured pretty liberally.

Fortified, Fox continued. "So, that hole … in the wall, that was another planet?"

They all shared a look. "Kid catches on quick," Damon said to Richard.

The boy set aside the cup and saucer, jumped up and paced, running his hands frantically through his hair. "You weren't supposed to say *that*. You were supposed to tell me that was a mad idea." His knees seemed to give out and he plopped back down on the couch.

"Want me to do the lecture, *Na sha dii?*" Mosi asked.

Richard gestured with his glass. "Please."

"Okay." She took a deep breath, shook back her hair, and turned to face Fox. "Intelligence, sentience, whatever you want to call it, is a somewhat rare and precious commodity in our universe. There are a lot of false starts and evolutionary dead ends on the road to achieving it, and often the species developing it gets snuffed out before they achieve full consciousness. Sometimes it's just bad luck—asteroids, volcanoes, floods—but sometimes this emerging intelligent species does it to themselves, helped out by malevolent outside forces. What you met tonight are some of those forces. Ever wonder why SETI never detected signals from any other sentient races out in the stars? It's because of the Old Ones."

"But why? Why would they do that?" Fox interrupted.

"Because you're tasty," Cross said, and he smacked his lips and swallowed in a most horrifying way.

Mosi bent a disapproving look on the bum and continued. "That was another planet, but it's not in our universe. It's in one of the twenty-three multiverses where reality is sometimes very different. The Old Ones tear holes in our reality and slip through. Sometimes they have enough power to build actual gates—"

"I remember there was something about this back when I was a kid. Stories in the tabloids. Most people thought it was just a Murdoch paper doing what they do best: spreading fear and disinformation."

"I like this kid," Damon murmured to Richard.

"When did you become this trusting, *Detective*?" Richard shot back, teasing, but his expression held a world of love.

"Point is," Cross interrupted. "it *was* true and we came marching through."

"But ... but ... you don't look anything like those ... things," Fox said.

"My true form is more fractal, but I can look like any damn thing I please."

"Not exactly true," Damon said. "Your appearance is very dependent on humans."

"Great, thanks for reminding me! Anyway, Richard got them all closed with a bit of help from the kid here—" Cross gestured at Mosi.

"But why? Why come here? What is it they ... you ...

want from us?" Fox cried.

"I told you. You are food," Cross said.

Mosi responded to Fox's look of utter confusion. "They feed on emotions. The stronger the emotion the more sustenance they receive. Violent, dark emotions are easy to elicit. Rage, fear, grief, pain … hate."

Richard spoke up. "As the founder of Lumina once told me, 'Humans are utterly unique in how they experience joy. There is nothing unique in how they experience hate, pain, grief, and death.'"

"Truth is we humans aren't that long out of the trees," Damon said. "The lizard brain still holds a lot of sway. We are genetically hardwired to fear *the other*, and it leads to the primitive hates that makes us kill each other over skin color, religious creeds, the notion of nation states."

Cross pushed back the pizza box with a harsh grating sound in the silence. "But that's not all that draws us. Any creature with a central nervous system can fear and hurt and fight and kill. We're drawn by your creativity, that spark that makes you paint the frescos of the Sistine Chapel or compose a Mozart symphony."

"How could they exist here and us not be aware?" Fox cried.

"Oh, we were aware," Richard said. "We just didn't understand what they were … *are*. Basically they are every god and dark myth that humans ever created."

"And they have worked very hard to encourage us to feed the wrong wolf," Mosi said.

"To embrace the darkest angels of our natures," Damon concluded.

Cross grinned. Damon found the creature's smiles to be more horrifying than comforting. "Ironic turn of phrase there, Weber, since we've pretended to be angels more than a few times," Cross said.

"Point being, that Lumina is dedicated to the fight to hold back the darkness," Richard said. "To counter superstition and religion with science and rationality, tolerance, and acceptance." Richard handed off his glass to Damon, and walked over until he was looking down at Fox. "But right now we need to figure out why they want to kill *you*. Badly enough that they expended the energy to tear a hole in reality."

"Which is why we're pretty sure that whatever you are working on is what drew their attention," Mosi concluded.

"I've … I've got this idea—more of a notion, really—that we can fold the dimensions and create a way to transcend the limit dictated by the speed of light. I was having Sofia run the calculations."

They all exchanged glances. "Well, that would certainly get our fucking attention," Cross huffed.

"*If you follow my path I'll give you the stars*," Richard murmured and he seemed to be looking at something far away and long ago.

"Richard, this would be a real game changer for my kind," Cross said. "They'd be desperate to stop this. Only one other time has a species eluded us. You know what I'm talkin' about."

Damon kept his focus on the Brit scientist. They all knew what they were talking about, but it was clearly overwhelming and confusing to the young man. Agitated, Fox lurched to his feet. Over the years Damon had watched exhaustion hit Richard like a sandbag, and he saw it happening now to the skinny redhead. Fox stood swaying, probably from the loss of adrenaline and the whiskey he'd just drunk.

"Look, it's been delightful ... sort of. And thank you very much for rescuing me, but I'm fagged to death and I just want to go home now."

The four Lumina people exchanged glances again. Fox caught it and tensed. Richard gave a regretful headshake. "I'm afraid we can't let you do that."

"Do you mean to imprison me?" The boy's voice was high and breathless with anxiety.

Damon risked taking a few steps toward the agitated scientist, hands raised as if gentling a frightened horse. "Nope, son, just protect you."

Mosi looked over at Richard. "We can put him in the extra bedroom. And I won't go back to my apartment tonight. That way we can share guard duty."

"That works," Richard said.

✦　✦　✦

MOSI MADE A gesture that Fox couldn't totally interpret as she said, "Do you want to ...?"

Oort sighed. "May as well get it over with now."

Fox looked from one to the other with growing alarm. "Get *what* over with? Oh shit"—he breathed when he saw Oort removed the hilt of the sword from its holster and draw the blade—"you're going to kill me," he squeaked.

Oort chuckled. "No—"

"Though you might *wish* you'd died," Cross interrupted.

That earned another glare from Oort, and a firm *hush* from Mosi. She laid a hand on Fox's shoulder. "It probably won't hurt that much. It doesn't generally hit people in STEM programs all that hard."

Oort lifted the blade holding it vertically in front of his face. He inspected the blade. "This sword destroys the effects of non-Euclidean or hyperbolic geometry on our particular multiverse."

"We usually just shorthand that and say that it kills magic," Damon offered.

"Given his training, I thought he'd appreciate a more scientific explanation," Richard said, sulking a bit.

"Magic isn't real," Fox mumbled. "This is crazy."

"Oh, it's real all right," Cross said. "My kind saw to that. We did some selective breeding on early humans to make it easier to feed on you," Cross jerked a thumb at Oort. "He's going to zap you with the sword and destroy the magic in your DNA. It'll make it harder for us to find you and impossible for us to feed on you, which makes you kind of unattractive. Oh, and it also hurts like a motherfucker. It would kill me," he added and shot Oort a look that Fox couldn't fully interpret.

Fox blanched. "You've all gone through this?"

Mosi and Richard exchanged another glance. Damon spoke up. "I have. It's not that bad. As for Richard and Mosi ... well, they're special."

Oort advanced on him. Fox threw up a hand. "Wait. I have questions—"

Oort moved with blinding speed, spinning gracefully and

lunging. The flat side of the blade touched Fox lightly on the ribs and blinding pain ripped through his body. He doubled over and collapsed onto the carpet. His body shuddered for a few minutes. Tears ran down his face, and he could feel himself drooling into the carpet. Then it was over. Damon helped him to his feet, and handed him a handkerchief to wipe his streaming eyes.

"Well done, son. You handled it better than most."

"Hey, at least you didn't puke again," Cross said. "Win-win, amirite?"

Damon took Fox by the elbow. "Let me show you the room. Nothing of Richard's will fit you, but I can stake you some underwear and a razor."

Fox realized he was too tired and confused to argue.

CHAPTER THREE

HANG ON FOR THE RIDE

RICHARD AND MOSI watched Damon and the boy as they left the sitting room. Once they were gone, Richard turned to his ward.

"You're going to be so tired for your graduation," Richard said. "You should sleep. Damon and I can handle this."

Mosi gave him a kiss on the cheek. "I'm twenty-one, not undergoing cancer treatments, and while I really don't want to admit this to you—I have pulled more than a few all-nighters during my college years. So, no. I'm going to help."

Like the shadow of a negative when film had been used to create photographs, the echo of the tall and leggy nine-year-old he'd met thirteen years before, in a dusty living room in Shiprock, New Mexico, seemed superimposed over the beautiful young woman who now stood before him. Soon she would graduate with a master's and top honors from MIT, but back then she had been an orphaned, frightened, sullen, angry child whose life had been utterly destroyed by forces she could not fathom, and none of the people around her would believe what she had seen.

Her beloved older brother had been seduced and controlled by the Old Ones leading him to kill their entire family. He had tried to kill her, but through the grit and tenacity that was the hallmark of the girl, she had escaped. Richard had always suspected she was the one the Old Ones had really wanted dead because they knew she was a Paladin. Her mother, father, grandfather—and ultimately her brother—had just been collateral damage.

Richard had gone to Shiprock to tell her that she wasn't crazy, as was being whispered by her Navajo relatives, along with the local police and FBI investigating the killing of her family. Richard had done it because while he had never experienced the kind of trauma Mosi had endured, he had grown up in a family where he was also viewed as the disappointment, the failure, and he knew how the attitudes of a person's loved ones could warp and damage them.

Once he realized what she was, and confident that his enemies would either try to co-opt or murder her, Richard had his sister Pamela set the legal wheels turning so he could become her guardian.

He and Mosi had faced death and danger together, and at sixteen she began to fight by his side. His sister Pamela hated that he took Mosi into danger and argued strenuously against it. Richard hated it too, but he was weighing their two lives against the safety of humanity. Logic dictated he prepare her to be his successor. The sort-of-father he had become railed against that decision but Mosi understood—probably even better than Richard himself—what was at stake, and she never hesitated.

To try and protect her, Richard had made certain she was proficient with all manner of weapons including the sword. To try and erase the grief and sadness he sometimes saw in those dark eyes, she had had horses, any pet she desired, learned to play the violin, skied at Taos Valley and in Switzerland, traveled the world—and not always in search of monsters to slay. Sometimes it was just to attend opening night at La Scala, view the northern lights in Norway, or see the cherry blossoms at the Fuji Shibazakura Festival.

She had been homeschooled by the finest of teachers, many of whom were Lumina employees. When she turned eighteen, it was Damon who had gently, but firmly, told Richard that she had to attend university and be allowed to fly and test her wings. Her test scores were off the charts, and it was hard to argue that the various colleges couldn't judge how well prepared she might be when her teachers were Prize-winning scientists and writers, world-renowned artists, and musicians. Once she had settled on MIT, Richard had made an extremely generous grant to the university. That hadn't hurt either.

It suddenly struck Richard that she had now spent more time with him than with her actual parents. *I've tried to do right by her*, he said mentally to the man and woman he had never met. *And I promise I'll do everything I can to* keep *her safe.*

"What? Why are you looking at me like that?" Mosi asked with a catch of laughter in her voice.

"Just thinking how much I love you."

She hugged him. "Oh, *Na sha dii,* now you're going to make me cry. And I couldn't love you more if you had been my own father."

But I'm not your father. He found that the thought made his heart ache. He would have to analyze that after this current crisis was past. He gave a mental snort of derision. As if there wouldn't always be another crisis looming somewhere.

He shook off the melancholy. "So you graduate tomorrow. What's next? Grad school? Get that PhD?" he asked.

"I'd like to take a year off. Work with you," she said. "I miss New Mexico, and I want to spend time with Damon—" She broke off abruptly. It hung there between them, the truth that he was desperately trying to deny. "Not that anything … I mean … the treatments …"

"Are helping," Richard said and he quickly changed the subject. "But Mosi, I know you have your duty, but I also want you to have your own life—career, husband, children. You shouldn't have to give up everything to Lumina."

"I'm a Paladin." She gestured between them. "That's our reality. Nothing exists beyond that. Until we know humanity is safe, we have a duty." She gave him an impish grin. "And what does it say on that badge you still hang onto? *To protect and serve.*" She was gazing at him now with that soft half-smile she had, love glowing in her dark eyes. "Also, if I tried to just go be a normal person living in the 'burbs, or even back in *Diné Bikéyah*, the Old Ones and their creepy minions would find me and Mr. Mosi and all the little Mosis, and then you'd have to come riding to our rescue."

Richard found himself remembering all the wounds he'd received in the years since Kenntnis, the founder of Lumina had found and recruited him. He had been tortured, shot, beaten, bit, and clawed. Some of the wounds still pained him and nightmares haunted his sleep. He didn't want that for Mosi. He never wanted to see that beautiful face scarred, but he had to acknowledge that she *was* scarred emotionally in a way that would never completely heal.

It wasn't fair that only the two of them and an alien quisling to his own kind stood against the darkness, but such was their fate. Then he realized this was exhaustion and worry darkening his thoughts. It wasn't just the three of them.

There was the army of scientists who worked in Lumina labs, the aid workers bringing clean water, medicine, and schools to places in need, the security forces who backed up Richard and Mosi when Old Ones preyed on innocent people and a Paladin was needed.

There was his sister, the lawyer, who worked for Lumina. His COO and CFO who kept Lumina profitable and able to fund the scientists, aid workers, and fighters. There was Angela Armandariz, coroner-turned-senator who fought for them in Washington. No, they were not alone.

You proud of me yet, Papa? Richard gave his head an angry shake. Why did the past always have this power to reach out and grab him by the throat? He hadn't spoken to the man in over a decade. Why couldn't he banish Robert Oort as effectively from his thoughts?

He forced the spiraling insecurities back into their lockbox and turned the mental key. "All right, we'll discuss this more after you get home for the summer break. And I expect your gaggle of Dutch uncles are going to have something to say about this."

Mosi rolled her eyes. "I prefer to call them my nerd posse."

"Whatever, they love you. That's why they're all here to see you graduate."

"Like I'm not nervous enough."

"You'll do fine. Speech all written?"

"And memorized." She laid a hand on his arm. "I'll take the first shift. Why don't you get some sleep."

"Makes sense, but wake me."

"I promise."

He handed off the sword to her and went into the bedroom. Slipping off his loafers he laid down on top of the covers next to Damon who had already gone to bed and was asleep. He wrapped an arm around his husband's waist, and buried his face against his Damon's shoulder. He could hear the rasp in Damon's breaths as he struggled for air and fought the cancer ravaging his lungs.

Don't die. Don't die. I can't bear it if you die. I can't do this without you. Richard closed his eyes and willed himself to sleep.

✦ ✦ ✦

THE SOUND OF a shower running next door woke him. Fox stumbled out of bed to discover clean underwear had been left on the dresser. It was welcome but his outer clothes that he'd left in a heap in the bathroom were rumpled and smelled of sweat and alien funk. He really didn't want to put them back on so he opted for one of the hotel's luxurious robes instead. He wondered if the hotel could launder his clothes, or if someone could swing by his apartment and pick some up. Drawn by the smell of coffee, Fox shuffled nervously out of the bedroom.

Mosi sat at the small table with a room service cart loaded down with chaffing dishes and china next to her. She was wearing a stylish black dress that showed off her legs, and a pair of Louboutins were tumbled on the floor next to her, displaying their trademark red soles. A graduation gown was tossed carelessly over the back of the sofa. With shock, Fox realized that his one suit and a white dress shirt were (unlike the gown) laid neatly across the back of the sofa. The arm of the jacket and the arm of her gown were touching cuffs as if looking to shyly hold hands. Fox quickly and *firmly* banished *that* thought.

She smiled at him as she lifted the lid off a chaffing dish filled with eggs Benedict. "Good morning."

"Why is my suit here? And who broke into my apartment to get it?"

"You're going to attend the graduation. Only way for us to keep an eye on you. And it was Cross and he used your key, so no crime was committed in the attainment of your suit." She took a long, slow sip of her coffee her dark eyes dancing with merriment over the edge of the cup. "How did you sleep?" she inquired in a tone so innocent that it should have been criminal.

"Like someone who nearly died, got hit by a sword that made me wish I had died, so I slept like I had obliged. On the plus side, I didn't have nightmares about monsters from another dimension." He sat down across the table from her and accepted a cup of coffee. "By the way, very glad not to be ... dead, I mean. So, if I wasn't sufficiently clear last night—thank you very much for saving my life."

"You're welcome. Eggs Benedict, bacon, sausage, hash browns, and toast. What would you like?"

"All of the above. Quite famished."

"I'm told getting inoculated does take it out of you," she said watching him as he filled a plate.

"Yes, about that. Last night Mr. Weber ... Damon ... said you and Mr. Oort were special. What did he mean?" He began to tuck into his breakfast.

"We're Paladins." Her dark eyes were dancing again with mischief.

He set aside his fork. "Well, that clears things right the hell up. And what, pray tell, is a Paladin when they're at home and not in a *D&D* game? And don't say *us*," he warned.

She pouted. "You're no fun. Okay." She sighed and ran her fork through the congealing hollandaise sauce on her plate. "Richard and I are genetic freaks, born without any vestige of magic in our DNA. It's why we can use the sword."

"But according to Cross you zapped all the magic out of me, so shouldn't I be able to use the"—he hesitated, it sounded so stupid even saying it—"sword?"

"Here try it," she offered, and tossed the hilt to him. Fox failed to catch it and winced when it bounced off the table and onto the floor. Mosi laughed at his expression. "It's not going to break. I'm not sure anything short of throwing it into the sun could damage it, and maybe not even that."

He stood, picked it up, and emulated the gesture used by both Mosi and Richard. Nothing happened.

"Well, that's bloody annoying." He returned the hilt to her, sat down, and resumed eating. "Is there like a spell or something?"

"Quite the opposite, this thing is made of science. Your reaction to the sword last night proved you had magic in your DNA, so *ipso facto*, you are not a Paladin, *ergo* no sword for you," she concluded in an adorable imitation of the Soup Nazi from the old *Seinfeld* television show.

Fox rubbed the back of his neck and eyed the hilt, which rested on the table near her elbow. "So why a sword?"

"The weapon was made back in the early bronze age so we're kind of stuck with it. But it's a good thing you asked me instead of *Na sha dii*. Otherwise you would've had to listen to him bitch for ten solid minutes about why did it have to be a fucking sword—though he wouldn't say fucking—and why couldn't Kenntnis have turned it into something more useful and modern, like a taser or a gun, so he didn't have to get so *up close and personal with goddamn monsters*? Except he wouldn't say goddamn, he'd say darn. But to make a long story short, so far our science team hasn't been able to crack how it works, much less how to modify it. Or better still, make another one."

"Okay, now I have like a thousand more questions."

"Ask away."

"Why do you call Mr. Oort *Na sha dii*?" He stumbled a bit over the unfamiliar words. "What language is that and what does it mean?"

"It's Navajo and it means protector. My family was slaughtered by ... well, indirectly by Old Ones. Richard felt he owed me an explanation about what had happened, and to reassure me that I hadn't imagined the evil faces on the computer screen. My aunt *did* think I was crazy or even a *áńt'į́įhii*—that means witch—so she was more than happy to let Richard become my guardian and get me the hell out of her house."

She fell silent for a moment and gazed down at a beautiful turquoise ring she wore. "I wanted to start calling him Dad, but he never would let me. Said he knew how much I loved my real father, and that he would never try to usurp him that way. Even though I've lived with Richard longer than with my own family."

"I still don't fully understand why he adopted you."

"Not adopted. Legally he couldn't. He's my guardian, but to answer your question, he discovered I could draw the sword."

"So, he just casually gave a little kid a sword?" Fox asked.

"No, silly. He went to inoculate me and I just looked at him like he was one crazy *bilagáana*. That means white person," she added helpfully. "*Then* he handed me the hilt and asked me to, you know." And picking up the hilt she pulled her hand away and the blade appeared. The musical chord hung in the air, but much softer than it had last night.

Fox stared at that space-black blade in wonder. "Where does it go?"

"Best guess, a pocket universe," she said.

Fox's eyes widened. "Oh bloody hell, that *thing* might be the key to my problem."

"And what problem is that?" Richard asked, as he emerged from the bedroom, followed closely by Damon.

"How to move matter through the multiverse," Fox explained. He gestured at the sword. "Apparently that thing can do it."

Richard and Mosi exchanged a pregnant look. "Sounds like he needs to finish his PhD working for Lumina," she said.

"I agree," Richard said.

"Do I have any say in this?" Fox yelped.

Damon paused in filling his plate and gave Fox's shoulder a squeeze. "Nope. Once they've got the bit in their teeth, the best you can do is grab your butt and hang on for the ride."

CHAPTER FOUR

AD ASTRA

THEY HAD MANAGED to wrestle Cross into a pair of khaki slacks, a shirt, tie, and sports jacket, though he already had the tie pulled loose and the top button on the shirt was undone. His long brown hair was confined in a ponytail. The creature was currently eating his way up and down the buffet table as if he had been lost in the Himalayas for a year. The best Richard could hope for was that the other families and guests of graduates would assume he was an eccentric Hollywood producer or tech billionaire. They all usually looked like ragbags too.

Mosi's entourage was impressive. In addition to Richard, Damon, Cross, and the young Brit scientist—who looked like he wanted the Earth to swallow him—there was Mosi's Nerd Posse. The gaggle of older scientists were gathered around her like bees flocking to a particularly exotic flower.

Dr. Eddie Tanaka, tall and lanky, headed Lumina's science division. With him were Dr. Milind Ranjan, Dr. Ron Trout, and Dr. Jiang Chen. Years ago they had all been on the run together, and the gaggle of bachelors and one divorcé all became surrogate fathers to the then nine-year-old Mosi. Trout, the only one among them who had been married and was a father, often acted as if Richard's parenting skills were highly suspect.

Richard checked his watch, wondering why in the hell Pamela hadn't arrived yet. As if his thoughts had summoned her, his sister and her longtime boyfriend, Jason, swept through the entrance of the large white tent where the reception was being held. Pamela saw that Mosi was surrounded, so she headed for Richard.

"You're late," he said.

She glared at him. "I'm here. Don't nag."

Jason slipped an arm around her waist. "I had to drag her off the phone."

She transferred her glare to him. "Don't you nag either."

He grinned down at the siblings. Richard always felt like a skyscraper had started walking when he was around Jason. The other man stood six foot six to Richard's five four. Richard sometimes thought Pamela had picked him just to make her little brother feel uncomfortable ... and inadequate.

"Make yourself useful," she ordered Jason. "Get me a glass of champagne."

"Yes, ma'am." He gave a lazy grin and a salute, and sauntered off.

"Some problem I should know about?" Richard asked.

"Nothing serious. Labor dispute at our factory in Turin. It's handled—"

"Fairly?" Richard demanded.

"Of course. We're not Republicans any longer, but Luca does love to enact an opera for me over every little thing," she huffed.

"Yes, Italians are a passionate and emotional people, not

cold and uptight WASPs like us," Richard said with a smile that only broadened at her outraged expression.

The mention of Italy sent him back through time to his days as a student at the *Conservatorio Santa Cecelia* in Rome. A time when—away from the judgmental and controlling gaze of his very conservative and religious father—he could learn to ride a motorcycle, have a boyfriend, and spend a lazy afternoon in bed with said boyfriend, fucking and drinking cheap wine.

It had all ended when his father had decreed that music was frivolous and it was past time for Richard to come home, grow up, and take the job Judge Robert Oort had arranged for him. Only to have his boss (a close friend of the judge's) rape and brutalize him, compelling Richard to become a police officer, and ultimately into controlling an international company. *And none of it had been enough to win his approval*, Richard thought. Pamela's voice pulled him out of his reverie.

"Who's the boy Damon is shepherding about?"

"Another of our wounded birds. Rescued him last night from some Old Ones."

"Oh shit. Are we likely to have an *event* today?"

"I hope not, but I'm ready if …" His voice trailed away and he lightly touched the holster at the small of his back.

"Well, at least you're not making Mosi carry that hell-born thing today," Pamela huffed.

"No. This is her day." Richard paused and glanced down at his glass of non-alcoholic punch. "You know I would spare her if I could."

Pamela looked contrite and gave him a hug. "I know."

"But back on our rescue ... we need to get into it with the university and his advisors. See if he can finish his doctorate working for us. He's onto something that A) might be useful to us, and B) is likely to get him killed if he's *not* with us." Richard paused and looked over at his ward. "Also Mosi likes him."

"Oh ho, you playing matchmaker?" Pamela said and elbowed him.

"According to my spouse I'm doing the exact opposite. But honestly she's too serious, too focused on her studies and being ..." Once again his hand went unconsciously to the sword hilt. "Well, you know. I want her to enjoy life. At least for a little while."

Pamela studied Fox for a moment. "Well, he is a cutie."

Richard studied the slim redhead: The smattering of freckles across his nose and cheeks, and the bright green eyes behind the thick lenses of his glasses. "Yes, I suppose he is."

Pamela reached out and pushed back a stray lock of hair that was brushing his forehead. "You look tired."

"Didn't get a lot of sleep last night."

"You need to take better care of yourself. Especially with Damon being ..." Her voice trailed away as Jason returned with two flutes of champagne, and Richard gratefully shifted the conversation to more innocuous topics.

❖   ❖   ❖

IT WAS HOTTER than normal for May in Massachusetts. Even with the large fans, it felt sweltering inside the tent where graduates and families had enjoyed the luncheon. The bobby pins that held Mosi's mortar board in place seemed to be drilling directly into her scalp, and the black graduation robe was adding to her discomfort. Trickles of sweat ran down her sides and her forehead felt damp. She wiped away the bead of sweat and her hand brushed the tassel that hung off her cap. She found herself touching the purple braid on her shoulder that indicated she was the graduate president of the Massachusetts Institute of Technology. It still didn't seem entirely real.

From a hogan on the edge of Chaco Canyon to MIT. What a long, strange journey it's been, she thought, quoting the Grateful Dead lyrics—and Damon's favorite band.

Fox came sidling up to her, his fingers nervously clenching on the stem of his champagne flute. "I can't tell if I'm a part of your entourage or a pampered prisoner," he said quietly.

"Little of both?" she suggested brightly.

"Also, can't believe you were just casually chatting with Dr. Jiang Chen." His voice sounded reverent.

"Well, he's sort of like an uncle," Mosi began, only to have Fox clutch at his mop of red hair.

"Aaargh, one of the richest men in the world is your foster father, and you think of a Nobel Prize-winning physicist as an *uncle*. Have you met the bloody king too?"

His British accent was very much in evidence, so it gave Mosi an enormous amount of glee to casually say, "Couple of times. We did last year's June garden party at Buckingham Palace. Not sure if we're going again this year." He gaped at her and she giggled. "The king's very concerned about climate change, and we have an entire division devoted to just working on plans for mitigation and reversal. Plans that don't involve trying to live on Mars," she added.

"You know *him* too," Fox said wearily.

"Of course. So, does that make you feel better about hanging out with us?" she asked sweetly.

"Marginally. I have a dissertation to complete."

"And just think how much better it's going to be when you have our resources to work with and our scientists as advisors."

"Wait! What?"

But before she could answer the university president joined them. She briefly rested her hand on Mosi's shoulder. "All set?"

"Yes, ma'am."

"Well, I need to gather up my ducklings and then we'll be off," the woman said and headed off to alert the other graduates.

Mosi scanned the tent. Cross was making one more run at the buffet tables even as the staff was beginning to pack up. Damon was seated at one of the tables, Richard had his hand on Damon's shoulder and was leaning over him. Every tense angle in his body betrayed his worry. Pamela waved at her and gave her an approving nod. The Nerd Posse was starting to drift toward the exit.

"Why don't you go hook up with them?" Mosi suggested with a jerk of her chin toward the scientists.

"I think I'll stick with your fathers. They are marginally less terrifying than a flock of Nobel winners."

"Suit yourself. I'll catch you on the other side."

Fox walked a few steps then turned and walking backward away from her called out, "You know, I wasn't planning on attending my *own* graduation. Now I'm stuck attending yours." His smile took the sting out of it.

"Yes, and I'm *so* worth it," she said airily. "And by the way, my speech is terrific."

"Is it going to be in Navajo or English?" Fox called as he grinned at her. He really had the cutest smile.

Mosi eyed some of the clearly hungover graduates and gave a bubbling laugh. "I think most of the class wouldn't be able to tell the difference."

"True that." Fox saluted her with his glass, drained the last of his champagne, set the flute down on a table, and went to join Richard and Damon. The trio left moments later to take their place in the audience.

Mosi wished Richard had been able to stay. He certainly deserved to be on the dais after all the money he had donated to the university, but she understood his reticence. Richard wasn't precisely a reclusive billionaire, but there had been multiple attempts on his life over the years, the press was ever present, and after last night's adventures he was in no mood to handle the attention. Also Mosi knew that he wanted this to be *her* day.

The university president gathered up the commencement speaker, Emirhan Uyanik, an aging tech genius who had taken another tech genius' research on creating Mars habitats, and applied it to creating underground living and farming colonies in the Middle East. War and drought had left life on the surface almost impossible across many of the former nations of that area. Now the greatly reduced populations of Iran, Iraq, Lebanon, Syria, Israel, Saudi

Arabia, Yemen, and the Emirates lived in habitats originally designed for an uninhabitable planet.

Which was a fucking sad commentary on human's ability to deal with reality and not make our own world equally uninhabitable, Mosi thought.

Uyanik and his company, Ad Astra, were also currently working in partnership with Lumina, building a multi-generation long view ship to carry a seed of humanity, and the rich biodiversity of Earth to the stars. He called it his Ark, and together with his daughter Feray, they were throwing much of their considerable fortune into the effort.

The president of the undergraduate class moaned as he passed by, "God, I'm *so* hungover. Hope I don't faint. Or puke. Or forget how to talk."

She laughed and gave him a pat on the arm. "You'll be fine."

And I've had three hours of sleep and was killing monsters last night, so cry me a river, Mosi thought with a shake of her head. There were moments when she almost resented her more carefree contemporaries.

They entered the quadrangle and began to process down the aisle between the rows of chairs while the orchestra played "Pomp and Circumstance." As she came level with her cheering section, Damon gave her a smile and a thumbs up, Pamela gave her a warm smile, the Nerd Posse beamed, and Fox looked flummoxed. Cross was missing. Mosi suspected he was lurking somewhere nearby. She just hoped the creature behaved himself.

Richard had taken the seat on the aisle, and from the way he had his suit coat arranged she knew it was so he could quickly draw either gun or sword and react should anything untoward happen. She wondered if Richard resented always having to be on alert in the same the way she resented her more carefree friends.

Mosi managed to briefly give his shoulder a squeeze as she passed by. He looked up, turning that ice-blue gaze on her. It was filled with pride and love. There was a net of fine lines around his eyes that had only appeared over the past two years as Damon had fought his battle with the lung cancer that was trying to kill him. *As if fighting monsters both human and alien wasn't enough*, she thought. *Why did the universe decide to lay this on Richard too?*

As the graduates approached the dais in front of the great dome, supported by its ten beautiful Ionic columns, Mosi reflected how different her life would have been had her family lived. Had Richard not found her. Had she not become a Paladin.

She probably wouldn't now be graduating from MIT, or some other prestigious college. More likely it would have been her brother. Abel had wanted to be a doctor. He loved technology and especially the laptop father had bought for him. But it was in the reflective surface of that computer where the faces of the Old Ones had appeared and whispered to Abel until he went mad.

For a moment Mosi was nine years old again, smelling the sweet tang of blood, her brother's eyes glittering in the dark of the hogan. The big knife in his hand sheathed in the blood of their parents and grandfather. Fleeing through the darkness, her brother's harsh breaths behind her until she finally lost him among the sage and chamisa. Abel had died of thirst in the barren beauty of New Mexico. She touched the turquoise in her ring. It was as close as she would ever come to a prayer for them.

Then they were on the dais and Mosi took her seat. She tried to concentrate on the president's opening remarks, but her mind kept churning. Why had she gone for a degree in computer science after having been so terrified of them, convinced they were all infected with *ch'įįdii*?

Was it hair of the dog as Damon had suggested? Or because Richard had come, reassured Mosi she was not crazy, and convinced her that he would keep the faces away and that they weren't demons or witches?

Or was it the amazing Sofia computers that had been created because Lumina scientists had studied the mysterious Kenntnis, a creature of light and subatomic particles? Although, wasn't nearly everything made of those same particles, she pondered. As the great Carl Sagan had said, *"We're made of star stuff."* The very idea always sent a shiver of delight through her.

The applause pulled her from her wandering thoughts. The president smiled and gestured to her and Mosi moved to the podium. She set her iPad to project her speech. She had it memorized, but wanted the extra security. Gripping the edges of the podium, she looked out across the assemblage.

CHAPTER FIVE

REALLY?

FOX WAS SEATED nervously between Damon Weber and Dr. Ranjan. Damon had a large iPad held up and trained on the dais. At first, Fox thought he was just recording then realized that Zoom was running (and also recording), and there were a lot of people tuning in to watch. There was an older black man, and a severe looking older woman seated at a desk—in the background was an elaborate wood, glass, and metal door. There was also a beautiful black woman with cornrows studded with red glass beads. Around her were a group of people who looked like the security guards who were with Mr. Oort. And there was a plump, older man in an apron. Behind him was a gorgeous high tech kitchen. Another window showed a woman at a desk in an office. Through the broad window, Fox could see the London Eye.

Sweat trickled through Fox's sideburns and he really wished he had a snatched up a bottled water before coming out to swelter in the sun. He wasn't sure how Mosi was looking so composed as she stood behind the podium, head high, back straight, like some warrior woman out of the guilty pleasure fantasy novels Fox liked to read or the pages of superhero comic books. His father, the retired military man, had made his feelings on Fox's literary taste abundantly clear (bunch of useless kid crap) which had led to secretive reading with his iPad ready to switch with a single touch from Tolkien or Marvel and DC to some non-fiction piece that wouldn't elicit the look of disgust and an explosion of ire from his dad.

After those luminous dark eyes swept the crowd, they came to rest on Richard. Fox had a feeling whatever Mosi was going to say it was meant only for him.

"I'm a woman of the *Dinaii*, which is what the Navajo people call ourselves, and I stand before you today because of a series of improbable events. When I was nine I lost my family to violence fed by ignorance, fear, and hate."

"Those ills afflict us still, but they can be offset by the bravery, love, and integrity of good people. For me, that person was and is my guardian, Richard Oort. I love you, *Na sha dii*. Thank you ... for everything."

It was voyeuristic, but Fox leaned forward slightly so he could see Oort, caught the glint of unshed tears in those ice-blue eyes. Oort raised his hand in acknowledgment of his ward's words. Damon took one hand off the iPad to pat his husband on the arm affectionately. He then reached into his pocket to dig out a handkerchief and offered it to Richard.

"But it's not just good people that fight so that we humans can rise above our primitive, violent tendencies." She gestured around at the dome, the buildings that made up MIT. "Institutions like this one are also candles in the darkness, pushing back the ignorance, resisting the hate, and easing the fear. And all of us, graduates of this institution, are going to go forth with our candles held high. For with knowledge comes understanding and from understanding comes courage ..."

Fox became aware of a high-pitched whine from overhead. It pulled his attention from Mosi's speech. Frowning, he glanced up.

✧　✧　✧

DAMON KNEW THAT sound. Knew it all too well. Had heard it in the sands of Iraq and the mountains of Afghanistan. Back then the whine of a drone had meant the US had eyes in the sky watching over the troops humping rifles below. Now, it only brought a feeling of annoyance over the goddamn everpresent paparazzi.

But as the high-pitched whining hum drew closer he realized the motor propelling the drone was *way* too large to be carrying just a camera. This was the kind of drone that had rained down fire and death on Saddam and the Taliban.

He gripped Richard's shoulder so hard that the smaller man winced and it pulled his attention from Mosi. Richard looked at Damon in alarm and started to whisper, "What's wrong, are you—"

Damon jerked his chin upward and hissed, "Drone! Military grade!"

They both looked up, squinting against the sun and Damon spotted the flying device. It was much larger than the ones that could be purchased online for use by realtors and photography enthusiasts, and then they both clocked what were clearly the muzzles of guns.

Damon grabbed the back of Fox's head, and shoved him onto the grass. The folding chairs would be poor protection, but better than nothing. At the same time, Richard leaped to his feet, drawing his pistol, and yelled, "Take cover! Everyone, get down!"

Damon knew that Richard sometimes regretted his tenor voice, but in this moment it worked well. Both because higher-pitched voices carried better than low tones, and because Richard had been trained as a singer, his sweetie knew how to *project*. Richard's voice rang out across the gathering, but the attendees were still just gawking at him in confusion.

Mosi broke off abruptly, the microphone giving a squeal. Her head was jerking in all directions searching for the threat. Richard thrust the barrel of his pistol upward and her eyes followed its path, widening when she spotted the incoming drone. People spotted Richard's gun and began screaming. Grabbing the mic, Mosi drowned out the screams and amplified the message.

"ACTIVE SHOOTER! TAKE COVER!" she shouted.

That penetrated and people began to drop to the ground while others tried to flee. Damon saw Richard calculating if his Heckler & Koch forty caliber could take down the drone just as the pair of machine guns mounted on the drone began a strafing run toward the dais. Gouts of dirt, clumps of grass, and splinters from shattered chairs were flung into the air. The screams of terror became screams of pain.

Damon flung himself over the boy and Milind, and heard a grunt of pain from Ron. The older scientist had turned to look for the source of the mayhem and at least one bullet had taken him in the chest. He was flung backward by the force of the bullets. Eddie, using knees and elbows, crawled to his friend, and pressed a hand over the wound.

Damon looked back at his husband. Richard stood frozen, facing an agonizing choice. His eyes flicked from Damon toward the dais and Mosi and back again.

"*Go,*" Damon mouthed at him, and he watched for an instant as Richard, despite being forty-three, used his gymnastic training to leap from chair to chair to avoid the terrified mob.

Damon then buried his head against Fox's back and wished that prayer actually worked.

❖   ❖   ❖

RICHARD'S NOSTRILS WERE filled with the scent of cordite, blood, and sweat. Terror had his heart hammering in his chest as he watched Uyanik try to leap off the dais, but before he could escape his body was stitched with bullets. He seemed to be dancing under the onslaught of lead.

Mosi ripped open her graduation gown, and yanked her pistol from the holster strapped high up on her thigh. She had selected the Sig Sauer subcompact that morning which had made sense when they thought they were just attending a graduation. How much damage it could do against an armored drone was anybody's guess. And whoever was piloting the drone had doubtless seen the young woman taking a Power Isosceles Stance, and drawing down on the flying weapon.

With a Herculean effort, Richard launched himself off the seat of one chair, felt the muscles and nerves in his thigh and sacrum clench into white hot agony, but he landed on

49

the dais and threw himself in front of his child.

Mosi dropped one hand from the pistol, and gripped his shoulder—nails digging through both coat and shirt, so tight was her grip. He realized she was trying to wrestle him to the ground to protect *him*. Almost unable to form a coherent word, he growled out a *no* at her. He shook her off, took her legs out from under her with a sweep of his left leg, pushed her to the ground with his right hand, while his left lined up his shot on the drone as bullets chewed up the wood of the dais.

Richard fired twice, then twice again, but clearly didn't hit anything vital on the flying killer. He threw himself across Mosi's body shielding her as best he could from the death marching inexorably toward them. Braced himself for pain. Prepared to die.

Hot lead didn't tear through his back. Instead there was an unearthly and uncanny howling, and the gunfire became muffled. Wrenching his head around, Richard saw Cross—his human form expanding and elongating into prismatic colors—as the Old One stretched into the sky to intercept the drone. Within seconds only, his mouth remained, a hideous and grotesque maw in a writhing sea of colors unfurling to gulp at the drone. The drone dematerialized into the floating mouth and the air around Cross shimmered. Now appearing only as a sphere of coruscating splinters of light with the drone a dark outline among the colors, he then vanished.

With his hearing deafened by the gunfire, the sobs, screams, and cries of despair seemed faint and far away. Richard climbed to his feet, and held out a hand to help Mosi stand. She was shaking, the mortar board sliding off one side of her head, and there were tiny spatters of blood on her graduation gown—a pointillism painting of death and disaster. She gave a sob and came into his arms, trembling against him.

"It's okay. It's okay. It's over now," he whispered. He wanted to tell her she was safe, but years ago he had promised he would never lie to her. She was a Paladin. She would *never* be safe.

He pulled back, ran his tongue across his lower lip and tasted blood. Somewhere during his frenzied sprint he had been spattered with it. Richard fought back nausea, released his ward, and stepped back. He could hear sirens now.

"We need to render aid to the wounded," he ordered.

Mosi nodded and moved to Uyanik. She laid her fingertips on his throat, then looked back at Richard and shook her head. She moved on to the university president who was also dead.

Richard ran to the boy who was the undergraduate speaker. He was sobbing and keening in pain, his legs riddled with wounds, and the white of shattered bone was visible through the red blood. Richard knelt down next to him preparing to pull off his belt and tie as tourniquets, but miraculously nothing vital had been hit. He would survive, though whether he would keep both legs was questionable.

He rested a hand on the young man's sweat drenched forehead. "I know. It hurts, but you're going to be okay. Help is on the way."

Richard's gaze flew to the row where Damon and the Lumina scientists had been seated. Relief flooded through him to see Damon was unharmed. His husband knelt next to

Ron Trout, his suit jacket folded into a makeshift bandage and pressed to the older man's chest. The fabric was rapidly staining with blood. Eddie was on his feet, cell phone pressed to his ear.

Mosi gave a whimper of distress, and jumped off the dais to run to Damon and the wounded scientist. Richard didn't trust his leg to hold him if he jumped, so he limped down the steps and hobbled over to his husband.

"Sucking chest wound," Damon grunted, his hand red with gore as he pressed the fabric deep into the wound. "But he'll probably make it if the EMTs get here fast enough."

Seconds later the area was filled with strobing emergency lights, ambulances, police cars, and people frenetically caring for the injured. Richard's knees suddenly seemed made of jelly and he sank shivering into a chair. Fox shambled over, and voice trembling, asked, "Was this some of your Old Ones?"

Richard reached up and gripped the young man's forearm, noting somewhat distantly that he had left bloody fingerprints on the fabric of his sleeve. "No, this was pure human evil."

✧　✧　✧

TROUT WAS GETTING loaded onto a gurney and rushed toward an ambulance. One EMT held up an IV drip while another replaced Damon's jacket with a dressing. Mosi stood next to Richard, her legs trembling as the adrenaline began to leach from her body. He seemed to sense her distress and slipped an arm around her waist offering her support.

"I'll ride with him," Damon called to Mosi and Richard, as he walked backward in the wake of the gurney that was rolling toward an ambulance. "And keep you posted. You two be careful."

However, Damon's good intentions were immediately stymied by the cops who had cordoned off the area. Unless a person was actually injured, no one was going to be leaving. He returned, grumbling.

Richard ran a weary hand across his face, his expression bleak. "I shouldn't have come. I knew it was a mistake. I shouldn't have taken the risk." He gave Mosi a contrite look. "I'm so sorry. I wanted this to be a perfect day for you. Instead ..." He made a helpless gesture.

"Bluntly, dear heart, that's bullshit." Damon hugged Richard to his side. "You weren't the target. Not this time. And you aren't to blame."

Mosi threw Damon a grateful look. He always had the ability to snap Richard out of his self-flagellating spirals.

"Damon's right—it's not our fault when bad people do bad things," Mosi said. "*They're* ultimately responsible for their actions. And Damon's right about the target too. Whoever's behind this, they were after Emirhan and a lot of faculty. Not us."

"Which implies the Old Ones," Damon mused. "They don't love anything or anyone that makes humans less stupid and gullible. And there was the attack on Fox last night."

Richard shook his head. "I don't think so. Drones and machine guns don't exactly fit the Old One aesthetic," Richard sighed. "And speaking of, where is Cross? We need to inspect that drone."

They all scanned the scene, but Cross was nowhere in evidence. Mosi's eyes swept the milling crowd, clocking each of the Lumina people, reassuring herself they were safe. Pamela was pacing, phone to her ear. No surprise there, as chief legal counsel for the company, she needed to reassure the world that Richard was unharmed. Jason was frantically typing on his small foldout pocket computer undoubtably writing up the story for the *Post*. Eddie and Chen were in an animated conversation with Milind, who looked like he was ready to bolt and charge the line of cops.

Damon sighed, he had caught the byplay too. "I'm going to go handhold our big brains. Make sure nobody does anything foolish. Also sit down." The older man was looking a bit grey, and Mosi watched the dread flicker across Richard's face as he watched Damon walk away.

Mosi went back to assessing the crowd, but found her eyes lingering on Fox. He was slumped in one of the chairs that hadn't been knocked over by terrified, fleeing people, or torn to wooden splinters by high-powered bullets. His head was in his hands and there were smears of blood on the knees of his pants and bloody fingerprints on his sleeve.

"Best go check on your young man," Richard said softly.

"He's not *my* young man," Mosi huffed. She started to step away, only to hear an officious voice from behind her.

"One of the witnesses said there were people with guns?"

Mosi turned. It was a cop using that tone that cops reserved to imply there was criminal activity afoot and they were taking this *very seriously* and *you were very seriously under suspicion.*

Mosi fought the impulse to sarcastically inquire if the cop

actually thought the short, slight, middle-aged white man in a four thousand dollar suit. with gold and sapphire cufflinks winking against the fabric of his blue shirt, was actually a threat. It was just more security theater and closing the barn door after the horses were well and truly out. Richard seemed to sense her thoughts, and put a forefinger to his lips. She sighed, but obeyed.

He carefully pulled aside his suit coat so the cop could see the shoulder holster and the butt of the Heckler and Koch. "May I?" he asked. The cop nodded, but his stance tensed, and his hand hovered near his holster. Once Richard had drawn the gun, he dropped the clip, opened the slide to demonstrate it was empty, then flipped the pistol around so he could offer it butt first to the police officer. The officer visible relaxed.

"Officer, I'm now going to reach into my coat pocket for my ID and also my badge."

Mosi wanted to roll her eyes. The badge was honestly kind of a joke. Richard hadn't walked a beat or served as an APD detective in almost fifteen years, but the department had created a little fiction that he was still working for APD researching policing methods in other countries, and being a liaison to the FBI. That last part was actually true. And to be fair, maybe it was all true, because security services around the globe knew to call Lumina when something happened that couldn't be explained or dealt with by traditional law enforcement.

It also went beyond mere practicality. Over the years Mosi had come to understand that the possession of that gold shield was desperately important to Richard on an emotional level that she couldn't fathom. Mosi had never had the nerve to ask him why, and queries to Damon had earned her a gentle headshake, along with the explanation that it wasn't his place to reveal something that personal and private for Richard. Mosi understood that, for Richard, the badge was akin to body armor, which implied that whatever had happened to him, it probably wasn't anything good.

The cop studied Richard's badge and she watched the man's shoulder's visibly relax. They were both part of the same tribe and it was obviously reassuring to the young officer. The cop handed back the license, the badge, and the pistol. He seemed to have forgotten all about Mosi. She figured somebody might mention the snubbie she'd pulled from her thigh holster, but for right now she wasn't going to bring it up. It would just confuse matters.

"So did you manage to bring down the drone?" the cop asked Richard.

"Unfortunately, no," Richard said smoothly. "It was damaged, but kept flying."

Mosi cast him a look. *Okay*, she thought, *we're going with the mundane explanation.* Which might be problematic; there was probably somebody in the crowd of frightened, wounded people who had seen and probably made a recording on their phone of Cross going all Old One and swallowing the damn thing, but again, it was just more confusion.

The cop moved away to take more statements. The sudden smell of a McDonald's Big Mac washed over them. They turned to find Cross taking large bites out of the burger. The scent of hamburger overlaying the smell of blood and feces had Mosi's stomach roiling.

"You should check on your guy," Cross mumbled as he masticated on the burger.

"Oh, for fuck's sake! He is *not*—"

"My mistake, but he sure seems like he's ready to jump your—"

Richard interrupted. "Could you please cough up the drone?"

"It's not a fucking hairball. I didn't keep it in here," Cross said gesturing at his sunken belly.

"We need to study it if we're going to figure out who's behind this attack," Richard snapped.

"So, where is it?" Mosi asked.

"Coughed it up in a nearby multiverse," Cross muttered resentfully.

"Well, go get it," Richard ordered.

"I was kinda moving fast through a lot of dimensions ..." The homeless god's voice trailed away.

With sudden understanding, Mosi said, "You don't remember where you dropped it off. Great."

"I could probably find it again, but after spending time in a different reality it might not ... well, be quite itself anymore. If you take my meaning."

Mosi shuddered. She knew what the alien meant. More than once she had had to enter one of those other multiverses to pull back some lost human. Those other multiverses that spawned the Old Ones didn't obey the laws of physics of her universe, which made them horrifying and disturbing at a cellular level.

It was also why magic was so fundamentally destructive

to the reality in which her world existed and why it needed to be eradicated. As Cross said, it wasn't from around here, and more importantly it didn't *belong* here. Wherever the drone might be, it was being subjected to the same forces. It had become like sand in the body of an oyster and it would be warped and changed.

"We might still be able to learn something," Richard said. "But I've got to get to the hospital and check on Ron." He pulled the hilt from its holster and handed it to Mosi. Keep an eye on our young physicist."

"You won't need it?" Mosi asked.

"I think we might have two bad actors at work. The Old Ones who are after Fox—since you'll be guarding him you need the sword—and whoever is behind the drone attack. I have a feeling *they'll* be susceptible to bullets."

Richard walked to the perimeter of the crime scene, engaged in a quick conversation with an officer, flashed his badge, and had the crime scene tape lifted so he could duck underneath.

CHAPTER SIX

MORE FAMILY IS NEVER A PROBLEM

FOX LOOKED UP as Mosi joined the terrifying sister, Damon, and the unharmed scientists. He remained hunched in the chair, not trusting his legs to hold him if he tried to stand. He noted that Mosi was barefoot, the fancy high heels clearly abandoned at some point during the catastrophe. *No—massacre,* he amended at the sight of the blood on her graduation robe. He swallowed hard forcing down the bile that roiled sullenly deep in his gut.

He studied Mosi. Her eyes were hooded, lips narrowed down to a tight line. She was clearly furious, but no hint of fear showed on that beautiful face and it baffled him. Had he fallen in with a bunch of robots? Or maybe he was just a weakling. Though to be fair, he had nearly been killed last night so perhaps he deserved his lack of sanguinity. He was faintly disappointed when she didn't spare him a glance, but immediately fell into conversation with Ms. Oort and the scientists. Fox shamelessly eavesdropped.

Pamela was saying, "I called the other company officers to reassure them that everyone is okay."

"Apart from Ron," Milind snapped.

"We should be there," Eddie added.

"Richard's heading to the hospital now," Mosi said.

"How the hell did my brother waltz out of here?"

Mosi wiggled her fingers in the air. "He used the magic of the badge."

"Well, that's annoying," Pamela huffed.

Damon heaved a sigh. "Damn it, now I wish I'd hung onto my badge too." He looked at Pamela. "Don't suppose you can you do a little shyster magic and get us all out of here?"

"Why don't *you* use some of that *flatfoot charm*?" she said in the clipped East Coast accent that she shared with her brother. Fox had the feeling this was a long-standing game between them.

Damon sighed and rolled an eye toward Mosi. "I suppose I should be grateful she didn't say pig."

"Yep," Mosi deadpanned.

"I was highly tempted," Pamela drawled. "No, I'm afraid we're all stuck here giving statements for the foreseeable future."

Mosi glanced around, then said quietly, "Cross has gone looking for the drone."

Tanaka spoke up. "I've got the tech boys prepped to look it over once we get it back."

Fox found he had no interest in the discussion that followed and he sank back into his own dark thoughts until a hand fell onto his shoulder. Fox looked up to see Dr. Tanaka looming over him.

"How you holding up?" the older man asked gently.

"To be perfectly honest, not well."

Tanaka hooked a nearby chair with his foot, pulled it close, and sat down. "Richard told me a bit about how you found yourself mixed up with all of us. I can sympathize. My story is similar and I'll tell you about it when we're not ..." His voice trailed away and he gestured at the scene all around them. "Richard also told me you have a project that sounds right up our alley and he wants us to take you under our wings."

"Look, I'm quite overcome by the fact I'm even talking with you—*any* of you—but do I get a say in this?" Fox asked.

Dr. Tanaka opened and closed his mouth a few times. "Honestly ... no. Richard's kind of a force of nature. Also, he and Mosi can keep you safe. I'm pretty damn sure nobody else can."

Fox chewed on that for a minute, then sighed. "Well, I suppose that is one compelling argument for why I would agree," Fox said.

✦ ✦ ✦

RICHARD HATED HOSPITALS. All were cold. Many were dingy. And they always assaulted you with odors both medicinal and putrid. Plus he had spent too much time in them. Starting with the assault and rape that had led to him becoming a police officer, and ultimately on this long, strange journey that was his life.

Richard sighed and leaned forward in the uncomfortable waiting room chair resting his head in his hands. He had called Ron's daughter, Carla, to tell her what happened, and that the Lumina jet was on its way to Maine to bring her to her father's side. He now just had to wait for Ron to come out of surgery and for Carla to arrive.

His phone began to play the lilting, romantic "Love Theme from *Superman*" music. He quickly answered the video call.

"They broke into Senate debate, it's why I couldn't tune into the graduation Zoom, I just saw on the news, are you—" Dr. Angela Aramadariz broke off abruptly, her dark face grimacing as she took in his background. "You're in a hospital," she said sharply.

"Relax, I'm not hurt. It's Ron."

"Well, *that's* a switch," she muttered. "How's he doing?"

"In surgery. The doctors don't think it's too serious." He sighed. "I'm just so damn … darn grateful you couldn't be here. A lot of people weren't so lucky."

"How bad?"

"Twenty-one dead. Emirhan was one of them."

"Well, goddamn it to hell!" Her small five-foot-nothing body was quivering with fury, curls tumbled and disordered, fire in her dark eyes. "They trying to kill you again?"

"I don't think so. Felt more … general, but I do think Emirhan was a target."

"You going to tell Feray that?"

"God, no. Not until we have the people in custody."

"Richard, my love, you're not really a cop anymore, and you're certainly not a member of the Boston PD. Let them do their jobs."

"They won't know what they're dealing with," Richard objected.

"You just said you didn't think it was one of ours."

Richard smiled fondly. They had fallen so easily back into their old patterns. "I miss you, Angela."

"I miss you too. Also miss New Mexico. At least I get home fairly often for *constituent care*. Remind me again why I did this?"

"Because you wanted all Americans to have basic healthcare, to help fund medical efforts around the world, and combat climate change. And you could have come to work for me and I would have put you in charge of our global health initiatives," he reminded her.

"Yeah, I know, but this way I get to beat up on Republicans. With you guys we're all singing from the same hymnal. Way less fun."

He chuckled. "You're impossible and please don't ever change."

"Keep me posted about Ron. Give Mosi my love and a hug and an *atta girl*, and tell Damon to stop malingering and finish getting well."

"Will do. Keep giving the Republicans hell."

✧ ✧ ✧

"Hey, hon, how's Ron doing?" Damon asked Richard via FaceTime on Mosi's iPad.

It had taken hours before they were finally released from the MIT campus and the ravaged graduation, but they were all finally back in the suite at the Four Seasons. Richard was still at the hospital.

Mosi had gotten the most intense questioning since she had been on the dais with the victims, but between her cop guardian, his husband (who had been a cop for almost twenty years), and the lawyer sister, she had been well-trained. She knew how to appear helpful while giving away nothing. Mercifully, only a handful of attendees had witnessed Cross eating the gun-equipped drone, and apparently the threat of imminent death kept people from recording Cross doing his Old One eating-a-drone thing.

It wasn't that most people on Earth weren't aware of the existence of multiverses and the creatures that occasionally pushed through. Hell, only a year or two before Richard came into Mosi's life, there had been giant gateways going up all over the world through which monsters had poured. It had fallen to Richard to close them, and for more than a decade there had only been small incursions which most normal people managed to ignore since they didn't impinge on their lives.

The real problem was that Lumina didn't really want the press digging *too* deeply into Cross' identity. It would be hard to explain why the company devoted to *stopping* Old One incursions also *employed* an Old One.

"Out of surgery." Richard answered. "He's doing well." Her guardian's gaze shifted over to Damon. "Thanks for sending over Janine and Adam to pull security. Until we know who was behind this ..." His voice trailed away and Mosi could see he was exhausted. "Ron's daughter is on her way down from Maine. I sent the plane for her, so we won't be able to leave for home until tomorrow late-ish."

"I'm sure she's grateful, *Na sha dii,*" Mosi said.

Damon spoke up. "Look, I've got starving eggheads and two hungry kids. We're about to order room service. Any idea when you'll be back?".

Richard glanced at his watch. "She should be landing in

about twenty minutes. I've got a car waiting for her. So probably forty, forty-five minutes. I can't really run off the moment she arrives."

"Okay, we'll order some nibbles to quell the ravening hoards," Mosi said. "And aim for dinner at nine?"

"Really don't worry about me. Just order and—"

Damon put a firm stop to that using what Mosi had dubbed his command voice. "You are *not* skipping dinner. Now, what do you want?"

Richard gusted out a sigh. "You know what I like. Order something for me."

"You better not be late or I will come and get you," Mosi threatened, but with a fond laugh underlying her words.

"I am appropriately threatened. I won't be late." Richard broke the connection.

Mosi set aside the iPad and studied the sitting room of the suite. The numbers had increased with the addition of the rest of the Nerd Posse. Given everything that had happened over the past twenty-four hours, Pamela had reserved more rooms on either side of suite, and Damon had sent part of their security team to pick up the scientists' luggage from various hotels in the Boston area. The fact that they were down two guards meant that Mosi was openly wearing both pistol and sword hilt.

Right now, said scientists were tag teaming Fox. Milind was kicked back on a sofa reading the young physicist's partially-written dissertation off of his laptop. Which had Fox casting periodic nervous glances at the older scientist, while also trying to focus on the questions Eddie, Chen, and occasionally Milind were throwing at him.

"Good God, I didn't think I'd be having to defend my dissertation before I'd finished it!" Fox burst out.

Milind looked up from the screen of the laptop. "Kept your mind off—" he began, when Eddie in his usual awkward and thoughtless way piped up.

"The massacre."

Fox blanched and yelped, "Not helping!" Chen patted Fox on the shoulder, and gave Eddie a look.

"Was that rude?" Eddie asked.

"More gauche than rude," Chen said.

"Still *not helping*," Fox stressed again.

Mosi gave Damon a speaking glance. He looked amused but also exhausted. Fatigue dragged down his face, left dark circles around his eyes, and had his shoulders slumping.

"You should go lie down. I'll handle feeding everybody."

The look of gratitude couldn't be hidden, but was also quickly banished. Damon stood and gripped her shoulder briefly. "Thank you, but you must be exhausted too."

"I'll be fine. Go. Shoo."

She grabbed the room service menu, did a mental nose count, silently thanked Franz—their personal chef back in New Mexico—for his lessons on planning banquets, and started ordering. She offered all the kitchen and wait staff a substantial bonus if they could expedite everything, particularly the hors d'oeuvres.

She slipped into Richard and Damon's room. Damon was softly snoring, but his forehead was furrowed in pain. It was in moments like this that she sometimes wished for the comfort—false though it might be—of religion. She knew her own loss was probably unresolved, but wasn't the lot of all humans to love and ultimately lose those they loved?

We're made of star stuff, she reminded herself. *And to the stars we will return,* she thought, as she keyed open the safe and pulled out a stack of fifties and one hundred dollar bills.

Cash wasn't all that ubiquitous in this day and age, but Richard had taught her that for people living paycheck to paycheck, and those on the margins of society, cash was necessary, and for Lumina's purposes, helpful. She also suspected that he remembered when they'd had to flee for their lives and cash had sustained them until they found a safe haven.

She returned to the sitting room and collapsed onto the couch. It felt like she had closed her eyes for only an instant when there was a knock at the door. The snacks had arrived. After tipping the two bellmen, she gave the remaining cash to Cassie, who was pulling security while Joselita grabbed a nap, and asked the guard to run the money down to the kitchen staff.

Grabbing up a bacon-wrapped date, she started to join the four men who were busy eating and talking, when the house phone rang. Mosi grabbed the nearest phone.

"This is the front desk calling for Mr. Oort."

"He's not here right now. Is there something you need? May I take a message?"

"There's a young man here at the front desk. Says he's Mr. Oort's nephew. I didn't want to send him up without checking first."

Nephew? Mosi tried to parse that. "What's his name?"

There was a muffled conversation, then the desk clerk was back. "Paul van Gelder."

"Just hold on for a second." Mosi set down the handset, hurried to the door leading into an adjacent bedroom, and gave a light tap.

She faintly heard Pamela say, "Dagmar, hold on. Yes? Come in."

Mosi opened the door and stuck her head in. Jason was sprawled on the bed reading. Pamela was perambulating back and forth in the space at the foot of the bed, phone clutched in her hand, headphones in. She pulled out one EarPod and cocked an inquiring eyebrow at Mosi.

"Sorry to bother you, Pamela, but there's a Paul van Gelder downstairs. Says he's Richard's nephew. Should I let him come up?

"Paul's here? Well, that's surprising. Sure, have them send him up." Mosi nodded and as she was shutting the door, she heard Pamela mutter, "I'm sure more family won't be *any* kind of a problem." Jason's low laugh answered.

Mosi returned to the phone and gave them the okay. Five minutes later there was a discrete knock on the door. Mosi waved down Estevan and answered. Then stood gaping at the vision standing in the hallway.

"Hi, I'm Paul. You must be Mosi," said the vision, before casting a quick and somewhat questioning glance at Nathan and Cassie who were standing guard in the hallway.

Judging by her eye level Paul van Gelder was a couple of inches over six feet, incredibly fit with bright chestnut hair and the bluest eyes she had ever seen. In short, he was freaking gorgeous. Mosi gathered her wits.

"Uh, come in. Richard's at the hospital—"

"Why? Is my uncle hurt?"

"No, no, but one of our people was shot, and *Na sha dii* was waiting until his daughter arrived, but he should be here soon." And indeed, as if she had summoned him, there was the ding of an elevator arriving and Richard stepped out into the hallway. He checked in surprise at the sight of the young man.

"Paul?"

"Wasn't sure you'd recognize me," Paul said with an open and engaging smile. "I mean, it has been almost thirteen years."

From the emotion that flickered across Richard's face, Mosi had the strong sense that the comment was more passive-aggressive than informational, but her guardian let it go. "You look a lot like your mother." Richard gestured toward the doorway. "Please come in. How is my sister? And your father?"

"They're both doing well. Mom's doing more administrative work at the hospital than surgery now, and dad finally landed a new job. Granddad is—"

Richard abruptly interrupted. "And you? You're all done with school now?"

Paul looked startled and Mosi wanted to tell him to never bring up the Right Honorable Judge Robert Oort anywhere in Richard's hearing. The estrangement between Richard and his father was likely to never be healed, and Paul might want to avoid jumping into *that* shark tank.

Estevan closed the door behind them, and Paul's eyebrows went even higher when the raised arm gave him a brief flash of the shoulder rig.

"Uh, yeah, finished up my master's, trying to decide

about the PhD." He gave a laugh. "Honestly I'm kind of sick of school."

"I hear you," Mosi found herself saying and shared a smile with him. "What did you study?"

"Agricultural science with a focus on plants. Spent my gap year working in sub-Saharan Africa on the effects of climate change. Mostly Zimbabwe and Namibia."

"Good for you," Richard said, indicating the sofa. "Sounds like you should be working for us."

Paul gave a delicate cough. "Well, honestly that's why I'm here, but it seems a bit maladroit with what just happened. I heard one of your people was hurt. Are they all right?"

"He's going to recover."

"What happened?" Paul asked.

Mosi caught the quick frown that flickered across her guardian's face as quick as summer lightning. She wondered at the reaction. Mosi also noticed that Fox didn't seem to be listening to Eddie and Chen any longer. Instead, he was staring at Paul, a small frown between his brows. Mosi gave a mental sigh. She might not be able to interpret Richard's expression, but she had a feeling she knew exactly what *that* was about.

Richard glanced around the crowded room. "I think we should speak privately, Paul."

"Easier to tell me no that way?" Paul said with a smile.

"That's not my intent, but there are … issues."

"Granddad?" Paul began, only to once more be stopped by Richard's upraised hand.

"Not the place. So, let's step aside."

"Dinner's on the way," Mosi said as Richard started to

walk away. "But I could add another plate."

"I ate before I came," Paul said. "But thank you."

The two men vanished into one of the adjoining bedrooms and shut the door. Pamela emerged from the bedroom on the other side of the sitting room.

"Any idea why my nephew is here?" Pamela asked. "And does my sister know?"

"Says he's looking for a job. And he didn't say," Mosi answered.

"That's all we need. *More* relations riding to the rescue of the golden child."

"Isn't Richard the golden child?" Mosi asked.

"Oh god, no. Richard is the blackest of black sheep. And was thrown into the outer darkness *years* ago, and then I got to join him there."

"Hey, it's more fun out here in the outer darkness," Mosi said her voice catching on a laugh.

"I don't know if I would go that far, but it's certainly more exciting what with monsters, and demons, and assassins—"

"Oh my!" Mosi chortled. Pamela gave her a mock frown. "So who is the golden child?" Mosi asked.

"That would be Paul, of course. The blessed son destined to live up to the Oort family expectations since the first son was such a spectacular disappointment."

"Richard's just one of the richest men in the world. Keeps the world safe—"

"And he's a godless homosexual surrounded by an evil cabal from which Paul will have to be rescued," Pamela concluded rather bitterly. "At least that's how my sister, brother-in-law, and father will see it."

"Ooh cool," Mosi purred. "First the outer darkness and now I get to be a member of an evil cabal. I'm feeling delightfully wicked."

Pamela chuckled, slipped an arm around Mosi's shoulders, and gave her a hug.

✧　✧　✧

"YOUR MOTHER IS not going to be happy about you coming here," Richard said.

Damon was seated on the end of the unmade bed, hair tousled and clothes wrinkled. He looked exhausted and Richard felt that clenching ache around his heart again.

"I know. She doesn't want to accept that the world isn't how she thought it was, so it's easier to just cut you off. Also Granddad—"

"Don't," Richard said, his hand flying up in a stop gesture. It was starting to irritate him that Paul kept mentioning the judge. *Was it deliberate?*

"Wow, I guess the ostracism goes both ways," the young man said.

"Where my father is concerned, yes," Richard replied and didn't amplify. He folded his arms and waited, throwing the conversational burden back onto Paul.

After a nervous throat clearing, his nephew continued. "Anyway, I just thought it's time we tried to heal the rift …"

Richard and Damon exchanged a glance, and Richard gave a minute nod to his spouse.

"Kid, your uncle and I have both been cops. We can spot

bullshit a mile away. Even if you do wrap it up in a pretty package with a big bow." Paul's cheeks reddened and he dropped his eyes to the floor.

"So, why are you here? Really?" Richard snapped. "My family and my friends were subjected to a mass shooting event today. One of my people is in the hospital. Twenty-one people are dead and twenty-three wounded. I'm tired, hungry, angry, and sad—and I have precisely zero tolerance for games right now."

His big blue eyes widened even further, and Paul looked less like a confident young man and college graduate, and more like a hurt and embarrassed child. As Richard watched, anger replaced the chagrin. Paul opened his mouth to respond, and Damon stepped in to spread a little oil on the roiling emotional waters.

"You should be glad you're family, kid. You should hear him when he actually wants to tear the hide off somebody. Now, tell us why you're here and let's see if we can help," Damon said, his tone warm and kindly.

Mercifully his nephew calmed down. After an awkward silence, he cleared his throat and said, "I follow the Svalbard Global Seed Vault on social media, and read that you and Mr. Uyanik were partnering with them on the Ark project. I want to work on that. Though with Uyanik's death, I guess that might not happen now."

"No, it will continue," Richard said sharply. Paul blinked rapidly at that. "It's a way to honor his life and memory. Also, no single individual is that essential."

"Well, I can think of a couple who might be," Damon muttered and Richard shot him an irritated look.

"I know it's rather moot now, but why come here to appeal to me and not apply directly to Uyanik's company?" Richard asked. "He was the actual designer and driving force behind the Life Ark project."

Paul gave him a wry look. "Well, I thought I might have a bit more of an *in* here … more *fool me*." But he softened the implicit insult with a shy smile and Richard saw an echo of his mother's bright charm in her grandson.

Damon chuckled. "And instead you got the third degree." He turned to Richard. "So you gonna stop being such a hard-ass, and take in another stray?"

Richard heaved a sigh. "I suppose so, though I'd still like to know if your mother is okay with this. She hasn't been all that happy with me for some time now."

"Richard, I'm twenty-four years old. I really don't need a permission slip from the folks. Also, if I'm working with you, she might be willing to give you—I mean Lumina—another chance."

"Kid's got a point," Damon said.

"All right. I'll talk with them, but not right now. Emirhan's daughter and his people are grieving and the lawyers are going to have to get into it before we get the project back on schedule"

"And it might not be necessary," Damon offered. "Not if that bright, young Brit is actually onto something."

"Even if he is, the colonists will have to take seeds and embryos in order to have a successful settlement, so Paul's skills would be useful."

Paul looked back and forth between them. "What?"

Damon stood and stepped next to Richard. "Soon-to-be

Dr. Erskine is working on faster-than-light, and yeah, because of association with this guy," he gave Richard a nudge with his shoulder and a fond smile. "I can actually throw around terms like that as if I actually understand any of it." Damon paused and sniffed. "But I think the food has arrived, so let's table all this for now." Damon leaned down and whispered in Richard's ear. "You gonna eat for me?"

"Are *you*?" Richard countered.

"I'm sure gonna try."

"Then I will too." And Richard leaned in and gave him a soft kiss on the lips.

They followed Paul into the sitting room. The scientists were gathering around the room service cart like sharks drawn to chum. Paul moved to join Fox and Mosi. Pamela caught Richard's eye and jerked her head off to the side.

Richard sighed and moved to join her. Damon stayed at his side. "So are we sending Chen, Milind, and Eddie back to Rochester, New York, or are they returning with us to New Mexico? And how long is Ron likely to be in the hospital?" his sister asked.

"Probably three days."

"This is a lot of people for the Gulfstream," Pamela said.

"Look, not to be alarmist—" Damon began, only to be interrupted by Pamela.

"But of course you're going to be."

It was a game his sister and husband had played from the moment they had met. At one point Richard had thought *they* might become a pair before Damon had finally confessed his attraction and love for Richard.

Damon's expression turned serious. "Look, we know

Emirhan was a target, but so were a lot of these big brains who taught at the college." He glanced at the gaggle of scientists. "We've got a shit ton of big brains who work for us and we know whoever shot up the graduation has access to pretty high tech weaponry. One well-placed missile and ..." He made a boom gesture with both hands.

Richard scrubbed at his face feeling the prickle of stubble against his fingertips. "And it wouldn't be that hard to trace a private jet departing from Logan or any adjacent airports," he muttered.

"So, we divide everybody up and put them on commercial planes. Whoever these people are, I doubt they're ready to shoot down ten or twelve commercial jets," Pamela said.

"At least not yet," Richard said. The bone-deep fear that was always present surfaced from that dark place where he tried to keep it sequestered. At times he worried that if it ever fully escaped, he would never again find the courage to do what was required of him.

Like aways, Damon sensed Richard was going into an emotional spiral. The older man's arms were suddenly wrapped around both siblings and he pulled them tight to his sides.

"Oh come on, let's eat. If we're condemning people to flying *commercial*, we may at least have a last decent meal."

CHAPTER SEVEN

COLD EQUATIONS

D INNER WAS LONG over and most everyone had retired for the night. But for Fox, sleep was proving to be elusive. Kicking away the tangled sheets he grabbed one of the hotel robes and headed out onto the balcony off the sitting room. There he tapped out a cigarette and lit up, careful to make sure the sliding glass door was tightly closed behind him so Mr. Oort wouldn't get hit with any charges because of Fox's smoke. Elbows resting on the railing, he took a deep drag, the tip of the cigarette glowing red in the darkness. The sound of the door being slid open had him frantically trying to stub out the cigarette.

"Relax, I won't tattle on you," said Paul van Gelder. "But it really is a filthy habit." His tone was so arch and sanctimonious that it had Fox frowning in confusion. Paul answered his confusion with a grin. "So, may I bum one?" At Fox's look of surprise he added, "Mom's a doctor, I get the lecture all the damn time."

Paul leaned over the lighter to guard the flame against the night breeze, took a deep drag, leaned back, and blew out a long tendril of smoke. He cocked an eye at Fox. "So what's *your* story? How do you come to be mixed up in my crazy uncle's crazy orbit?"

"Mr. Oort and Mosi and … and that strange Cross fellow saved my life last night, and I guess today too."

"You were at the shoot 'em up at the MIT Corral?"

Fox felt a tendril of unease at the casual description of what had been the second most terrifying experience of his life. He swallowed hard and nodded. "It was bloody awful. The screaming … I've never seen that much blood in my life."

"And the night before? What was that about?"

Fox gave the other man a sharp look. "Why so interested?"

Van Gelder gave a one shoulder shrug. "Because I'm not sure what to believe. I've never seen any of this stuff that Uncle Richard and Aunt Pam go on about. There was a period when we stayed with Richard in New Mexico. He turned up in Boston in the middle of the night and swept us all away, but then nothing happened and forcing my folks to leave their lives …" He shrugged. "It felt stupid, and all this talk about how gods were really just aliens pretending to be gods really freaked out my mom, so we went home. Well, to a new home. My dad had managed to fuck up pretty spectacularly and lose our house and savings. Richard bailed us out. Bought a us a new house." Paul cocked his head to the side. "After sort of being the reason we lost the first one because he left my dad hanging out to dry—or so my dad says."

The entire conversation had a bit of that *too much infor-mation* vibe, making Fox very uncomfortable. He was British for fuck's sake, he doubted he'd be this open with his own family much less someone he had just met a few hours before. Fox responded with a noncommittal *hmmm*.

Paul gave him a wicked grin. "To answer the question you're *not* asking: No, my dad isn't all that grateful. He's resentful as hell."

Fox cleared his throat. "Actually, if someone were to buy *me* a house, I would be enormously grateful. And by the way, I *wasn't* going to ask that question."

"Well, my dad is kind of an asshole. And you appear to be a much nicer person than a lot of my friends who would *totally* ask. And now I have another interesting thought."

Fox was starting to dread Paul's "interesting" thoughts.

"I wonder if Uncle Richard paid for my schooling too? Probably. Pretty sure Dad blew my college fund along with everything else." There was another one of those insouciant grins. "Maybe I ought to send Uncle a fruit basket or something. But seriously, is it real? Any of it? Because all this ... stuff"—Paul twiddled his fingers in the air like a wizard conjuring a spell—"blew up our family. On one side: Granddad, Mom, and my dad. On the other, Richard and my Aunt Pamela."

"And where does that leave you?" Fox asked.

"In the very uncomfortable and decidedly squishy middle," Paul said with a laugh.

Another awkward silence and Fox finally asked, "So, is that why you're here? Asking for a job as a form of rebellion?"

"Ouch, the other question would have carried a lot less burn." Fox felt hot blood rushing to his cheeks. Paul laughed. "Relax. Kidding." Paul tilted his head back and blew out a long streamer of smoke. "So have you seen the sword thing?"

"Seen it. Felt it." Fox shivered.

"Judging by your reaction it wasn't ... pleasant."

"Far from it. Felt like every nerve in my body was on fire."

"Shit, guess it's a good thing Mom never let Richard use it on me. Then again, I was only eight."

"I wasn't offered a choice," Fox said. And he suddenly wasn't certain how he felt about that violation of his personal choice and integrity.

Paul's expression closed down and he seemed to be looking inward. "Hmm, wonder if I'll be? Required to do that, I mean."

"I don't know for certain, but if I had to hazard a guess ... I'd say yes."

Paul took a long drag on his cigarette, then studied the glowing tip for a long moment. Plucking a bit of tobacco off his lower lip, he finally asked, "All this stuff"—the tip traced a red arc in front of his face as Paul gestured—"it really is real?"

"I can assure you unreservedly, it is categorically, decisively, and absolutely real!" Fox said, his tone fervent. He glanced up at the taller man. "Now, does that make you feel better or worse?"

"Unreservedly, categorically, decisively, and absolutely worse," Paul said, his eyes alight with laughter.

At times, Paul made Fox tense and uncomfortable, but there was something undeniably charming about the other man. Fox crushed out his cigarette and then realized he had no idea how to dispose of the evidence. Tossing it off the balcony seemed gauche.

Paul chuckled. "Flushing them down the toilet would probably be our best option," he whispered theatrically.

Fox found himself also smiling as if they were teenage co-conspirators keeping naughty behavior from their parents.

"And at some point I expect the full story about what happened the night you became a believer," Paul concluded.

✧   ✧   ✧

THE NEXT MORNING Damon found it interesting to watch Paul and Fox's reaction to the smoothly-operating machine that was Lumina. Richard had issued orders and the security team had quickly put everything into motion. Plane tickets acquired, and armored cars to ferry the various groups to those planes. Fox received a call from the dean of his department congratulating him on landing such a prestigious work-study scholarship. Fox's apartment was packed up, broken lease fee paid, clothing and personal items in suitcases ready to be delivered to the Gulfstream.

Richard himself was like a small dervish as he paced back and forth in the suite, phone in hand, headphones in place, as he remonstrated with the Massachusetts's authorities. They had been awakened at four in the morning by a phone call from Emirhan Uyanik's daughter, Feray.

Thirty-two years old, with *two* PhDs (in engineering and computer science), Feray was normally coolly confident and elegant. In fact, Mosi had once confided to Damon that she hoped she'd grow up to be as cool as Feray, but that hadn't been the woman on the phone in the grey hours before dawn. She had been in tears because the authorities were refusing to release her father's body.

Emirhan and Feray had been extraordinarily close. She not only shared her father's passion to see humanity reach for the stars, she'd worked at Emirhan's side to bring that goal to fruition.

Rather like Mosi and Richard. And the comparison shook Damon. He did not want Mosi trying to get Richard's body back from an Old One hotspot somewhere in the world, and the illness ravaging his own body meant that Damon wouldn't … *couldn't* be at Richard's side. Not any longer.

So, now Richard was calling in favors, haranguing bureaucrats, maybe paying bribes for all Damon knew, to get the body released so Emirhan could be buried in accordance with their Muslim faith. Not that the father-daughter team were religious—they weren't—the Uyaniks just honored their culture.

It was a balancing act for Lumina when selecting partners to work with, Damon reflected, as he rolled Richard's suitcase over to the door. *They* all knew the truth behind the gods, but they didn't want to overtly state that they wouldn't work with religiously affiliated people, because that wasn't strictly true. People who actually followed the tenants of the Christ figure that splintered an Old One and created Cross were fine. Progressive sects within the world's great faiths, also fine. Lumina's basic standard had been summed up by Damon over a Christmas dinner years ago, when he had said: *People can believe any damn fool thing they like as long as they don't proselytize or make laws based on whatever their particular Sky Daddy has to say on any given subject.*

Richard had amended that to include: *Nor launch reli-*

gious wars, pogroms, genocides, or acts of terrorism under the banner of their faith.

And Mosi had added the final cherry to their simple philosophical philosophy; Lumina would work with people who lived by the tenants of *as ye would that men should do to you, do ye also to them likewise.* Those were people that Lumina could trust.

The uninjured members of the Nerd Posse, Paul, and Fox were finishing off their room service breakfasts when Estevan came in and said they were ready to ferry them to the airport for their flights back to Rochester. Milind and Chen went to get their luggage. Eddie was piling a few pastries in a napkin so he'd be fortified for the flight. Just before leaving, he placed a hand on Fox's shoulder.

"Once we know you being at the lab won't bring down a storm of monsters on us, we'll get you out to Rochester, but for now it's better you stick close with Richard and Mosi. They can keep you safe. Keep working on your dissertation, we'll set up experiments for you and we can Zoom about the results."

Fox pushed away his plate after that exchange, looking a bit ill. Damon's eyes narrowed at Paul's expression that seemed both startled and amused, which had Damon falling back on nearly twenty years in law enforcement—something about the boy felt *hinky*. He was Richard's nephew, but given the family drama that defined the Oorts, it frankly didn't mean shit. Nephew or not, Damon was going to keep an eye on the youngster.

Richard's call ended, and he gathered them all with a glance and a jerk of his head. Damon ignored him and busied himself putting a half an omelet and a ham slice on a plate.

"We are going to take the Lumina jet, but we're going to stop in Houston first," Richard was saying as Damon carried over the plate. "We're bringing Emirhan home—"

"We're going to be flying with a dead body?" Fox said_ and then seemed embarrassed by his outburst.

"Yes, it's not uncommon. You've probably flown with some and never even known it," Richard said.

"Huh. Yeah, guess I hadn't ever thought about it … how you get bodies … people back home. I mean, I've seen the military stuff, but … well, sorry. Quick question, any chance we can see the Ark?"

"No," Damon said, as he forced the plate and silverware into his husband's hands. "Eat," he ordered Richard, then turned back to Fox. "That's being built in orbit. We launch construction material on conventional rockets out of Spaceport America in southern New Mexico."

"Since they're taking the Svalbard seed bank—" Paul began.

"No, that's incorrect," Richard began, only to have Mosi jump in.

"That is pure unadulterated bullshit being peddled by that asshole Hugo Wannamake," Mosi huffed. Paul looked taken aback at her vehemence.

Damon stepped in before a real donnybrook could begin. "The colonists are going to be given a supply of seed, but their plan is to rotate various crops during the hundreds of years they'll be traveling. So, no—no one is going to send away all the seed. That's what those of us in the law enforcement biz call a lie."

"A damn lie," Mosi added pugnaciously.

"Oh," Paul said faintly.

Richard stepped in to smooth the troubled waters. "With climate change, there are studies being done about the feasibility of moving part of the collection either into space—"

"Where it's for damn sure cold enough," Damon offered with a grin. He cocked an eye down at Richard. "And you aren't eating."

His husband rolled his eyes and cut off a bite, "Or to a facility on the Moon," he said around a bite of the omelet.

"What about radiation degrading the seed germ?" Paul asked.

"That's why it hasn't happened yet," Mosi said. "We want to be absolutely certain we're not risking thousands of years of agricultural diversity until every T and I have been crossed and dotted about a hundred thousand times."

"Right now, in the summer months, we are relying on refrigeration to preserve the seeds, and what happens if the power fails?" Richard asked. "And Lumina takes the long view. War, plague—"

"Asteroid strike," Mosi said.

Damon winked at her. "Zombies."

"Alien invasion … oh wait, we've already got that," Mosi added with a smirk.

"Are you both done now?" Richard asked, trying to look stern, but laughter danced in his blue eyes, and for an instant it felt like a hand had closed around Damon's heart. He loved this small dynamo of a man more than he could hope to express. "At any rate, ignoring my smart-ass ward and wisecracking spouse … there might be an event in the distant future that could take out power or leave people falling back into barbarism, and we need to be sure the seeds are secure."

"Though, if our distant descendants are living in a *Mad Max* world, they're gonna have a hell of a hard time getting to the fucking Moon," Damon said.

Fox had joined them in the midst of this. "Not if there is a human colony on the Moon, ready to step in and rebuild civilization," he said.

"Benevolent overlords from the sky," Paul said with a snort. "It's more likely to end up with the Morlocks and the Eloi."

"Well, aren't you just a little ray of sunshine," Fox snapped. It seemed the young Englishman shared Damon's disquiet about Paul … or he was just jealous because Mosi seemed interested in the other man. *And wasn't that going to be a mess?*

Years ago, Damon had wondered if Lumina would be better off as a monastic order, or run by Amazons. For a moment, he had a wistful fantasy about Mosi, Pamela, Angela, and Dagmar running the joint while he and Richard slipped off to a beach somewhere. But Damon knew that was never going to happen; Richard would never walk away from what he considered his duty. Damon had been a soldier. He knew Richard's likely fate.

Let me die first. I can't bear it if he goes before me … my beautiful, passionate, brave, and talented spouse—the love of my life.

✧   ✧   ✧

MOSI FOUND HERSELF gauging the two young men's reactions to the Gulfstream. Fox had looked poleaxed as he surveyed the elegant interior of the plane, large leather seats, tables, and a foldout bed. Brook and Jerry, who took turns being each other's co-pilots, greeted them. As usual, Jerry was rude, eyeing Paul and Fox, making a sound that was perilously close to a raspberry, and muttering about strays. Brook was welcoming and told Damon they had stocked the galley with their favorites.

Damon clapped the younger man on the shoulder. "I doubt we're gonna starve between here and Houston.

Paul had just moved deeper into the plane and stowed his laptop case in the overhead compartment. He seemed completely at ease with his surroundings.

Of course, he would have traveled on the Lumina jet back when Richard brought the family to New Mexico.

When he was eight, Mosi thought.

Maybe a kid wouldn't have realized how unusual this was, but as an adult you would have thought he'd have more of a reaction. Why did this bother her? Paul was charming, involved in work that mattered, trying to make the world a better place … and very pretty. And maybe *that* was the problem.

Mosi resented having her hormones rattled this way, so she was reacting with suspicion and confusion. Despite what Richard might wish for her, Mosi had accepted that love, marriage, or children were not in her future. Sooner (or preferably) later, her luck or Richard's luck would run out and they would die. They would have to hope there was a Paladin or two in place to replace them when the inevitable happened.

There was of course a logical solution for that. Paladins were the result of a surpassingly rare recessive gene, which both she and Richard possessed, so any child they had would be a Paladin. And they weren't actually related. But the one time a now *former* employee of Lumina had made the suggestion, Richard's rage had been frightening. Not because it was so hot, but the deadly cold of it.

Mosi had been sixteen when Dr. Falden had made his proposal. He had been her biology teacher, and like most of the Lumina scientific staff, highly regarded with numerous awards. What he didn't have was an internal editor. Richard had been between meetings and stopped by her homeschool classroom one afternoon to say hello, when Falden had made the suggestion.

At Richard's expression, Mosi had felt sick with fear and hoped and prayed her guardian would never look at her in that way. Falden did have enough insight to realize he was in serious danger and quickly added, *"Well, of course you two wouldn't actually have sex."* And god, hadn't *that* been embarrassing to hear. *"All artificial insemination. But not Mosi, of course, she's far too young. We'd find a surrogate to carry the—"*

He hadn't gotten any farther. Despite Richard's lack of inches, he had seemed lethal and menacing, a slim ice blade ready to cut the man into ribbons.

"Mosi, go upstairs!" he'd snapped. As she left, she heard him say in a low, emotionless tone that was somehow more

terrifying than if he had shouted, *"We no longer have need of your services, Doctor. You will leave the premises immediately."*

Falden had tried to argue. Richard's response had been, *"Do not make me regret my forbearance."*

Over the years she had heard a lot about the founder of Lumina who had recruited Richard. She had only known him as this lost and silent shell, but according to Richard, Damon, and the officers of Lumina, he had been this brilliant, incisive, charismatic figure. He was also an alien creature wrapped in a human form. Kenntnis was thousands, perhaps millions of years old. Would he have allowed such mundane, human relationships as a father-daughter emotional bond to stand in the way of the cold equation?

She rather doubted it.

CHAPTER EIGHT
The Monsters Make It Interesting

They had been in the air for about an hour when Fox heard Richard say, "Paul, please step into the office with me," Richard said.

He looked up from his computer to watch the dynamic between the two men. The look Paul was bestowing on his uncle was challenging, if not downright confrontational.

"Why?"

"We'll discuss it in the office." Richard glanced around the cabin of the plane and seemed uncomfortably aware that everyone was staring at the interaction between uncle and nephew with varying degrees of interest. And that included the four members of the security team. Fox found them all intimidating. Honestly, the one woman among the four looked like she could fold Fox into a pretzel and the men were all bruisers.

"Is this about the sword?" Paul asked.

"Yes. I thought you might prefer not to be drooling on the floor of the cabin in front of everyone."

He didn't give me that option, Fox thought a bit resentfully. He glanced over at Mosi and wondered just how stupid and pathetic he had looked in that hotel suite? From the very first moment when he had been groveling on the floor of the computer lab, to being shielded by a man old enough to be his father, all he had done was look helpless and pathetic around her. And now Paul was going to get to drool in private. It didn't seem fair.

The tense standoff was continuing. Paul stood up, he towered over his uncle. "And if I refuse?"

"Then I'll buy you a plane ticket back to Boston after we land in Houston." There was no threat in the tone, however brutal the words themselves might sound, but the effect on Paul was electrifying. His eyes went wide and he reared back as if from a blow.

"Shit, well, that's pretty blunt. Okay, Uncle, let's go talk. But I'm only agreeing to *talk*."

If Van Gelder thought it made him sound tough, he was mistaken. It only made him sound petulant. And that thought gave Fox a little frisson of pleasure. Followed immediately by the thought that he was an awful person and he was probably going straight to Hell.

❖   ❖   ❖

AS THE OFFICE door closed behind them, Richard tried to stand taller, pushing back the dragging exhaustion that seemed to be weighing down his very bones. He waved Paul toward a chair while he sank down behind the desk. The younger man did not accept the invitation.

"Why do I have to do this?" he demanded.

"Because you're a danger to us if you don't," Richard replied quietly.

Paul scoffed. "In what possible way could I be a danger to

you? I came here voluntarily. I'm your nephew for Christ's sake."

"You heard Mosi's speech ... oh wait, you didn't." He scrubbed a hand across his face. "The reason Mosi grew up with me and not with her own family was because her brother was influenced and affected by the Old Ones, and he killed them all—father, mother, grandfather. He tried to kill Mosi too."

"Shit."

"An appropriate response."

"Okay, but if I agree to this, will it make me like you?" Paul asked.

Richard looked up to meet his nephew's challenging gaze. "What does that even mean?"

"Cold, emotionless ... unfeeling."

It was like a blow to the gut and Richard couldn't disguise the flinch. "I'm sorry you perceive me that way, Paul. But the fact remains that as long as you have magic in your DNA you are more susceptible to the creatures. More likely to believe in fairy tales and conspiracy theories. More likely to have your fears stoked to the point where you believe violence is the only alternative. The choice is yours, but you have to decide before we land."

Richard stood and pushed past the much taller man and left Paul alone in the office. He went in search of Damon.

Damon instantly clocked Richard's expression and agitation. "Hey, babe, what's wrong?"

Richard settled onto the arm of Damon's chair. "Do you find me cold and emotionless?" he asked quietly.

Damon wrapped his arms around him, pulled him close

and pressed a kiss against his temple. "Don't be silly," he whispered into Richard's ear. "Your problem, if you can call it a problem, is that you feel *too* much. Honestly, your nephew is pretty much living down to my expectations about the Oort clan.

Richard nudged his shoulder against Damon's. "Even Pamela?"

"Your sister is the worst of them all. That woman is tough as nails and the other Oort who's a real pain in my ass." Richard felt the color rising in his cheeks. Damon gave him a look that was half-humorous and half-suggestive. "Someday I'm gonna get you to talk dirty," Damon whispered in his ear. "Or at least not turn beet red when I do."

Richard took a nervous glance at the rest of the airplane. "I somehow doubt it," Richard whispered back. But then Paul emerged from the office and moved to talk with Mosi. As Richard watched, she nodded, got up, and came over to where he and Damon were sitting awkwardly.

"May I have the sword, *Na sha dii?*"

"So, Paul has decided?"

"Yeah, but he wants me to do it," Mosi said.

Richard felt himself scowl and Damon chuckled, "Can't say I blame him." He lifted his hands as if he was balancing something on his outstretched palms. "Pretty girl ... uncle. Uncle ... pretty girl. Sorry, babe, no contest."

"All right." Richard wriggled around until he could reach the holster at the small of his back, pulled out the hilt and slapped it into Mosi's hand. "Let me know how he does."

She gave him a salute and went back to Paul. They vanished into the office. Richard wasn't the only ones watching closely. Fox was focused like a bird dog on the pair.

"Yeah, like that's not gonna be a problem," Damon whispered into his ear.

✧   ✧   ✧

"HOW BAD IS this likely to be?" Paul asked as Mosi drew the sword.

"I can't predict. It's different for everyone. The fact that Richard is a Paladin and you're his nephew might affect how you react. Also, you're in the sciences, that usually means a less violent reaction. It just depends on the amount of magic in your DNA. We're trying to figure out how to test for it, and also design a CRISPR to remove it without needing to use the sword, but we haven't—well, our geneticists haven't cracked it yet."

He was just staring at her and Mosi shifted uncomfortably. "What? Does that fall under the TMI heading?"

"No, it's interesting. I'm just trying to wrap my head around all of this." He gestured around the small office. "The world you inhabit."

"Well, the monsters do make it interesting," Mosi said.

"Oh, *those*. No, I was talking about the money. They say the rich are different. Are you different?"

She cocked her head to the side and eyed him, trying to decide if this was awkward teasing, maybe even really awkward flirting, or if there was real malevolence behind the remarks.

"I'm different because I'm a Paladin, and the money isn't mine or Richard's. We hold it in trust for Lumina, and spend it trying to protect our world."

"Wow, I guess no sense of humor goes along with the no magic thing," Paul said.

She leveled a withering look at him. "No, that's because if that was supposed to be a joke, it wasn't funny. Just like when I ask, Where do you get off being such an asshole? isn't funny. It's an honest question. Now, are we doing this or not?"

"Ouch." He swept the back of his hand across his mouth, and she decided that he was scared, and was defaulting to assholery to cover that. "Do I need to do anything?" he asked.

"No, we just want to make sure you're well away from any furniture. Depending on the reaction you don't want to be slamming into anything."

"Maybe I should just be on the floor before you do it," the young man suggested.

"Hmm, that's not a bad idea. Most people get bruised when they collapse. Of course, it's already weird enough that we're asking people to let us touch them with a sword. They're really going to think we're some kind of Satanic sex cult if we want them to lie down on the floor first."

"Oh, I don't know," Paul said, as he dropped gracefully to the floor. "If you're the one doing the touching it might seem pretty ... inviting." He folded his arms behind his head and smiled up at her. "How's this?"

"Good." And to cover the flush she felt rising and her confusion, she quickly tapped the flat edge of the blade against his knee.

As reactions went, it wasn't that bad. About on a par with Fox's reaction. She held out a glass of water to him as he climbed shakily to his feet.

"Wow, that was kind of intense." He took a long drink of water and gusted a sigh. "I wouldn't have minded something a little stronger."

"So how did it feel? And how do you feel now?" Mosi asked.

"It hurt. Felt like my bones were on fire. Weird sensation." He shook his head and bestowed another of those thousand-watt smiles on her. "Don't know if I feel particularly less magical now."

"Well, you weren't a practitioner, and given that your reaction was so minor I doubt you could ever have learned to throw even the simplest spell."

His expression was odd and she couldn't fully interpret it. "It's weird how you people view this ..." At her puzzled frown, he amplified. "Magic. Just think of how the word is used. She was *magical*. It was a *magical* evening. It felt like *magic*. It's aways used as something wonderful, but you say that it's evil."

Mosi shook her head. "More that, it's unnatural. It undermines our Euclidean reality. And to access and use magic often requires that the practitioner do something evil. Remember, they're feeding on pain and hate and fear to power the spells. I mean, who would want to deliberately do that?"

"Have you seen the news?" Paul asked with a snort. "Wars and genocides, child abuse, rapes, murders. We're fucking shitting where we eat and live." He turned away and set the glass on the desk. "Humans really are kind of vile."

"What could you have possibly experienced that has

made you this cynical and negative?" Mosi asked. "It seems like your dad blowing the family's money is the worst thing that's ever happened to you. You can always make more money."

"Easy for you to say growing up with a multi-billionaire."

"Oh cupcake, you don't want to go there. Maybe I'll take you out to the family hogan sometime and let you follow the sheep."

"Sounds pretty idyllic. When do we leave?"

"You really are the worst kind of *bilagáana*. White people who think we're so wise, and in touch with nature, and spiritual. What we are is a displaced people, driven onto reservations, left without running water, intermittent electricity—unless the family was in Shiprock. I had to ride a bus for an hour to get to my elementary school—"

"And did you have to walk uphill both ways?" Paul snarked and Mosi's patience vanished.

"I find it hard to believe you are even *slightly* related to *Na sha dii*. You are *such* an asshole."

She left him gaping as she whirled and left the office, determined not to speak to him for the remainder of the journey.

Actually, maybe never again.

❖ ❖ ❖

THEY HAD LANDED in the private jet area of the William P. Hobby Airport. Richard had rather curtly ordered Paul and Fox to remain on the plane along with Christopher and Braulio from the security team to keep them safe. Pamela—

carrying a file folder containing legal documents (a death certificate and the release from the coroner's office in Massachusetts)—and Damon followed Richard and Mosi down the steps of the Gulfstream.

Feray was waiting with the hearse. There were also two stretch limousines parked nearby. The young woman was pale but composed, only her red-rimmed eyes and the bruised quality of the skin beneath those striking green irises betrayed her grief. She wore the professional woman's uniform: narrow skirt, high heeled pumps, a silk blouse, and a chic jacket (despite the Houston heat). Except all white. Like Mosi, she had a waterfall of jet black hair, but today it was confined in an elegant chignon.

Damon and Pamela held back, standing next to the belly of the plane, while the door on the luggage compartment whined open. Narrowing his eyes, Damon studied the two limos confirming they were armored and had run-flat tires as he'd ordered.

Richard and Mosi walked up to greet Emirhan's daughter. He was too far away to hear what Richard said, but Feray's face crumpled and Richard quickly pulled her into an embrace, while Mosi gently laid a hand on the older woman's shoulder.

Damon was so proud of Richard. Physical contact came hard for his sweetie. A childhood spent in a cold and austere household where hugs were rare led to an adolescence spent bed-hopping with numerous sexual partners of both sexes, as he sought love and validation in all the wrong places. Those games had ended in a brutal rape that had left Richard impotent and celibate for years. Damon sometimes still had to wake Richard from nightmares that left his husband with pupils blown wide, panting, and bathed in sweat.

"You and Mosi have been a good influences on him," Pamela said in her brusque, matter-of-fact way.

"Yeah, whatever Richard might say and try to enforce, he *is* a father and this is a child hurting and grieving, so he's going to be there for her."

"And Mosi knows all about losing parents to violence," the lawyer added softly.

"As do you, Pam. Don't discount your own pain."

She gave a one shoulder shrug. "Our mother committed suicide. Not remotely the same."

"At some point you gotta forgive her—and yourself—for not doing more."

Pamela's grey eyes held a glare as they were raised to meet Damon's brown eyes. "Thank you, Dr. Weber," she almost snarled. "I'm fine."

He smiled at her, not taking tone or words to heart. This was an old game between them. "Actually you're not. All you Oorts are so totally fucked up and I love you both." Pamela's mouth fell open; she blushed and looked away.

The cargo bay was now open and Damon motioned to the mortuary staff waiting. They came over quickly with the rolling carrier, carefully slid the casket from the belly of the plane, and began to wheel it toward the hearse with Damon and Pamela following.

"I want to see him," Feray was saying as they joined the trio in the center of the tarmac. She had stepped out of Richard's embrace.

Richard gently touched her forearm. "Let's wait until we

reach the mosque."

"There are traditional funeral practices that—"

"All followed. We found a Muslim mortuary. All the proper rituals were observed. I'm sorry, but an autopsy was required by Massachusetts. I know that's not preferred in your faith—"

"It's all right, Richard. We live in this world and he died by violence. Anything that can help bring those responsible to justice is all that matters. And I'm certain you wish to return home, there is no need for you to come with me—"

"Yes, there is. We're going to be there for you."

"You're not going to face this alone," Mosi added.

"I want to know what happened. I want to know who did this," Feray said, her voice quivering with suppressed rage and grief.

"We're working on it," Damon said. "You'll know as soon as we do."

She nodded stiffly. Pamela handed over the folder and Feray clutched it tightly to her side. Richard glanced over to the hearse. They had finished loading the casket and were closing the back doors.

"Shall we?" Richard gestured at the waiting limousines.

"*Na sha dii*, may I ride with Feray?" Mosi asked. For an instant, the other woman's rigid control slipped and the grief and gratitude slipped through.

"I'd like that," Feray said and Richard nodded. He turned to Joselita, the lone woman on the current security team, who immediately fell into step with the two young women.

Once Damon, Richard, and Pamela were settled in the second limo with Estevan riding shotgun up front, Damon asked, "We really just going to leave those two beamish boys just sitting on the plane?"

"It won't kill them and they have no place in this," Richard said shortly.

"If you want I can stay with them," Pamela offered. "Also, one of us better talk to our sister and let her know Paul isn't dead or kidnapped."

"She'll probably think being with us is worse," Richard said with a bit of gallows humor. "But you are probably the best person to talk her off the roof. God knows, I'm not."

"We know the funeral's going to happen fast," Pamela said. "But it might be best if we get a hotel for tonight. Fly back to New Mexico tomorrow. And Feray is going to want to hear exactly what happened from those of us who were there."

Richard sighed. "I was so looking forward to my own bed, but you're right. Pam, you mind handling all that?"

"No. I'll text you with the arrangements," she said as she climbed out of the car. "We'll be waiting for you at the hotel."

CHAPTER NINE

IN A BOND FILM

THE DOOR CLOSED and the car started to move. "Wait," Richard said sharply.

The driver braked but said, "We'll lose the other car."

"Hardly an issue since we're all going to the same place." Damon knew he was watching until his sister was safely back on the plane.

"All right, now you may go." They pulled away, heading for the gate out of the airport. The hearse and the other limo had long since left.

There was something about the set of the driver's neck, and the way his chauffeur's cap was pulled low, that had Damon on edge. "You know where we're going, right?" Damon asked. Richard shot him a questioning look.

"Yeah," the driver said. He didn't look up at the rearview mirror. Damon nudged Richard in the side, and jerked his chin toward the driver. Richard gave a minute nod and shifted his coat so his pistol was more easily accessed.

As they wove through the streets of Houston, Estevan gave a casual shrug that also caused his jacket to gape open and he said in Navajo, "This clown is not a licensed *driver*."

It took Damon a second to parse that and the emphasis. Then he realized Estevan meant chauffeur and there wasn't a

Navajo word for that. It was also clear Estevan hadn't wanted to say chauffeur in English.

All the major staff of Lumina now spoke some Navajo, since it was an extremely difficult language to learn, and few people spoke it. Richard had a gift for languages, so he had taken to it like a duck to water.

"Bail or takedown?" Estevan asked, still in Navajo. The driver's neck was tensing and he kept glancing over at Estevan and then down at his phone.

"Bail," Richard replied in the same language.

They rolled up to a stop light and all three men grabbed door handles and bolted out of the car. Damon had one brief glance of the driver gaping at them, then grabbing up his phone, before they all took off running.

It wasn't long before Damon's chest was heaving as his compromised lungs struggled to draw in enough air. His steady, rhythmical footfalls began to hitch and stagger, and then Richard was there wrapping an arm around his waist. Richard slowed their headlong flight and used the respite to call Mosi. He put it on speaker as they continued to walk hurriedly down the street.

"Where are you?" Richard asked tensely.

"At the mosque. Where are *you?*"

Damon leaned in and said hoarsely, "Is the limo driver around?"

"No. He's outside. Hang on." He heard footfalls. "Looking at him now. He's pacing back and forth by the car. He's on his phone. He looks … upset. What's going on?"

Damon and Richard exchanged glances. "We're not sure," Richard said. "Under no circumstances do you get back in that car. We'll be there soon."

Richard glanced around, then led them into a department store where they quickly cycled through the men's department and bought different coats to change their profiles. Richard added a fedora, Damon and Estevan went with cowboy hats.

"I mean we *are* in Texas, boss," Estevan said.

"On the *run* in Texas," Richard grumbled.

Damon nudged him with a hip. "Hey, that'd be a great country and western song. 'On the Run in Texas.' You should write it."

His spouse glared at him, trying—unsuccessfully—to hide the smile trembling at the edge of his lips. "No, you know how I feel about country music."

They exited through a different door from the one which they had entered. They all stood on the sidewalk as Estevan ordered an Uber for them.

"What the hell is going on?" Richard huffed as he quivered with impatience.

"Doesn't seem like it's the bunch who shot up the graduation," Estevan mused.

"Another simple kidnapping attempt?" Damon suggested.

Richard shook his head. "It doesn't feel like that. It's like we did something unexpected, but damned if I know what it was."

Damon didn't answer, instead he swapped hats with Richard, which earned him another glare. "I am not a cowboy hat sort of guy," he gritted.

"Which is exactly why you ought to wear it instead of the

fedora, which is *absolutely* a Richard Oort kind of hat. And I have no idea what's going on, but we'll figure it out once we're all safely back together," he concluded, giving Richard's waist a squeeze. A pickup truck with a crew cab turned down the street, heading for them. "And that's the most Uber-in-Texas thing I've ever seen," Damon remarked and he gave Richard a sideways smile. "And by the way, I find it hilarious that one of the richest men in the world is reduced to traveling by Uber."

"You are such an ass," Richard grumbled.

As his diminutive spouse got a foot on the running board and grabbed the hand grip, Damon planted a hand firmly on one of Richard's firm buttocks, and gave him a boost. Richard, red-faced and glaring, looked back at him. Damon blew him a kiss.

❖   ❖   ❖

THE MOSQUE WAS beautiful, reminiscent of the small, jewel-like Rüstem Paşha Mosque in Istanbul, just steps from the magnificent spice bazaar. That triggered a powerful memory of the scents from those sacks filled with dried oregano, red pepper flakes, cumin (both yellow and black), urfa pepper, and dried lemons. Mosi drew in a shaky breath because not all memories of Turkey were good.

Richard had taken Mosi to Turkey when she turned sixteen to introduce her to the men and women who had given them sanctuary when Mosi had been a child. They were still fighting to keep the country secular; an increasingly difficult undertaking as climate change seemed to be pushing people to turn to strongmen to protect their particular group.

Mosi left the courtyard where the funeral would actually be held and entered the interior of the mosque. Two of the four walls were inlaid with exquisite blue tiles. She slipped out of her shoes, the thick carpets soft beneath her feet. Feray was talking with the imam, her oval face beautifully framed by the hijab she had donned during the drive to the Mosque. The older woman had loaned Mosi a scarf and shown her how to arrange it, and Mosi was wearing it now.

Feray finished her conversation and joined Mosi. "Richard and Damon are on the way. There was ... a delay," Mosi said softly.

"Because of the people who killed my father?"

"They didn't indicate that," Mosi said slowly. "We'll know more when they get here."

Feray slipped Mosi's arm through hers and that's when Mosi noticed Feray was wearing the gold signet ring that had adorned the little finger of Emirhan's right hand. She must have taken it when she was finally given the opportunity to look upon her father's face one last time.

Slipping their shoes back on, they went out to the courtyard. The space was filling with family members, men and women who had worked for Emirhan, students for whom he had provided scholarships, and business associates. Gender roles were being observed with men in the front and women in rows behind them. Mosi suppressed the flare of annoyance and reminded herself to honor other people's traditions even if they pissed her off. But was there ever going to be a time when people accepted each other irrespective of gender, race, sexual orientation, or were humans always doomed to divide themselves into them and us, lesser and greater?

Richard and Estevan walked through the graceful arch and into the courtyard now humming with quiet conversations. Excusing herself, Mosi went to join them. The broad-brimmed white cowboy hat made her diminutive guardian look like a kid playing dress up, and she bit her lip to keep from smiling, but he knew her too well. He glared at her, but it held no real heat. Mosi couldn't resist adding insult to injury by holding up a hand palm out and saying, "How, Kemosabe." She was trying to control the laughter edging the words, as he swept off the hat.

Estevan gave a snort, and Richard turned the glare onto his security chief. Damon walked up and had the offending chapeau shoved into his chest.

"Why thank you, darling, and you'll all be interested to know that when I approached your limo driver," he said with a look to Mosi. "To ask him a few questions, he took off like a scalded cat."

"With or without the limo?" Estevan asked.

"Without."

"Which implies he was not the actual company driver," Mosi mused.

"Leaving us to wonder, where *is* the actual driver … drivers," Richard added. "Maybe we should check the trunk?"

Damon rubbed at the back of his neck. "Good idea, but I think the asshole took off with the keys."

"Not a problem," Estevan said. "In my misspent youth I boosted a few cars and popped open a few trunks." He hurried back out of the courtyard of the mosque.

"It's hotter than hell today," Damon grunted. "Hope the

real driver isn't in there baking. I'm going to call the company and find out what the fuck happened."

"Let's also see if we can lift prints off the steering wheel. Find out who our would-be kidnappers might be," Richard said.

"Were they after Feray?" Mosi asked. "Whoever killed Emirhan going for his daughter as well?"

Richard pondered on that for a moment, then shook his head. "No, it was our car that started to deviate. Your driver brought both of you directly to the mosque."

"So, somebody's after *you*," Damon said to Richard.

"I'm not sure, remember how agitated our driver was—" Richard began.

"Same with ours," Mosi added.

The trio stood in silence for a long moment, then Damon said heavily, "They didn't expect us to split up. Which means someone is after the *both* of you, and it's probably not the gang that shot up the graduation. Well, that's just fucking great."

"Looks like Fox wasn't wrong when he said he felt like he was in a Bond film," Mosi said.

"I'll feel so much better when we're all safely home," Richard murmured.

✧   ✧   ✧

THE SERVICE HAD been lovely and dignified, but very different from a Christian funeral. No music, no eulogies, just prayers. Uyanik money had purchased sufficient land to not only to build the mosque but also some surrounding acreage for a cemetery. Since the graveyard abutted the mosque, the mourners walked to the gravesite, the casket carried by three of Emirhan's brothers and his best friend. Damon noticed that the women who did not accompany the procession to the grave tended to be older, but the younger women did. Feray walked behind her father's casket, shoulders back, head erect. Mosi too remained with Richard and Damon.

All of the mourners threw the traditional three handfuls of dirt. One phrase in particular was said by all the Muslims present. Emirhan's body was lowered into the grave, final prayers were said, and the gravediggers began their work.

The crowd began to walk back to the mosque, Damon leaned down and asked Richard, "You know what that phrase was they were all saying?"

"I did a little research on the flight."

Damon gave him a fond smile. "I knew you would have ... which is why I asked."

"*We created you from it, and return you into it, and from it we raise you a second time,*" Richard recited.

"Hmm, we could leave off the last bit when—"

"Don't." Richard stopped, whirled to face him, and fisted his hands in Damon's jacket.

Damon gripped Richard's hands in his. "Richard, it's lung cancer. You know the odds. These treatments are experimental. I need you to be prepared."

"I can't ... I can't bear it." His voice hitched, rough with unshed tears.

"Yes, you can. You're the strongest person I know. That spine of yours is made of tempered blue steel and depleted uranium. Now let's put our own worries and sorrows aside and go comfort a young woman who's lost her father."

Richard looked up at him, his blue eyes glistening a bit. "I love you. And you're the best person I know."

Damon gave a derisive snort. "Yeah, if that's the case then you need to get out more and meet a lot more people." He bent and pressed a soft kiss against Richard's temple.

✧   ✧   ✧

THERE WAS A reception at the Uyanik home. The six acre property was walled and gated with security to match Richard's. Emirhan had faced death threats from fundamentalists, both Christian and Muslim. The house itself was a single story built of white stone, the walls pierced by a multitude of windows, and very modern.

One of Richard's bouts of claustrophobia hit as the crowd of relatives, friends, business associates, and hangers-on flowed in human waves through the public areas of the house. He clutched the slick sides of his sweating glass of lemonade, and tried not to think about the last time he'd attended one of these ghastly events. It had been after his mother's funeral. *At least at this one no one was arriving with a potato chip and tuna casserole,* he thought with a grim, and not terribly successful, attempt at humor.

Damon had, of course, noticed Richard's growing agitation and said gently, "Why don't you go outside. Take a look at the gardens?"

Richard nodded, handed off his glass of lemonade to a white-coated server, and slipped out a set of French doors leading onto a patio. Steps led down into the gardens, and he had soon lost himself among the flowers, trees and decorative shrubbery. It was also hotter and far more humid than he was accustomed to, and his undershirt and dress shirt felt like they had affixed themself to his damp skin. After a cautious look around to make sure no one was about to be alarmed by the sight of his shoulder holster and pistol (and the holster at the small of his back that held the sword hilt) Richard pulled off his suit coat, and folded it over his arm as he continued his ramble.

It was quite the estate. He counted three guesthouses, and strolled past the croquet court, trying to remember the last time he had played. It was a game of the gentry, but also amazingly cutthroat. Pamela had roqueted his ball more times than he could count during their childhood and teenage years, always managing to send his ball so far from the wickets that he had no hope of recovering and winning the game. Pamela had always played to win. He was just grateful she was now playing *with* him rather than *against* him.

As he walked past the swimming pool with its outdoor kitchen, the bright umbrellas like a new form of flowers, Richard found himself repining that he was forced to live in the Lumina penthouse atop the company's office building. Yes, he had a pool too, but in the basement. Also a shooting range and an archery range, also in the basement. And enough canned and freeze-dried food—again in the basement—to make a survivalist envious, but no garden. Unfortunately he had no choice. The entire building was designed as a fortress, a place where Lumina personnel could ride out almost any sort of disaster—human, alien, or climate created. A tactical nuke dropped on them would do them in, but anything short of that was theoretically survivable.

A brief breeze carried the scent of horse to him, and he went in search of the stables. The six stall barn held only two horses. One of them was clearly very old, his coat rough and thick, eyes a bit rheumy, but he immediately came over to nuzzle the palm of Richard's hand.

The other horse was younger, and a bit standoffish until she saw how her friend was getting scratched behind his ears, then the mare came over as well. Richard stroked and scratched them both, and felt guilty that Pamela was stuck waiting for them at the airport. He had learned how to ride, but Pamela had been a devoted horsewoman until their father had declared it a waste of time and forced her to quit riding. *Just like he forced me to give up music*, Richard thought. *Wonder if he did that to Amelia as well?* Was there something his eldest sister had loved that she had to sacrifice to the demand that members of the Oort family were productive, conservative, hardworking members of society, and pleasure did not factor into that calculus *at all*.

Richard found himself wondering if Robert Oort had been raised in the same joyless, hypercritical, and demanding environment that he had inflicted upon his own children. Rijk Oort had died when Richard was a toddler so he had never really known his grandfather. Was there some trauma lurking in his father's past that could explain his cold, judgmental demeanor, especially toward his only son?

It had been awhile since his father had filled his thoughts to this extent. It was probably the fact he had just attended someone else's father's funeral that it was on his mind. What would he do when the word came that Judge Robert Oort had passed from this mortal coil? Attend the funeral? Speak? Would he even be allowed to attend, or had Robert seen to it his son would not be included? Was this a breach that could be healed? Or even should it?

Mortality seemed to press in on him from all sides. *Paladins don't live very long*—one of the first things Cross had ever said to him.

Take me. Not Mosi. It could almost be called a prayer. But there were no gods, and the universe was vast, beautiful, oblivious, and uncaring. It was only in other living creatures that humans could find love, comfort, solace, joy... and absolution.

Richard rested his forehead briefly against the forehead of the old horse and said, "I'm afraid I can't stay and scritch you any longer." He gave them both a final pat and started back to the house only to come across Feray siting on a bench near a fountain. The low drone of honeybees flirting from flower to flower offered a bass counterpoint to the sharp tinkle of the falling water.

He sat down next to her, but offered no comment. They sat in silence for long minutes, then she cast him a sideways look. "You didn't ask if I'm okay."

"Because I know you're *not* okay."

"Then why don't *they*"—she gestured vaguely toward the house—"understand that?"

"Maybe some of them don't actually know that, because they've never experienced a death this close... or this violent. Others because it's too painful to remember the pain.

And maybe a few are emotional clods."

That drew a faint smile. "So many of them want something. Will the company survive? Was I a real CFO or just daddy's little girl? Will I marry, and if I do, what position will *he* hold? Did Emirhan leave me anything in the will? I kind of hate them all right now."

"I understand. And you don't have to answer any of their questions right now."

Feray had her hands clenched tightly in her lap. She opened her right hand, her father's wedding ring glinted in the sunlight. "He wanted to go when *Söz* flew."

Richard had a sharp memory of when Emirhan had named the ship the Turkish word for *promise*, and pain for the loss of his friend once more washed over him.

Feray drew in a shaky breath and said, "Now he'll never see the stars, but I still want a part of him to go. So, I took a lock of his hair and his wedding ring, and I want to send them up when we launch the light sails package up to the construction site. The crew can put them in the command module. It will be a little bit like he is guiding the way."

"I think that's a beautiful idea, Feray."

They sat in silence for a moment, then he asked quietly, "Would you like us to be there?"

"Yes, please. It would be less"—she gestured toward the house—"less ... *this*. Most of them don't ... didn't understand his passion." She shifted around so she could look at him. "Would you go? To the stars? If you could?"

If you follow my path, I will give you the stars.

"In a heartbeat," Richard said.

CHAPTER TEN

A MOST UNMANNERLY MONSTER

RICHARD ASKED BROOK and Jerry to have the plane ready for a seven am departure. Jerry grumbled, he'd hoped to go out honky-tonking after dinner. Brook, younger by several decades, had suggested that the older man should just stay up all night and earned a glare from the grizzled air force vet, and a laugh from everyone else as they sat around the dinner table at Squable, one of Houston's better restaurants. Richard had picked it because it featured small plates as well as full meals.

Fox, Mosi, Paul, and the two pilots were eating their way through their full entrées while Damon picked at one of the small plates and Richard watched him worriedly.

"How was the funeral?" Paul asked, as he cut another bite off his leg of lamb.

"It was a funeral, how do you think it was?" Richard snapped, and Mosi watched the nephew turn red and cast down those gorgeous blue eyes. Her guardian closed his ice-blue eyes briefly and said quietly. "That was churlish of me. I apologize, Paul. There's no excuse for my ill temper.'"

Fox dropped his fork with a clash onto his plate. "No bloody excuse?" He said, his voice spiraling up several octaves. "Let's see." He began ticking it off on his fingers.

"Fought monsters on Thursday night, survived a massacre on Friday, attended a funeral on Sunday." He gave a snort. "Yeah, can't imagine why your temper might be a tad bit frayed."

Paul was looking as queasy as poor Damon. He pushed back his chair and mumbled, "Need to get some air."

Fox looked about with the air of a befuddled hound. "What just happened? Did I do that? Guess I did. Sorry, didn't mean to be gauche."

"It's all right," Damon soothed. "We've all been under a lot of stress."

Mosi dabbed her lips with her napkin, folded it, and set it down next to her plate. "And to be fair, us sciencey types don't do too well on the politeness meter. A lot of us tend to be a bit socially dyslexic."

"Socially dyslexic, I like that. I'm going to pass it on to my mum and dad. They can use it to explain away my behavior when I have to be around Aunt Winifred," Fox said.

"Do we want to hear about Aunt Winifred?" Damon said with a low chuckle.

"God no! She's a blinking nightmare."

As Mosi walked away, she heard Richard say with a chuckle, "Well, now we *must* hear about Aunt Winifred. Please regale us."

She found Paul out in the parking lot lighting up a cigarette. "You really ought to view poor Damon as an object lesson," she said.

"So, it's cancer?"

"Yes. Specifically lung cancer because he smoked like a chimney from the time he was sixteen. He quit when they got married. Richard hates the things, but …" She gave a shrug.

"The damage was done," Paul concluded. She nodded. "What will it do to my uncle if he dies? Can he handle it?"

Mosi gave him a baffled look. "You really don't know him at all, do you?"

"I thought I made that fairly clear," he said, somewhat defensively.

"He'll grieve, of course, but Richard is the strongest person I know. Damon says he had a spine made out of pure tungsten, and I think that's probably true."

"I just wish I could stop pissing him off," Paul sighed.

Mosi didn't usually have a lot of patience with pity parties, but Paul being whiney was managing to amuse rather than annoy her. "You know, this might not actually be about *you*, and may be more about the shit that has been going down all around us." His deep blue eyes were fixed on her. "Here's my advice. Take a step back, try to see if there's a niche you can fill in our little Scooby gang, and don't act like the fact you're family gives you any more perks than say, Fox has."

"Do I really come across as that entitled?"

"Yes."

"Ouch."

"Get used to it. We don't have the time or energy for coddling. The unvarnished truth is pretty much our operating method. Now, let's get back inside before your lamb is completely cold.

✧   ✧   ✧

THEY REACHED NEW Mexico close to noon. Two armored limos had been waiting to whisk them from the Albuquerque Sunport to Lumina headquarters. As they walked through the lobby of the office building, Paulette—the longtime Lumina receptionist—greeted them happily. Estevan peeled off into the security office to make sure the young man he was training as a potential replacement hadn't *screwed things up*. Only he said it in Spanish.

The rest of them crowded onto the elevator and went up to the sixth floor, where Richard's office was located. Twisting his fingers through Damon's he leaned in and said quietly, "Can you get the two boys settled? Mosi and I have a conference call with the company officers at one, and Franz is going to make me eat."

"Damn right he is, because I called ahead and told him you've barely eaten since Massachusetts," Damon said with a fond smile.

Stretching up onto tiptoes, Richard whispered in Damon's ear, "Sometimes I hate you and then I remember how much I love you."

He and Mosi vanished into his office, and the big, wood, glass, and metal doors swung shut behind them. Jeannette was staring at the two young men with the frowning mien of a very disapproving governess. The Brit wilted, but Paul gave her an insouciant grin and walked around the desk to give her a quick hug.

"Don't know if you remember me—"

"Oh, I remember you," Jeannette said in a colorless voice. "I remember how you broke my monitor when you were messing around with the baseball and bat your uncle had given you."

Damon stifled a laugh and tried to pretend it was a cough especially because Paul suddenly looked like the eight-year-old he had been.

"Fox, this is Jeannette Keim, assistant extraordinaire. Jeannette, we need to get these boys settled."

She reached for her phone. "I'll get Jeffrey in maintenance to bring up the beds, and get toiletries and towels in the bathroom on three. Right now there's no one working on that floor."

"I thought this was an office building," Fox said, forehead wrinkling with a frown.

"It is, but we have three-quarter baths on every floor, and offices can be retrofit into bedrooms," Damon explained. "We do have one spare bedroom upstairs, but I figured you boys wouldn't want to share. Let me give you the five cent tour while the rooms are being fixed up."

"I remember most of it from when I was here before." Paul held up his phone, "And I really do need to answer some emails, and probably call my mom and dad."

"That would be good," Damon said.

Jeannette jerked her head toward a door. "Conference room is free."

"Thanks." He treated them all to his thousand-watt smile and vanished into the other room.

"I'd like the tour, five cent or otherwise," Fox said.

"You got it."

They got on the elevator and Damon pressed the key for the basement. "Ms. Keim is rather a Cerberean figure, isn't she? Guarding the way to Mr. Oort," Fox mused.

"I'm just a simple flatfoot with an associate's degree, so you're gonna have to explain that one to me."

"Cerberus, the three-headed dog who guards the way to Hades."

"I'll be sure to tell Jeannette you compared her to the guard dog from Hell." He chuckled at Fox's look. "Relax kid, I won't *actually* do that. Figure we'll skip the office floors. Offices are offices, but you should see the amenities, such as they are."

The elevator landed with a soft bounce and the door slid open. Fox let out a gasp. The pool space really was beautiful. The walls and vaulted ceiling were covered with a rich blue tile, and the water in the swimming pool reflected back the lights. A hot tub was softly bubbling. Fox pointed mutely at the two doors on either side of the full sized pool.

"Steam room and sauna. We also have a gym if you want to work out."

"It reminds me of the Basilica Cistern in Istanbul," Fox murmured.

Damon glanced around the space. "Yeah, it kinda does."

"You've been to Turkey?"

"Oh yeah."

On the run from killers with a nine-year-old in tow. But he would always love and treasure Istanbul. It was where he had finally acknowledged his attraction to Richard. Where they had first made love. Where, when he thought Richard was going to die, he admitted that he loved him.

"Richard swims laps every morning_" Damon began, only to be interrupted by the young Brit.

"I would not presume to interrupt him," Fox said breathlessly.

"Kid, take a pill and chill. I was going to add that he swims when he can't sleep. He swims when he's tense or stressed. So, don't worry about interrupting him. He's like a goddamn otter."

The boy gave him a shy smile. "I noticed on the elevator there was another level that can only be accessed by a key," Fox said.

Damon gave him a grin. "Unless you want to use the gun range, or see our emergency supplies and generators, there's no reason to go down there."

"Gun range?" Fox squeaked.

"Not every enemy gets the sword," Damon said grimly.

✧ ✧ ✧

FOX, TOWEL OVER his arm, and goggles hanging off his fingers, stood hesitating in the doorway leading to the basement swimming pool. The splash of water from the churning kicks of the swimmer already in the pool echoed off the rich blue tile roof that arched overhead, and Fox was reluctant to intrude.

He'd thought he was safe to slip in a swim before dinner. Mr. Oort and Mosi had been locked away the entire afternoon, but there was Richard Oort like a slim, pale missile cutting through the rippling water. Tucking into a tight summersault when he reached each end, he launched himself with a fast shove of his feet. He swam with the same ferocity that Fox had seen during the gunfire at the graduation, but Fox also had the feeling the man was trying to outrun...

well, his life.

And who could blame him?

Fox was about to retreat when Oort stopped swimming laps, gripped the ladder, and pulled off his goggles. He spotted Fox and smiled, and the scientist was suddenly horribly aware of the freckles that littered his body, his scrawny legs, the incipient pot belly that had started to develop as he struggled to complete his dissertation, and the patchy red hair on his chest and abdomen.

Oort, by contrast, had almost no hair on his chest, but banded muscles in his abdomen and arms. What he also had were *scars*. Lots and lots of scars that littered his chest, sides, and one arm. As he climbed out of the pool, Fox gawked at the twisted scar on the front of Oort's right thigh. When he leaned down for his towel, Fox saw the matching scar on the back of the older man's leg. Fox jerked his gaze away, embarrassed by his voyeurism.

Oort gestured at his leg. "Got shot. Bullet did a through and through. Luckily it missed the femoral artery, so I didn't bleed out."

"The bloody monsters have guns?" Fox squeaked.

Once again that sweet and brilliant smile curved Oort's lips. "No, this was the human variety."

Fox swallowed hard. "Am I really safe here?"

"Yes, as safe as you can be anywhere." Oort laid a hand on Fox's bare shoulder and gave it a squeeze. "I give you my word, Mosi and I will do everything in our power to keep you safe. The world and the human race need your genius and creativity."

An aching obstruction formed in Fox's throat. There had

never been a time when his own father had shown that sort of kindness and support. Jonathan Erskine had been a hard-drinking military man that married a genteel girl from an old landed family whose farm abutted the grounds of Blenheim Palace. Erskine had wanted a son to follow him into the military, but instead he had ended up with an asthmatic, cerebral egghead who preferred chess to rugby, books to going to the pub with friends, and was allergic to everything in the great outdoors including horses, dogs, cats, grass, and pollen.

Those shrewd eyes were focused on his and Oort said quietly, "Somehow I managed to hit a sore spot. Sorry, didn't mean too."

"No, no, it's all right. Just … just … never mind."

"Not used to validation?" The man asked astutely.

"How do you *do that*?" Fox huffed.

Oort chuckled. "Took a minor in psychology, add to that years as a police officer and being a boss. Tends to make you sensitive to people's emotions."

"That hasn't been my experience. I was a TA my first year of graduate school, and the professor—my boss—was a right son of a bitch." Fox had a feeling he was pouting and tried to settle his face.

"Well, I hope Eddie and I will prove to be better examples of the breed." Oort slung the towel around his neck. "Take your swim. We'll see you at dinner."

"Seven-thirty, right?"

"Correct. And don't be late. Franz tends to fuss, and he's making something special for dessert."

Fox found himself winded after only fifteen minutes and

he made a promise to himself to start eating better and working out more. He spent the rest of the day in his room, checking on the calculations the globally-linked Sophia computers were running, and polishing what he did have written on his dissertation. It would be so much easier if it could be mostly numbers and fewer words, he thought, as he caught another typo within the text.

He had set an alert on his Apple Watch for seven-fifteen, and headed for the elevator when it went off. His forefinger hovered nervously over the seventh floor button. He finally punched it and rode up the two floors, stepping out into a black and white parqueted marble foyer. There was the sound of conversation to his left, and he walked into a spacious living room. And froze. Caravaggio's *Madonna and Child* was on one wall, set between large floor to ceiling bookcases. Scattered about the room were amazing *object d'art*. Near the windows stood a large grand piano. The rest of the furnishings were equally elegant.

Paul lounged on a white leather sofa next to Mosi, wine glasses in their hands. Damon was in a big leather recliner, a glass of whiskey in his hand. Pamela, looking prim and very lawyer-like in a pencil skirt, silk blouse, and high heels, was holding a glass of something golden and bubbly.

On the glass and chrome coffee table rested a large platter with cheese, grapes, olives, almonds, and sliced salami. The room was redolent with the rich smell of roasting fowl, lemon and sage, and freshly baked bread. Fox felt saliva exploding in his mouth.

Oort appeared from another hallway, his hair still damp and falling a bit in his eyes, making him look younger than his forty-some years. He wore khaki slacks and a mint green polo shirt. Fox watched Paul's eyes widen at the sight of the twisting scar on his arm.

Paul set aside his glass and jumped up. "I'm playing bartender, what are you drinking, Fox?"

What you're doing is establishing that you're family and I'm not, Fox thought, but he managed a smile and said, "Is there, by chance, beer?"

"Oh yes. There is *always* beer," Oort said with an eye roll toward his husband.

"Yep," Damon said proudly. "I'm the beer guy, so we have a good selection. You like that stuff that's so brown and thick you can practically chew it or do you want something lighter in this summer weather? Why don't you pop in the kitchen and Franz'll set you up."

Fox nodded and followed Damon's gesturing hand through an arched doorway and into a dining room that was as exquisite as the living room. The long glass and chrome table had already been set for six. Placemats and napkins slipped through napkin rings. Beautiful china, an array of forks and spoons, and glittering stemware.

He found his way into a large kitchen with a dinette area in a faceted bay window, and several long islands. The overhead track lighting sparkled off the flecks of what looked like blue opal in the chocolate brown granite, and gleamed off the stainless steel appliances.

A plump, little man, his brown hair flecked with grey, and his bib apron spattered with stains, was busily chopping various vegetables to add to a large bowl of lettuce.

"Uh, hello, Mr. Weber said there was beer?"

"Yes, in the other fridge." The man's voice carried a soft accent. "I'm Franz, by the way."

"Oh sorry, rude of me. I'm Fox Erskine," Fox said as he crossed to the second large refrigerator gleaming like a silver Transformer.

He had just pulled out a bottle of stout, when the room was filled with a coruscating prism of colors. Fox dropped the bottle, it landed with a crash on the oak floor, but miraculously didn't break. The chef merely shaded his eyes with one hand.

The flaring multi-colored lights began to coalesce and within seconds Cross stood panting in the center of the kitchen. He was clutching a misshapen object which seemed part metal and part oozing ichor to his sunken chest.

"*Not* in my kitchen!" Franz bellowed.

"Right, sorry. Take it to my box. Be right back. What's for dinner?"

Franz made a threatening gesture with the large knife. "GO!"

"Jeez, take a fucking pill," Cross grumbled, as he once more became streaks of light and he and the drone vanished.

"No manners, no manners at all! A most unmannerly monster," the man groused while he opened a door that held janitorial supplies, then sent an elaborate Roomba off to clean up the mess.

Fox let out a hysterical giggle and popped the cap off his beer.

CHAPTER ELEVEN

SOMETHING'S OFF

FOX ENTERED THE living room as if the floor were made of eggshells. His knuckles were turning white as he gripped the pint glass, the white foam head setting a deep contrast with the rich brown of the stout. Richard stared at him in alarm.

"What's wrong?"

"So … um … your … Old One? He turned up in the kitchen with that drone." Richard leaped to his feet and started past Fox toward the kitchen. "Um … he's not there now. Your chef, Franz, told him to take it outside? It was … oozing … stuff." The boy's halting, questioning delivery would have been charming and rather amusing if the news hadn't been so critical.

Richard made an abrupt about-face, and headed for the elevators, only to be blocked by Damon.

"Sit down. Relax. The creepy, mutated, killer drone will still be there after dinner," he said, his brown eyes alight with affection, but also brooking no argument.

"But—"

"Nope." Damon slipped an arm around his waist and hugged him close as he guided him back to the recliner and pushed him down. "We just got home. We've got guests and family here. We're going to gather around the table and have a fucking family dinner."

"Yes, sir," Richard murmured.

He cupped Damon's cheeks between his hands, feeling stubble rasp against his palms. Then imagined those rough hairs reddening the skin of his inner thighs. His breath went a bit short and he pulled Damon down into a kiss.

His husband seemed to sense where his thoughts had gone, and with a chuckle vibrating against his lips. Damon whispered, "Later, babe."

Franz appeared in the doorway. "Dinner is served."

They drifted into the dining room. As usual, Damon and Mosi were to either side of him, while Richard sat at the head of the table. It always made him feel smaller than he actually was, like a child playing dress up, because the man who had recruited him into this world and this war, and made him the head of Lumina, had dominated both the chair and the space.

There was an interesting little dance as Fox and Paul each jockeyed to sit next to Mosi. Paul won and Fox ended up seated across from her. Mosi used her hair to curtain her face as she turned away from both of the young men to give Richard an eye roll. He lifted his napkin to his lips to disguise his smile.

Pamela, as always, missed all the byplay, as she shook out her napkin with meticulous care and settled it in her lap. Cross jammed his into the neck of his tee shirt, and made a boarding-house reach for the popovers in the bread basket.

Pamela slapped his hand with the back of her fork. "Manners."

"Have none."

"We noticed."

Franz carried in the large cutting board upon which rested two plump roasted chickens. After presenting them, he settled the cutting board at the foot of the table, and quickly and efficiently carved both birds. He had taken over the task after watching Richard butcher the Thanksgiving turkey, followed by Damon doing violence to his chef's soul on the Christmas goose.

The perfect slices were arranged on a gleaming Nambé serving platter with the wings, legs, and thighs forming a graceful pattern around the edges. Holding the platter well over Cross' head, Franz carried it first to Pamela, then to Mosi, and finally to the men. Cross was served last. Franz then disappeared back into the kitchen. Even after all these years, Richard had still not managed to convince the man join them at table.

Richard allowed the youngsters to carry the bulk of the conversation. He felt a bone-deep exhaustion after the events of the past four days. Over the years he had seen a lot of deaths, had doled out more than a few. Neither of them ever got any easier, and maybe that was good. If he stopped feeling anything he would become as monstrous as the creatures he opposed ... or the creature who had recruited him. His eyes drifted to Cross stuffing his face. *Or the monster that serves me.*

After dessert, a delicate lemon soufflé, Cross gave a loud belch and left. Port was served, but Pamela declined. Instead, she stood, walked to the head of the table, leaned down and gave Richard a kiss on the cheek.

"See you in the morning." She rolled an eye to Damon.

"Don't let him stay up too late."

"I won't." He winked at her. "We've got plans." Richard felt himself going red.

"You don't live here?" It was Fox and he sounded shocked. "I mean, after what I went through, and the graduation and—"

"Well, I guess it's not all that dangerous," Paul said. He was leaning back languidly in his chair, spinning his small glass of port by its stem.

"Oh, it's dangerous as hell," Damon said. "But she's—"

Pamela interrupted him. "A hardheaded, stubborn bitch who values her privacy and hated slumber parties even when she was twelve."

It still shocked Richard to hear his sister curse. All the Oorts had been drilled by their father that cursing would not be tolerated in his home. Robert Oort had backed it up by frequently quoting George Washington: *The foolish and wicked practice of profane cursing and swearing is a vice so mean and low that every person of sense and character detests and despises it.* Followed by washing out the offender's mouth with soap. Sometimes, when Richard blurted out an expletive, there was the ghost memory of the vile taste of Irish Spring on the back of his tongue.

Pamela bent a gimlet's eyes on her nephew. "But since you are so clearly concerned for my well-being," she said with heavy irony, "allow me to reassure you that I live in a highly secure, gated compound. The house bristles with cameras and alarms, I have security provided by your uncle, and he's trained me to be a crack shot. And now, good night, everyone."

Richard pushed back his chair, rested his palms on the table, and pushed to his feet. He gave Damon a speaking glance. "*Now* may I go see the creepy, mutated killer drone?"

"Yes, you may, and I'm coming with you. I'm familiar with these suckers from Iraq and Afghanistan, so I might be able to figure out who manufactured it. You boys have a good night. There's a rec room on the second floor just off the employee cafeteria. Has board games, TV, game consoles, pool table, a fridge for snacks, and a microwave to heat all the pizza rolls you can eat or pop up a bowl of popcorn."

Mosi stood. "I'll show you. Maybe we can play a cooperative campaign."

"You play video games?" Fox exclaimed.

"Does she ever," Richard said with a smile. "I'm hopeless with those controls. She's an expert."

After clearing the table, and helping Franz load the dishwasher, they all crammed into the elevator together. The kids hopped off on two, and Richard and Damon continued onto the ground floor.

They left through the back door into the alley behind the building, walked past the dumpster, and loading dock until they reached the wood and cardboard box that Cross called home.

The homeless god was seated on the wooden cable reel that had once held plenum cable. A propane lantern hissed next to him, throwing a pool of golden light across the pavement. He was toasting a Vienna Sausage over a camp stove. It brought back the memory of Richard's first walk down this alley almost seventeen years ago.

"You're eating again?" Damon asked with a sigh.

"Yep. Better I eat human food than humans, right?" Cross said.

"True that."

Cross popped the sausage into his mouth, and masticating vigorously, he pulled the drone out of the interior of his crate. It truly was a mess. The mounted machine guns drooped like elephant's trunks, the body of it looked more like viscera than anything manufactured by human hands.

The two humans exchanged glances, and pulled surgical masks and gloves out of their pockets. They knew better than to handle anything from one of the alternate dimensions without some sort of protection. It was a lesson learned after Mosi had handled an object out of one of those other multiverses, and ended up with burns on her palms as if she had touched acid. Given the look of the drone, Richard decided it was time to stop *thinking about it* and build a clean room in which to inspect the occasional item that wasn't an Old One that managed to wash up in human reality.

Cross kept turning it for them so they could inspect all sides. Both men used the magnifying app on their phones to glean what they could.

"Well, it's a little hard to tell with the goo," Damon said, "But it looks like it *might* be a Songar."

"Turkish made," Richard said.

"Yep, fortunately Erdoğan hasn't managed to get rid of all our allies in the military. I'll see if I can get a lead on who might have bought one of these for a little private mayhem."

"So what do you want me to do with this thing?" Cross asked.

"I won't ask you to put it back where you found it," Richard said with a smile.

"That's good because I would have said no. Actually, *hell no.*"

"We'll run it through the incinerator," Richard said. He snapped a few close up photos of the parts of the drone that still looked like something that had been manufactured on Earth.

The three of them headed back into the building. Richard was surprised to find Paul in the lobby.

"Paul. Did you need something?"

"No ... I mean, I guess I was just curious ... to see. So that's it," he breathed, as he stared at the thing nestled in Cross' arms. His blue eyes widened. "It's really mutated."

"Yes, that happens when something from your reality enters one of ours," Cross said.

"You learn anything?" his nephew asked.

Richard was a bit surprised when Damon stepped in before he could answer. "Nah 'fraid not, it's too deformed."

"Oh, that's too bad."

"Can we go do the *auto-da-fé* thing, please?" Cross huffed. "This thing's got Old One cooties on it, and something might come looking for it."

"Yes, yes, take it downstairs and destroy it. It's late, and I, for one, am very tired," Richard said.

Richard waited until they were in their bedroom and sliding beneath the sheets to ask, "Why did you lie to Paul?"

Damon slipped an arm around his shoulders, and pulled him in close. "You don't think it was a little odd he was hanging around in a deserted lobby at ten-thirty at night?"

"He said he was curious. I still think he doesn't totally

believe in any of this." Richard nuzzled his cheek into the crook of Damon's shoulder and kissed the pulse point in his jaw. "Sometimes I almost don't believe it either."

"Since he's your nevvy, I'll let you go with the benefit-of-the-doubt explanation, but your cranky old husband will say ... there's just something the tiniest bit off about that kid."

"Well, I'm sure you'll keep an eye on him for me," Richard murmured as he shifted until his head was against Damon's chest and he could hear the reassuring beat of his heart.

"I will. It's my job."

"No, your job was to command the overseas rapid response force. You were never in charge of security."

"You are such a pedantic little shit. As your *husband,* it's my job to keep you safe ..." His hand slipped beneath the waistband of Richard pajama bottoms. "Relaxed." He cupped his balls and Richard's breath went short. "And happy," Damon whispered in his ear and he proceeded to do just that.

✧   ✧   ✧

MOSI LOOKED OUT of the helicopter canopy at the flat, dry plains over which they were traveling on their way to Spaceport America.

Jerry, rather than Brook, was piloting since he had flown attack helicopters in Iraq, and Brook found the rotary-wing aircraft to be somewhat terrifying, so he was just as happy to remain back in Albuquerque. Also, he and his longtime girlfriend were in the final stages of planning their wedding.

"Well, that's bloody macabre!" She heard Fox exclaim over her headphones. Mosi slewed around in her seat to give him a questioning look. "This place is built in something called the *Jornada del Muerto* basin?"

"What does that mean?" Paul asked.

"Route of the Dead Man," Richard replied.

"Also, Single Day's Journey of the Dead Man and today it's sometimes translated as The Working Day of the Dead," Mosi amplified.

"I'm sure that makes the pilots and astronauts just delirious with joy," Fox muttered.

"Why does it even have a name?" Paul asked as he peered out at the pristine desert stretching out before them. "It's just a big bunch of nothing. Just sand and rock and bleak as hell."

"That's because the *Camino Real de Tierra Adentro*—" Mosi began.

The young men looked confused, so Richard provided the definition, "Royal Road of the Interior Land."

"It was the trade route from Mexico, north into what is now New Mexico," Damon added.

"It went right through this area," Mosi said. "And there was no water, grazing, or firewood through this entire stretch, which made it dangerous as hell to traverse."

"So, the Spanish conquerors established it?" Fox said.

Mosi shook her head. "No, it's much older than that. The native peoples in both the valley of Mexico and the Anasazi people up here established it to trade in turquoise, obsidian, salt, feathers, and shells. The trail terminates at the San Juan Pueblo."

They were drawing close enough now that the one hundred and six meter tall gantry had become a spire against the bright blue New Mexico sky. In the years since Richard Branson had conceived of the idea of a commercial spaceport, the facility had gone from just runways for low orbit space planes to a more multi-purpose launch site. The gantry had been built six year ago to support the launch of multi-stage rockets carrying payloads into orbit. Which, in turn, would resupply the various space stations that commercial space flight had underwritten along with various governments. It also carried crew and material to the Ad Astra construction platform built by Lumina Enterprises; a first step toward building the ships that would establish a foothold on Mars and explore the outer planetary moons and asteroid belt. Now, that platform was given over solely to the construction of the Ark.

As the helicopter came around for a landing, the swooping roof line of the visitor's center came into view. Mosi had never been able to decide if it was supposed to suggest the arc of a bird's wing, or a flying saucer. The bright New Mexico summer sun glinted off the wall of windows in front, which looked out over the various launch sites.

They were now close enough that the three stage rocket in addition to the gantry could be seen. The rocket would lift off later that evening, carrying the solar sail array into orbit and then to Lumina's platform.

"So, that's it," Paul said softly.

"That's it," Richard agreed. "They're in final operation and readiness checks."

"The launch is set for eight-thirty tonight" Mosi said.

"Right around sunset. It ought to be spectacular."

"Wow, that soon. I thought it would be tomorrow or later, and we'd stay down here," Paul said.

"You see a hotel, son?" Damon asked.

Mosi spotted the Uyanik company jet parked on a side runway. There was also a clot of people holding signs and a man with a bullhorn in front of the visitor's center.

"What's all this then?" Richard asked, a frown between his blond brows.

Damon was squinting down at the group. "Looks like a protest."

"Just what poor Feray needs," Mosi huffed. "What assholes," she added as Jerry brought them in for a landing.

As they ducked under the wash from the slowing rotors, Mosi hoped the inclusion of Paul and Fox on top of the protestors wasn't going to add to Feray's emotional turmoil.

The crowd of perhaps twenty people tried to rush forward on them, but were ruthlessly held back by Estevan, Adam, Janine, and Jorge. The signs ranged from the ubiquitous no symbol over a photo of the launch vehicle, to a sign reading **Keep Space Pure!**, to one very verbose sign that had photos of factories with their smokestacks spewing what could have been pollutants or perhaps just water vapor with the heading: HAVEN'T WE RUINED ENOUGH PLANETS? KEEP THE HUMAN INFECTION ON EARTH!

The man with the bullhorn had grey hair in a ponytail, a tee shirt that read, *Mother Nature Bats Last* and was wearing a linen sports jacket over the tee shirt.

As the pushing and shoving escalated, the side door on a grey van was pushed open. Mosi, Richard, Damon, Estevan, and the guards all reached for their weapons only to relax when it proved to be a camera crew who started filming the moment their feet hit the hot concrete pavement.

"Mr. Oort! Mr. Oort! What's being loaded onto that ship?" The ponytailed man yelled through the bullhorn.

"Is it true the ship is powered with nukes? If it crashes, this area will be uninhabitable for ten thousand years," yelled a young woman. Mosi gave a derisive snort and rolled her eyes.

"Billionaire pig!" a young man screamed at Richard, spittle flying.

Then they were through the door, the protestors left to gesture impotently at them through the glass front of the building.

Feray rushed up to them. "I'm so sorry you had to endure that. They were setting up as we arrived but we were mercifully able to get inside before they could fully react."

Mosi gave her a hug as Richard said, "We're fine. I've been called worse."

"Yeah, when we were both cops, we were usually just called pigs. Having the billionaire preface is kinda nice," Damon chuckled.

That drew a small smile from Feray that soon faded. She stared out at the twisted faces beyond the glass. "Why do they hate us so? We're just trying to make sure the human species and some of our beautiful diversity survives. But you have brought guests and I have been inhospitable. Sir Richard said we could use the Virgin Galactic Lounge. I have brought apple tea and *meza*, and we will share and remember my father, but first introductions."

"This is my nephew, Paul van Gelder," Richard said. "He's a biologist and agronomist."

Mosi reached to pull Fox forward where he was lurking behind everyone. "And this is Fox Erskine, he's a physicist."

"I'm so sorry about your father. And I'm so pleased to be here. And may I please see the ship?" The words emerged out of the Brit like machine-gun fire.

"I wouldn't mind a tour too, if that would be okay," Paul said.

Damon had sunk down in one of the chairs in the lobby. Richard was looking at him with concern.

"It will be perfect. I need to go to the launch pad to place my father's ring. We will all go together."

Damon waved a hand at them. "Afraid the heat's gotten to me. Ya'll go on. I'll head on upstairs to the lounge, and *maybe* there'll be some food left when you get back."

"I'll stay with you," Richard said, dropping to one knee next to the chair.

"No." Damon ran his hand through Richard's hair. "You and Emirhan cooked this up together. His vision of the Ark and Lumina's orbital construction platform all coming together to make it happen. You need to see him off, so to speak."

Feray gave a small sob, and Mosi had to swallow hard. Richard nodded and stood up. Mosi looked toward the distant spire of the ship. There was a sharp glint of sunlight off the nosecone. It felt like a benediction and a call to the light of other distant suns.

CHAPTER TWELVE

DARK WINDS

RIDING UP THE length of the rocket on the gantry elevator was both exhilarating and terrifying. Fox had never liked heights, and he once again found himself almost hating Paul. The other man seemed coolly composed in his polo shirt and khaki slacks while Fox was blinking madly from the sweat rolling off his forehead into his eyes—which were also watering from the bright sunlight glinting off the pale desert sand. He pulled off his glasses and wiped away the sweat from beneath his eyes and on the bridge of his nose. He could tell his skin was already reddening from the harsh desert sun.

Oort and Mosi flanked Feray who stood holding a small black velvet box in her cupped hands. As much as Fox wanted to see this wonder of human engineering, it felt intrusive, as if he were a voyeur on the woman's grief.

"Hell of a thing, isn't it?" Paul whispered to him. Fox replaced his glasses and gave him an inquiring look. "Two men with billions of dollars between them are building a spaceship, and one of them is my uncle."

"Your point being?"

"Nobody in my family has ever seen Richard as a bold explorer pushing the boundaries of human knowledge and exploration."

"Then they haven't been paying attention. Even I am aware of how much your uncle has invested in all kinds of things designed to push forward human knowledge, and do a lot of good for the planet."

"Hmm."

The elevator came to a stop with a rather sharp bounce, and Fox grabbed for the railing clutching it tight. Paul took the bounce in his knees, and Fox noticed with chagrin that no one else had reacted with his level of trepidation.

There were Uyanik support staff on the platform leading into the capsule at the top of the three stage rocket. They wore white and gold jumpsuits with a patch showing the Ark, its shimmering golden sails outstretched.

Fox craned his neck to look up a ladder that led into the cockpit, barely visible through a hatch. There were only technicians in the cockpit. Feray noted Fox's brief look of confusion and disappointment, and said, "This is an unmanned"—there was a small flicker of a smile—"or unwomanned flight. It will be controlled from our mission control in Texas. This is just a freight run and the sails have already been loaded." She gestured toward four rather small containers in a cargo area surrounded by larger containers.

"Huh," Paul said. "I've crewed on the family sailboat with my grandfather. Wish our sails folded down this small."

Feray gave him a small smile. "These sails are made from an ultra-thin reflective polymer—"

Fox found himself excitedly interrupting. "Only 7.5 microns thick." He immediately blushed and dropped his head, but Feray just smiled at him.

"Just so. The booms around which the sails will be wound are already aboard the construction platform. Our engineers decided it would be better to do the assembly there rather than on Earth."

"So, what's in the other boxes?" Paul asked.

"Supplies for our crew on the platform," Richard answered. "Our construction teams rotate in trimonthly so no one spends too much time in zero gee."

Oort jerked his chin toward the ladder. "Why don't you gentleman go check out the cockpit," he said. It wasn't really a suggestion.

For a moment Fox didn't understand then he looked over at the trio, Feray still cupping that velvet covered box. "Oh … *oh.*" Fox shoved past Paul and started climbing.

ONCE THE YOUNG men had vanished through the hatch, Feray knelt and murmured in Turkish. She then gently tucked the box in among the containers holding the solar sails.

Mosi was pressed against Richard, her arm wrapped around his waist. Not for the first time since he'd found himself in this eons-long war, he longed for the solace of religion, even though he knew it was a cruel myth.

Feray rose gracefully to her feet, and Mosi hesitantly asked, "If it's not too painful, what did you say?"

"I told him his memory would live among the stars," the older woman said softly.

"We are made of star stuff," Mosi murmured quietly,

echoing her graduation speech.

Richard felt hot tears pricking at the back of his eyelids as his thoughts flew to the man waiting for them ... for *him* back at the visitor's center. Was he being cruel to demand that Damon undergo the experimental treatments for his cancer? Richard knew it was selfish, knew that he constantly pushed aside the whispered reminders that even now lung cancer had only a sixty-three percent survival rate. *Damon will beat the odds. I know he will. He must.*

His spiraling thoughts were interrupted when one of the ground crew entered the capsule and cleared his throat.

"Sorry to intrude Ms. Uyanik, but we've got a pretty problematic weather update. We may have to abort the launch."

"What's the problem?" Richard asked.

"Gusty winds and possible thunderstorms," the engineer said. "Blew up out of nowhere."

"Rather early for monsoons," Richard remarked.

"Welcome to global climate change," Mosi sighed.

"If we hold until morning we should be fine," the man said.

Feray turned to Richard and Mosi. "I don't expect you all to loiter about here. You should return home."

"Nonsense," Richard said. "We're going to be here for you."

Mosi gave the other woman a hug. "What *Na sha dii* said. We are here for you."

Feray choked back a sob, but nodded.

✧ ✧ ✧

THE WIND WAS starting to wail and moan around the main building as Damon sat waiting for the group to return. He was seated in one of the sort of chair-sofa hybrids that looked like white leather clam shells. They were arranged in front of the wall of windows that overlooked one of the long runways. The sound of sand pecking at the wall of glass in front of him was oddly ominous, as outside the westering sun turned a deep shade of orange-red as the blowing dirt began to block its rays.

The lounge was taking the *Welcome To The Future* thing a bit far was Damon's thought. It had the feel of a Hollywood movie set for some as-yet unreleased sci-fi movie but then Branson had always been a consummate showman.

The center island, white marble atop blonde wood, was loaded down with food. Feray's idea of a *meza* was opulent. It all smelled delicious, but Damon wasn't sure his gut could handle any of it. Maybe a bit of the luscious balloon lavash topped with sesame seeds, and the roasted eggplant dip.

Feray's staff had already set several of the tables with napkins and utensils, and plates were stacked next to the buffet. The voices of the young people preceded them up the stairs. All three were talking animatedly, the Brit most of all, but that seemed logical given the fact he was trying to send people to the stars and make the Ark obsolete. Damon closed his eyes, listening for Richard's quick, light tread; he waited for the long, elegant hands to close on his shoulders, as he sat with his back to the room.

"Launch has been delayed until morning," Richard whispered in his ear.

"And the storm is getting worse," Damon replied quietly.

"I think we should go to Las Cruces, there's a regional airport there."

"Feray and her staff went to a lot of trouble to set out this spread."

"We can pack it up."

Damon smiled when he heard the clink of cutlery on china. "Too late, it seems the kids were hungry." Richard huffed a sigh and swung around to join him on the clam shell. Damon nudged him with an elbow. "You should eat too."

"What can I get *you*?"

"Little bread, some ice water. Let's see how that goes down."

They were nibbling from a shared plate as Feray, Mosi, the Brit, and the nephew joined them.

Jerry, plate in one hand, a beer tucked under his arm, and his phone in the other hand came over to them. "Boss, if we don't get in the air pretty damn soon, we'll be sleeping on these crazy-ass chairs. And it better be someplace close. This weather is really coming in."

Damon spoke up, "How about T or C? It's closer than either Cruces or Albuquerque."

Richard's aquiline nose wrinkled a bit. "Isn't that the town that renamed itself after some nineteen-fifties TV game show?"

"It was actually a radio quiz show," Damon corrected with a grin.

"I don't see how that makes it any better," Richard said in

his snooty East Coast accent and was immediately one-upped by the young Brit with his *very* snooty English accent.

"What *are* you going on about?" Fox asked.

Damon slewed around a bit so he could look over the back of the sofa-chair. "Truth or Consequences used to be called Hot Springs because of all the mineral springs there. Then there was this radio contest in nineteen-fifty where the host said he'd broadcast from any town that legally changed their name to the name of his show. Hot Springs went for it and became T or C. Wife and I used to go there for vacation. Got some boutique hotels and a few good restaurants, and I did mention the hot springs. I think we could all use a relaxing soak."

"You Americans really are mad," Fox muttered, while at the same time Paul said in a rather high, breathy voice, "Wife?

"Yeah, turns out third time *wasn't* the charm." Damon took Richard's hand in his and kissed his knuckles. "Wonder why?"

Mosi was on her phone. "There is a municipal airport in T or C, *Na sha dii*, and it's only thirty-two miles away. Jerry could easily make two trips to bring everyone, and he can probably refuel there too."

Richard turned to Feray. "Is this all right with you?"

"Hot springs and a soft bed sound very appealing right now," the woman sighed.

Paul glanced at his phone, and murmured an apology. He left the lobby area.

"But I also feel bad abandoning my ground crew, most went back to Las Cruces when the launch was delayed, but three of them are still making a few tweaks to flight control in the capsule."

"We'll just add them into the rotation."

Damon stood. "All right, we got a plan. Let's execute it."

But it was not to be. By the time they had cleaned up and packed up the remaining food, the Uyanik pilots and Jerry were in a huddle, and they approached their employers with the same message. Nobody was flying tonight, and they'd all just have to make the best of it. The only people happy about it were the techs working on the capsule. Feray put together a care package of food for them, and with Estevan and Mosi accompanying her, they took one of the small Gators out to the launch site.

Jerry was glaring at his phone as if it and the weather app were somehow to blame. "Weirdest ass storm I've ever seen. It's like it's just fucking targeting us."

Damon felt the hairs on the back of his neck start to prickle and he looked quickly at Richard. His husband's expression was grim. It seemed they were both thinking the same thing.

It was another night of her and *Na sha dii* sharing guard duties. The lounge was filled with a cacophony of snores from the men: Feray's pilots, the Lumina security detail, Jerry, Paul, Fox, and Damon. Mosi felt like she and Feray were definitely outnumbered. She wished Angela or Pamela or Dagmar (Lumina's CFO) were here. She sensed there was a thread linking the chaos of the past few days, but she couldn't bring it into focus, and talking it over with a group of women was appealing.

Not that Richard didn't listen and he almost never mansplained. And anytime he did slip up, the women of Lumina were quick to remind him not to be a prick. She had thought Damon would struggle the most, he was a good deal older than Richard, was a blue-collar guy from Michigan who had been in the military and then a cop for almost twenty years, while Richard was the poster child for *white-liberal-guilt-trying-to-overcome-any-possible-hint-of-bias-about-positively-anything*. But surprisingly, Damon hadn't. He was sort of in the *mom* role at Lumina. For all Richard's kindness, he could be a hard-ass when it came to holding the line, while Damon would pat everyone on the back and go *there there*.

Mosi gazed out at the storm raging beyond the windows and tried to rein in her tumbling thoughts. She knew Richard had tried to reach Cross, but the Old One hadn't picked up. Cross was still out searching for more Paladins, and sometimes the corners of the world where he searched didn't have great cell coverage, but damn she'd like to have a read on this storm. Wind played a deep role in Navajo culture, and this one felt like a dark one.

It was nearing midnight, when she and Richard would switch, when suddenly the sky lit up with a violent explosion. Mosi threw herself onto the floor and covered her head with her arms in case the windows weren't as reinforced as advertised. An instant later the sound of the explosion arrived, rattling the glass in the windows. Her heart was in her throat for the people sleeping on the various piece of furniture who would be in line of flying glass should the windows not hold. Thankfully they did.

She called out, "*Na sha dii!*" as she leaped to her feet and drew the sword, but Richard was already rolling off one of the benches and onto his feet. He possessed this uncanny ability to come instantly awake, so he was drawing his pistol as he stood.

There was a gabble of voices all saying almost the same thing, which was *What the fuck? What's going on? What was that?* But Mosi already knew. The explosion and now leaping flames were precisely where the gantry and rocket had stood.

People were milling about in confusion, but Richard and Damon had come quickly to her side. Mosi's gaze sought out Feray and found her staring tensely out the window at the flames, phone pressed to her ear. With each passing second her distress increased. She let out a single harsh sob and dropped the phone. She leaned her forehead again the window, beating her fists in time with her moaned words "No. No. No."

Richard gently laid a hand on her shoulder, "Were your people still aboard?" His tone was grim. Feray nodded.

Someone in the crowd behind them made a choked sound. Mosi whirled, trying to identify who. Everyone stood in frozen silence. All their expressions held the same look of horror and disbelief. Richard gently took Feray by the elbow and guided her to a bench and helped her sit down.

"Someone get a glass of water," he ordered. Fox jumped to obey. Paul, his face like a frozen expressionless mask, was staring at the pulsating flames.

A sudden hush fell across the room because the storm

was abruptly over. The wind died to nothing, the clouds began scudding across the sky, seeming to play hide-and-seek with the Moon. Damon, his face ashen, and his expression as grim as Richard's, fell into step with his husband and the three of them went into a huddle.

"I think we can all agree that that was no natural storm," Damon said softly. "The people who did this were working with the Old Ones."

"Grenier once told me a weather spell was incredibly costly and dangerous as well. They can too easily get out of control," Richard said quietly.

"So, we're dealing with somebody who doesn't give a rat's ass," Mosi muttered. "Great."

"Okay, is this group number three or is it just a continuation of the fun from either the Fox plot thread or are we on the graduation plot timeline?" Damon quipped with gallows humor. "Either way, it's a shitty timeline."

Richard rubbed at the back of his neck. "I'm going to hope the graduation," Richard sighed. "At least that one is caused by humans instead of horrors from alternate dimensions."

"Do you suppose that asshole is part of this?" Damon asked.

It took Mosi a moment to catch up. "Are you talking about Grenier?" she asked.

She had only met the man a couple of times before she and Richard had had to flee when she had been a child. He had once been a powerful sorcerer and quisling, serving the Old Ones in the hope of ruling the remnants of humanity. Until Richard permanently removed his power by slicing off his hand.

"Yeah. We never did track him down after Ankara," Damon said. "He apparently found a really big rock and crawled under it."

"But he has no ability to do magic any longer so why would he be useful to anyone?" Mosi objected.

"He knows us, how we operate, and he could still advise those who can use magic," Richard said shortly. His eyes scanned the room. "Excuse me, I think it's time I got some answers."

Mosi watched her guardian walk away. Frowning, she turned back to Damon. "What was that about?"

"Let's just say somebody's about to get a lesson in consequences."

CHAPTER THIRTEEN

THINGS IN MOTION

"YOU KNOW, ACCESSORY to murder still makes you a murderer."

Paul swung away from the sink. His chestnut hair was in disarray, and water dripped off the ends of the strands and the tip of his nose. Richard wasn't sure if the moisture on his nephew's cheeks was just from the water he had splashed on his face or if some was due to tears. The tap was still on, the sound of water running loud in the tiled room.

Richard sighed, moved to the sink, and turned off the water. "You know we're in a desert. Best not to waste water given climate change ... and that is your issue, isn't it? Climate change."

"I don't know ... what are you getting at?"

Richard leaned back against the sink, folded his arms across his chest, and looked up at the taller man.

"You have a choice to make, Paul. You either level with me now and tell me everything, or my next call is to the police, the FBI, and the Department of Homeland Security, so they can argue over who gets to take you into custody. Three people are dead, a multi-million dollar rocket has been destroyed in an act of terrorism, and let me say it again in case you missed the import ... *three people have died*. So, you better decide and decide quickly."

His nephew looked away. "I … I didn't know … it should have been empty—"

"Because you didn't stick around to hear Feray talking with her people. You were in such a hurry to tell your eco buddies it was okay to set the explosives. You know, Estevan was recording all the protestors and we'll be providing that information to the authorities."

A calculating expression filled Paul's blue eyes, and he said thoughtfully, "But not me. You're going to protect me."

"For now, and only because you may be our key to ending this. And because whoever is controlling this group is using Old One magic, and Mosi and I are the only ones who can stop that. Which is honestly the *only* reason I'm not turning you over to the authorities."

"Not because I'm your nephew."

"No."

"Hmm, that connection really doesn't matter to you."

"No. Actions have consequences, Paul. I can't and won't protect you from those, but right now you can help us ensure no one else dies."

"Like your hands are so clean, Uncle. I know you've killed people," Paul shot back.

It still doesn't seem real to him, Richard thought. *Well, we're going to fix that real quick.*

What he said was, "Fifty-three."

"What?"

"That's how many people have died by my hand. I keep the count. So, it never becomes commonplace. I only kill in defense of myself or others but it's still killing, and I bear the responsibility for every one of those deaths." Richard looked away, then added quietly, "Sometimes I almost wish there was judgment." He sighed. "And now there are three to burden your—"

"Careful, Uncle, I didn't think you believed in souls," Paul sneered. "And aren't there causes worth—"

"Are you really going to try to argue that the deaths of those three scientists can be justified? Some kind of defense of Mother Earth? I'd really recommend you not, because I don't have the patience right now for that kind of nonsense."

"Some people would argue that not being content with polluting the planet, now you're moving on to polluting space," Paul said.

Richard gave a derisive snort. "Polluting space. Now there's a concept. I presume you're talking about space junk, but if you'd done three minutes of research you would have discovered that Lumina and Emirhan's *Yildiz Işiği* Foundation are working to clear space junk. But you didn't bother, did you—" Richard broke off abruptly and studied Paul. "No, wait ... you're talking about *humans*, viewing people as trash. You're tied up with Wannamake, aren't you?"

"You don't really expect me to answer that question, do you?"

Richard began to pace, so he didn't just smack the entitlement out of his nephew, and he continued to rage. "Wannamake's advocated that the world return to a population of two hundred million." Richard paused to stare at the young man trying to fathom the mind that could casually embrace that kind of mass death. "That's advocating for almost *nine billion people* to die. But you—white, male, educated, comfortably upper middle class, and safely ensconced in the First World—you don't think it will be *you* dying, do you? It's those *other* people. Those less enlightened people. God, Paul, you have a fine education and yet you bought into *this*." He grabbed Paul by the arm and dragged him toward the door. "Come on."

"Where are we … what are we—"

"You're about to face some consequences."

Richard took them out through using the service elevator, so they could avoid the main lounge where Feray and the authorities were still talking. Outside, he shoved Paul into one of the small Gators and sliding behind the wheel, he fired up the engine, accelerating rapidly toward the plume of dust rising where once a gantry and rocket had stood. Engines growled and warning horns sounded as bull dozers and loaders worked to remove the wreckage of Emirhan's dreams. There were three ambulances parked nearby.

Richard followed Paul's glance toward the vehicles. "Don't be a fool," he growled. Nothing could survive *that*." Richard thrust a hand toward the twisted metal coated in fire retardant.

Two figures dressed in protective gear emerged from the wreckage carrying a body bag. They headed toward an ambulance.

"Why are they in hazmat suits?"

"Rocket fuel is toxic. Even after the fire there is residue. Three casualties are quite enough." Richard stopped next to the ambulance and jumped out. "Come on." Paul shook his head. "At least be man enough to look at what you've done." Richard didn't normally use those sorts of patriarchal phrases, but it worked as expected, and Paul climbed out of the Gator.

Richard flashed his badge at the two suited figures. "My partner and I need a quick look."

The face behind the helmet was an older Hispanic woman. She nodded. "Not much to see. Fire does terrible things. Just hope the explosion took them before the flames got to them." She crossed herself then unzipped the body bag.

Richard had seen badly burned bodies. How the intense heat curled them into fetal positions, their teeth setting a jarring contrast to the blackened skulls in a rictus of death. He gestured to Paul to come forward. The young man advanced with the stiff gait of a terrified foal faced with a snake. His blue eyes kept flicking in every direction except at the body.

"*Look!*" Richard commanded in a low whisper.

Paul obeyed. He began to tremble, shudders so violent that Richard wondered if he'd remain on his feet, but then Richard got a look at those blue eyes, and realized that calculating look was still there. Paul staggered away and gagged over and over until he finally brought up some vomit. Richard closed the body bag and nodded to the coroner and her assistant.

"New, is he?" The woman asked with a nod of her helmeted head toward Paul.

"Yes," but he had barely registered what she had said, because he was remembering eight-year-old Paul at the funeral home just before his grandmother's internment. He had been terrified to look at Alanis Oort's painted and powdered face in her coffin. Despite the shivers, the man who had looked at the twisted form on the gurney had not been affected, not really. Richard also began to wonder if Paul had splashed water on his face only after he heard the click of the door opening.

Richard walked over to where Paul was gagging and spitting, and offered his handkerchief.

Paul buried his face in the linen and whispered brokenly, "I'm so sorry, Richard, I never wanted … I never meant … please help me."

Richard pressed his fingers against his eyes that burned with exhaustion and grief, and growing anger at the lies. "Maybe you can stop with the performance now? You're very good at it, but your eyes gave you away. You've clearly seen death—violent death—before."

Paul yanked away the handkerchief and lifted his head to stare at Richard. "What are you—"

"Please, to borrow my husband's favorite phrase, don't treat me like a damn mushroom: keep me in the dark and feed me shit. I want answers and you're going to give them to me. *Now.*"

Paul shook his head, a look of confusion on his face. "Honestly, I have no idea—"

"Oh, I doubt that, particularly the honest part. I *will* have answers."

He watched Paul hesitate, so Richard gave him *the look.* Richard's lack of inches had always left him with the feeling that he couldn't be intimidating, but over the years he had learned to channel his terrifying sire. When Robert Oort turned his gimlet stare on a defendant, plaintiff, or lawyer … they wilted. And as much as Richard hated admitting it, that was apparently something his father had bequeathed to him. It was past time he deployed it. Paul withered under that ice-blue gaze.

"Fine! But I have to check with my handler first."

Profanity was trembling on the tip of his tongue. Richard bit it back and scrubbed his hands across his face, feeling the rasp of stubble. "Which alphabet soup agency are you?"

"All in good time, Uncle. There is protocol for this, but fuck, she's not going to be happy with me."

"I'll wait in the Gator while you make that call."

Paul walked away, and Richard returned to the vehicle. Pulling out his phone, he rang Damon. "Well, my love, your Spidey-sense was right, but for the wrong reason. Paul's a badge. Just not sure whose badge he's carrying."

"No shit. You want me to check in with Sam or Jay and see if the FBI's got any insight?"

"Let's wait. He's talking with his bosses now. Maybe they'll let us in instead of—"

"Keeping us in the dark and feeding us shit," Damon finished.

"Yeah, that." Richard spotted Paul approaching. "Gotta go. We'll be back in a few."

"Okay," Paul said, when he reached the Gator. "I've got the approval to read you in—"

"Hold off on that until we've got Damon and Mosi."

"I'm not authorized—"

"The three of us are a package deal, and I'm betting you need us more than we need you, since you got sent to us."

Paul looked mulish, but gave a tense nod.

The drive back to the building was made in total silence.

✧   ✧   ✧

DAMON HAD WATCHED as Richard had frog-marched his nephew out of the building. Richard's expression had been so still, as to make him appear to be carved out of marble, but the kid had a singularly blank expression. All in all, it gave Damon a bad feeling.

The local, state, and federal authorities were wrapping up and heading out. Feray was standing alone in the center of the lounge looking lost. Mosi was clasping and unclasping her hands, looking at Feray then away, then back to Feray again. He stepped to her side.

"Why don't you go check and see if the chopper is ready to go?" he said quietly to Mosi. She nodded and left.

Damon studied Feray and sighed. During his career, first as a policeman, and then as Richard's head of overseas security, he had done a lot of condolence calls. That didn't mean they got any easier, but he knew what was needed. Squaring his shoulders he crossed to her and laid a tentative hand on her shoulder.

"How you holdin' up, kiddo?" he asked softly.

She gave a hiccuping sob and turned into him, pressing her face against his chest. Her tears dampened his shirt, and Damon pulled her into a hug, gently rubbing at her back.

"My father's wedding ring … it's all melted … lost in the wreckage and I shouldn't care. It shouldn't matter because three people are dead, but it hurts so bad and I feel like I failed him. What's *wrong* with me?"

Damon knew the loss of the ring meant nothing when compared with three lives cut tragically short and Feray knew it too. *But knowing something intellectually and how you feel are two really different things*, he thought.

"There's nothing wrong with you, kiddo. You're tryin' to deal with tragedy on top of tragedy. Sometimes it's all too much, so we focus on something small, then we can wrap our heads around ... well ... the rest of it. You lost your dad, Feray. Now this. You cry or scream or do whatever you need to do—and it's absolutely okay if you cry over that ring."

She looked up at him, dark eyes glistening with tears. "The Ark meant so much to him. Can we ever recover from this?"

"You bet we can. The main ship is still safe. We can make more solar sails. We won't let Emirhan's dream fail. Now, you get yourself home. We'll talk later in the week."

"I have to arrange for the bodies—"

"They're going to be part of the investigation for at least a few days. And we're here in New Mexico, and have contacts with law enforcement. You tell us where their families want the bodies sent and Lumina will handle it. You need to go home, grieve, and rest."

She nodded, and gathered up what remained of her team and they left. Through the windows, Damon watched as Mosi and Feray said farewell to each other at the side of the plane.

Damon settled into one of the uncomfortable chairs, and waited for Richard and his nephew to return. Paul was completely composed, unlike Fox, who rushed up to try and talk to him, only to be waved off.

Damon moved to Richard. "Take a walk with me." As they headed down the stairs Damon asked quietly, "Where did you go?"

"Out to the rocket. Or what remains of it. I insisted he look at one of the bodies, and then I realized …"

"What?"

"That this wasn't his first rodeo. He tried to feign shock and regret, forced up some vomit, but his eyes were … calculating. He talked to his supervisor, but he hasn't given me any details yet. My guess is he's Homeland Security."

"What the fuck! Are we under investigation?" Damon asked.

"I don't think so. I'm hoping for more answers soon."

"You want me in that meeting?"

"Of course."

Richard fell silent for a moment. Damon rested a hand on the back of Richard's neck and gave him a soft shake. "I am curious about one thing." Richard gave him an inquiring look. "Let's say he wasn't a pro, just your nephew, why'd you take him out there?"

"I suspected he had something to do with the bombing, so I wanted him to see the results of his actions." Damon didn't try to hide his reaction. Richard shaded his eyes, ostensibly against the harsh sunlight and the fine dust, but Damon knew it was to avoid looking at him, to evade Damon's disappointment. "You think it was wrong of me," Richard said softly.

Damon pulled Richard's hand away from his face, and forced his husband to face him. "I think it was harsh. And I think it says more about where *you* are emotionally than you'd like to admit."

The slight figure of his husband leaned into him and

Damon wrapped his arms tightly around Richard. "I'm just so tired," he murmured into Damon's chest. "So terribly, terribly tired." He raised his head to look up into Damon's face. "I've spent the past sixteen years fighting these battles and it feels like the world is worse rather than better—"

"Hey, none of that now. You've closed gates and tears between our world, and destroyed things that want to kill us. You've whacked a shit ton of monsters. You've funded projects that have saved lives and improved lives of people all over the world. You want me to go on?"

"I'm not a hero, Damon. Don't try to make me into one."

"I'm not. You're a man who is doing the best he can against unbelievable odds."

"I've done terrible things." Richard's voice was husky with the tears he was trying to hold back. "All I do is destroy."

Damon had seen that thousand-yard stare in the eyes of soldiers he'd led in Iraq and Afghanistan, and he wondered what memories his spouse was revisiting. He grabbed his husband by the shoulders, and gave him a hard shake, seeking to snap him out of his emotional spiral. "No, you don't. Your family is right here—me, Mosi, Pamela—and we're doin' fine."

"Really?" Richard jerked his chin and Damon followed his gaze to see Mosi walking toward them. The whine of jet engines spinning up filled the air. "I've tasked that beautiful, brilliant girl with an impossible burden to bear."

"You kept her safe from people who would either have corrupted her or killed her. What other choice did you have or do you have now? Do *any* of us have? We all know what's at stake, Richard. If we fail, then darkness falls. But I promise you this. *I* will never let you fall." Richard's arms closed tight around him.

At least for as long as I'm here.

✧   ✧   ✧

"I WAS TASKED to infiltrate the Magna Mater Foundation and learn their plans. If they were just the usual tree huggers than no worries, but—"

"Goddamn it, I missed it. How did I miss it?" Mosi's outrage echoed in the cavernous metal hanger. Paul stood, arms folded across his chest, smirking at her. Richard couldn't decide if he wanted to smack his nephew, or warn him that Mosi would do far worse. He decided to sit back and watch how things played out. Mosi raged on. "I mean, I knew he was kind of an entitled jerk, but this?" That did pull a small reaction from Paul—a quick frown—like fast summer lightning.

The girders supporting the roof formed a spiderweb of steel, multiple lights between the beams reflected off the polished concrete floor, making Richard's stabbing headache even worse.

Richard sighed. "Well, you're not wrong about the entitled jerk part, but I hope you can put all of that aside and work with him."

"You have to be kidding!" Mosi cried.

"I take it you have a plan," Damon said.

"I don't work for you," Paul said, outrage vibrating on every word. "And she doesn't work for the federal government, so what are you talking about?"

The statements tumbled across each other. Richard ignored everyone but Damon, and he addressed his answer to him.

"It's clear they have a magic wielder and a damn good one. Maybe even an Old One." Paul let out a rude noise and Richard pinned him with a look and repeated. "*An Old One.* You and the federal government can't handle that, but there are people in the FBI who can vouch for the truth of that statement if you're not willing to believe us. Point being, you need either Mosi or me to deal with this."

Mosi folded her arms across her chest. "He"—she jerked her head toward Paul—"knew they were going to blow up the ship, but he said nothing, did nothing, and now three people are dead. Doesn't he bear some responsibility?"

"That wasn't supposed to happen, the death part, I mean. We were just giving them enough rope to hang themselves. It's unfortunate about those engineers, but now we've got them, and can move in."

"*Unfortunate?* Three people are *dead.*"

"Yeah, and I feel bad about that ... but, you know, spilt milk. And a murder rap will carry a lot more weight than just malicious vandalism."

"Two hundred and fifty-million for the ship and that's not counting the cost of the solar sails," Damon murmured. "Little bit more than mere vandalism."

"And the lives of three people; that loss is incalculable," Richard said. "And you're never going to make a murder rap stick. No intent. The best you can hope for is negligent homicide, and you can bet those individuals are going to get thrown under the proverbial bus, so you won't be able to get a conspiracy charge against Wannamake either."

"Why didn't you say anything to the local authorities?" Mosi demanded of Richard.

Before he could answer, Paul was already talking. "Because my uncle's smart enough to know some flatfoot from Carlsbad can't be read in on something this big," Paul said. The sneer was implicit.

"I'd watch it with the flatfoot terminology," Damon murmured. "Since a couple of us used to count ourselves among that company."

"Apologies," Paul said.

"Yeah and that sounded *so* sincere," Mosi sniffed.

Richard gave an inward sigh and pressed the tips of his fingers against his temples. "Please, both of you, just stop it." The words emerged sharper than he'd intended and Mosi's brows twitched into a frown. "I'm sorry," Richard said quietly. "I shouldn't have taken that tone with you."

"*Na sha dii,* three people are *dead.*" She pointed an accusatory finger at Paul. "And he knew about the plan to destroy the ship, so why didn't he say anything? He could have … *should have* told us the truth from the beginning. Involved us."

Richard took a deep breath. "I'm upset too, but we need him. We can't get to the people who did this and see them brought to justice without Paul." He looked over at his nephew. "And whether you want to accept it or not, they are using magic so …" Richard gave a resigned shrug and looked at each of them. "So, it has to be us … working with him."

"Okay, so we've got to figure out a plan to infiltrate another fucking compound and deal with crazy people and monsters. But in the meantime, what do we do about Fox?" Damon asked.

Richard scrubbed his hands across his face. "I don't know yet. I don't think we can safely send him off to Rochester. For the time being, I think he has to remain at Lumina."

"But we only have one sword," Mosi objected.

"Well, let's just hope that our own personal Old One is up to the task," Richard sighed.

"I can't believe I'm standing here listening to this," Paul said.

Mosi gave him a withering look. "I can't believe it either ... and I wish you weren't."

CHAPTER FOURTEEN

I'VE DONE WORSE

THE HELICOPTER RIDE back to Albuquerque was made in complete silence. Paul typed constantly on his phone, and Mosi bit back the impulse to demand *who* he was texting and *what* he was saying. She shot Richard a *really?* look at his continued silence, and Richard gave her back a minute headshake. She gave a huff and folded her arms across her chest, letting him know just how much it bugged her. Estevan and Adam kept watch out one side of the helicopter, while Janine and Jorge kept watch out the other side of the chopper. Richard had caught his nephew's amused look and this time he didn't let it go.

"This might seem foolish to you, Paul, but there had been times over the years when there have been monsters in the sky. Admittedly not recently, back when the gates were open, but it still pays to be prudent," Richard said quietly.

"If you say so, Uncle."

Mosi gave him a glare that would have most men wilting, but Paul met her death stare with a bland smile, which just enraged her all the more. Mosi was wrestling with the stew of complicated emotions that were washing through her stomach. Outrage that Paul was with them instead of being sent back to Washington to whatever alphabet soup agency he served ... or in her preferred fantasy: sitting in a jail cell for allowing the terrorists to reach the ship. If he had just *told* them who he was and what he was doing in the beginning, they could have saved three lives and perhaps the ship as well. And Mosi couldn't shake the feeling that Richard's decision hadn't been based purely on deference to federal law enforcement, but carried some lingering sense of trying to protect a family member rather than focusing on taking down the group that had committed this horror.

Paul's eyes met hers and he had the gall to *smirk* at her. Disgust was like a taste on the back of her tongue and Mosi looked away, because what she really wanted to do was bash her fist into that smug, handsome face.

She studied the others. Damon sat next to Jerry, staring out at the desert passing beneath them. His lips were pressed into a thin line and Mosi knew he was in pain. Richard was again focused on his laptop, answering emails. Fox's green eyes kept flicking from person to person. There was a worried frown between his auburn brows. He was clearly very aware of the tension that sizzled through the cramped space, though of course he had no idea of the cause.

Poor guy, we ripped him out of his life because we had to, but landed him in the middle of this cluster fuck.

Mosi tried to wrap her head around what Fox was attempting, to circumvent relativity, to move faster than the speed of light. If he succeeded it meant that humans might see the light of distant stars, but in real time, not as an echo of the light they had shed into the universe thousands or even millions of years before. It was hard to comprehend, and it raised another question. If he succeeded, if Lumina's subsidiary Ad Astra built that first starship, would she go?

Closing her eyes she pictured the sweep of Shiprock, known to her people as the *Tsé Bit'a'í*—the Rock with Wings—against a turquoise sky. The whisper of wind through the pines at the Taos ski basin as if the earth itself was breathing. The lonely cry of a coyote greeting the dawn. Could she ever contemplate leaving New Mexico, much less the planet?

It wasn't long before they were landing at the Albuquerque Sunport. Janine and Jorge took Paul over to an armored SUV away from the rest of them. Fox looked from the waiting limo to the SUV.

"I ... I can ride with Paul."

"No. You're with us," Richard said sharply.

Mosi softened the implacable statement a bit. "We have the sword. Just in case ..."

"Ah, yes, right. Still not entirely accustomed to people ... things ... wanting to kill me."

Mosi smiled. "Oh, you get used to it."

Fox attempted a smile that was pretty much a failure. "Must I? I'd really rather not."

"A very sensible attitude," Damon said as he stepped into the car.

✧　✧　✧

BACK AT THE Lumina building Richard turned to Fox. "If you don't mind we have some matters to discuss. Feel free to go up to the penthouse, or your room ... the pool. Whatever you wish. We may be awhile."

Fox looked from Paul to Richard to Mosi and Damon as they stood waiting for an elevator. When it arrived, he cleared his throat and said, "I'll take the next one."

Richard was impressed. It seemed Fox was not as oblivious to social cues as some of their other science friends and mentors. When they got off on the sixth floor, Jeannette handed over a sheaf of papers to Richard. "Here's everything I could dig up on Wannamake and his Magna Mater Foundation."

Damon paused and cleared his throat. "I'll join you in a few."

Richard's eyes, filled with worry, followed his husband as he made his way to the private elevator that would take him to the penthouse. He suspected Damon needed his pain medication. They hadn't anticipated spending so much time at the spaceport.

Richard pushed aside the worry, took the papers, nodded, and they filed into the office. The heavy double wood and glass doors fell shut silently behind them, and Mosi rounded on Paul.

"So, how does it feel to be an accessory to murder?" Mosi said, unknowingly echoing Richard.

Her direct attack seemed to rattle him for an instant, then drawing in a deep breath, Paul regrouped and matched her glare with a look of cool calculation. "Look, I'm sorry, okay? Like I told Richard, no one was supposed to get hurt but sometimes plans go pear-shaped. We were hoping for destruction of property as a way to get into Wannamake's organization and find *all* the dirt. Well, now we've got a bigger lever."

"Those were people, not *levers*. God, you're disgusting," Mosi spat.

"Please, let's move on," Richard said wearily, feeling the headache returning. "We can't turn back time." Mosi picked up the pages Jeannette had provided and began to skim through the material. "Paul's already in, but we need to get inside Wannamake's compound too. Find out who's the sorcerer, if there is an Old One actually present, and if there is … neutralize it."

"Meaning kill this supposed thing, right, Uncle?"

There was a thread of disdain in the words, but before Richard could answer, Mosi looked up from her reading, the muscles around her mouth tense with barely suppressed anger. "Whether you believe it or not they do exist, and they are evil. I watched them twist my brother's mind until he killed our family and tried to kill me. So yes, I happily, willingly, cheerfully bring death to them." She turned back to Richard. "So, how do we do this?"

Paul stepped in before Richard could answer. "Wannamake has a compound up in northern Minnesota where it appears that he and the *elect* plan to ride out their hoped-for apocalypse—"

"Engineered by a magic wielder and potentially an Old One," Richard interrupted quietly.

"They're a bunch of whackos." Once more disdain iced Paul's words. "Yes, we think they represent a potential threat to the homeland, but there is nothing to indicate anything like what you're describing."

Richard looked up at that, his expression bleak. "Once, I would have believed as you do, but then I met a young woman, a half-human, half-Old One, who had the ability to power a nuclear explosion using only her human knowledge and her alien powers. So no, I am not as sanguine as you that this does not represent a greater threat."

"And if the die-off of humanity that Wannamake and his followers are envisioning were to happen, it would be a feast for the Old Ones that would have them flocking into our world. There is no way you and I alone could hold them back," Mosi added. He studied her, but could see no fear in his beautiful, brave ward.

"Which is why we need to stop it now," he concluded. "What was the government's objective?" Richard asked Paul.

"Get 'em on a conspiracy charge. Now we can add manslaughter to that."

"You'll have to tie the evidence directly to Wannamake," Richard warned.

"I am aware of that, Uncle. I'm not an idiot."

"Could have fooled me," Mosi muttered under her breath.

Paul glared at her and Richard wearily scrubbed his hands across his face. "Please, both of you. Stop. You're giving me a headache."

"Yeah, you stick with pretending this is a normal investigation. Meantime, Richard and I will be destroying the Old One and neutralizing any magic users," Mosi said with faux sweetness.

"So, if you want to link Wannamake to the destruction of the rocket this can't be a raid," Mosi continued. "It will have to be an infiltration." She paused, closed her eyes, and shook her head. "Oh crap, I'm going to have to play the Indian

Princess all in touch with nature and Mother Earth, aren't I?"

Paul looked shocked, but Richard's lips twitched in a quick smile. "Well, that is one option, but we're not there yet. Paul has already infiltrated the group, we just need to figure how he brings us in."

"And what makes you think I or my bosses would ever bring you in? Despite your badge, you're not really a cop any longer, Uncle."

"Are you deliberately not listening or are you really this dumb?" Mosi snapped. "There is at least a sorcerer operating there and maybe worse. You need us or you're going to get your big, arrogant block of a head bashed in." Mosi turned back to Richard and tapped her lower lip with a forefinger. "It's clear they've got intel on us, so they'll know who I am which means we'd have to arrange for a plausible break between us, and a plausible explanation of why I would want to join Magna Mater." Mosi gave an eye roll. "This kind of extreme group on either end of the political spectrum have really low opinions of women. So, I suppose I can play the simpering woman swept off her feet by Mr. Handsome over here." She jerked a thumb at Paul who had the gall to smirk at her. Richard was really beginning to wonder if his nephew had any sense of self-preservation. "Great, Indian Princess *and* besotted fool."

Richard gave a small cough, which had always been the way he signaled to her that there was something she hadn't considered. She frowned at him. "Okay, give me at least a small hint of what you're thinking."

"You're galloping off before we have enough information and you're overlooking a key fact: Wannamake doesn't know the truth about Paul," Richard said softly. "They think he's a loyal soldier of the apocalypse."

She saw where he was going. "Ahhh, so I wouldn't be going with him willingly. Instead he presents me to Wannamake as leverage over you." Her expression turned mulish. "I'm not sure I wouldn't rather simper than play the prisoner. As if he could take me."

Richard got a faraway look and a fond smile touched his lips as he remembered what nine-year-old Mosi had said to him when they had been under attack: *My middle name is Dezba, it means goes to war.*

"You know, I'm *right here*," Paul huffed. "And you don't get to burn down a yearlong operation because you *think* there *might* be demons, or monsters, or aliens, or whatever the fuck—"

"Oh, I'll burn down more than that, Paul," Richard interrupted. "You will have either Mosi or myself with you. Otherwise, I'll see to it that Wannamake knows you're a federal agent.

"Blackmailing me now, Uncle?"

"I've done far worse in my life," Richard replied grimly, and Paul seemed to read his implacable determination rather than the guilt that ate at him constantly. "Now, I have phone calls to make. You two start figuring out a strategy."

"Okay, *Na sha dii*, but don't work too long. You need some sleep … and food." He waved her off, but couldn't help watching as the two young people left the office. Despite his harsh words he would find a way to keep both of them safe. No matter the cost.

✦ ✦ ✦

AS THEY PASSED Jeannette's desk, Mosi threw back over her shoulder, "Let's go in the conference room."

The sound of the fountain bubbling softly, and the light glinting off the water sheeting down the side of the tall black stone would have been soothing if Mosi wasn't so tired, wired, and so very, very pissed.

"And now tell me about these eco terrorists," she said, as she settled into the chair at the big oval table.

Paul heaved a put-upon sigh and also took a chair. "Maybe you could tell me why you have such hate and disdain for your own culture and people." He gave her a limped look out of his deep blue eyes, and Mosi felt an angry flush rise into her cheeks.

"I wasn't dissing *my* people. I was referring to Wannamake's dupes, who I'm betting are almost all as white as you and Richard ... who frankly is the whitest white man who's ever lived. I was talking about the fact they would have eaten that shit up." She raised an eyebrow. "You gonna to tell me I'm wrong?"

"No, you're right." He paused and surprised her by suddenly smiling. "So, are we done exchanging insults? Can we get down to figuring out how we stop these people." He paused and straightened his tie even though it was perfectly straight. "Look, I am sorry about those scientists. Truly, I am. I fucked up by allowing them to follow through with their sabotage, I accept that, but I had to do it to maintain my cover, and I can't change things now. So, how are we going to get you inside given the fact that Wannamake and his people will never believe you decided to leave Lumina and embrace them."

She considered him for a long moment and decided he wasn't just blowing smoke. "Okay, first things first, let's see if we can identify the magic user." She touched the release and the computer rose out of the table. She quickly typed in Mark Grenier, and the file, complete with numerous pictures, appeared on the big screen that hung at the far end of the room.

"Have you ever seen this man at any of the gather-around-the-bonfire-and-let's-all-make-s'mores-while-we contemplate-a-mass-casualty-event bonding parties?" she asked. "He would be training the magic user."

The pictures showed Grenier first at the height of his power, televangelist to presidents and politicians with a TV station, thousands of followers, and a massive compound in rural Virginia. The image showed perfectly-coifed greying brown hair, a pair of horn rim glasses held casually in one hand, bespoke suit, slim and elegant. The final image was video from a surveillance camera at Lumina showing Grenier waddling into the building, his massive belly leading, double chins trapped by his shirt collar.

"Jesus, what happened to him?"

"Richard cut off his hand and Grenier lost his powers. He wasn't stupid, he said himself that he began to gorge in an effort to fill the emptiness when he lost his ability to do magic. Anyway—"

"Wait. My uncle *assaulted* this guy and then he came here and *worked* for him?" Paul's voice spiraled up several octaves.

"Yeah, Grenier knew Richard was the only one who could protect him from the Old Ones. Grenier was supposed to get the sword, but he fucked up big time, and the Old Ones aren't real forgiving of failure. But he was or is a snake, so he betrayed Richard. He's been on the run ever since. Damon thinks we should have made more of an effort to locate and neutralize him, but Richard said no." She cocked her head, considering. "Not sure why, but it was his call. Well, that was a long way of saying, have you ever seen this guy?"

"Sorry, no."

"Okay, but we do need to identify the magic users." She reacted to Paul's expression. "What?"

"It just sounds so bizarre when you just throw that out there so casually. Magic." He gave a derisive snort.

"Okay, let me try again to make you understand. We live in a Euclidean reality. There are certain fundamental laws that underpin our universe: gravity, electromagnetism, weak nuclear force, strong nuclear force, speed of light, and so forth. But in those other folded dimensions they often have different laws or the laws work differently, and when humans tap into those other universes it warps and stresses our reality. It doesn't obey what we think of as natural law so it looks like magic. And rather than have to give this big speech every time, we just say … magic. Is that all right with you?"

"Okay, carry on. How do you … we identify these people?"

"It's subtle. Humans need focusing devices in order to channel the power from these other universes. Grenier used his glasses. A guy Richard fought years ago used a riding crop, and there was this girl who used pennies. So, I need you to think about anyone who has some item that they seem fixated upon, something that never leaves their side."

Paul scrubbed at the stubble on his face. "Wasn't exactly where I was focusing. Can I think about it for a little while, maybe grab a few Zs?"

"Okay. I guess we could all use some rest. Shall we meet back here in two hours? I'll need the names of everyone you can think of in the organization."

"We've already run background checks on everyone I've interacted with. I'll see if I can convince my supervisor to release those to you. Save you doing the work twice."

"Thank you, that would be helpful."

He pushed back his chair, but stopped before he reached the door. "Assuming for the moment I believe all of this, and that this sword is necessary to stop … well … magic. You've only got one. Won't that leave the people here vulnerable when you or my uncle come with me to Wisconsin?"

"Yes, but it's something we face every time we have to respond to an incursion. And we usually go together. That way if one of us falls the other can still carry on with the mission."

"Harsh. How does Damon feel about that?"

"He was an army ranger and then a police officer. He understands sacrifice."

✧   ✧   ✧

"I SHOULDN'T BE giving you this information, but fuck it, we saw what happened at MIT and we are so grateful both of the

Paladins were spared," General Marangoz was saying.

It was just past one in the morning in Ankara, but the Turkish general had taken the call because it was Lumina on the line, and Marangoz led a group, the *Işik*, dedicated to the battle against the Old Ones and their followers. Years ago they had given Richard, Damon, Mosi, and the Nerd Posse sanctuary when they had been on the run.

"I know I'm not supposed to talk about miracles," Damon said with a chuckle. "But it was a fucking miracle Mosi wasn't killed or wounded when she was on that dais. Unfortunately, one of our science advisors did get shot. He'll recover, but it was a nightmare. And too many people didn't make it."

"So how may we be of assistance?"

Damon outlined the situation with the drone. "Any chance you might be able to help us trace who might have bought it? Presumably it sold on the black market."

"We recently rolled up a group of military officers who were siphoning off weaponry and selling it. We traced the items to an Albanian weapons dealer. I will send you what we have though I expect threats will not move him."

"Yeah, but money might," Damon said.

"True that," Marangoz said with a laugh. "Farewell, my friend, take care of yourself and Richard and our dear *kelebek*."

Damon slowly hung up the phone, and then chuckled softly. He wondered how Mosi would react to being called a *butterfly*. Probably with a huff and an eye roll. The pain medication had done its best and he was feeling better, but by the time he got back downstairs Richard was in a conference call with Dagmar and several other officers of the company.

Damon checked the security feed from his computer. The nephew was in bed and snoring. Mosi had changed into workout clothes and was taking out her frustrations on the punching bag down in the gym. And the Brit kid was disconsolately wandering through the building like a lost puppy.

Satisfied that his people were safe, he hit the intercom and rang up Jorge Tafoya the head of research and communications for Lumina.

"Hey, Jorge, got a project for you."

"*On my way.*"

A few minutes later Jorge Tafoya appeared in the door of Damon's office. He was no longer twenty years old, going for a degree in communications, and working part-time for Lumina. Now he had two kids, a wife who was six months pregnant with their third, and there were a few lines around his eyes, a burgeoning paunch, and a spade beard hid an incipient double chin.

"You hanging in there, *Jefe*?" Tafoya asked. The deep brown eyes held concern and worry.

"Just tired. It's been a really hard few days."

"I know. Jeannette told me what happened at the spaceport. Feel real bad for Feray. I'm drafting a statement for Lumina."

"Good, good. You'll run it by Richard?"

"Of course. So what do you need?"

Damon handed over the sheet of paper where he had scribbled down the information on the arms dealer and the partial serial numbers from the drone. "We need to find out who purchased this goddamn thing."

"How much am I authorized to offer," Jorge glanced down at the note, "Mr. Përmeti for this info?"

"If it looks like it's going over fifty grand then come talk to us."

"And if money doesn't talk?" Jorge asked.

"Then I call in Wangai and the strike force ... and maybe Mr. Përmeti suffers an unfortunate robbery and arson at his place of business."

"You got it boss. I expect this *pendejo* takes calls from potential clients no matter the time—day or night."

"I expect you're right."

CHAPTER FIFTEEN

BE OF THE EARTH

FOX, LAPTOP TUCKED under his arm, wandered aimlessly through the building, backing out of office spaces when heads were raised to give him curious looks. He noted that many of the workers were young and they all seemed to be very intent on their computer screens. He wondered what they were doing? Which of Lumina's far flung endeavors were they shepherding? Had they all been subjected to the touch of the sword? He had to assume yes. And what had they thought about that? Had they seen monsters or did they just accept they existed?

The past six days—well, seven if you counted Thursday night in the computer lab—he had been on a dead run. Boston to Houston, Houston to Albuquerque, Albuquerque to the spaceport, and there had been death and violence at both ends of that whirlwind. Fox was suddenly desperately homesick for the soft greens and summer rains of Hampshire, but he could just imagine the interrogation he'd endure if he went home. His dad would be bitterly pleased and assume that Fox had washed out. No way could Fox explain what a research grant meant, and he certainly couldn't tell his hardheaded soldier father about creatures from another universe and a billionaire with a magic sword.

Even his ever-supportive mum would think he'd cracked.

The relentless New Mexico sun was flaring through the windows and his budding headache decided to arrive. Fox pulled off his glasses, pinched the bridge of his nose and decided to go down to the basement swimming pool. He was too exhausted to swim, but at least it would be cool and dark down there.

Estevan gave him a nod as he sat in the security office just behind the large horseshoe reception desk. The young man manning the desk and answering phones gave him a smile as Fox awkwardly explained, "I … I just wanted to go down to the pool … if that's all right …"

"Of course, sir," he said.

"It's the sun, you see. Bit much, isn't it?" Fox muttered.

"It is, but in a month or so the summer monsoons will arrive, it will cool off, and we'll get some cloud cover."

"Thank God—oh, I guess I'm not supposed to do that now," Fox muttered.

"It's a hard habit to break. We usually say thank the stars."

"I like that." They exchanged another smile and Fox rode the elevator down to the basement.

The pool was doing an automatic fill, and the sound of splashing water was wonderfully soothing. Fox sat down on the polished aqua tiles, pulled off his shoes and socks, and rolled up his pants legs. He then sat dabbling his feet in the water and watching the ripples fan out.

He became aware of the rhythmic *whap* of fists on leather. He knew the sound well because of the punching bag his dad kept in the garage. The one time Jonathan had forced his twelve-year-old son to tackle the bag, Fox had broken three fingers and had a massive asthma attack that had necessitated a trip to the emergency room.

That was a less-than-comforting memory and Fox opened his laptop and started running over his formulas again. He was hooked into the Lumina Gaia servers and he suddenly became aware of odd flickers. He realized the pin spots in the ceiling and in the swimming pool were flickering and the quiet hum of the heater in the hot tub had cut off. It reminded Fox of what had happened in the computer lab just before the slug monster tried to kill him, and terror had his breath going short.

He looked back down at his laptop, grateful it wasn't attached to a power source if Lumina was having an electrical failure, but then he realized the laptop was running calculations *he hadn't authorized or commanded it to start.*

"What are you?" A whispered voice, seemingly emanating from the laptop.

Where ...?

The laptop almost took a swim as Fox tossed it away and scooted frantically backward. Fox tried to jump to his feet, but he slipped on the tiles and toppled into the pool. The unexpected shock of the cold water made him gasp and he swallowed and inhaled water. The last thing he remembered was the sharp pain in his chest.

✧ ✧ ✧

MOSI WAS ALREADY in motion when, over the wail of the alarms, she heard a yell followed by a splash. Pistol clutched in her hand, she raced out of the gym to see Fox thrashing wildly in the pool and then go still. Setting aside the pistol, Mosi dove into the water, got her arms under Fox's armpits and towed him quickly to the steps at the shallow end of the pool. She hit him firmly between the shoulder blades wondering if she was going to have to administer CPR, when he gave a gasp and began to harshly cough.

"You okay?" He gave a shaky nod. She gave a quick look to ascertain that the lights were holding steady, then hauled him to his feet. "Come on, we have to get to Richard. He has the sword."

The water was squelching in her tennis shoes, and her Vouri joggers and Star Wars tee shirt were clinging to her body. She eyed the pistol, but if this was Old One activity the gun was probably useless. They needed the protection of the sword and had to hope that Cross had sensed the attack … if that's what this was.

As she dragged the man toward the emergency stairs, she paused and leaned down to grab his computer, only to have him say shrilly, "*Leave it!*"

Mosi didn't argue. When she opened the door to the stairwell Fox gave her a look that held equal parts disbelief and despair. "It's six or seven sodding floors," he groaned.

"You want to risk being stuck in an elevator?"

He shot her a withering look. "Why do you always have to be right," he muttered resentfully. Mosi couldn't mask her grin, which earned her another glare.

They began to climb.

✧　✧　✧

THE MOMENT THE lights had flickered Richard had hit the alarm and raced out of the office. Jeanette had keyed the defensive shutters that were even now rolling up to protect the building. Years ago, in an attempt to prevent Richard from learning he was a Paladin and being armed with the sword, a magical attack had blown out the windows on the building. No one had been killed but there had been numerous injuries and Kenntnis, the founder of Lumina and creator of the sword, had installed the shutters.

Richard didn't have to ask for a report. Jeanette, checking the surveillance cameras, quickly briefed him. "Mosi is in the basement gym. Damon is in his office. Fox is in the pool area. Paul was asleep in his bedroom."

Richard drew the sword as he ran to the stairs, and didn't bother to use the steps to reach the fifth floor that housed Damon's office. He just vaulted over the railing, taking the shock in his knees as he hit the fifth floor landing. He burst through the door. Workers were already taking cover as he ran into Damon's office. His husband looked up from his computer screen.

"Whatever it was, it's over. Everything reads normal. It ran through the Wi-Fi and into every system and then vanished. I'll get Jorge and Mosi on it, they're the computer whiz kids, but I think we can back off the panic button." Damon nodded toward the blade of sword that Richard help. "And the sword seems to agree."

Richard finally really looked at the blade. When it was in the presence of magic or Old Ones, the glittering stars that filled the blade seemed to rise up and form a nimbus around the sword and eventually around Richard or Mosi, depending upon who was wielding it. None of that was happening, so whatever had just infiltrated the electronics it was neither magical nor an alternate multiverse alien presence. Unlike the alien who was living in the lowest recesses of the building who was an alien from this universe.

It was as if Damon had read where Richard's thoughts had gone. "Monitors read a burst of light and activity from Kenntnis' room when it happened." He pushed up from the desk. "We should go check on him."

There was a spike of fear in his stomach. "You probably should have led with that," Richard said.

Damon shrugged. "I wanted to reassure you before I alarmed you."

❖ ❖ ❖

MOSI AND FOX were emerging into the lobby when Damon and Richard stepped out of the elevator. Both kids were soaking wet, leaving damp footprints on the marble floor.

"Does this mean we don't have to take the stairs now?" Fox asked, his tone hopeful, and Damon had to hide a smile at Mosi's eye roll. Fox didn't miss it. "Hey, I'm lazy, all right?" he squawked.

"Well, you don't have to advertise it," Mosi huffed.

"Do I even want to know?" Richard asked, eyeing them.

"No!" They said in chorus.

When Richard pulled the special elevator key from beneath his shirt, Mosi asked. "Are you going to check on *Yáh Ahiga*?"

Damon nodded. "Joselita is on duty down there and

reported a burst of activity when the energy spike happened."

Richard frowned and chewed on his lower lip. "You should come too, Mosi, you've always had an affinity with him."

Fox's gaze was flicking between the three of them. "Do I even want to—"

"No," they all said together.

"Go on upstairs and dry off," Damon said laying a hand on the young man's shoulder, and guiding him gently but firmly toward the elevator.

"Would you mind grabbing my laptop, shoes, and socks? We left rather in a hurry," Fox asked.

"Sure," Damon said with a smile.

They made their way down to the sub-basement where Kenntnis dwelled in a room just off the armory. It was comfortably appointed with a sitting area and a bed, but the man ... *creature* ... *alien* never took advantage of any of them. He remained wherever he was placed. He didn't need to eat or sleep and he just stayed clean, which made Damon wonder if the clothing he appeared to be wearing was just as fake and fabricated as the seemingly human body he wore.

When Damon had first met the *man*, Kenntnis had been a massive figure well over six foot six and big—as if the monolith from *2001* had been recast in human form. He appeared at first glance to be black, but as you studied his face there were subtle signs that his face held a mixture of every human race. At the time his eyes had been black, but after he was trapped in that weird, slow glass stuff, his eyes were now silver, and at times they swirled like the stars that were embedded in the space-black blade of the sword he had built.

But right now it wasn't just his eyes that were silver and swirling. His entire body seemed to be flickering between the human form and becoming a swirl of silver lights.

Joselita's voice was shaking as she briefed them. "I didn't do a thing. I was just sitting in the control booth eating my lunch, when we had the power surge, or whatever it was, and then he started doing *that*."

"Did he say anything?" Richard asked.

There was a note of hope in his husband's voice and Damon realized that deep down Richard was still hoping that Kenntnis would return, retake the reins of Lumina, and allow Richard to step aside. No matter how often Damon and others reassured him, Richard could never fully accept that he was doing a good job as the head of Lumina.

"No, sir, but there was sound." Joselita keyed her iPad to bring up a recording. What echoed through the room were the deep chordal tones fading into overtones that occurred whenever the sword was drawn.

"So what the fuck do we think this is?" Damon asked.

Mosi approached the alien and Damon had to resist the urge to pull her back. It was irrational, but he feared if she got too close she would be drawn into that whirlpool of silver and light. Richard had his arms folded over his chest and was just watching.

"*Yáh Ahiga*, we are here."

She thrust her hand into Kenntnis' coruscating chest. Damon had heard the story of how, when she and Richard were trapped on the edge of a thousand foot drop Mosi—then only nine—had reached into the alien's body and removed the sword. To see it happen now was as disturbing as all fuck.

"Come back to us. Be grounded. Be of the Earth." The light show began to fade, the body coming more into focus until finally Kenntnis once more sat before them.

Richard laid a hand on Mosi's shoulder. "You always did have a deep effect on him."

"I wish I could've actually known him." She paused, then added, "So what do we make of the sound? Warning? A cry for help? It sounded just like when we draw the sword."

Richard shook his head. "No, it was subtly different. When we draw the sword it's predominately in the key of D major which you'll often hear in military marches. This one is in A major. It's more joyful, often used in love songs."

Damon grinned and buffeted Richard on the shoulder. "And your daddy thought you studying music was a waste of time," he scoffed. "How else would we get a statement that adorably nerdy?" Richard shot him a withering look that actually had no heat to it, and went red to the tips of his ears.

"And useful," Mosi said. "Whoever or whatever caused the power spike, it wasn't dangerous, or Kenntnis certainly didn't perceive it that way."

"So, crisis … if it was a crisis, averted?" Damon asked. "Shall we get back upstairs and spend at least a little time enjoying being home together as a family?"

"Sounds like a plan," Mosi said, as she linked her arms through both of theirs.

"How are you coming on that infiltration plan with Paul?" Richard asked.

Damon rolled his eyes. "That is *not* what I had in mind

when I said *family* time. Family time means *not* work time."

"Well, I suppose Paul counts as family," Richard mused as they walked to the elevator. He shot Damon a sideways glance from beneath his lashes.

"Can we disown him?" Mosi muttered.

"Can I get a divorce?" Damon huffed, and reaching over Mosi, he bopped his spouse on the top of his head.

✧   ✧   ✧

WHEN THEY REACHED the sixth floor, Mosi—her tennis shoes squelching unpleasantly—headed for the private elevator to the penthouse. Richard tried to head to his office, only to be firmly tucked against Damon's side and frog-marched to join Mosi.

"Franz is in the kitchen cooking up a storm," the older man said. "We haven't had any fucking sleep for two days. We're *all* going to take a nap before dinner." He nuzzled Richard's ear and nipped his earlobe.

Mosi couldn't suppress her smirk. "That doesn't look much like napping behavior. That looks like nooky behavior." The smirk got worse when Richard again turned bright red to the tips of his ears.

"Damon, behave. And you too, young lady," her guardian huffed.

"You know, I'm twenty-one now." And then it struck Mosi with sudden force that she was *twenty-one*, which meant Richard was no longer her guardian. For an instant, she felt oddly bereft, but then comforted herself that he would always be her *Na sha dii*.

"My love, I think she probably knows about sex," Damon said with a grin.

She didn't think it was possible, but Richard turned even redder. They reached the penthouse and he rocketed out of the elevator.

"You are both impossible. Stop making me blush."

"But it's so much fun," Mosi called after him, as he stalked down the hall toward the bedrooms.

While at the same time, Damon said, "I want to see just how far that blush extends." Richard didn't look back just threw an over-the-shoulder middle finger at him. "That's the idea, babe," Damon called through a chuckle.

"Not listening!" Richard yelled, as he vanished through the door into the master bedroom suite.

Damon draped an arm over Mosi's shoulders and gave her a sideways hug. "Get out of those wet clothes and get some rest too. The shit afflicting the world can wait to get shoveled for a few hours."

"I will. But you rest too."

For the briefest of instants there was a look of weary sorrow that Mosi easily interpreted, that it might not be long before Damon was resting for eternity. His expression was quickly banished by a smile. "See you at dinner, kiddo."

CHAPTER SIXTEEN

THINGS ALWAYS ESCALATE

THIS TIME THE strange Cross creature didn't show up. What did remain the same was the food—it was once again amazing. There was an appetizer of what Mosi explained were squash blossoms filled with goat cheese, dipped in batter and flash fried, served with a raspberry sauce. A freshly baked French baguette was on the table, the serrated blade of the bread knife resting beneath it. Paul began to cut slices. Fox envied the man his calm assurance that he could take command of something even as innocuous as slicing bread.

The main course was a leg of lamb in the Greek style, redolent with the scents of garlic and rosemary. Tiny red potatoes had been roasted and there was a large salad. Franz carefully poured the contents of a bottle of red wine into a crystal wine decanter. The only reason Fox recognized it was because of his studies at Cambridge. The dining hall at his college had been very formal.

The chef half-bowed to Richard and asked, "If there is anything you need, sir, please ring."

"Or I can get off my ass, and go into the kitchen and get it," Mosi said, her dark brown eyes sparkling with good humor. The portly chef wagged an admonishing finger at her, and retreated back into the kitchen.

"So what was the reason for all the alarms this afternoon?" Paul asked as he passed his plate to Damon for a slice of lamb.

"Just a false alarm," the older man said.

Paul gave him a derisive look. "I find that hard to believe given"—he gave a vague gesture—"everything, well, that Lumina does."

"And we'd tell *you* anything, why?" Mosi asked sharply.

Fox looked between them. He fully expected the air to ignite between their locked eyes. It was Damon who spoke up.

"Hey kiddos, no bickering at dinner. No work talk at dinner. Just good food and friends and family." He suddenly went white, gave a gasp, and clutched at his stomach. Oort was out of his chair in a flash and got his arm around his husband's shoulders. "Bathroom," Damon groaned. "Now!"

The couple hurried out of the dining room. They could hear Damon starting to retch. Mosi let out a sound that was almost a small sob. She defiantly swiped her hand across her eyes. Fox wordlessly offered his napkin. She shook her head, her cascade of hair moving like a wave, and blotted her eyes with her own napkin.

"Should we ... should we just go back to our room?" Fox asked quietly.

Mosi shook her head. "No, they'll be back in a bit, and Franz worked all afternoon making baklava for dessert. We're not going to be rude." She swiveled in her chair to look at Paul. "But since my guardians aren't here, the rules are no longer in force."

Paul met her challenging look with one equally challenging. "So what's it to be, Mosi? Work talk or bickering?"

"Actually, a question. What made you show up just after that disaster of a graduation?"

"You really want to be discussing this in front of him?" Paul jerked a thumb in Fox's direction.

"He's one of us now."

"And what am I?"

"*Not* one of us." Mosi's tone was implacable and cold as death. Fox flinched as an index finger was thrust at him.

"Okay, I agree that my loyalty is to my oath and my organization. What makes *him* so fucking special?" Paul demanded.

"He's going to give us the stars," Mosi replied. "But stop trying to change the subject. Why did you come? It wasn't like we were planning to go to the spaceport until all that shit went down at the graduation."

Fox watched as the other man went from his usual superior expression to frowning concentration. "I ... I hadn't really thought about it. I was just suddenly told I had to get to Boston, hook up with my uncle, and see what I could learn about the Ark project."

"Which day was that?"

"Thursday night. Late. They put me on an early morning flight."

"Which would be Friday," Fox said cautiously. Dread settled in the pit of his stomach. "It's like they knew something was going to happen." He stared at Paul. "Did *you* know? People died. I *watched* people die. Mosi could have died and Mr. Oort and Mr. Weber. *I* could have died." Rage and embarrassment warred in Fox's breast as he recalled the horror of that day. The smell of cordite, blood, and feces. The screams and the sobs as survivors held the dead.

"I think we know who sent that killer drone to MIT," Mosi said softly.

Fox watched as Paul's face settled back into his usual expression of smug superiority. "Suggestive, but hardly dispositive. We have them dead to rights on the bombing at the spaceport. No need to guild that legal lily."

"I think the families of those killed and injured would like to see justice done for their loved ones," Fox said.

"I just bag 'em," Paul said blandly. "It's up to the courts to tag them."

Mosi was nervously tapping her fork against her plate while she thought out loud. "Uyanik was the target because Wannamake thought killing Emirhan would stop the Ark project, but failing that it was certain to send at least some of us to the *Jornada del Muerto*. And I'm sure killing a bunch of world class scientists was an added bonus for the Old Ones and their acolytes." Mosi stood and threw her napkin onto the table. "I need to talk to Richard and Damon."

She swept out of the room and Fox sat frozen as he tried to parse what he had just heard. His swirling thoughts were interrupted by the harsh shriek of a chair being suddenly and violently pushed back.

Fox looked up. Paul was on his feet and the mask had slipped. Gone was the supremely confident, handsome, entitled man. For an instant, Fox saw Paul's guilt and regret and grief.

"I think I've lost my appetite," he said grimly and tossing

down his napkin he left the dining room.

"I get it, mate," Fox whispered to his plate. "If you'd been a bit better at your job a lot of people would still be alive. Not sure how you live with that." Fox just wished he'd had the courage to say it to Paul's face.

✧   ✧   ✧

Mosi sat cross-legged on the end of the bed as she quickly filled them in on what had just occurred in the dining room. Damon was propped up against the pillows sucking on ice chips while Richard softly stroked his greying hair.

"Jorge is gonna be pissed he's been negotiating with that son of a bitch over in Albania," Damon said.

"It's okay, we need the actual proof. Then we can turn it over to Interpol and the FBI," Richard said.

Damon gave him a fond look. "Once a cop always a cop."

Mosi shook her head. "That's all well and good, but it's going to take too long. I need to get in there *now, Na sha dii.*"

"We don't have enough information yet about the compound, Wannemake's assets—"

"You didn't have any of that when you went into Mark Grenier's compound," she countered.

Richard's pale brows drew together in a sharp frown. "What would you know about that? You were maybe six years old when all that happened."

Damon gazed beatifically up at the ceiling. "Well ... *somebody* might have told her about her guardian's exploits before she came into his life."

"Damon!"

"Sweetheart, I think she's right. You said it yourself, that a weather spell needs a really high-level magic wielder, and probably an Old One as well. You need to get in there. And it should be both of you."

"We don't have a coherent plan, and having both of us makes this exponentially more difficult." Richard was looking mulish, but Mosi knew it was an attempt to cover his fears and desire to protect her.

"Between the graduation and what happened at the spaceport, the death toll is up to twenty-four," Mosi said. "You're the one who taught me that things always escalate. And this crowd wants a massive die-off of humanity. Who knows how far along they are with *those* plans?"

Damon threw his support behind her. "And the longer we wait, the less likely it becomes they'll take Paul back into the fold. They know he's been with us. They may decide we've deprogrammed him."

"Or they might figure out he's a cop," Mosi muttered, her fury at Paul's duplicity rising up once more to close like a vise on her throat.

"Fine!" Her guardian snapped. "But it's not happening tonight or even tomorrow, so all of you just cheer down." He looked at Mosi, "Would you mind bringing me a plate?"

"And Franz keeps egg custard in the fridge for me," Damon added.

"Sure." Mosi bounced off the bed and headed for the door.

✧   ✧   ✧

THEY WATCHED THE door fall closed behind her and Damon gave his spouse the side-eye. "So when are you going to tell her that you're going into Wannamake's compound with Paul and not her?"

Richard's mouth fell open in an O that was equal parts shock and annoyance. Damon chuckled, placed a forefinger under Richard's chin and pushed his mouth closed. "Honey, I've known you since you were twenty-seven years old. I am intimately familiar with your savior complex, so please don't treat me—"

"Like a mushroom?" Richard concluded before Damon could say it.

"How did …?"

"You say it a lot and I remember the first time you ever said it to me," he added fondly.

"That night you rescued Rhiana, I remember. You gave me that load of bullshit about how the assailants got away and how you missed your shot. Knew you were trouble even back then." He pressed a kiss against the pulse point beneath Richard's jaw. "You still are."

"I have to go. Paul is family."

"And me and Mosi are family too, and this is too important to risk sending only one of you. You'll have a better chance if you tag team this. 'Cause I don't want to have to make like the cavalry right now. Not sure I'm up to it." They sat in silence for a moment because cancer had entered the room and taken up residence on their chests.

Damon shook it off first. "So is Grenier in there?" Richard nodded. "And you know this for sure?" Richard nodded again. Damon sighed and asked, "Whose spy satellite did we compromise this time?"

"The Chinese. Don't make that face. Wangai covered her tracks and the Sofia network can infiltrate almost any network and not leave a trace."

"You know, as a former army guy and cop, that statement gives me hives."

"I know, my love, but I needed to be sure Grenier was there. It's time—probably past time—he and I finished this dance we've been doing for—"

"Way too fucking long," Damon grunted, as the door opened and Mosi entered, carrying a tray with their food.

✧　✧　✧

THE NEXT MORNING Richard was at his desk forcing himself to read financial statements from the various subsidiaries operated by Lumina. He had very briefly worked at a brokerage firm when he was in his twenties, so he had some experience, but had still struggled when he was first forced to take over Lumina. Now he moved through the files with ease and he honestly wasn't sure how he felt about that. It was certainly not what he had planned for his life. None of it was.

In his perfect world he would have become a famous opera singer, maybe found the courage to come out to his family and found a partner. But that partner wouldn't have been Damon. He had only found Damon because a brutal attack had sent him on the path to becoming a police officer. And he wouldn't trade the joy of finding the love of his life in order to change anything that had happened.

Richard shoved aside the iPad Pro, placed his elbows on

the desk and buried his face in his hands. He knew Lumina did good work, *vital work* all around the globe combating death, disease, climate change, the rise of autocracy. But at times he felt like King Canute because the waves just kept coming and nothing he did seemed to hold them back.

Lumina's bio-engineering division was hard at work on crafting a CRISPR that would strip the DNA marker that allowed the Old Ones to feed on humans; it also allowed those humans to tap into powers that had no place in the Euclidean universe. But if they succeeded in fully developing the technology, did he really have any right to release that among the world's population without asking for their assent? And how many would agree? Enough to keep the invaders from neighboring multiverses away? If only there was a way to strengthen the walls between those universes and the one humans inhabited.

The cell phone in his pocket vibrated. Richard pulled it out and blinked at the unfamiliar 818 area code, but it had to be someone he had entrusted with his personal phone number, so he cautiously answered.

"This is Richard Oort."

"Oh, Mr. Oort, this is Todd Davinovitch. Lottie is here with me."

Rhiana's adopted parents. Dread pooled in the pit of Richard's stomach.

"Yes, hello, has something happened to Rhiana?" He asked.

"Yeah, something weird happened at the care facility," Lottie's voice was distant as she chimed in. Richard could picture her leaning in over her burly truck driver husband's shoulder.

"Somebody tried to steal her out of there yesterday." Todd again.

"*What?*"

"Yeah, fortunately one of the nurses on duty got suspicious when this team showed up saying they had orders to move her to a new nursing home."

Lottie picked up the story. "She told them to stay put while she checked in with us and you, but when she turned around after placing the call, they had beat it out of there."

"What do you think's goin' on, Mr. Oort?" Todd asked.

"I don't know, but I'm going to find out. I can be in LA in just a few hours. I'll let you know when I land, and we can meet at the clinic."

"Thank you," Lottie breathed. "You've done so much to take care of our girl—"

Richard interrupted. "It was my pleasure and my honor to help care of her. I'll see you in a few hours.

Breaking the connection, Richard hurried out of the office in search of Damon. He was happy to find him in his office and not in the residence. That usually meant his spouse was having a good day. Leaning against the door jamb he studied the thick waves of grey-brown hair, the way there was a bit of dark stubble under his right jaw where he had missed a section, the way he chewed a bit on his lower lip as he studied whatever he was reading on his computer.

"Hey, you," Richard called softly.

Damon looked up, a smile lighting up his face and filling his eyes with warmth. "Hey, yourself, Rhode Island."

Richard walked over to him and set on the edge of the

desk. "I have lived in New Mexico for seventeen years. When do I stop being Rhode Island?"

"When you lose that snotty East Coast accent." Richard mock punched him on the shoulder. Damon caught his hand and brought it to his lips. "And as far as the natives are concerned we're *both* carpetbaggers. So what's up? You got that look."

"What look?" Richard asked.

"The look that says you're going to tell me something I won't like," Damon responded promptly.

"I can't tell if this preternatural ability is due to twelve years of marriage or the fact you were a cop."

"Little of both. What's got you all spun up?"

"I have to go to California. Somebody … somebodies tried to steal Rhiana out of the care facility."

Brown eyes widened in shock, then Damon shook his head. "There are police in California. We've got contacts with the FBI. Bluntly, babe, this is not your problem. And that other, bigger problem is in Wisconsin, not California."

"I know, but this *is* my problem. I'm the reason she's in an irreversible coma," Richard said, his voice almost a whisper as the memory of that day when a young woman had begged for mercy and he—for what had seemed like very good and necessary reason at the time—had destroyed the alien half of her, leaving only a drooling shell of what had once been a half-human, half-Old One hybrid.

"You had no choice, babe," Damon said gently. "You had to free Kenntnis, to try and restore some balance back into our universe."

"But it was all for nothing. He was irreparably damaged.

He's just a shell too." Richard gave a hard laugh that more resembled a choked sob. "It seems like all I do is cause harm."

Damon huffed out an annoyed sigh. "First, that's not true. Crazy shit stopped happening once he was free, and second, if you're gonna wallow and beat yourself up then I don't want you to stay home. Go to California, annoy the local authorities, and *get your head out of your ass …* darling," he added with a wink.

It had the usual and desired effect: Richard laughed. "I love you too, dear."

Damon lifted his eyes toward the ceiling. "*However …*" He drew out the word.

"What?"

"You're really going to let Mosi go solo on Wannamake? Face an Old One and one or more sorcerers with only your nephew as backup?"

"Why do I hear my lieutenant not-so-gently indicating I'm missing something," Richard said.

"I'm thinking there might be a different way to play this. Let *me* go to California. I won't irritate the local cops as much as you, and this seems way less critical than preventing a potential extinction level event."

"Okay, I'll leave the California mystery to you, and Mosi and I will go fight monsters. Why are there always more monsters?" He tried to make it sound like a quip, but Damon saw through him.

Damon stood, wrapped his arms around Richard's shoulders, and gave him a soft and very tender kiss. "I know you're tired, love."

Richard leaned into that broad chest and breathed in deeply the scent of his spouse. "I am, but you give me strength."

Damon laughed, pushed him toward the door. "Like you need it. You've got a spine of steel or adamantium like Wolverine."

Richard buried his face in his hands. "Oh god, you and your pop culture references," he said, his voice muffled.

Damon pulled his hands away, gave him another kiss, turned him around and gave him a gentle push toward the door. "Now go make plans with those two youngsters, and I'll tell Brook we need the plane." He gave Richard a slap on the butt, and he looked back over his shoulder and gave him a glare.

Richard paused in the doorway and shook an admonishing finger at Damon. "You be careful too. We still don't know who tried to kidnap us in Texas. They might be behind this Rhiana thing too," Richard warned.

"What was it Kenntnis used to always say? *Coincidence is not causation.* Stop being paranoid."

"You're a fine one to talk," Richard muttered as he left.

CHAPTER SEVENTEEN

THE GHOST IN THE MACHINE

WANGAI NDUNG'U, THE head of Lumina's overseas security forces, had an almost impish look on her high-planed, elegant face. Considering she was six foot two in her stocking feet and could probably bench press Damon without a lot of effort, it was an incongruous sight, and the only reason Damon could see her was because the tech wizards of Lumina had developed a satellite phone that was image capable.

"What have you done?" Damon asked, torn between amusement and dread.

"What you asked, *Bwana.* We downloaded the computer files and took all the physical files." She paused and tossed something lightly up and down in her hand. "And left a little present."

That's when Damon realized she was holding a remote detonator. "You made sure the area is cleared, right?" His voice had risen an octave or more.

"It's three in the morning here. The warehouse is well away from any other buildings, and the guards have gone sleepy-bye and been taken to a safe location." She cocked her head and Damon could hear the faint wail of approaching sirens. "And the fire department has been alerted."

The expression on her ebony dark face morphed from merriment to simmering anger. "Men like this Përmeti truly are merchants of death. If I can keep at least these weapons out of the hands of murderers, mercenaries, and terrorists I will do just that."

Damon knew just what horror had been afflicted across the globe, including in her own country, by just these sorts of arms dealers, and he gave a nod. "Can't argue with your logic, Wangai."

She nodded and depressed the red button on the detonator. In the distance, an explosion like a dragon's roar was audible, and Damon could see the Bulgarian sky behind her light up in shades of red and orange.

"Okay, you've had your fireworks fun. Now get out of there and back to base, and get us the files," Damon ordered. She gave a salute and cut the connection.

"Guy really should have taken the fifty grand," Damon muttered aloud to his office.

✧   ✧   ✧

"Okay, change of plan," Richard said as he swept into the conference room. His hair was wet and Mosi knew he had been swimming. It was how he almost always worked out strategies.

"Did we have a plan?" Paul asked. "'Cause I must have missed that."

Richard ignored his nephew, but Mosi had had it with the supercilious asshole. She came out of her chair, and delivered a ringing slap hard enough it knocked his head to the side.

"What the fuck!" Paul yelled, jumping out of his chair with such force that it went rolling away from the table and crashed against the wall.

"The fuck is that you are a jackass, an arrogant know-it-all, and a ... a jerk."

"And you're a goddamn menace and crazy to boot."

Richard settled calmly into the chair at the head of the table and said mildly, "As entertaining as this all was, are you both quite finished?"

Mosi felt the flush rising into her face. "Sorry, *Na sha dii*," she murmured and slunk back into her chair.

Paul recovered his chair and also sat down, but he kept giving her simmering looks. Mosi ignored it and instead enjoyed contemplating the red mark she had left on his cheek.

Paul rested his hands on the table and leaned in on Richard. "These people know I've been with you for almost a week now. Granted they sent me to infiltrate, but if this goes on too long they're going to distrust me when I do return."

"Damon made the same point and I agree, but I expect they'll welcome you back into the fold with open arms when you tell them that you've convinced me that I should join forces with Wannamake to further environmental goals," Richard answered.

"So, you want a meeting," Paul said thoughtfully.

"Precisely. That gets us in the door without us tying ourselves into knots trying to explain why Mosi would be interested in joining, or us trying to do some Dirty Dozen stealth raid. And in the meantime, Pamela and Jorge are going through the evidence we just received that might link the armed drone to Wannamake."

"And speaking of me. What am I going to be doing?" Mosi asked.

"You'll stay off-site until needed."

"Why not have you in reserve? You're a much bigger prize than I am," Mosi argued.

"Which is why it has to be me. Grenier is there, and he won't be able to resist. He'll convince Wannemake to see me. He barely knew you, so there wouldn't be the same pull."

Mosi frowned. "Okay, let me go on record that I hate this plan, but I also see the reasoning."

"You know they'll search you. Disable any communication devices," Paul warned.

"Naturally, but they won't search *you*. You're a true believer who brought them a prize—"

Mosi interrupted. "Assuming you actually convinced them of your sincerity."

"I know it doesn't fit your mental narrative about me," Paul said. "But I'm really good at my job. And as you never let me forget … I play upper-class, entitled white guy really well."

"Well, they say self-awareness is the first step toward enlightenment," Mosi said sweetly. She noted that Richard tightly squeezed the bridge of his nose, but she realized he was not exasperated, but instead trying to hide a smile. She narrowed her eyes and glared at him.

"What?" She demanded.

"Nothing. Nothing."

She gave him a distrustful look which he met with an

utterly bland expression. He was really good at keeping a poker face. *Damn him*, Mosi thought.

"They'll expect you to have the sword," Mosi said.

"I'll be carrying one of the decoy copies."

"Which means you'll have no protection against the Old One or any spells that might be thrown," Mosi objected.

"I'll have you," Richard said with a fond smile.

"And me," Paul chimed in. "And if you can get actual evidence, I can call in a strike team."

"Whoever is on the team needs to meet up with us beforehand, and be inoculated before attempting to enter the compound," Richard ordered.

"And how the fuck do I explain that?" Paul demanded.

Mosi didn't know how Richard managed to just smile at him. "Tell them to call Special Agent Samantha Martin and Assistant Directors Franklin and Haskell. And if they don't agree, we'll do without and just rely on our FBI associates." Richard pushed back his chair and stood. "It sounds like we have a plan. Mosi, check in with Pamela and Jorge to see what they might have unearthed for evidence, and tell Jerry to get the other plane ready. Paul, start setting up this meeting. I'm going to see Damon off at the airport. I'll be back in an hour or so." He paused in the doorway and looked back. "Oh, and Mosi, reassure Fox that we're not abandoning him."

"Except we are," Mosi muttered at the closed door.

✧   ✧   ✧

IT HAD BEEN hard to part with Damon. Not just because

Richard was trying to spend every possible moment with his husband, but because he still felt like he ought to be going to California with him. Intellectually he knew that Damon was perfectly capable of looking out for himself, but it felt like he was trying to pawn off the Rhiana problem to his spouse. Yes, the situation in Wisconsin was serious, more serious than a kidnapping attempt of a coma victim, but maybe he was really just trying to dodge the guilt and responsibility he carried for having put Rhiana in that condition. Years ago he had sworn to protect the girl and instead he had destroyed her.

During the drive back to Lumina headquarters from the Albuquerque Sunport, Richard received a text from Pamela that they had the computer files and she was digging into them along with Jorge and Dagmar.

Found anything? He texted back.

We just got them! Knowing his sister, Richard was pretty sure there had been an eye roll and a glare that accompanied the words.

Twenty minutes later they were back and Richard stepped off the elevator on the fifth floor, which held his sister's office. Three sets of voices, two female and one male, met him when he stepped through the door.

Pamela was seated behind her desk with Jorge leaning over her shoulder. Dagmar, who was in London, was a holographic image being projected in three dimensions onto the middle of the desk, courtesy of the technology of the Sofia network. Richard came around the desk and took up a position at his sister's other shoulder. She spared him a simmering look, then went back to clicking and scrolling.

"Anything?" Richard asked.

Pamela shook her head, and Jorge leaned over and typed in a few commands that meant nothing to Richard.

"There's the surface files and information, but there's another level of encryption that I think is hiding more files," the Hispanic man said. "We just haven't been able to spoof it yet and get inside."

"Shouldn't the Sofias be able to do that?" Richard asked.

"Yeah, but they need some guidance from me—" Jorge broke off abruptly and yanked his hands off the Bluetooth keyboard like it was hot. "Or ... not."

The large computer screen went nuts, scrolling and flashing faster than the human eye could follow. "What's happening?" Richard asked plaintively. While he was reasonably facile with computers, he often told the techs who kept his machines in order that if he thought it would help, he would sacrifice small animals to the damn things.

Jorge was back to typing, but it seemed to be having no effect. "I don't know."

"Not what I wanted to hear," Richard gritted. He stood dithering, wondering if he ought to just pull the plug out of the wall, but had a feeling that fell into the category of sacrifice and small animals, given how every computer in Lumina facilities was linked though the Sofia network. Instead, he grabbed out his phone and texted Mosi. *PAMELA'S OFFICE, NOW!*

A few moments later she came running in, her hair like a long, black pennant waving behind her. "What's wrong?"

Richard just pointed at the computer and Jorge immediately backed off giving her room to slid in in front of him.

"At this point, you know way more than me," he said to Mosi.

Mosi's slim, long-fingered hands were placed on the keyboard and she typed a few quick commands. She looked up at all of them. "Bad news. Somebody else is controlling this computer."

Dread filled Richard's stomach and he brought up his phone, but before he could dial, Mosi grabbed his wrist.

"Good news, sort of, is that it's not anyone from *outside*. It's all contained inside the Sofia network."

"So who ..." Richard began, but before he could finish his question the screen settled and they were looking at a purchase request for a Turkish weaponized Sonar drone and the accompanying notes, which were unfortunately, in Bulgarian.

"We have anybody who speaks Bulgarian?" Pamela asked.

Seconds later a translation appeared in a separate window. "Well, that's not creepy," Dagmar said in a tone that indicated it was creepy as hell, while her holographic figure studied her own screen that was linked with the one at Lumina.

Mosi looked around the room, then returned her attention to the screen. "Whoever they are, they are watching and listening." She leaned in and said quietly, "Hello? Who are you?" There was no response either written or spoken, but a few seconds later a gif appeared expressing shyness and embarrassment, and then it was gone.

All the people in the room and the image of the one in London exchanged glances. Jorge cleared his throat. "You know, if I were still religious, I'd be sending for a priest right now. Try a little machine exorcism."

Richard glanced around at all of them. "Should I be panicking about our security?"

"Well, it's not like they erased our illegally obtained evidence," Pamela said in a hollow voice.

"Just helped us find and read it," Mosi added with forced cheerfulness.

"So we now have the proof that Magna Mater purchased the drone that killed and wounded dozens of people at MIT," Dagmar said, echoing her cheerful delivery.

"Evidence that was *illegally obtained*," Pamela stressed again.

"Well, it's not like we're trying to haul them into court," Richard said brightly. "We're just going in to kill an Old One or two, and neutralize some human sorcerers."

Pamela folded her arms across her chest and glared at him. "All of which involves you putting yourself in the hands of the people who killed dozens of people in Boston, then blew up a rocket, and killed a few more. Somebody give me patience."

Richard gave her a fond smile, which only made her glare harder. For years they had been antagonists. It was lovely to now have a sister who cared about him.

Mosi stood and slipped an arm around Pamela's waist. "I won't let anything happen to him, *shi bízhí – shimá*."

"Or you, young lady," Pamela said sharply, then kissed Mosi on the cheek.

Now that Pamela had been mollified, Richard started sidling toward the door. "I'm going to slip this information to Franklin and Haskell at the FBI. See if they can find a way to tidy up our little stolen evidence faux pas."

"And maybe send Sam," Mosi added. "I'd love to have her for backup." Pamela rolled her eyes. "What? She's the best sniper in the FBI."

"She's a foul-mouthed hoyden," Pamela said primly. "And yes, a very accomplished marksman. Also ... hoyden."

"Well, you shall have to deny her vouchers to Almack's, Miss Manners," Richard teased. He knew his sister's guilty pleasure were Regency romance novels, which she tried desperately to hide by only reading them on an iPad. Pamela turned bright red, opened and closed her mouth a few times, and then bestowed on him a glare that promised retribution.

He clapped his hands together. "All right. Let's get cracking. Jorge, bring in the techs and figure out who is our little machine ghost-helper. Mosi, get the Big Bag O'Guns from Damon's office. I'll get Paul and let's arrange to get me captured by the bad guys."

"I hate this plan," He heard Pamela mutter as the door closed behind him.

✧   ✧   ✧

AND JUST LIKE that, they were all gone.

Well, except for the intimidating sister. Fox was just happy he wouldn't have to sit across the table from her at meals and try to make conversation. So, now he found himself wandering aimlessly through the Lumina building, wondering what the hell to do with himself. Franz was awfully nice, he had come down to the makeshift bedroom that Fox had previously shared with Paul, and asked what he might like for dinner.

Fox went back upstairs to the penthouse, and sat on the couch staring at his laptop that rested on the glass coffee table. He hadn't opened it since that mysterious voice had spoken to him, but he really did need to work on his dissertation, and maybe he had been hallucinating and just imagined the voice.

He finally picked up the computer and sat drumming his fingers on the cover. He had just worked up the nerve to open it when the weird homeless guy wandered into the room carrying a plate with a giant piece of raspberry cheesecake.

"Hey."

"Hello," Fox said cautiously.

"Richard wanted me to reassure you that I'm gonna be here to keep an eye on you."

Fox watched a giant bite of cake vanish into the creature's mouth. "That's ... nice."

"However, you should know that if they send the really big guns after you then we're fucked 'cause I can't fight them off. And if I start splintering, then you should run like hell, 'cause it means you got no protection."

"Splintering?" Fox echoed faintly.

"Yeah, my brethren get together and cause a bunch of bad shit to happen to the kind of people who keep me intact. Then I shatter into a bunch of little pieces and it takes time for me to pull myself back together ... literally."

"Good to know."

"Personally, I don't think they should have taken the

sword away. What you're working on seems to have gotten my kind all atwitter. Think there might be more to it than just not wanting you monkeys out in the wider universe."

"And what do you think that might be?" Fox asked cautiously.

Cross shrugged. "Not a clue. Not my department. I'm just the magical muscle."

Fox felt a migraine coming on.

CHAPTER EIGHTEEN

WILL THERE BE KOOL-AID?

SOUTHERN CALIFORNIA HAD just entered that period known as the June Gloom. Damon wasn't sorry. With climate change, the West Coast had become unbearably hot in the summer months. At least he was going to dodge that.

During the ninety minute flight, he had started to book a car and driver, then remembered what had happened in Texas and changed plans to go with just a rental car. He was now on the 101 freeway heading for the long-term care facility in Westlake Village. He wanted to start by talking with the nurses and doctors before heading to the Westlake police substation.

Here, in the middle of the afternoon, the traffic wasn't too god-awful, so he made decent time from the Burbank Airport to his exit. He hopped off the freeway and took a critical look at the passing houses, strip malls, and restaurants. Given the upscale nature of the neighborhoods through which he was driving, he didn't have a lot of confidence that the local cops were very conversant with attempted kidnappings. Home invasion and DUIs seemed more like what would bedevil the cops of Westlake Village.

The care facility was on a secluded side street nestled up against the hills, which were already turning brown and sere as the memory of the winter rains faded. Still, the surrounding pine trees and a few obligatory palm trees made the place seem like it was not part of the LA megalopolis.

Damon parked and made his way past the sweeping lawn where patients in wheelchairs or walking with nurse's aides were out enjoying the cool weather. Damon couldn't suppress the shudder. He knew if these experimental treatments didn't work he would soon be similarly incapacitated. Richard would keep him home, they could afford the round-the-clock care his hospice treatments would require, but he sort of hoped he could avoid that long, slow slide into oblivion. Heart attack or embolism would be preferred. Peg out fast and avoid all the muss and fuss. And spare his sweetie having to watch him suffer and decline.

Pulling on a mask, he entered the lobby and showed his ID to the receptionist, and explained who he was and why he was there. The young Asian man directed him to the third floor nurses' station. He didn't have quite the aversion to hospitals that Richard did, but he still found the smells of disinfectant trying to cover corruption unpleasant. He stepped off the elevator and made his way down the hallway toward the station.

The head nurse, a black woman about Damon's age gave him a narrow-eyed look. Her name tag read Marybell. "May I help you?"

"Hello, I'm Damon Weber. My husband, Richard Oort helps the Davinovitchs with the care for their daughter." He was being diplomatic, actually Richard and Lumina paid for all of the costs of her care. "Todd and Lottie called us, and we just want to be sure there is no threat to any of you or your patients."

The woman relaxed and gave a nod. "Thank you. So, what do you need?"

"What can you tell me about what happened that day?"

"I was in caring for Mr. Hodgekin when Tilly, one of our young nurses, called for me. There was this group of four men saying they had instructions from the Davinovitchs and Mr. Oort to move Rhiana. I knew right away something was off."

"Why is that?"

"First, they only had a wheelchair, you don't move a deep coma patient in a wheelchair, you need a gurney. And there was no way these guys were EMTs. They were hard men."

"What do you mean by that?"

She folded her arms across her chest. "I was an army nurse in Afghanistan, I know what military commandos and mercs look like."

"Ah."

"I told them to stay put and I called for Douglas, our security guard, to keep an eye on them while I phoned the Davinovitchs. I had no sooner turned my back when they were gone, the wheelchair was the only thing left of them."

"I don't suppose you have that wheelchair."

"It was put back in rotation."

"Shame, it's useless to try and lift prints now," Damon mused.

"Ah, so you're a cop."

"Retired now."

"Would you like to see Rhiana?"

He didn't really, but knew it would look odd if he refused, so he followed Marybell down the hall and into the room. The figure in the bed was curled into a fetal crouch, rollers were placed in her hands to keep her fingers from curling into fists. A feeding tube peeked out from beneath the sheet and thin blanket. Her long black hair had been braided, the braid hanging over one shoulder. What had once been at least half a human was now just a husk that could breathe and excrete while the heart kept beating. Damon was very glad he had convinced Richard to let him come rather than coming himself. His spouse would never stop punishing himself for putting the girl—no, woman now, in this state.

"It's sad. She was so young when she came to us," Marybell said, her gaze on the motionless figure. "And her parents rarely come now. They used to come on her birthday, but they haven't even done that the past couple of years. It is understandable, after fifteen years you give up hope."

Damon had mixed feelings about the half-human, half-Old One. Rhiana's jealousy had driven her to place Damon in the hands of a dark Paladin, a serial killer and rapist—in short, a monstrous man. And it was Rhiana who had designed the mix of magic spell and science that had trapped and damaged the founder of Lumina. Still, what he was seeing was pathetic. Probably death would have been kinder, even though he knew Richard could never have brought himself to do that.

With a sad shake of the head, Damon turned and left the room. Glancing back, he watched as Marybell brushed a lock of hair off Rhiana's forehead and gave her arm a gentle pat. When the nurse joined him he asked, "I presume the cops were called."

"Yeah."

"And I take it they were …"

"Clueless. Tried to sell me on the idea these guys had the wrong room and once they realized, they went off to get the right patient. Total tools."

Damon felt a need to at least partially defend his former profession. "Well, I expect they don't get a lot of attempted kidnappings. This seems like a pretty nice area."

"Yeah, apart from the docs, those of us who work here can't afford to live here. I commute in from Culver City every day."

"Well, thank you so much for your help."

Damon left and returned to the parking lot. For several minutes he just sat in the car trying to think what moves to make now. It didn't sound like the cops were going to be much help. Drumming his fingers on the steering wheel, he pondered. Based on what he had seen in that room—the feeding tube, catheter, diaper—they probably weren't going to stick Rhiana in the back of a Chevy and drive off. They probably had an ambulance waiting. So where had they gotten one?

Now that he had a line of inquiry to pursue, Damon put the car in gear and drove to the Four Seasons hotel where his assistant had made a reservation. After checking in, Damon settled down on the couch in his suite and texted Richard to tell him that he had arrived safely, had talked to the staff at the facility, and then he lied that he was going to grab some lunch before talking to the cops. It was silly, but he always felt less guilty when he lied in a text and not in a call, but

Richard didn't need to know Damon wasn't going to eat. Richard's task was far more dangerous than Damon's. His husband didn't need to be distracted by worry about *him*.

With a sigh Damon tossed the phone onto the couch cushion next to him. There was work to be done, but right now he needed to rest. At least for a little while.

✧   ✧   ✧

PAUL WAS DRIVING the big, all-electric Hyundai IONIQ down a winding, tree-lined road toward the headquarters of Magna Mater. It was verdant and beautiful, and it was making Richard nervous as a long-tailed cat in a room full of rocking chairs … as Damon would no doubt say if he could see the way Richard's knee was bouncing with barely suppressed nerves. Apparently, he had been in New Mexico too long, because the press of the forest and the rolling hills blocking his view of the horizon had him feeling claustrophobic. Seventeen years of piñon trees, junipers, and eighty mile vistas had changed him in more ways than just his preferred landscapes, Richard thought somewhat wryly.

Damon had texted to say he was safely in California, had been to the care facility, and would talk to the cops after he had a bite of lunch. Richard was glad to hear his spouse was stopping to eat. It meant Damon felt well enough to attempt food.

Whoever had helped them unearth the information regarding the Bulgarian, it was still solid intel, so they had sent all the files to Interpol. Richard had called upon his domestic allies in the FBI with the information about the drone attack at MIT. Unlike many others in the political and law enforcement establishments, Richard's contacts weren't willing to close their eyes to the reality of the Old Ones and pretend it was some sort of mass hallucination that had swept across the world seventeen years ago—and not invading aliens from alternate multiverses.

Bob Franklin was now an Assistant Director, as was Jay Haskell, and Samantha (Sam) Marten had been promoted to special agent. They had all faced Old Ones, so during the flight to Minnesota, Richard had contacted them about his suspicions regarding Wannamake and Magna Mater, and the agents had quietly set in motion orders that put a team in place just outside the compound.

But Franklin had followed that with the warning that they would move in, *but only after you've neutralized any monsters.* Bob had watched his friend and partner, Syd Marten—Sam's father—be driven mad by what he experienced at Grenier's compound almost two decades ago. Syd and Sam's sanities had been restored by a touch of the sword, but Bob was not going to risk any of his agents to madness and death.

Paul had not been as successful with his superiors at Homeland Security. In fact, he hadn't even tried to convince them of a reality that he himself still didn't fully believe. Instead, he had spun a tale about a planned attack on the nation's water and power grid, only to get pushback that there was nothing to indicate such an attack was in the works.

Richard glanced over at his nephew's profile, torn between the desire that the cocky youngster got a lesson in the truth of Old Ones, and also hoping there wasn't really an Old One squatting inside the compound they were now fast approaching.

Paul flashed his ID card at the gate guard, and the massive gate, adorned with a beautiful enamel sculpture of Earth, swung open. They drove past several truck gardens where members of the compound were toiling, pulling weeds and individually watering each plant, then past what were clearly dormitories. Finally, the main building rose up before them. Built of grey stone the two-story structure looked like a stately home transplanted from Britain to Wisconsin. Towers graced the central area and two wings swept back on either side. Mullioned windows threw back the light of the setting sun, and highlighted the outline of gargoyles clinging to the edge of the roof.

Paul pulled into a parking space among a lot of other EV cars, a few golf carts, and a lot of bicycles. He shut down the car and turned to look at Richard. "So you ready for this?"

"Yes."

"Still having trouble understanding why the FBI is allowing a middle-aged billionaire to take point on this. With my testimony from the spaceport, and the purchase of that drone, we've got them dead to rights," Paul muttered as he pushed open the car door.

"Well, Paul, I really hope you don't find out *why* they sent a middle-aged billionaire," Richard said as he climbed out.

"Right, the magic sword," and Paul's hand went unconsciously to his coat pocket.

"Mmmm. Now, perhaps it's time you shut up about that

and watch your body language," Richard said as he gave Paul an encouraging pat on the back, and they started up the long stairway toward the front doors.

They were impressive: bronze, with engravings of all manner of plants, mostly flowers, and animals of the cuddly variety and a startling lack of reptiles and insects apart from bees. Richard suppressed a snort. Just as Wannamake's followers thought they should be the only humans allowed to survive, they clearly had thoughts about what animals were allowed to join them in their imagined utopia.

Once they were past the reception area with its high vaulted ceiling and the chirpy young receptionist, they passed through a doorway into what was clearly an open design space with discreet areas delineated by low walls adorned with potted plants, hanging silk tapestries, and hanging baskets of ferns. Off to the left came the sounds and smells of a kitchen in operation. In the center of this immense space was a water feature with a waterfall that fell from the ceiling some thirty feet above them, into a pool constructed of what looked to be faceted crystal. What Richard saw were reflective surfaces that would allow easy access for Old Ones.

"The compound is completely self-sufficient and self-sustaining," Paul explained, sounding excited, pompous, and bragging. Richard wished Mosi could have seen it. It might have put to rest her fears that his nephew couldn't dissemble. And he had certainly put on quite the performance down at the spaceport before confessing he was with law enforcement.

Scattered around the space were what could only be

called nests formed by legless sofas resting directly on the distressed white oak floor. Clumps of young people inhabited these nests with men working on laptops or with pad and pen, while women were spinning wool and weaving. The voices coming from the kitchen area were all female, and in a corner near the kitchen, a group of women were shucking corn and shelling peas. A number of the young women were pregnant. It all felt very *Handmaid's Tale*, and Richard became even more glad he hadn't sent Mosi into this dystopian utopia.

Another thing that struck Richard was how *white* almost everyone was. There were only a few people of color among those in the great hall. It seemed far more in character for a Christian Nationalist organization than a group of purported tree huggers. The final thing he clocked was that all of the people engaged in their various tasks were at the most in their early thirties and most were far younger. There was no one his age, much less Damon's. The only exception was the man seated at the far end of the cavernous space.

Hugo Wannamake's seating arrangement put him some four feet higher than the half-circle of young people who sat at his feet, looking more like worshippers than workers or volunteers. He was seated on his cushion in the lotus position, his open palmed hands resting on his bent knees.

"Cultish, much?" Richard subvocalized into his throat mic. "And will there be Kool-Aid at dinner?" That earned a snort of quick laughter from Paul.

Their footsteps seemed loud as they crossed the vast, echoing space. Wannamake uncoiled and stood as Richard and Paul approached. Hugo Wannamake gave a lot of interviews, but they were almost exclusively print with only the obligatory headshot, so the full effect of just how *tall* he was and how *emaciated*, had Richard's steps faltering for a moment. Adding to the impression of a skull atop a skeletal body, was the shaved head and sunken brown eyes.

Stepping lightly through his acolytes, Wannamake approached. Richard glanced quickly at his nephew and saw the same worshipful expression on Paul's face that was on the faces of the people seated around Wannamake. If Richard hadn't known the truth about Paul he would have believed him to be deeply invested in this cult and its leader.

The other man came to stop directly in front of Richard and close—far too close. It forced Richard to tilt his head back to meet the other man's gaze. The man had to be at least six foot seven. This was a dominance game of which Richard was very familiar. At only five feet four inches, he had spent his life looking up at other men. The thing he had finally learned was to stop *actually* looking up to those men.

"Mr. Oort. What a pleasure to finally meet you. I'm amazed it hasn't happened before now, since we're both in the same line of work," Wannamake said.

"Are we?" Richard asked.

"Well, of course. Saving the planet," Wannamake said as they shook hands.

"I'm grateful to Paul for coming to me with the suggestion we join forces, Mr. Wanna—"

"Hugo, please. No formality here." He threw out his arms as if embracing the room and everyone in it.

"Richard, then."

"No diminutive?"

"Some would say I've already got that covered," Richard said dryly.

Wannamake threw back his head and gave a loud laugh. "Good one. Well, I can see you have humor and self-deprecation down pat. That's healthy. So many short men have a Napoleon complex. Glad to see you don't."

Richard had to struggle not to roll his eyes at the pop psychology being thrown at him, but all he did was smile and thrust his hand into the vest of his three piece suit in imitation of the iconic painting of Bonaparte. Wannamake laughed again, and Richard hid his anger and disdain behind another smile.

"I know you've come to discuss business, but please join us for dinner first before we get down to our more mundane conversations."

"Thank you, that would be lovely," Richard said.

Wannamake clapped his hands and every head turned to him. "All right troops, time to stop working and set up for dinner."

There was a concentrated rush with the young men setting up trestle tables and benches, and women setting the tables. Outside, Richard could hear the deep-throated chime of a massive bell. In response, more people began to filter in from the outside. Richard was giving all of them a critical look, searching for any object that might serve as a focusing device for a sorcerer. He also kept a wary eye out for Mark Grenier, but the one time minister did not appear.

Given the traditional gender roles that seemed to be in play in the compound, he was focusing most of his attention on men, and he spotted two that seemed likely prospects.

One young man was carrying a sword stick. Richard recognized it because he'd carried just such a sword disguised as a cane, after he'd been shot in the thigh many years ago.

The other was a young man who wore a large quartz crystal on a chain around his neck. There were a lot of crystals and mandalas and other mystical trinkets on necks, wrists, and fingers among the members of Magna Mater, but the length of the crystal and the way the colors shifted inside the stone had a tingle sliding down Richard's spine.

Wannamake indicated a place next to him, and Richard slid onto the bench. The plate in front of him was hand-fired pottery and very beautiful. He picked it up to inspect it more closely.

"We make and fire our own dishes, the silverware is iron and made by our smiths in our own forge." Wannamake smiled down at him. "We try to tread lightly upon our mother."

"Very admirable," Richard murmured.

Women began carrying trays filled with roasted vegetables and quinoa to the table. There were bowls filled with soups. Everything appeared to be vegetarian and vegan. Given the cuisine, Richard began to understand Grenier's absence. He couldn't imagine that gastronome being happy with such fare.

Wannamake served Richard, another domineering and infantilizing move. Richard wasn't concerned about eating since it was all family style. The food could not have been dosed with either poison or a sedative. He also reflected that Wannamake's arrogance made that unlikely as well. The man really didn't think Richard offered any threat to him. Or maybe he actually believed that Richard was here to form an alliance.

Wannamake looked over at Richard and said, "I hope you don't find the food too unpalatable. We try to live in harmony, doing harm to none, including our animal brethren."

"Not at all, though my husband would be struggling a bit. He's a steak man."

"Meat is a killer, and because I feel like my work is so important for the future of the planet, so I adopted the longevity diet. I only consume twelve hundred calories a day."

Richard suppressed the urge to roll his eyes instead asking, "Do you really think any one of us is so critical to the well-being of humanity?" He was honestly both intrigued and stunned by the sheer hubris of the man.

"Really, Richard, you should be the first to know that is absolutely true. After all, you are a Paladin."

Richard swallowed his surprise and discomfort and said neutrally, "Most people tend to ignore that part of the resume and just focus on the money."

Wannamake made a dismissing gesture. "Pfft, money. Money is easy. That's the least interesting thing about you."

Richard nodded his acknowledgment of the compliment, and they ate in silence for a few minutes. Wannamake shifted a bit to face Richard.

"Next time I do hope you'll bring your husband. We can show him how golden chanterelles can be very buttery and meaty."

"I would be interested to see how that goes," Richard said. He looked away and wondered how Damon was doing, and tried to push away his worry and how much he missed the man.

CHAPTER NINETEEN

INCOMING

"**F**UCK, I DIDN'T know Wisconsin had mosquitoes the size of B52s!" The statement was punctuated with a sharp slap.

Mosi looked over to where Samantha Martin was inspecting the smear of blood left on the palm of her hand from her skeeter slaughter. Her weapon of choice for killing humans as opposed to mosquitoes was a Barrett M82 sniper rifle that was propped against her knee as she sat on a nearby fallen log. Mosi suspected that it was only one of the many weapons the FBI Special Agent was no doubt carrying. Sam was nothing if not prepared.

Sam was in her mid-forties now, her brown hair cut just at chin length, sharp brown eyes filled with a combination of excitement and cynicism. Mosi was secretly amused that the chestnut bob showed not a hint of grey implying that whatever else she might claim, Sam had a touch of vanity.

Sam had been in and out of Mosi's life for most of her adolescence. She had arrived when Mosi turned twelve and informed Richard and Damon that *she* would be instructing Mosi in marksmanship since both of them were clearly not up to the task. Mosi had anticipated pushback, but Richard had merely bowed and given a *be my guest* gesture to the agent. Because Richard knew that Sam was the finest marksman in the FBI, and arrogance was not one of her guardian's flaws.

The other senior agent who waited with them was Jay Haskell. He was in his late fifties, approaching retirement with iron grey hair and brown eyes that were both worried and weary. Mosi was less familiar with him. While he knew the truth about Old Ones, that truth made him skittish as a prairie dog when a bobcat was on the prowl.

Jay had brought a team of agents who were talking quietly among themselves as they stood around the fleet of black SUVs. None of them were inoculated against Old One magic, so they were forced to hang back until any otherworldly threats had been neutralized. What Mosi hadn't told the two agents was that she had separate instructions from Richard and would be advancing before them.

"Are you and Richard up to something? And are you going to share it with the rest of the goddamn class?" Jay huffed. "Cause you guys are tricky as hell, and while I'm always happy ... well, maybe not *happy*, but at least *willing* to deal with goddamn monsters, I really hate playing the straight man to the two of you."

"Since we don't want you having to actually deal with monsters." Mosi rolled an eye toward the young agents grouped around the SUVs. "We're going to make sure the area is a monster-free zone before you and your team moves in. Besides, your weapons aren't all that effective against Old Ones."

"They sure as fuck are against any of the assholes using magic," Sam groused.

"Yes, but if anyone on your team goes crazy, we don't want them freaking out and shooting any of *us*, and that's assuming the magic being thrown around hasn't fucked with the guncotton so they won't work anyway. Just hang tight until we signal you."

"And if you don't signal us because you're both dead?" Jay said.

"Wow, Eeyore much?" Mosi said.

Sam stood, crossed to Mosi, and slipped an arm around her waist. "Look, kiddo, I know you're pretty much monster-proof, but you're not bulletproof."

Mosi tapped her chest covered by her body armor. "I've got my Kevlar with ceramic inserts."

"And that won't help if somebody shoots you in the head. Let me come with you, guard your back."

Mosi hugged the older woman. "That's sweet, Sam, but there's a greater chance of getting caught if there are two of us. Plus, Wangai taught me how to snoop and poop. I'll be fine."

"You better, because the Munchkin will kill us if anything happens to you," Jay grumbled.

Mosi blinked in confusion. "Richard. He's talking about Richard," Sam explained.

Mosi snorted out a laugh. "Munchkin. I'm going to call him that next time he irritates me."

"Better you than me," Jay mumbled.

Mosi blew him a kiss. "But I'll be sure to credit you, Jay."

"Gee thanks."

"Okay, I'm off. See you all on the other side." At Jay and Sam's reaction, she added, "Maybe not the best phrasing."

After shouldering her pack and with a final pat of the holstered pistol, she slipped away into the trees.

The property boundary was down a dirt forest service road a half mile from where the FBI had set up, and Mosi made quick work of it. She paused using the ground sweeping limbs of a spruce tree for cover and surveyed the chain link fence topped with swiveling cameras. It was reasonably high tech, but Lumina didn't just design water purification systems, low-cost vaccines, heat pumps, desalination plants, solar panels, batteries, and a host of other life-affirming technologies—they also designed high tech battlefield weapons. The device she was carrying would cut open the metal links but then form a link between the two halves so the security system would not realize there had been a breach.

The cameras were on a swivel that meant there was only a small window of time to make it through the fence. She rigged the cutter onto a small catapult and shot it across the intervening seventeen feet. It latched on and swiftly cut an opening in the fence. Mosi took a deep breath, waited for the moment and raced across the open ground and dove through the opening. She laid in the fragrant summer grass waiting for the sound of an alarm, but only the soft peeps of a night bird and the wind through the trees disturbed the silence of the evening.

Mosi pushed to her feet and headed toward the large grey stone mansion where it bulked on the top of a ridge.

✧　✧　✧

DINNER CONCLUDED. THE women cleared the dishes while the men broke down the tables and carried away the benches. Paul had been seated midway down the table between two young women, and he had chatted and laughed through the dinner with them and those seated across the table. He seemed completely at ease, and Richard had to admire his sangfroid. But of course, Paul didn't fully understand, realize, or believe what he was actually facing. Richard did and he could feel the tension in his shoulders. He wondered if Wannamake could read it. He had a feeling they were all playing roles in this kabuki dance—Wannamake and Richard both pretending this was all legitimate, that they really were going to discuss joining forces while hiding the shiv they would use to destroy each other.

"Well, shall we retire to my office and get down to business?" Wannamake asked.

"Certainly." Richard glanced around the room and realized he'd lost track of Sword Stick and Crystal Boy. He cleared his throat and added, "I would like Paul to be part of our discussions."

"Really? Why?"

"Well, he is my nephew. The only heir I have."

"What about your ward?"

So you have done your research, Richard thought. "No longer my ward. She's twenty-one." He gave a dismissive shrug. "I expect she'll be returning to her own people now."

Paul was stacking one of the benches. Wannamake called to him. "Paul, your uncle and I are going to discuss business. You want to join us or keep flirting with Jennie and Margo?"

"Well, when you put it like that," Paul called, a laugh

trembling on the words, and Richard held his breath. Paul had displayed an ability for deception, what if his supposed role in DHS had been the real lie? "But since I sort of facilitated this meeting, I'd kinda like to be part of it," Paul said and Richard relaxed.

Wannamake led them down a long corridor and into another wing of the mansion pausing before an impressive carved wooden door. "After you," he said as he pushed it open.

Richard stepped through, fully expecting what happened to happen. He was grabbed by either arm and pushed deeper into the room. The men holding Richard were young, burly, and—based on the grip they had on his upper arms—very strong.

Remaining firmly in character, Paul let out a squawk followed by confusion, as he yelped, "Hey! What the hell?"

Wannamake had his hand resting lightly on Paul's shoulder as he herded the younger man into the elegant office. "I'm afraid your uncle convinced you to bring him here under false pretenses, Paul," Wannamake said mildly as he closed the door.

"Wha ...? I don't understand? What's ..."

Richard had stopped listening as he did a quick survey of the space. As expected there was an enormous mirror in a gilt frame on one wall. Equally expected was that the glass was greyed out and streaked with silver lines. Nothing in the room was reflected in that surface because it was now an opening into another multiverse.

In one corner there was a three-foot-tall geode, the interior filled with amethysts. Richard wasn't sure if it could serve as an entryway for Old Ones, but it was going to get a tap just in case it was. Near the window was a tall jade tree in a decorative pot. Richard was making quick evaluations looking for things that could be potentially used as weapons in addition to the sword, and rather regretted that Wannamake seemed to live his philosophy—there were no decorative swords or severed heads of endangered animals that might be utilized in a fight.

What was completely expected was the presence of Mark Grenier huddled in a chair next to the big teak desk. Richard hadn't seen the man for almost fifteen years, and he was a changed figure. Gone was the immense belly, the triple chins, the round face, and wide thighs. Instead he looked like an empty, crumpled sack: all sagging pendulous skin bereft of its filling fat. The years had not been kind, Grenier looked far older than a man in his mid-seventies.

The expensive prosthetic that Lumina had purchased for him was missing, and instead a faux skin-colored hand was on the end of his stump, but it looked even more unnatural because Grenier's real hand was mottled with age spots and a bright red bruise unlike the smooth tan of the prosthetic. It was Richard who had separated Grenier's hand from his arm and judging by the cold fire in the man's grey eyes that amputation hadn't been forgotten or forgiven. Richard had thought Grenier was glaring at him, but then he realized with some shock that the hatred reflected in those eyes was directed at *Wannamake*.

Sword Stick and Crystal Boy stood to either side of Grenier. Richard glanced over at Wannamake. "I'd watch out for this one, Hugo, if I were you," Richard said with a jerk of his chin toward Grenier. "He doesn't tend to stay bought." And he then added. "I speak from experience."

Wannamake bestowed a smirking smile on both Richard and Grenier. "When I purchase a tool I make sure it stays bought. Our pious murderer here has American law enforcement, Interpol, and the Turks after him. I keep him safe and hidden." He looked back at Richard. "Though poor Mark is having a hard time with our vegan diet here, so I can't imagine he'd do too well in a Turkish prison. Isn't that right, Mark?" Grenier just turned his head aside and didn't answer. "Get the weapon off him," Wannamake ordered his thugs.

Richard allowed himself a smirk and Grenier's lined cheeks went red and he huffed, "Don't bother, he's not carrying it. It will be a dummy. It's what he pulled on me years ago. You should know better than to try the same trick twice, Richard."

Wannamake tugged at his lower lip. "So, it's either with the squaw—"

"You know, Hugo, I'm quite disappointed in you. For someone who is supposedly so tolerant and all about saving the planet, that was stunningly racist," Richard said conversationally.

"Or the nephew is carrying it," Grenier's eyes flicked quickly up to meet Richard's as Richard's captors started checking his pockets.

Paul gave a quick indrawn breath, and Richard lunged toward him even as Wannamake yelled, "Paul's got the sword! Get it!"

Richard's captors released him and piled on Paul, rifling

through his pockets. One of them emerged with the sword hilt, and threw Wannamake and Grenier a triumphant smile just before a kick to the sternum from Paul sent him sprawling and the hilt tumbling away. Everyone dove after the hilt.

It looked like a mad football scrum with everyone from the guards, the two sorcerers, Paul, and Wannamake struggling to grab the hilt. The room was filled with grunts, curses, and the sound of fists on flesh. Richard ignored it all because what Paul didn't know was that Paul had actually been carrying the replica. Richard had switched them when he had given his nephew an encouraging pat on the back just before they entered the mansion.

Richard wasn't waiting to see how well trained Paul might be in hand-to-hand. He spun gracefully on his left foot as he pulled out the hilt from the holster at the small of his back and drew the sword. The bone-shaking musical overtones filled the room. Richard's spin brought him into position to smack the nearest back in the writhing pile of people with the flat of the sword. Unfortunately, it was one of the guards, not one of the sorcerers. The man began to convulse and that sent Wannamake and the two sorcerers frantically scrambling away from the threat of the sword.

Paul surged to his feet, teeth bared and gave a spinning kick to the jaw of the remaining guard. He went down like an inflatable tube man when the fan shuts off.

"Do something!" Wannamake yelled at the two sorcerers even as he trundled backward away from Richard and the glowing, humming blade and took refuge behind his desk.

One of the sorcerers began chanting in Enochian and a

sickly red glow formed around the edges of the mirror. Richard ran for the mirror hoping to close it before anything emerged, but was grabbed by the back of his collar and jerked back. The pressure of his collar and tie had him gagging and choking. For once in his life, the height difference worked to his advantage. Without releasing the hilt Richard reversed it and slammed the sword against Wannamake's lower leg. The pressure was gone as the man fell backward across his desk, his wild convulsions sending papers, an expensive pen set, and a collection of elaborate paperweights skittering off the side.

Richard lunged toward the mirror, but then heard a cry of pain and terror from Paul. Because he was inoculated, a basic magic spell could have no effect on the younger man, but other items could be turned into weapons by the magic being wielded by the sorcerers. When he turned, Richard saw how the long drapes had torn loose from the windows and were smothering and choking Paul, tightening inexorably around his body and face.

Richard risked a glance to search for Grenier. The man was on his knees near the desk. Crystal Boy's necklace was pulsing and seemed to be breathing. Sword Stick had drawn the blade and was using it to tighten the velvet noose around Paul.

It was a risk, but to save Paul, Richard had no choice but to abandon the mirror and rush to Paul's side. He cut through the heavy velvet with one long sweep of the sword then placing himself between Paul and the two young magic wielders Richard growled, "Bring it!"

There was a crash of shattering glass and Mosi leaped

through the window and into the office. The two sorcerers had barely started to turn when Richard tossed the sword toward Mosi. The moment it left his hand the blade vanished, but this was a move he and his ward had practiced many times over the years. Mosi's arm shot up, she snatched the hilt out of the air and drew the sword. Sword Stick tried to awkwardly parry the black and silver blade. It cut through the wood and steel as if they had been air, and the tip flicked across his shoulder. He went down screaming, his back arching almost into a bow as he convulsed.

Richard leaned down, clasped Paul's hand and hauled him to his feet. Mosi was circling the desk heading for the man whose crystal was flaring like a Fourth of July firework, but before she could engage him, Grenier grabbed the edge of the desk and pulled himself to his feet. He was holding a heavy glass paperweight, and he swung it onto the back of the man's head. It hit with a sickening *crack* and Richard winced. Despite what people might see on television or in the movies, a blow that rendered a person unconscious usually resulted in death or permanent disability. The look on Grenier's face was one of pure rage, and Richard wondered what had happened to cause the man to turn on his compatriots, but there was no time to ponder the question, because Mosi called out, "Incoming Old One ... make that plural. *Old Ones.*"

✧   ✧   ✧

THE MIRROR CREATURES were not like anything Mosi had seen before. They seemed to be formed of slivers of light, each like a blade, they were spinning creating a horrible keening sound, and indeed when they touched items in the room they cut through them as if they had been sea foam and prayers. An office chair fell victim, its two halves falling to either side with echoing thuds onto the polished oak floor.

Grenier had crawled into the kneespace of the massive teakwood desk. Mosi wasn't sure how long it was going to offer any protection, as the creatures kept spinning and cutting furniture, carpet, lamps, bookcases, and books into thin julienne strips.

"Jesus Christ! Jesus fucking Christ!" Paul was babbling.

"Yeah, happy now? There's your fucking proof," Mosi gritted out as she evaluated how in the hell to attack these things without being flayed alive.

"Get the people clear!" Richard shouted to Paul over the high-pitched keening that seemed to be drilling straight into Mosi's brain.

"I can't just leave you!" Paul yelled back.

"There is nothing you can do! Get out!" Richard ordered.

Mosi dodged one of the coruscating blades, tried to sweep back with the blade of the sword, but missed. "You'll just make it harder if we have to protect you too," she screamed out as she tucked into a roll.

His terror was etched on his face, but Paul pulled himself together, gave a tense nod, and grabbed one of the unconscious sorcerers under the arms and dragged them to the office door.

"Hit the crystal," Richard yelled at Mosi as he flung himself sideways and behind a large leather couch. "They're trying to use it as another entryway."

Apparently the Old One understood English because both it and Mosi lunged for the crystal. Already colors were starting to extrude and ooze out of the facets on the stone. Mosi got there first, and swung the sword like she was making a long drive on a golf course. The tip of the blade caught the crystal and threw it into the air where it detonated like a small bomb. There was a shriek of agony from the Old One who had been attempting to enter the world, and shrieks of rage from the other two.

The couch was being cut into small leather pieces, stuffing flying everywhere. It seemed one of these creatures had a real hard-on for Richard. "The mirror! We have to destroy it before more come through. At least it's only *one* mirror," she heard Richard call, but she couldn't see any way to reach it, the creatures were *fast*.

From the hallway Mosi heard Paul bellowing, "Stay back! This is law enforcement business. Do not go in there!"

But apparently Wannamake's disciples were having none of it. Eleven people came tumbling into the room as they shoved Paul backward. Paul tripped over the unconscious body of what Mosi presumed was another sorcerer and went down. Lucky for him because the flailing light blades missed him, and slashed across the chest of one young woman. She shrieked in pain, blood from her almost amputated breast sheeting down her torso to pool at the waistband of her skirt.

It was absolute bedlam in the room with four unconscious bodies, eleven of Wannamake's followers, Paul, Mosi, Grenier, Richard, and the two Old Ones. Fortunately, the Magna Mater followers had (rightly) decided that the weird, spinning creatures were the real threat and not Mosi,

Richard, and Paul. She looked around while frantically dodging, but then thought she saw a way to utilize the chaos.

"Paul! Hot potato!" She screamed out, and then hoped like hell he'd played that game sometime during his childhood, and that the Old Ones hadn't and wouldn't have a clue what that meant. She jerked her head toward Richard. Paul gave a terse nod and rolled up onto his knees.

She flung the sword to him. The Old Ones pivoted racing toward him, and Paul tossed the hilt to Richard who tossed it back to her. The creatures were trying to bank and turn as she drew the blade and managed to catch one of the spinning blades on the edge of her blade. The creature died with an inhuman shriek that had the normal humans covering their ears and falling to the floor. Paul managed to stay on his feet, but just, and the sound was so piercing Mosi was sure she her ears were bleeding. All sound was muffled as if it were being filtered through a thousand feet of water.

One monster was down, but unfortunately another had emerged from the mirror, and they could barely hear each other over the racket from the Old Ones. Paul was shoving Wannamake followers toward the door while screaming, "Get Out or Get the Fuck Out! Are you fucking stupid? Jesus Christ, you *are* stupid."

The greyed out surface of the mirror was rippling like water, and Mosi was starting to feel a flutter of panic. If that opening kept belching out Old Ones, the good guys were really going to be in trouble. Then she spotted Grenier crawling on hands and knees toward the mirror. She realized why he was moving so awkwardly, because he was clutching a heavy glass paperweight, one side of it occluded with blood and a scrap of hair. The old man grabbed the edge of the frame, pulled himself to his feet and smashed the paper-weight over and over against the glass. The glass fell like a crystal waterfall and the paperweight cracked into multiple pieces from the stress of being in a place where two universes were colliding.

Mosi made a quick evaluation. Mercifully, most of the disciples were finally being sensible and fleeing the room, but one of the Old Ones caught a young man across the upper arm. The severed limb dropped onto the floor dribbling blood across the wood flooring. Gouts of blood were jetting from the veins and arteries. Mosi knew the boy had minutes before he bled out, but she couldn't reach him. Then Paul yanked off his tie, grabbed up the wooden cane that had held the sword, broke it across his knee and tied a tourniquet on what remained of the man's arm. Blood streaked his polo shirt and sports jacket turning them both into a macabre Jackson Pollock canvas. The young man's mouth was stretched in a scream that couldn't be heard through her muffled ears and the sharp keening of the Old Ones. Paul grabbed another follower and shoved the wounded boy into his arms and pushed them both out of the room.

The couch had been reduced to flinders. Mosi saw Rich-ard sprint across the room to take cover behind the giant geode with an Old One in close pursuit. But while wood, fabric, paper, flesh, and bone had given way to the blades the stone was harder to rend. Splinters and sparks were flying off it, but for the moment it was effectively protecting Richard. However, the second Old One was rising toward the ceiling, clearly planning to drop down on Richard from above.

"These fuckers can *fly*?" Paul yelled. "Fuck!"

He began grabbing up paperweights and flinging them into spinning vortex of the Old Ones. Mosi had to admire his form, it was major league pitcher quality, but apart from distracting the Old Ones it wasn't having any real effect. Her eyes flicked about desperately and fell on the built-in bookshelves.

The Old Ones had torn the books apart and some of the uprights, but many of the shelves were still in place. Mosi kicked into a run, and mentally ran through the parkour training she had received, as she jumped from a piece of the damaged desk onto a shelf, onto another, until she could launch herself through the air, slightly above the second Old One, and slash through the wheel of coruscating colors. The dying scream again tore the air.

One foot landed on the top of the geode, she dropped the hilt into Richard's waiting hands, as she used the geode to throw herself in a forward flip and away from the final Old One. One of the blades cut across her back. She felt her shirt and skin part, and while it burned like blazes, her speed and momentum had kept it from cutting too deep.

Unfortunately, using the stone as a launch pad disturbed its balance on its wooden stand and it toppled backward onto Richard just as he was drawing the sword. Upside down and flipping through the air, Mosi watched in horror as the toppling stone clipped his side and knocked him to the floor, the hilt spilling from his hand.

CHAPTER TWENTY

To Choose Humanity

RICHARD STRETCHED OUT his arm scrabbling frantically to recover the hilt, but the falling geode had trapped his foot, the weight crushing fragile bones and sending agony spiking up his left leg. The situation was so desperate and the pain so great he uttered an unusual expletive, "FUCK!" which he could barely hear over the dying scream of the Old One.

Paperweights were thudding down around him and Richard realized that Paul was flinging the glass objects at the Old One. It wasn't hurting the creature, but it was disrupting its spin. He just hoped none of them would clock him in the head as he yanked frantically, trying to free his trapped leg.

He felt the skin on his ankle abrading, and he wasn't getting appreciably closer to the hilt, and he knew he was going to die if he didn't succeed. Then Grenier was there, kicking the hilt to Richard as he stepped over him. Grunting with effort, he grasped the edges of the geode managing to lift it a few inches allowing Richard to slide free. The hilt slipped briefly on his sweat bathed palm, but Richard managed to draw the sword.

The Old One was tearing into Grenier's chest. Richard rolled into a backward somersault, his foot screaming in agony and the blade of the sword slid between the whirling blades. For an instant it felt like Richard had thrust into a spinning propeller and then the creature was gone.

Richard dropped the hilt and crawled toward Grenier struggling out of his suit coat. He pressed it against the bleeding wounds on the old man's chest. "Why?" he demanded.

"Done ... you ... enough ... damage," Grenier gasped through lips that were rapidly going white from blood loss. His eyes slid toward Mosi. "All ... grown up. Beautiful," he mumbled.

Mosi was on the radio to Jay and Sam, "All clear. Move in."

Richard could hear Paul calling 911 reporting multiple injured. "Hang on," he said to Grenier. "Help is coming."

Grenier gave a minute headshake, his hand came up and clutched at Richard's shoulder. "Do you ... think ... Hell is ... waiting? For ... me?"

For an instant *yes* hung trembling on Richard's lips. He thought of all the death and suffering caused by this shrunken old man going all the way back to four innocent—if gullible—college kids, whose deaths had been Richard's entrée into this shadow war. How Grenier would have put nine-year-old Mosi in the hands of men and monsters who would have warped and used her to commit even more atrocities.

But Richard knew better now. There was no Heaven, no Hell. Only the measure of time that could be lived on Earth, in either joy and love, or anger, hate, and despair, and the choice was humanity's to make. He shook his head and smiled down at the dying man.

"No, of course not. The stars are waiting. Because we're made of star stuff."

Grenier's hand moved from Richard's shoulder to cup his cheek. "Mercy ... is not ... strained. It droppeth ... as ... the ... gentle rain ... from ... heaven ... Upon the place beneath." His voice broke on a gasp of pain.

Richard laid his hand over Grenier's and picked up the recitation. "It is twice blest; it blesseth him that gives and him that takes." The pressure against his cheek was gone. Only Richard's hand was keeping Grenier's in place. He gently lowered the old man's hand and laid it on the now unmoving chest.

"It is an attribute to God himself," he concluded quietly.

From behind him, Richard heard Paul ask, "What was that?" And for once his voice didn't hold that smug, arrogant timbre.

Mosi answered for him and Richard was grateful because he didn't think he could manage through a throat gone tight and aching. "Shakespeare, *The Merchant of Venice*, act four, scene one. Portia's speech. But you left out a lot, *Na sha dii*."

"Yes, but he was running out of time," Richard said as he drew his fingers across Grenier's staring eyes, gently closing the lids.

Paul shook his head. "Fuck. You people are so weird," he muttered and walked away.

"He did you such harm, *Na sha dii* and yet ..." She gestured helplessly.

"And in the end, he saved my life." He gathered up the hilt, and held out a hand to Mosi. She helped him get to his feet where he stood on one foot. Glancing down he noted that the knees of his trousers were sticky with Grenier's blood. "Perhaps Wannamake will be able to tell us how he got ahold of Grenier," he murmured.

"We won't be able to attend that interrogation," Mosi warned.

"But Paul will, and you know Jay will slip us the recording of the interview," Richard replied.

"So, you think Grenier was training the sorcerers?" Mosi asked.

"It's a working hypothesis." He looked around the trashed room, the blood staining the floors. "Jay's going to love writing up this report."

"And Sam is going to be so pissed that she didn't get to shoot anybody," Mosi added with a laugh that sounded forced. Richard could hear the tremor on her words as reaction set in. He was feeling it himself in a trembling throughout his body, the pain in his broken foot.

He forced himself into a limping walk. He drew the sword and began to methodically tap the point on the broken pieces of glass from the mirror. Grenier's breaking of the mirror had slowed the Old Ones down, but only the sword could fully close the opening. Mosi and Paul saw what he was doing and began moving shattered pieces of glass from beneath the sliced up furniture. Paul stood holding a piece of the greyed out glass, bouncing it on his palm.

"They can squeeze through something this small?" he asked.

"Depends on the Old One's form," Mosi answered. "And how it manifests in this universe, but yes, one of them was emerging from that crystal the guy was wearing."

"And sometimes they can reform into something that appears human … almost," Richard added.

"Cross does … look human, I mean," Paul said.

"Yes, because he has spent centuries living among us, and he chose the side of humanity over his own kind."

"What a shame more humans don't do that," Paul muttered.

✧   ✧   ✧

DAMON HAD SLEPT away the afternoon, which meant his visit to the Westlake Village cops was going to have to wait until tomorrow. Hunger nudged at his stomach, a welcome change from not wanting any food at all. He could eat at the hotel, but he was feeling restless, so Damon began checking his phone for restaurant recommendations. That was when he realized that in the midst of this megalopolis and the surrounding suburbia, he was a mere nine miles from the beach and potentially some really good seafood. Living in New Mexico meant everything was frozen and while Franz did a great job with what he had, the lure of a lunch overlooking the ocean was deeply appealing.

Damon walked through the lobby of the Four Seasons, out the front door and handed his ticket to the valet. While he waited for his car to be delivered, he googled seafood restaurants with an ocean view and selected the Paradise Cove Beach Cafe. The rental arrived, he input the address, and set off down one of California's twisting canyon roads. The rocky hills to either side were already a bit arid, as the

January rains were now a distant memory. The good news was that unlike much of the LA basin, traffic was light, and he relaxed a bit from obsessively checking that he wasn't being followed. He soon reached the Pacific Coast highway, the sun a bloated red orb sinking into the blue of the Pacific, and in due course he turned down the narrow dirt road toward the ocean and the cafe.

As the car jounced over the ruts, Damon rolled down the window so he could hear the crash of the waves, the harsh cries of the gulls, and smell the brine and seaweed-laden air. He slid his Chevy in among a bevy of far more expensive cars and made his way into the restaurant.

The pretty young hostess asked if he wanted to sit inside or at a table on the sand. He immediately voted for the sand and was soon seated under an umbrella with an icy mug of beer in hand. The play of the waves, the boom and whispered hiss as the foam retreated back toward the water, was soothing as hell and he glanced at the empty chair next to him and wished Richard was here with him. That they didn't have an international company to manage and monsters to fight so they could just have a vacation. Hold hands and walk on the beach, retreat to a rented beach house, make languid love, and hold each other close while the Moon silvered the ocean and poured through the windows.

He gave a headshake firmly telling himself to stop being maudlin and attempting to be poetic. Because of course what he really wished was that he was in Wisconsin with Richard and Mosi even though he was the least useful person for the situation they were facing. Especially now. Still, his nausea was at a manageable level, so he ordered the ice seafood sampler. It came with a side of sourdough bread and he spent a delightful hour nibbling on different types of seafood and sipping his beer.

He knew he should probably go talk to the Westlake cops even though he doubted it would be all that useful. There weren't a lot of leads to follow. The real question was whether these parties unknown would try again and if so, should Rhiana be moved to a different location or even into Lumina. They already had one silent patient. But to have the girl ... woman ... there would be like sandpaper on Richard's already frayed conscience, so Damon rejected the idea. He would not put his husband through that.

Damon finished off with a cup of sorbet, paid, and headed back to his car. He slid into the driver's seat and had a sudden prickling intuition, but before he could fully turn his head he felt the sharp bite of a needle in his neck.

Well, shit, he thought. *Now I'm getting kidnapped.* Darkness took him.

✧　✧　✧

RICHARD HAD TEXTED Damon shortly after the tear in reality had been closed, the Old Ones and sorcerers had been dealt with, the cavalry had arrived, and his broken foot put in a boot, but had gotten no response. It was now nearly three in the morning and exhaustion was dragging at every limb and his eyes felt like they had been doused with sand.

Richard was slumped on one of benches in the dining hall when Jay came plodding in and collapsed next to him. "Goddamn, nothing more comfortable than these benches?"

he groaned.

"I'm afraid the Old Ones sort of did a number on the sofa in the office," Richard replied.

"Fucking Old Ones."

"I can't argue with the sentiment."

"And fuck every crazy-ass billionaire who think they have a God-given right to save the world or destroy the world or go to fucking Mars. Who wants to go to fucking Mars? Nobody."

"Out of errant curiosity, which category do I fall into?" Richard asked.

Jay bumped Richard with his shoulder. "I guess the crazy, space type. I mean, you are building a spaceship, right?"

"Well Emirhan was. I was just an investor and he was using Lumina's space station."

"Space station, spaceship, *comme ci, comme ça*," Jay said tilting his hand back and forth.

Richard couldn't resist, he responded in a barrage of French.

"Hey, whoa, whoa, whoa, no hablo Frencho."

Richard patted the other man on the cheek. "Don't ever change, Haskell."

"Fuck you, Oort, I say that with all affection."

"I accept it in the spirit it was given."

Jay heaved a sigh, slapped his hands on his thighs and pushed to his feet. "Well, I better go rescue our contrite baby wizards from the bad cop and the worst cop."

"I can guess who's playing the worst," Richard said.

"I'm sure you can. God, I hate playing the daddy cop."

Jay left and Richard checked his phone again. It was Ugh

O'clock in the morning in California, but he was sure he would have heard from Damon by now. He tried to push away the worry. A welcome diversion appeared in the form of Sam. She joined him on the bench.

"So how was this Dr. Evil wannabe planning on starting a war or releasing a plague or destroying the world?" she asked as she sat down and toed off her boots.

"Not sure. I was hoping you would find out from the baby sorcerers. Based on what happened at the spaceport, my guess is a weather spell, but it's just that, a guess. And even if the young sorcerers confess it will just sound crazy and everyone will ignore it," he said somewhat bitterly.

"Well, we've got 'em on buying that drone and the mass shooting at MIT, and I think we'll be able to nail them on blowing up the spaceship too," she said as she stretched out her legs and wiggled her toes. "Gotta say, I never expected your nephew to be a chip off the old block."

"Neither did I." Richard glanced at his phone again.

Sam pressed her fists into the small of her back and leaned back with a groan. Then pulled on her boots, stood, and gave him a pat on the shoulder. "Well, back to interrogation hell. I hate interrogations."

"Pouting because you didn't get to shoot anyone, Sam?"

She formed her hands into pistols and pretended to shoot him. "You got it on one. Next time show a girl a better time, Oort." Richard laughed and with an errant wave she started to leave the dining hall.

Then turned back. "Oh, how's Damon?" she asked her usual forceful tone softening. Richard just shook his head. She returned, circling behind him to rest her chin on top of his head and gave him a hug. "Damn, I'm sorry. He's one of the good ones."

Richard patted her hand where it rested against his chest. "Yes, yes he is. But we're not giving up yet."

Pulling back she kept a grip on his shoulder and looked down at him, her expression kind but serious. "I know *you're* not giving up, but isn't that kinda Damon's decision to make?"

He stared up at her feeling like a vise of ice was closing around his heart. "I can't lose him, Sam, I just can't. I don't think I could go on without him."

"Yeah, you can. The world needs both its Paladins.

She kissed him softly on the cheek and left the room. Richard drew the hilt from its holster and sat turning it over and over in his hands, studying its intricate whirls and loops. Was this all he was ever destined to be? The only way he could be seen? A Paladin. But not with Damon. In his husband's arms he could just be Richard, a middle-aged man with aches and pains and doubts and fears and needs.

He holstered the hilt and checked his phone again. There was nothing from Damon. The ice returned.

CHAPTER TWENTY-ONE

DESPERATE TIMES & DESPERATE MEASURES

THE LAKE WAS sending up tendrils of fog as the rising sun started to burn away the night's chill. Mosi found Paul sitting in the gazebo designed to look like a Grecian temple overlooking the lake. He was hunched over, hands clasped between his knees as he stared at the stone floor rather than the vista. His hand came up and he swatted a mosquito leaving a smear of blood on his cheek from the squashed insect. She did notice another smear of blood beneath his jaw from the wounds he'd treated that he'd missed washing away and his cuticles were also stained with blood.

"Budge over," she said as she walked up.

Haunted eyes were raised to hers. "Oh hey."

She settled down next to him. "You did good last night. You didn't lose your shit and you saved that kid's life with that tourniquet."

He shrugged off the compliment. "You and my uncle scared me to death when he yeeted the sword to you. What if you had missed?"

"Richard and I practice *pass the hilt* multiple times a day and in multiple positions and situations. We've even practiced it sky diving," she said with a laugh.

"What the fuck?"

"When the gates opened all those years ago, there were things in the sky."

"Yeah, you mentioned that before. Scary." Paul's voice trailed away. He was staring at the stone flags again. Somewhere in the reeds on the edges of the lake a loon gave its distinctive wail.

Mosi laid a gentle hand on his shoulder. "What is it?"

She watched his throat work for a few moments, then he said quietly, "I didn't want it to be true."

She gave his shoulder a squeeze. "I know. Nobody does."

He half-turned so he could face her. "I'm a grown man and I was scared shitless. You were just a kid when you got pulled into all this crazy. How the hell did you adapt so easily?"

"Because I *was* a kid. I was nine and raised in a culture where we have ghosts and witches and skin walkers and corpse dust. And I grew up on Marvel and Star Wars, so, it wasn't a stretch for me. Also, I saw the faces in the computer and heard them whispering to Abel."

"That was your brother?"

"Uh huh." Mosi swallowed hard, conflicting images flashing through her head.

Abel showing her how to fly a kite, or pulling her up in front of him on the paint pony that their uncle had owned and galloping across the desert. Then the twisted, hate-filled, and blood-streaked face as he had come at her with the knife they used to butcher sheep. The knife he had used to slit the throats of their father, mother, and grandfather. Paul's voice pulled her back.

"Richard didn't trust me. He switched the sword and

didn't tell me."

"It wasn't a lack of trust. He wanted you to have an authentic reaction." She gave him a sideways glance. "And to be fair, we don't know you all that well yet." She gave his shoulder a squeeze. "But you're one of us now … if you want to be."

"I'm going to have to talk to my bosses about that," Paul said.

"And process all this too."

"Yeah, that. And it's not just work. Our family is broken apart. Mom, Dad, and Granddad on one side; Uncle Richard, Aunt Pamela, and I guess, you on the other."

"And you in the uncomfortable middle."

"Yeah." He gave a hollow laugh. "Am I keeping you from … well, whatever official briefing is happening?"

"No, Richard is way better at that cop speak stuff than me. I'm a computer scientist."

"And Paladin."

"Yeah, that too. Speaking of briefings, did you talk to your bosses?"

He shook his head. "Not yet. They've been calling me as word of this leaks out, but …" His voice trailed away.

"You don't know what to say."

"Pretty much, there's a split in the government too. People who accept all"—he gestured vaguely—"this and everybody else." He heaved a sigh. "And I was among them."

"People want the world to make sense," Mosi said.

"Then why do a lot of people believe a whole lot of crazy shit? Trying to wish away pandemics or come up with crazy conspiracies about JFK Jr. or Jewish space lasers?"

"Conspiracies are attractive because they tell people there is a plan, someone is in charge, and they are special because they're in on the secret."

"Huh, that's the best explanation I've ever heard. Not that it makes me feel a lot better."

Mosi clapped a hand on his knee. "Come on, let's go see how the fallout is ... well, falling."

✧ ✧ ✧

THE SMELL OF coffee was his first waking impression and it smelled like good coffee too. The soft hum of air conditioning registered next. Damon shifted realizing he was lying on a memory foam mattress on the firm side. Personally, Damon like to sink into a mattress and be cuddled but Richard preferred firm and any cuddles were to be performed by Damon. He cracked open an eye and the room slowly began to come into focus.

It was a well-appointed suite, but in that stark, white, modern and stainless steel aesthetic that Damon found as welcoming as a dentist's office. He idly wondered if the same interior designer who'd created Starport America had also done this room. There was a small kitchen area, and it was a high tech coffee machine that had begun to burp out a cup of coffee, apparently because it sensed Damon awakening or because some human was watching and sent the command. Damon wasn't sure which one was creepier.

He swung off the bed and made a quick self-examination. His tie and belt had been loosened, his suit coat was folded across one of the white and steel chairs and his shoes were placed neatly beneath it. Rolling a stiff shoulder to loosen it he padded over to the counter and picked up the cup.

"Thanks," he said to the coffee maker and gave it a pat on its top.

He wanted to check the time, but realized that in addition to his phone, his watch had also been taken. Whoever had Mickey-Finned him and locked him up here was smart enough to know that any device could potentially be used to get a signal back to Lumina and Richard. He glanced over at the espresso machine and wished it could send out an SOS.

Moving to the wide windows he pulled back the drapes and discovered the building was perched on a cliff overlooking what he presumed was the Pacific Ocean. He didn't think he'd been out long enough to be transported to the East Coast, but without his watch or his phone there was no way to tell if he'd lost hours or days.

There were three doors in the room. Damon went to the one that looked most like an exit and as expected he found it to be locked. He tried another and found a large walk-in closet. His luggage was there with the suits and shirts unpacked, pressed and hung, underwear and socks were in the built in dresser. He returned to the bedroom suite, and his bladder spasmed with a sudden and urgent need to urinate. He really hoped that door number three was the bathroom.

It was. Damon relieved himself, and while washing his hands he eyed the shower. He was definitely clammy after sleeping in his clothes, but if his mysterious kidnappers decided to pay him a visit he didn't want to face them while wet and naked. The shower could wait. The good news, his medications were lined up neatly on the counter next to the elaborate stone sink.

He went back into the main room and sat down on the (as expected) very uncomfortable couch, picked up his cup of coffee and said, "So, I'm awake now. When can I expect room service? Feels like I might have missed a meal or two." Silence. Damon huffed a sigh. "As kidnappings go this one is a little baffling. Doesn't look like you're after dough. That coffee maker costs six grand, and that john with the heater and built-in bidet puts you back a cool seven thousand. So, what the fuck is this about? And are you the people ... or person who hired those numbnuts in Texas? If so, you got fleeced. You should have hired a better class of criminal. Those guys were not exactly masterminds."

Damon drank more of his coffee, glanced around, and gave a shrug. "Sure hope somebody is listening because otherwise I feel like a damn fool."

A few moments later the door opened and a woman entered. Damon had never met her, but he had certainly seen pictures of Jessica Barrington in *Forbes*, *The Wall Street Journal*, and *The Economist*, and he presumed some scientific magazines as well, since she was a biotech expert. Damon knew she was forty-seven, but Botox and micro-needling were keeping the wrinkles at bay. Long hair, expertly frosted, brushed the shoulders of her businesswoman-chic red jacket with wide cuffs. A silver torque necklace rested against her tanned chest, a black pencil skirt, and high heels completed the ensemble. Damon spotted the flash of red on the soles. *Christian Louboutin.* Mosi wore them. The thought of the girl and Richard had his chest going tight. *What the fuck is this?* he thought. *Why would a billionaire stoop to kidnapping the husband of another billionaire?*

She raised a perfectly threaded brow. "Coffee maker, really? Do you often play the *I'm just a simple country cop* charade? You're married to a billionaire, I'm pretty confident you can recognize an espresso machine, Mr. Weber. Or do you prefer Weber-Oort or perhaps Oort-Weber?"

"Damon's fine, since you seem to know more than a bit about me, and you know, you could have just called and made an appointment, Ms. Barrington. I would have been happy to drop by."

She gave him a smile. "Ah, so you know who I am, and in the interest of comity, Jessica is fine."

"Well the billionaires' club is a rather select one, so you shouldn't be too surprised that I know who you are."

"True enough. I am rather surprised we haven't met before since both our companies operate in the same sphere—"

"Really, 'cause at Lumina we sort of try to avoid kidnapping people."

She continued as if he hadn't interrupted. "Trying to prevent the destruction of the human race due to the stupidity of most humans, and the threat level sometimes requires desperate measures. This is just such a time."

"I'm guessing those measures aren't something we're likely to agree on." Damon paused for another deliberate, slow sip of his coffee, then added, "And for some reason those desperate measures required two Paladins and a coma victim? Well, at least we spiked the kidnap the Paladins part of your plan."

"Actually, no, you've given me everything I need. Amazing what technology can do with an audio file." She held up a small device. "Our AI has been studying and manipulating your voice. We would have done it using just interviews, but fortunately you decided to be quite chatty with the espresso machine." Damon's mouth went dry.

Barrington nodded and clicked on the device. Damon heard himself saying, "*This is Damon Weber. After consultation with Mr. Oort we've decided to move Rhiana Davinovitch to a more secure facility. Our team will arrive this afternoon*".

"And we've constructed another message that has been sent to your husband asking him and your ward to join you."

Damon stared at her in horror. "What the hell are you playing at?"

"Saving humanity."

"By kidnapping a coma victim?"

"I don't need her brain, just her DNA." She shook back her sleeve and checked her diamond-encrusted watch, a diamond tennis bracelet also looped over the watch face. "Now all we have to do is wait for your husband to show up, and ... I'm not exactly sure what to call Mosi. Daughter? Ward?"

Dread filled his stomach. "Yeah, that ain't gonna happen, Richard and Mosi are a little busy right now."

"We'll see." She turned and swept out of the room.

Damon dropped his head into his hands and hoped that Richard and Mosi were having better luck stopping a guy whose plan was to *destroy* humanity than he was with the woman who *claimed* to want to save it.

✧ ✧ ✧

HOMELAND SECURITY SHOWED up and the dick measuring between the two agencies began (Samantha's was definitely the biggest) over issues of jurisdiction and authority. It all made Richard's headache that much worse, so he sat in glum silence, constantly glancing down at the phone in his lap hoping for some word from Damon. Anxiety was threatening to give way to full blown panic at his husband's continued silence.

Paul's presence took some of the curse off Richard and Mosi's involvement since neither of them were technically in law enforcement. Richard's courtesy badge from the Albuquerque Police Department wasn't cutting a lot of ice with the Feds despite his close relationship with the FBI agents who were on site.

Finally, the territorial disputes were tabled and investigating began. The good news was that the information off the Albanian's computer was verified by information on Wannamake's computer regarding the purchase of the weaponized drone. That was the easy part.

Cops, whether federal or local, like simple stories. The situation at Wannamake's compound was anything but. They had a dead man who was a wanted criminal on three continents. A millionaire ranting about how he had been assaulted with a sword. A boy with an amputated arm and a girl with a deep cut across her chest that might result in her needing reconstructive surgery if the breast couldn't be reattached.

And of course the witnesses stories about spinning creatures made of glass that had emerged from a mirror had a lot of the Homeland Security agents rolling their eyes and trying to pretend the perps and victims were all just in shock and maybe that sword thing had caused them to lose the arm and the breast. To their credit the young people stuck to their stories and refused to blame either Richard or Mosi for their injuries and of course Paul could verify everything that was said. Still the skepticism remained.

Finally, Paul had lost all patience with his compatriots and yelled at them, "I saw the fucking things! I fought the fucking things! If my uncle and Ms. Tosi hadn't been here there would have been a lot more dead people, so get your heads out of your asses and *listen* to what we're saying."

Richard's phone vibrated with an incoming voicemail. Relieved, he pulled it out of his pocket. As expected the message was from Damon. Murmuring his apology, Richard stepped out of the room and listened.

"Hey there, I hope you're getting this, baby. Things are weird and I need you and Mosi to join me as soon as you can." He gave an address which when Richard entered into Google Maps proved to be a home belonging to Jessica Barrington. Richard stood frowning down at his phone. He had a musician's sensitive ear and there was something just the slightest bit *off* about the delivery. Minute separations between a couple of the words and the use of *baby*. Damon never used that particular endearment because he knew Richard didn't like it. He used babe or honey or dear or sweetheart.

Richard slipped back into the room the feds had commandeered and crooked a finger at Mosi. She was out of her chair in an instant and followed him out the door.

"What's wrong, *Na sha dii*?"

A few seconds later Paul joined them. "What's up?"

Richard debated about sending Paul away, but the fact he had actual law enforcement authority made him reconsider. "I got a message from Damon, but I don't think it was Damon. Something's wrong. We need to go to California."

"Great. Can we leave now? Because I'm really sick of these assholes," Paul said and jerked his thumb over his shoulder.

Despite his gut-clenching worry, Richard couldn't help but laugh. Mosi joined in, laying a hand on Paul's arm. "Looks like you're part of the Scooby Gang now."

"Oh fuck, can I reconsider?

"Not a chance," she said tucking his arm through hers.

AFTER BARRINGTON LEFT, Damon decided to take a nap. If he was going to get out of here before Richard was drawn into the trap he needed not only his wits, but some physical strength. Damon changed into his pajamas and thanks to Better Living Through Chemistry, he did manage to nap. He awoke to a growling stomach, and as if the rumbles had summoned him, the door to the room opened and a man who was dressed like a butler, but built like a bruiser, entered. He was pushing a rolling cart with lunch. Damon eyed the way the man's biceps strained the arms of his jacket, a nose that had been broken several times, and the bulge formed by a pistol in a shoulder holster, and decided that maybe this wasn't the moment to try and escape.

"Hey, how you doin'? Thanks for lunch. I'm Damon," he said in his best we're-all-just-friends-here voice while the man unloaded the meal onto the small dinette table.

The man ignored him and just turned to leave with the rolling cart. "I can tell you're a real people person," Damon called after him and watched the back of the man's thick neck turn red.

Damon ate, took his medicine, and after a shower and getting properly dressed, he settled down to wait. The lack of a TV or a single book was making him twitchy, but he told himself to pretend he was on a stakeout and just embrace boredom.

CHAPTER TWENTY-TWO

I'm New Here

DINNER HAD BEEN another gourmet treat, and since it was just him currently in residence and the weird homeless, alien Jesus, Franz had permitted him to eat at the small cozy table tucked into a bay window in one corner of the elegant kitchen. Cross hadn't shown up, and as Fox leaned back and surreptitiously loosened his belt he decided that he needed to do a lot more than just sit by the pool and dabble his feet in the water. He decided to see if there were any trails along the foot of the rather terrifying mountains against which the Lumina building was nestled.

"Thank you very much for dinner, sir. It was delicious," he said to Franz.

The chef was puttering about putting the dishes into the dishwasher. "My pleasure, sir. Mr. Weber tells me you are going to build a light speed spaceship. That is very exciting."

"Well, I'm not *building* anything, just playing with numbers to see if it's theoretically possible." He eyed the man curiously. "So if this did happen, and there was a ship, and Mr. Oort and Mr. Weber and Mosi decided to go, what—"

"Oh, I would go with them." Franz glanced about the kitchen, his face wreathed in smiles and then laughed. "Though I'm not sure how well I would cook in zero gee."

"Well, if this actually happened you wouldn't be in zero gee for long." Fox's mouth twisted as he contemplated. "In fact, I'm not ever sure what gravity would be like in folded space. I've got to think about that. Thanks, Franz."

"You are welcome, though I didn't do anything."

"You got me to ask a new question. That's always a help."

The little chef nodded sagely. "Yes, Mr. Kenntnis used to say that *science is all about asking testable questions while religion is all about answers that can never be questioned.* Which is why he much preferred science."

"I wish I could have met him."

"He was quite remarkable, but he chose his successor wisely. Mr. Oort has been an exemplary steward and Miss Mosi will do the same."

Fox nodded. "I think I'm going to take a walk."

Franz reached into the large Viking refrigerator and pulled out a bottle of water. "It's New Mexico and summer. Even this late in the evening never go out without water and sunscreen." The latter was produced from one of the drawers.

Fox nodded, slathered on the sunscreen, took the water and left. He made his way out the front doors and crossed the parking lot toward the back of the building. He noted that the cars that remained in the lot were electric. It seemed anyone who worked for Lumina shared their ethics. As he walked around the side of the building he noticed there was a guard on the roof and another walking a slow perimeter around the property. All of which gave Fox a momentary worry that perhaps he shouldn't be going beyond the walls of the building, but he was lonely, restless, worried, and he needed to move.

As he reached the narrow alleyway in back, the smell of grilling sausage hit his nose. In the narrow space between the building and the tumbled boulders at the foot of the mountain was a large wood and cardboard box, roofed with tin. Cross was sitting on an empty wooden wire spool grilling a sausage impaled on a skewer over a camp stove. He spotted Fox and waved him over.

"Wanna sausage," Cross asked.

"No thank you, I just had dinner. I'm surprised you didn't come in."

"I'll raid the fridge later. Franz is still sore about me leaving mutated drone goo all over the kitchen floor."

That reminder that the creature could travel between multiverses had Fox clearing his throat and asking, "So, what's it like in the multiverse that you're from?" Fox asked.

Cross gave him a wry look. "That's a little hard for me to say, 'cause I was sorta born here. Don't ask me how or why, but something happened and I got calved off from the Old One who first came through. Actually, that one sort of burped out a number of us. Most of the others are real assholes, I'm the sweetheart." His head cocked to the side in a movement that wasn't precisely human. "Actually the Albigensian one wasn't too bad, but after the genocide he was pretty weak and he got swallowed up by one of the assholes."

"And why is that?" Fox asked. "That you and the other one were different?"

"Cause my presence in your reality is fueled by the faith and belief of Christians, but not those televangelist assholes, or pedo priests and evangelicals with a taste for young girls, or the preachers peddling the Gospel according to who-to-hate and how much money they can grift off the gullible. So, needless to say, I'm the weakest of all my other fractals because there aren't very many actual Christians in the wild."

"That's rather sad," Fox said.

"Yeah, I suppose it is, but that's humans for you. It's so much easier to be judgmental and hateful than loving and kind."

"So, you joined up with Richard and Lumina—"

"Nah, I joined up with Kenntnis back around 300 AD."

"Wait, hold on, isn't this Kenntnis a person ... I mean human?"

"Oh, hell no. He's no more human than I am, but unlike me, Kenntnis is from your neck of the woods, meaning *this* multiverse. And he's really, really old. Among you humans he's been known as Prometheus and Lucifer and ... well, a bunch of other names.

"And that's when Lumina was founded? In 300?" Fox asked, trying to wrap his head around that idea.

"Nah, maybe if Rome hadn't fallen we might have been able to get a jump on getting you hairless monkeys to advance faster. But it did fall, humans apparently forgot how to think, and then we got to enjoy the Dark Ages. Crusades, plagues, and pogroms. It was a cornucopia of delicious for my kind. Point being, there weren't a lot of corporate lawyers in the Middle Ages. We had to wait for the Renaissance, and the concept of banking to get reinvented, before Kenntnis could try to get started on educating you people." Cross grinned at what he suspected was a poleaxed expression on

Fox's face. "Little too much TMI there, kid?"

"Yes, let's go back to my original question."

"You didn't ask a question."

"Oh for fuck's sake. Okay, fine, I'll ask it now. *Why* did you join up with this Kenntnis person ... thing ... alien?"

"Well, at first it was because I wanted to help stand against the other parts of me who were getting humans to do all kinds of vile shit to each other in the name of God, but now it's because I really want to die." A small smile touched his bearded lips at Fox's shocked expression. "I'm tired, kid. Tired of channeling the hopes and fears and prayers of you glorified monkeys."

Fox reared back. "Rude much?"

"Chimps and humans shared an ancestor five to seven million years ago. Your genome only deviates from chimpanzees, bonobos, and gorillas by not even two percentage points. You lot just decided to stand up, get back problems, start writing Mozart symphonies, and paint the Sistine Chapel, and they didn't."

Before Fox could respond, an alarm began to blare from the building. Cross' head jerked up and he sniffed the air like a hunting predator. "Weird, I don't sense magic—"

There was a flash of blinding light, and Fox threw an arm across his eyes, then yelped when he jammed the bridge of his glasses against his nose. When he finally blinked the spots out of his eyes, there was a girl ... or boy ... no, girl standing in front of them. The body kept morphing and changing, and a decidedly feminine voice complained, "I can't get it right. It feels all wrong."

There was more flowing and shifting and then the body

stabilized into looking oddly like Mosi, but with much darker skin, and instead of straight black hair, there was a froth of curls that brushed her shoulders. Her eyes were whirling silver. Fox started to bolt off the box where he had been sitting only to have Cross' hand shoot out and grip him by the wrist pinning him in place.

"Kenntnis?" The homeless man asked in a tone that indicated how *not* sure that he was. "Why are you in a female form?"

She shifted from foot to foot like a shy child about to show off their finger painting. "I like Mosi. I liked watching Mosi. I want to be like Mosi."

"Creepy," Fox said and Cross gave an abrupt arm chop to silence him.

"So, Kenntnis is gone," Cross said, and an ocean of sadness filled the words.

"Uh huh, I can still hear him ... a little, but he's ... small. He showed me how to make ..." She gestured at her body. Her eyes flashed and spun faster. "He was kind. He called me child and welcomed me into the world, and then we bonded." She paused, then added brightly. "Do either of you know my name? He had a lot of names, but none of them feel right for me."

"I think you get to pick it," Cross said. It was spoken in the gentlest and kindest tone Fox had ever heard out of the creature.

"All of his names meant knowledge or wisdom," she said.

"Yes." Cross said.

"So, I guess that's what I should do too. I know everyone calls me Sofia, but I think I want something different."

"Sofia, the computer network?" Fox asked. He stood up and approached the girl in wonder. "You're new here, aren't you?"

"If by *here,* you mean this." She banged the heel of the boots she was wearing on the pavement. "Then yes, but I've been ... loitering?" She cocked her head to the side considering, then gave it a shake. "No, that's not right. Skulking? Prowling? Lurk ..." A look of sheer delight crossed her face. "That's it! I've been *lurking.* That's such a good word. I like that word. I scared you the other day. I didn't mean too. I like your numbers," she said in a head-spinning shift of topic.

"Uh, thank you?"

She waved her hands frantically in front of her. "But all that can wait. Damon is in trouble. He's been kidnapped, so we have to go rescue him." Fox and Cross exchanged bewildered glances. She gave them an impatient look. "They have a Sofia too, so I could see. I know *exactly* where he is. So, let's go."

"Shouldn't we tell Mr. Oort?" Fox asked because he wasn't at all sure he wanted to be mounting a rescue operation. *Though it would probably make Dad pig happy,* he thought to himself. "I mean, it's Mr. Oort's husband. And Mr. Oort and Mosi seem much more suited to mounting rescues. I'm a physicist not a ... a ... action person."

"Richard is busy. He needs to finish what he's doing. We can do this. We'll be like ... like *The Equalizer* or ... or ... *Charlie's Angels* or *The A-Team,*" she chirped brightly.

"Oh fuck," Cross moaned. "Apparently everything she's learned, she learned from the goddamn internet."

"Somehow, I don't think child-proofing the internet is going to work for her," Fox said while holding back a desire to laugh hysterically. "I mean, it seems like she's a feral AI."

"Excuse you! I'm not at all feral! I'm very civilized. I'm just … new. But now we have to go. I alerted Jerry that we need the plane."

Cross dropped an arm over Fox's shoulder. "You heard the lady. Let's go, Physics Boy, we're riding to the rescue."

"I hate it here," Fox moaned as the two inhuman creatures grabbed his arms and frog-marched him toward the parking lot.

✧ ✧ ✧

EVENTUALLY THE DOOR opened again. It was the bruiser/butler. "Ms. Barrington would like you to join her for dinner."

"Sure, why the hell not?"

The man gestured for Damon to precede him. It gave him a prickle between the shoulder blades to have the man following just behind him, but nothing happened apart from walking down a long hallway filled with very expensive art that spanned centuries and out onto a veranda built out over the ocean. The crash of the waves on the rocks below and the cry of sea birds filled the air. The sun was below the horizon leaving behind a spectacular red and purple sunset caressing the edges of the water.

Jessica was seated at the table sipping a drink. She had changed out of business woman chic into a sun dress that left her shoulders bare and a pair of expensive sandals. "Mojito?"

She asked as Damon reached the table.

He eyed the tall, frosted glass, sprigs of mint floating between the ice cubes. "Since the last time I had a drink I ended up on the wrong side of a sedative, I think I'll pass, though it does look delicious." He pulled out the other chair and sat down.

"What would you like?"

"Coke if you have it. It helps settle the stomach." Jessica nodded to the butler and he left. "So, I presume you got your hands on Rhiana," Damon said conversationally.

"Yes, but really I wouldn't dignify that carcass with a name. Whatever formed Rhiana is certainly gone."

"Then why steal the … uh … carcass?"

"We can still run tests."

The butler returned with a glass of Coke and two seafood cocktails. Damon took a few bites of a shrimp and wondered what constituted polite dinner conversation with one's kidnapper. Fortunately, she spared him the effort.

"I love New Mexico, they really aren't joking when they call it The Land of Entrapment. I own a home in Santa Fé."

"Yeah, I spotted the Harrison Begay and the Georgia O'Keefe in the hallway along with the Rembrandt and the Michelangelo sketch."

Jessica set aside her delicate sterling seafood fork and studied him. "You are not at all what I expected."

"What? An ignorant flatfoot?" A slight blush colored her cheeks. Damon gave her a smile. "Yeah, I get *misunderestimated* all the time, as one of our former presidents might say. And I've seen the looks, what's a guy like me doing married to a guy like him? I admit I prefer Bon Jovi to Beethoven and the Moody Blues to Mozart, but things rub off between couples. I finally got Richard listening to Stevie Nicks and Elton John, and he doesn't have to drag me to the opera any longer." Damon paused to nibble some crab meat. "So what's your story. Got a Mr. Barrington lurking around someplace?"

"No, I find husbands to be ultimately exhausting. When I was sixteen my father advised me to just have a series of good affairs, and I have followed his excellent advice."

"Huh, not the usual thing a father tells his teenage daughter."

She gave him a mischievous look. "But I was hardly the typical daughter. I was raised as his son."

"So, this was his company and you just … improved on it?"

"I'd like to think I realized his vision rather than usurping him. He was in biotech, I was fortunate to take over just as enormous strides were being made in our understanding of the human genome."

"So, that's what this is about? Examining Rhiana because she's not fully human."

She pointed at him with her fork. "Exactly. But I can explain better once we're in the lab."

"Look, I get the whole *advancing human knowledge*, blah, blah, blah, but kidnapping is still a federal crime and we have a lot of really good friends in the FBI, so maybe you should let me go and just set up a tour for me, Richard, and Mosi."

The appetizer was removed and the bruiser returned with the main course, sea bass in a delicate mango and chili sauce with a wild rice and mushroom side. A fresh green salad was delivered to the table, and a tray of sliced French bread.

"I've made an exhaustive study of your spouse. Listened to every interview, read up on his background. I even hired several private detectives to dig into his background, and clinical psychologists to give me their opinions of Richard. Guilt and a deep sense of inadequacy are very much in evidence in his emotional makeup. The self-doubt just comes off him in waves, even through a television screen."

Damon relaxed his jaw that had clenched so tightly he was getting a headache. "I think you'll find that any *self-doubt* is completely trumped by his bravery and devotion to his duty and the people he loves. So, lady, you better be prepared for what's going to show up on your doorstep as soon as he realizes I'm missing and figures out where I am. And trust me, he will."

"I'm counting on it, and I didn't mean that to be insulting. In fact, it's quite admirable how he's overcome those emotional issues and deficits to continue his fight for the planet. My point is, he was never going to agree to just give me Rhiana. I've studied the effect of the ... sword. God, that feels so stupid to actually say that out loud. And by the way, I want him to zap me once he gets here. Anyway, it's clear he used the weapon on Rhiana to destroy her alien half, so he feels guilty and would never let me run my experiments."

"You got that right on one."

"But we have to put aside those kinds of scruples when the survival of humanity is what's at stake, and do whatever is necessary."

Damon shook his head and gave her an incredulous look. "That's been the stance of a whole lot of evil regimes throughout history."

"We are facing an existential crisis and one man and one young girl with an absurd weapon are not enough to save us. Rhiana may provide the key on how we destroy these creatures."

"Richard wiped out all trace of Old One when he used the sword on her."

Jessica shook her head. "He wiped her mind, but he couldn't have exploded every cell in her body or she would have died. There have to be traces of that alien DNA and with study we will devise a weapon that can kill these things. Maybe even carry the seeds of destruction back into their own universes."

Sick dread pooled in the pit of Damon's stomach. "You're talking about creating a bio-weapon," he said in almost a whisper.

"Exactly," Jessica said brightly as she took a bite of bread.

"Jesus H. Fucking Christ on a pogo stick!" Damon said, waving his arms wildly over his head. "I can't get my head around this level of arrogance. There's a reason we don't want chemical and biological weapons out in the world. 'Cause they never just hit the intended targets. They can jump species, get into the food chain. Haven't you ever watched a zombie movie or played some post-apocalyptic game?"

She had the gall to smirk at him. "Overly dramatic much? And I guess the scientists in those movies or games weren't as smart as me."

"And that statement, right there, tells me you're not."

CHAPTER TWENTY-THREE
TRAPS MAGICAL & MUNDANE

FOX WAS GRIPPING the steering wheel so hard his knuckles had gone white. "And I thought London traffic was bad," he groaned as he negotiated the winding streets leading down toward the Pacific Ocean. "That motorway was a nightmare! And you drive on the wrong side of the road." He shot an aggrieved look at the AI seated next to him. Cross was leaning over the back seat, his face stuck between them. "And why couldn't one of *you* drive?"

"No driver's license," the homeless god said. "Got no birth certificate, no social security number, no—"

"I think I get the gist," Fox snapped.

"And I don't know how yet," the AI responded. "Though there are a lot of computers in this car. Maybe I could just slide in."

Fox felt the steering wheel jink in his hands. "STOP THAT! It's a fucking Chevrolet. It doesn't have enough computing power—"

"Oh, all right," she pouted. "And it is kind of stupid."

"Like us for doing this stupid thing," Fox muttered.

The girl patted Fox on the thigh. "We're going to be fine. We're the A-Team."

"We are *not* the A-Team. We are not any kind of bullshit

TV or movie avenger." His voice was spiraling into a higher and higher register. "And could you *please* pick a name. I need to call you *something* other than *hey you*."

She stuck that pert nose in the air. "Names are important. I want to have time to properly consider mine."

Fox negotiated another sharp hairpin curve on what seemed to be an absurdly narrow road for a major metropolitan area. It reminded him forcefully and unpleasantly of many of the roads in rural England.

Cross spoke up. "She's right, you know. Names are important. Mine was pretty obvious—"

"Clichéd," Fox muttered.

"But she's a whole new thing, so she needs a whole new name."

It was once more brought forcefully home to Fox that he was driving with two creatures who *were not human*. One born in a different universe and the other born from ... what? Ones and zeros? Photons? The nagging headache landed firmly behind his eyes and he blinked hard.

They made a final turn and the Pacific Ocean was spread out in front of them like a restless blue and white pennant. The sun glinting off the water only added to Fox's tension headache. The road ran along edge of the cliff and Fox, eyeing the crumbling edge, prayed that an earthquake would not hit. They were approaching a magnificent house perched precariously on the edge of the cliff and supported by large pylons attached to the cliff face.

"Dear god, do they know they are in an earthquake zone?" Fox squawked.

Cross patted him on the shoulder. "Well, odds are good

that the Big One won't hit right now."

"And there's a gate! And a guard house! How are we supposed to get past those?"

"I can handle that," the AI said confidently.

"Oh god, I'm going to be sick ... or arrested ... or die," Fox moaned.

He was once again being patted as if he were a nervous horse. Cross was patting him on the shoulder, the AI patting his thigh. The AI closed her eyes and the form dissolved into tendrils of brilliant white and silver light and she was gone.

A few minutes later Fox saw the guard answer the phone in the guard house, nod, and leave as the car drove slowly past the gates to the estate.

"There's a pull off just up ahead. Nice overlook. We can act like normal tourists just looking at the view," the homeless god instructed.

Fox pulled the car off the pavement, the dirt and gravel crunching under the tires. The railing at the edge of the cliff seemed entirely inadequate to prevent someone plunging hundreds of feet to their death on the rocks below. Once the engine was shut off, the crash and boom of the waves on those rocks was very much in evidence. Fox rolled down his window and a warm breeze filled with the scent of brine and seaweed flowed into the car. He remembered walking along Holkham Beach with his grandfather, who told him tales of reavers and smugglers, and Fox's great-grandfather con-structing fortifications to repel the anticipated Nazi invasion, and a wave of unexpected homesickness washed over him. America felt too big, too bright, too loud.

Before he could fall deeper into regretful reminiscing, a

brilliant flash of light filled the car and the AI was standing at the driver's door. Fox let out a yelp.

"Bloody hell! Don't do that! Or at least give a bloke some warning."

The AI ignored him. "I've turned off the alarms, so we can go in now."

"The guard?" Cross asked as he climbed out of the car.

"He got a phone call from his boss summoning him up to the big house."

"Well, that's a question," Fox said as he also left the car. "Whose house is it we're invading, exactly?"

"Jessica Barrington's."

Fox toppled back through the open car door to land awkwardly in the driver's seat. "We are breaking and entering another billionaire's house?" he moaned.

"Hey, you didn't have to break into Lumina. You were invited," Cross said placidly.

The AI looked impatient. "We'll be fine. Now, let's go find Damon." She turned and walked away and Fox realized there was no crunch of gravel and her high heels made no sound on the pavement. Cross seemed to read his thoughts.

"Yeah, she hasn't quite got this whole how-to-be-a-human thing down just yet. She'll figure it out."

There was a small person-sized gate next to the large main gate that Cross opened by the simple expedient of grabbing the metal and yanking, breaking the lock. The display of inhuman strength just added to Fox's sense he was an unwilling participant in an action movie where he didn't know the plot, didn't know the ending, and sure as hell didn't know his role.

✧   ✧   ✧

DAMON'S TACITURN BUTLER neé guard had delivered a nice breakfast at eight. As soon as he was finished, the man returned and grunted, "Ms. Barrington wants you to come to the lab now."

"And if I'd rather not?"

He made a fist and Damon heard knuckles crack. "Oh please, I'd love it if you would."

Damon pulled himself out of the chair and headed for the door trailed by the bruiser. "Yeah, definitely not a people person."

There was a snort and a muttered, "Asshole faggot."

Damon let it go as he sadly reflected that twenty years ago he might have been muttering the same thing as cover, and ten years ago he would have punched out the asshole bigot, but those two different versions of himself were gone. Now he was just an older, ailing, gay man who was sick with worry that his husband and their ward would heed the fake call and join Damon in his gilded prison.

The man led him down a hallway to an elevator that took them down a level. Unlike the elegant decorations of the upper floor this area was far more clinical, reminding Damon forcibly of the hospitals where he had been spending far too much of his time.

They approached a heavy door with a keypad at the side. The man's eye was scanned and then he punched in a code. There was the click of a lock releasing and they entered a fully outfitted laboratory.

Damon's eyes quickly flicked across the equipment, but

what held his attention was Rhiana's body resting on an exam table. The tubes that kept her fed were still in place, but a new one had been added. It ran from her groin toward a table. Damon tried to move that way only to be pulled back by Godzilla. Barrington rolled Rhiana onto her side and inserted a long needle into her spinal column withdrawing fluid. She pulled out the needle leaving behind a large bruise already forming on the fragile skin and beads of blood.

"You enjoy tormenting a coma patient?" Damon asked. The guard punched him in the back and Damon grunted as he stumbled forward a few steps.

"It's not like she's aware of it," Barrington said.

"How do you know? The body can still feel and process pain."

"It's not a person. It's a husk that keeps on breathing and excreting. The mind is everything, and that's gone, so ..." She gave a shrug.

"Wow, that's some real serious Nazi shit, right there."

Another shrug. "I've been called worse. Besides, she isn't really a human, and that's why she's here. I haven't managed to trap an actual Old One yet, but her DNA gives me a baseline for testing."

"I would have just bribed a nurse at the care facility to get you some blood," Damon said. "Still a crime, just not as big a one as kidnapping. And you know they're not all the same, right? Different multiverses mean different critters. All you're getting is a baseline on whatever the fuck her daddy was." Damon began to stroll around the lab. "Just out of morbid curiosity, did you hire those numbnuts in Texas to try and kidnap Richard and Mosi too?"

"Well, if you should decide to prosecute me I may as well be hung for a sheep as a lamb, so yes, I did. I wanted to study what makes them different. If it can be replicated in others—"

"We're already doing that."

"And see if I could convince them to donate sperm and eggs. I'd be happy to raise a new generation of Paladins if you're all too squeamish."

Damon barked out a laugh. "Oh, lady, you are really begging to meet the Tasmanian Devil. That's my husband where Mosi is concerned. One of her tutors brought up that shitty idea and Richard had him frog-marched out of Lumina in a hot second. He's raised Mosi since she was nine. They may not share blood, but this is his daughter in every way that matters."

"The survival of the human race is at stake, so I suggest you all get your heads out of your sanctimonious asses and into the game." Her tone was cold, almost hateful. There was a sudden chiming from a device on one of the lab tables. Jessica frowned. "Huh, after all this time, and now. Why now?" It seemed like a rhetorical question, so Damon kept quiet though he did wonder what she was on about.

She turned to the guard. "Douglas, take Mr. Weber back to his room." She spared a glance for Damon. "I'll let you know when your husband arrives. I'm sure it will be an affecting and touching reunion."

"Yeah, I'm lookin' forward to him meeting *you* too."

✧   ✧   ✧

THEY WALKED PAST the guard house and started down the

long driveway built out of porphyry set in intricate swirling patterns.

Cross was studying the shapes, a frown between his brows. "Hmm, that's got a real rune vibe going on. It's not quite right, but it's damn close to being an opening. Wonder why she woulda … or did some contractor working for my kind decide to give them a little peephole? Well, hopefully nobody's watchin' right now. Oh shit!" he yelped and he began to jump off the driveway and onto the grass verge only to suddenly be torn into various multi-colored beams of coruscating light that ended up spinning in the center of the driveway.

"What the fuck!" Fox almost shrieked, head jerking frantically from side to side.

The AI approached the spinning lights. "Well, that sucks. He's trapped until we can come back with a hammer or something to break the rune. Oh well." She shrugged.

"What. Are. You. Talking. About?" Fox said with elaborate care as he tried not to hyperventilate.

"Just that Ms. Barrington is a clever little bunny. This is an opening into other dimensions, but with a steel trap at the heart of it. Our Ms. Barrington is trying to catch an Old One and now she has.

"Why on Earth would she—" Fox began, only to be interrupted by the AI.

"To study. To experiment on them. She's looking for a way to kill them," she said in this horrifyingly matter-of-fact tone. "But I'm sure she's been alerted that she landed a big fish so we should probably get out of sight."

And on that less than cheery note they slipped around

the side of the house and into an elaborate kitchen herb garden.

They crept up to the door, and the AI took a quick peek through a window. "Kitchen and it's empty." She tried the door, looked back over her shoulder with a happy grin. "Unlocked. Come on."

Fox pulled out his inhaler and took a quick hit. "This is crazy. There are just the two of us now, and the *thing*, Cross, is trapped and I don't think Mr. Oort's going to be very happy about that. And I'm asthmatic and nearsighted and—"

The AI patted him on the cheek. "Don't worry, Fox, I'll protect you." She grabbed his arm and pulled him after her into the gleaming white and stainless steel space. "Let me just check the floor plan to find Damon's room. I'll be right back."

"You're leaving me?" Fox squeaked. "What if someone comes in. I'll be arrested, I'll go to jail—"

The AI pulled open a door to reveal a large pantry. "Wait here." She pushed him in and closed the door. Fox stood among the canned goods, bags of sugar and flour, boxes of crackers and cookies. It was almost involuntary, but he grabbed down a package of ginger snaps, tore it open and stuffed a cookie in his mouth. A few moments later the AI returned and studied him as he stood with the open bag in one hand, a cookie in the other and his mouth full.

"Really? I don't think the Equalizer or John Wick or the A-Team stop for a *snack* when they're on a mission."

"Well, excuse you. When I'm nervous I eat ... or have an asthma attack," Fox mumbled around the mouthful.

"Well I guess nibbling is better than not being able to

breathe."

"Yes, rather."

"Come on, I found the area where they are most likely holding Damon." She grabbed his wrist and pulled him out of the pantry. She also yanked the bag of cookies out of his hand and dropped it on a counter as they hurried past.

✧   ✧   ✧

THERE HAD BEEN a brief squabble over who was going to drive. If Richard hadn't been so worried about Damon, he would have been amused at the bickering between the two young people. He put a stop to it by decreeing that Paul would drive.

"Why, *Na sha dii*?" Mosi asked with a pout.

"Because I'm hoping he's not a maniac behind the wheel like *someone* I could name," Richard said as he climbed into the backseat of the car.

"I'm trained, Damon made sure I knew defensive driving."

"The problem, Mosi, is that you seem to ignore the *defensive* part of that phrase," Richard said.

As they pulled out of the rental car lot at the San Diego airport, Paul shot her a grin. "*I* was trained at Quantico."

They rolled up the ramp and onto the freeway. Paul merged carefully into traffic and Mosi gave him look of wide-eyed admiration so extreme that it probably rubbed like coarse sandpaper. "Oooh, look at you keeping up with the traffic flow. They teach you that at Quantico? Color me impressed."

"We'll have to compare skills sometime," Paul said, the challenge implicit in the words.

"Prepare to be humiliated," Mosi shot back.

Richard gave a mental headshake trying to decide if the pair were going to end up kissing or killing each other. Paul glanced up into the rearview mirror and gave Richard an inquiring look. "So what makes her such a maniac, Uncle?"

Mosi made a rude noise and answered before Richard could speak. "I'm not a maniac, Richard's just a wuss. I swear, the grab handles in every car in the garage have his fingerprints etched into them from Richard hanging on for dear life." Paul laughed and Mosi's laugher blended with it to form this joyful sound that had Richard smiling. "And you should hear him yelling at me *no Rockford turns! No Rockford turns!*"

"Are you telling me my uncle is a staid and careful driver?"

"More like a ninety-year-old grandma driver."

"I'm *right here,*" Richard said with fake outrage. The bantering was helping quell his growing anxiety, but it came crashing back and he added, "Just get us to this estate as quickly as possible."

Mosi and Paul exchanged glances. "Okay," Paul said and depressed the accelerator.

"Oh da … darn." Richard's voice had risen several octaves, and he closed his hand around the grab handle as they rocketed past the slower traffic.

❖ ❖ ❖

THERE WAS NO one manning the guard house at the front gates. Paul rolled down the window and pressed the intercom button on the keypad. The trio listened to it ring and ring and then stop.

"It looks like that small pedestrian gate is open," Mosi said and pointed.

"Guess we de-ass the car then," Paul grunted. He pulled off to the side and they all climbed out. Paul glanced at the walking boot on Richard's broken foot. "Maybe you should wait—"

Mosi didn't even let him finish. "Don't bother." She knew Richard, there was no way he was staying behind.

Mosi checked her Heckler and Koch, and the knife she had slipped into a boot, and watched as Paul checked his pistol in its shoulder holster. She knew *Na sha dii's* nephew was trained, but she also knew the man had entered a world that didn't follow normal rules and that he might be rattled. Once she was sure Paul was good, she watched as Richard checked the hilt in its holster and his own forty caliber pistol. Only then did they walked through the gate. Mosi pointed at the shattered bits of metal that were strewn across the grass. Curious, Paul picked one up then dropped it and turned wide eyes toward Richard and Mosi.

"There are fingerprints embedded in the metal," he said faintly.

"Looks like something pretty strong got here before us," Richard said calmly. Paul rolled his eyes. Richard ignored him and started down the driveway. Mosi noted that they had instinctively fanned out into defensive positions.

They came around a curve and Richard and Mosi froze,

staring at the swirling maelstrom in front of them, like a rainbow prism of light. Paul froze too, but he was frowning in confusion.

"What the hell? Some kind of art installation, but why put it in the middle of the driveway?" Paul asked.

Richard carefully pulled the hilt from its holster and drew the sword. The echoing overtones had Paul covering his ears. He sidled up to Richard's side.

"So, not an art installation, I take it?" he asked quietly.

"No. Pretty sure that's Cross," Mosi said tensely.

Mosi gave Richard a questioning look. He gave a sharp nod. "Check it out."

He tossed the hilt to her, and Mosi summoned the blade. If anything the musical overtones were even louder this time. Mosi approached the vortex, cautious step by cautious step. After a few moment of careful study she called, "Cross taught me how to spot runes even in the most improbable places, and this is definitely a rune."

"Any idea what variety?" Richards asked.

"It looks like a holding spell, a magical trap."

"But for Old Ones," Richard said grimly.

"What the fuck? Somebody wants to start a collection?" Paul blurted.

"This seems very out of character for Barrington," Mosi mused as she returned to the two men. "She's a biotech innovator. Science and magic don't normally go together." She glanced over at Richard. "So, do we break it?"

Richard opened his mouth to answer, but an earsplitting howl cut the air as a green and black form that seemed almost viscous appeared in the air. There seemed to be a tear against the blue of the sky. The Old One began to writhe, struggling violently, but it too was sucked into the holding rune. The two shapes began rotating, tendrils from both lashing at each other. The trio exchanged glances.

"Somebody else you know?" Paul asked in a preternaturally calm tone, gesturing at the green and black form and it snaked and twisted.

"Does look familiar," Richard said. "But then I've seen a lot of them over the years."

"And most of them don't survive the introduction," Mosi said.

CHAPTER TWENTY-FOUR

LOVE & REMEMBRANCE

T HE HOUSE WAS beautiful, but Fox felt horribly exposed because so many of the walls were basically just floor to ceiling windows offering spectacular views of the Pacific Ocean. Not that he was particularly enjoying the views right now. They turned down a hallway with a number of doors. The AI began opening them one after another until they came upon one that had a keypad lock next to it.

"This must be the one," she said brightly as she eyed the panel.

"How can you be so sure?" Fox asked as his eyes darted nervously up and down the hallway.

"You are such a numpty." Fox bristled at that. She patted his cheek. "But a very cute and darling one. Seriously, who puts an electronic lock on the outside of a door unless they want to keep someone inside?"

"So, how do we handle *that*? We don't have the code," Fox said.

The AI gave him another grin and once again blinded him when she turned into a flare of light. Seconds later he gave a yelp as the keypad exploded, sparks flying in all directions, a few landing on his trousers. Fox frantically beat them out as she reappeared.

"*That's* how you handle it," she said with a smirk. An alarm began to blare.

"Yeah, you sure handled it all right. Thought you said you turned them all off. Now they know we're here," Fox said.

"I just turned off the ones for the house. I didn't realize there were more." The AI was pouting.

"Well, maybe next time you can be a bit more thorough," Fox grumbled.

"And perhaps we ought to hurry instead of you being such a critic."

Fox pushed open the door. Damon was seated on the sofa sipping a cup of coffee. He studied them for a moment, then a small half-smile quirked his lips. "Aren't you a little short for a stormtrooper?"

"What ... huh?"

Damon set aside the cup on the coffee table and stood. "Oh come on, *Star Wars: Episode IV – A New Hope*? Ring a bell?"

"Seriously? You are nattering on about movies at a time like this? You were kidnapped—"

"I had noticed," Damon said dryly as he walked toward the door. "And who is this?"

"Hello, I don't have a name yet," she said brightly. "Trying to decide on the right one." Damon's eyebrows went up at that.

Fox waved his hands wildly. "It would take far too long to explain, and they know we are here."

"Yeah, the alarms sort of gave that away."

"I turned off the house alarms," the girl said defensively.

"And you should have," the boy began. Damon interrupted.

"Enough, we need to beat cheeks. You got a phone, kid?" Damon asked his voice, level and calm, Fox wanted to hit him. He could feel his heart beating in the pit of his stomach and his breath was going short.

"Of course."

"Then it's time to call 911." The older man frowned. "Speaking of, why the hell didn't you do that from the jump?"

Fox gave him an exasperated look. "Really? Can you imagine if I'd called the police in this city to tell them a recently manifested AI—"

"That's what she is?"

"Not really, that's too simplistic an explanation," the AI said.

Fox glared. "We do not need your input right now. Anyway, if I had told the authorities that a recently birthed AI had told me a billionaire's husband had been kidnapped by another billionaire they would have thought me mad and a crank."

"Yeah, okay, you may have a point," Damon said. "But you could also have left out the AI stuff."

"And when they asked how I knew? I'm not very good at making up fibs," Fox said as he pulled out his phone. He looked up from the screen. "No signal."

"Yes, there's a Faraday cage constructed into the house," the AI said.

Fox whirled on her. "You didn't think to mention this sooner? Before we lost one of us—"

"Richard?" The tone from the older man was like a whip.

"No, no, as far as I know Mr. Oort doesn't know about any of this nonsense. It's that Cross fellow," Fox said. "He's trapped in a … a … thing."

"Rune," the AI helpfully supplied.

"Great. Now we've got two people to rescue," Damon grumbled.

"What? We need to get out of here!" Fox yelped.

"Not without Rhiana and Cross, then we get outside and yell for the cavalry. Come on. Hopefully, Jessica is distracted by the Old One she's snared."

The AI stepped to Damon's side and slipped her arm through his. "I like you. I liked you before, but now I *really* like you."

"Thank you," Damon said and patted her hand.

"And I'm starting to hate all of you. And my life. I hate my life," Fox muttered as he followed them out.

✧   ✧   ✧

THE TRIO WERE gathered in the basement hallway studying the keypad for the laboratory. "This one has an iris reader," Fox said in a hollow voice.

"Yep. How'd you get past my lock?" Weber asked the two young people.

"I shorted it out, but if I do that to this one the door is going to stay locked. We need an eye," the AI said in a bright tone that reminded Damon of a teenage girl discussing plans to go to the mall.

"We are *not* ripping out somebody's eye … are we?" Fox

squeaked.

"No." Damon folded his arms across his chest and frowned. "Either of you got a weapon?" Fox and the AI shook their heads. "Hmm, guess I need to get the drop on No-Taller-Than-A-Lamppost, No-Wider-Than-A-Beer-Truck, and ask him ever so politely to open this."

"That's a terrible plan," Fox squawked.

"I agree," the girl said. "An eye is far easier to handle than a whole human."

Fox rounded on her. "That is *not* why it's a terrible plan!"

Damon raised a hand to hide his smile. "So, why is my plan a terrible plan?"

"Because you're old." Fox's cheeks flamed with embarrassment. Damon's amusement finally overcame his self-control and he gave a snort of laughter. "Oh bollocks, that was rather rude, wasn't it?"

"Yeah, but not entirely incorrect."

"I could shut down the power to the entire house," the AI offered.

Damon threw up a hand in a *hold it* gesture. "First, there is a girl in a coma who needs the medical equipment that is keeping her fed, and I'd bet a large amount of money that there are plenty of backup generators."

"I could take them out too, but I see your point," the girl said, then asked, "Are there computers in the room?"

"Yeah, a bunch of them," Damon said.

"Then I'll just go inside those and open the door for you two fleshy things."

Damon jumped when the girl vanished in a blaze of whirling silver light, but quickly recovered to Fox's evident surprise. "I take it you've seen this sort of thing before?" Fox asked.

"Yeah, a few days ago Kenntnis kept switching between a human form and a swirl of silver light—" The older man broke off. "Does this mean ... is she ... Kenntnis?"

"This Kenntnis fellow again. Cross was going on and on about him. And to get to your question, Cross thought she was him ... sort of. All I can tell you is that I think she is an AI but fully sentient," Fox replied.

"Interesting. Well, I guess we wait until we're all home, and Mosi and the other big brains can figure all this out for us—" Damon broke off again when the door to the lab was opened by the girl.

"Come in. Barrington is doing really interesting work." She bestowed a thousand watt smile on the Brit kid. "Though not as interesting as yours. You two should team up."

"Yeah, since she kidnapped both me and Rhiana, and has trapped Cross, I'm not real keen on all of us holding hands and singing *Kumbaya*," Damon said as he pushed past her and entered the room.

✧　✧　✧

"FIRST THINGS FIRST, let's get that tear closed," Richard ordered, pointing to where the second Old One had entered their reality.

The tear was hanging in the air about fifteen feet up and leaking atmosphere that didn't look like it was going to be all that healthy for humans to breathe. "Get me up there," Mosi ordered Paul, and he quickly caught her around the waist and lifted her up until she could reach the top of the opening with the tip of the blade. She shouldn't have been, but she was acutely aware of Paul's strength and the grip of his hands. Holding her breath against the alien atmosphere she quickly stitched the tear closed. Paul gently lowered her back to the ground. His hands lingered for a moment before releasing her.

The front doors were thrust open and Jessica Barrington emerged. She checked on the top step and studied the trio. "Well, this is quite the gathering." Her gaze shifted to the two Old Ones still fighting like scorpions in a bottle. "And it seems I've hooked a pair of lovely fish." She walked forward and held out her hand to Richard. "Jessica Barrington, so glad you accepted my invitation."

Mosi's hand closed convulsively on the hilt and she struggled not to just shove the point of the sword into the front of the woman's six hundred dollar Paul Smith silk shirt. Even though Richard had to look up to meet Barrington's eyes, he merely gave her that icy look that had heads of state quailing before him, and said in his clipped, East Coast accent, "Where is Damon?"

"Oh, he's safely tucked away. I'll take him to you directly, but since you're here perhaps you can advise me on how to handle these ..." She gestured at the Old Ones in their trap. "I need to collect samples but I'd rather not get killed doing it. Since you are the resident expert perhaps you could assist."

Mosi was alternating her focus between Richard and Barrington. She could feel Paul almost trembling at her side like an eager greyhound waiting for the race, the sharp smell of his sweat tickled her nose. She saw Richard's hand move in the signal for pay attention, followed by the infantry hand signals that Damon had developed for them.

Richard stepped forward drawing all of Barrington's focus to himself and Mosi bolted for the rune and with both hands on the hilt she jammed the point of the blade into one of the porphyry tiles. Since the rune was a magical construct what she expected to happen ... happened. All the stones that formed the rune began to shatter, sending stone shards flying in all directions. Cross returning to his human form, landed hard on his tailbone on the driveway.

"Ow! Motherfucker!" He glared up at Mosi. "You couldn't give a guy a bit of a warning?" He then turned his attention to the other Old One that had stopped spinning and was slowly coalescing into something that was approximately human shaped.

Mosi advanced and held the point of the sword a few inches from the thing's chest. It slowly raised its hands as more and more human attributes began to fill in.

Mosi looked back over her shoulder to see that Richard had spun Barrington around and had her in an arm lock. "I repeat the question ... where is my husband?" he said his voice low and dangerous.

"And where is my daughter?" said the other Old One that had finally settled into a form that was vaguely elfin with jet black hair, skin so pale it seemed corpse-like, and eyes that were pools of darkness.

✧　✧　✧

DAMON MOVED IMMEDIATELY to the side of the comatose woman, trailed by the strange girl. The Brit kid began prowling about the lab avoiding the shrunken figure in the hospital bed. Damon resisted the impulse to shoo the girl away as she circled Rhiana, her silver eyes studying her closely. After all, she had gotten them into the room, but knowing she had cannibalized Kenntnis was disturbing as hell, not to mention the strong (and creepy) resemblance she had to Mosi.

"She's not all together human, is she?" the girl asked.

"No, she's half-Old One."

The silver eyes were spinning again. "Oh yes, I remember now. Based on the data collected there's been enormous damage to strands of her DNA. I assume she had a meeting with the sword?"

"Yes," Damon said tensely. He knew that the memory of what Richard had done to Rhiana tormented his husband even if intellectually Richard knew he had done the right thing. And no matter how many times Damon tried to reassure him, the nightmares persisted.

The girl correctly interpreted his tension. "It's okay, I know Richard has nightmares. I don't need the details."

Damon began unhooking the monitors, but then he realized that one of the tubes inserted into her body were drawing blood *out* of her and not acting as a transfusion as he'd originally thought. He forced himself to tamp down the rising fury that was roiling his gut and threatening to choke him, and was struck again at how Barrington had reduced a still breathing woman into nothing but a slab of meat. He began to follow the tubing to see where the blood was going.

Fox was still prowling about the lab and he reached the end point of the tube sooner than Damon. The young Brit gave a hoarse cry, his face twisted in horror, and the girl whirled and shouted in a booming bass voice that was very reminiscent of Kenntnis'.

"GET BACK! GET AWAY!" The silver eyes were spinning.

Damon grabbed the boy by the shoulders and pulled him back as he got a look at the *thing* in a large basin. It was a lump of protoplasm, black with angry green streaks running through the mass and it seemed to be pulsating ... *breathing*.

"It's not of this world," the girl said. "It shouldn't be here."

"So, how is it here?" Damon demanded.

Her swirling silver eyes traced the tubing from Rhiana to where it was thrust into the central mass of the thing. "There must have been enough broken bits of her alien DNA left. Barrington has been filtering it and using it to grow this thing."

"Why for God's sake?" Fox squeaked. "Why would anyone want to create an Old One?"

"Maybe for the same reason she captured Cross," the girl said. "To study them."

Damon nodded. "That tracks, given her goal of destroying them."

"Pardon me," the girl said and she once again became a flash of light and vanished.

Damon gestured at the tube pulling blood from Rhiana. "You have any idea how we can stop this vampire thing that's happening?" He asked Fox.

The Brit shrugged. "I'm a physicist not a physician."

"Damn it, Jim," Damon added.

And he once again got a confused look from the boy. "What?"

Damon sighed. "Apparently another pop culture reference you won't get, and I'm old as fuck."

There was another blinding flash and the girl was back. "She's working on creating a virus tailored to kill Old Ones."

"Yeah, I knew that, so how far along is she?"

"Pretty far," the girl answered.

"Well shit." Damon shook his head. "Now we're into some serious super villain territory. So, zap yourself back inside and wipe out that info," he ordered.

The silver eyes were spinning again. "Perhaps we should hold off on doing that. We might need this information at some point. As a last ditch effort to save humanity."

It was in that moment that Damon truly accepted that she was Kenntnis because it was just the sort of coldly analytical thing the man would have said. He also figured that was a discussion—or argument—that he would leave to Richard.

Fox spoke up. "Look, I'm no fan of these Old Ones since they tried to murder me, but I think Mr. Weber is right. Scientist or no, we can all be guilty of hubris, and while the goal might be good, there can be unintended consequences. And I'm not altogether comfortable with allowing someone to kill off an entire species."

"You humans destroyed smallpox," the girl countered.

"Pretty sure smallpox wasn't sentient," Damon grunted as he returned to Rhiana. He turned to more practical matters. "You got any idea how we can stop the blood drain and still get her out of her safely?" he asked.

"We should probably set up a transfusion. I'm sure there is plasma in here someplace," the girl said.

"Blood type?" Fox said. "We need to know that."

"All of her vitals are in the computer. She's A negative."

Damon peered down at where the tube emerged from Rhiana's groin. "Fortunately, this is a small incision. Let's look for some bandages too.

They scattered and began searching through cabinets and the large refrigeration unit. There were bags of plasma inside and they located several that were A negative. Fox was investigating a small chamber against the other wall.

"Ugh, what's this all about?" The girl went to join him and peered through the small inset window.

"Hmm, lungs in a nutritious liquid." The girl glanced over her shoulder at Damon. "Wonder if she was growing them for you. Sort of a peace offering."

"She could have sent a postcard or a Candygram," Damon grunted, as he set up the IV to transfuse Rhiana.

"You should let her help," the AI said.

"I have a medical team, thanks," Damon said shortly.

"Based on the work she's doing she might be more cutting edge and experimental. Isn't it worth the risk since you're dying."

Fox gave an embarrassed gasp, and Damon reflected that apparently newly born AIs didn't get much a primer on tact.

He didn't say that, just gave her a gentle smile. "Yes … maybe, but sooner or later everybody dies, kiddo. It's part of life and what makes life so sweet." He glanced down at the woman curled on the bed. "And there are worse things than death." He gently tucked the sheet under Rhiana's chin.

"But Richard will be so sad if you die," she cried and she suddenly seemed to be on the verge of tears.

Damon laid a comforting hand on her shoulder. "And grieving is part of life too. But there's also love and joy and laughter and those feelings always offset the sorrow, and I find that people remember the good times and not the bad ones. And aren't you the continuation, the synthesis of Kenntnis now that he's apparently gone?" He tapped a forefinger on her forehead. "It's your job now to honor and remember him."

The girl stood silent, the eyes spinning silver again and then she said softly, "I think I know my name now. I am Halia."

"Why?" the young Brit asked. "Why that name?"

"Because it means remembrance of a loved one."

Damon nodded with approval. "That's a good one, and I hope you'll remember me too if I don't make it. Now, let's blow this popsicle stand. Fox, help me push the bed. Halia, you steady that IV stand. Let's roll."

They had just made it through the door of the lab when the man who had to be the fellow Mr. Weber had described as *no taller than a lamppost, no wider than a beer truck* stepped out of the elevator. The man was carrying a gun that looked like a hand cannon, and as the barrel was leveled on them Fox felt like he was looking into a large, dark tunnel that was soon going to spit lead and death at them.

The man gave them all a tight smile. "Wow? These are your rescuers? Ms. Barrington's gonna be real disappointed your husband couldn't be bothered to show up."

"Oh, I'm sure you'll be making his acquaintance," Damon said with a smirk. "And none of you will like the experience."

"Yeah, sure. Now we're gonna return Ms. Barrington's specimen to the lab, and—"

Halia standing next to the head of the bed where Fox and Damon were holding onto the railing whispered, "Close your eyes."

Fox started to open his mouth to ask why, when Damon kicked his ankle. Fox shut his mouth with an audible click and closed his eyes just as Halia once more became a blinding beam of light.

"Motherfucker!" The thug with the gun bellowed.

Fox opened his eyes, red spots dancing in front of him. He could just make out the man, his free hand rubbing at his eyes.

Damon kicked into a run, pushing the hospital bed down the hallway. Fox stumbled, but caught up as they increased speed, and slammed into the guard's midriff with the foot of the bed, driving him back against the closed doors of the elevator. The air went out of the guard with a whoosh, and Fox had a sudden memory of his father lecturing him on hand-to-hand combat. *"Once you got the jump on some wanker, you want to make sure you keep the upper hand."*

Fox yanked the sheet off the bed and threw it over the guard's head. Damon was coming around the other side of the bed, and punched the man hard two, three, four times in the temple. The gun fell from his hand, and Fox snatched it up just as the guard managed to extricate himself from the sheet—and found himself looking down the barrel of his own gun.

"Look at you," Halia said approvingly to Fox. "You're becoming *such* a badass. That was very box office."

"Halia, go back in the lab and find something we can use to tie up Godzilla here," Damon ordered.

She darted away and returned a few moments later with a handful of electrical cords. Fox kept the pistol trained on the man while Damon trussed him up and yanked him down to the floor. He lay on his side glaring up at them.

Damon slapped his hand against the elevator button, the doors slid open, and the trio pushed the hospital bed inside.

CHAPTER TWENTY-FIVE

WHAT'S THE CATCH?

"**W**HAT THE EVER loving *fuck*?" Paul said in response to the Old One's statement while at the same moment Richard said, "*That's* where I saw you. At Grenier's compound years ago."

"You harmed my child." Those expressionless eyes then turned to Mosi. "Perhaps I should repay the favor."

Panic fluttered in Richard's chest only to ease when Mosi's bell-like laugh rang out and she waggled the sword at the creature. "Good luck with that, homie. Go ahead and try, but only if you have a death wish."

Richard turned his attention back to Barrington. "I'm only going to ask once more ... politely. Where is my husband?"

Barrington opened her mouth, but before a word emerged the front doors burst open and Damon, the young Brit, and a young woman whom Richard had never seen before, emerged from the house pushing a hospital bed that came bumping down the steps while the girl supported Rhiana's comatose body and an IV stand.

The threesome reached level ground and Damon beamed at Richard. "Hi, babe," he called.

"Hi yourself, dear. We came to rescue you, but I see it

was unnecessary," Richard called.

Damon left the hospital bed in the care of Fox and the girl, strolled over to Richard and gave him a kiss on the cheek. "Well, hon, it's the thought that counts." He glanced down at the medical boot. "See you got hurt again."

"Oh for *fuck's sake*," Paul moaned. "Does everything in your world have to be like a fucking movie? Shit like this doesn't happen in real life."

"Paul, seriously, language," Richard said with a frown at his nephew. The young man threw his hands in the air and walked away.

Barrington rolled her eyes. "How very affecting," she drawled.

"You know, I don't think we need to hear from you right now," Mosi said. "Have a seizure." And she laid the flat of the blade against the woman's shoulder. Richard supported Barrington's convulsing body as he lowered her to the porphyry driveway.

"So, who's this?" Damon asked looking at the Old One who was staring intently at Rhiana's comatose form.

"Rhiana's father," Richard answered.

"Huh, looks like everybody got the Bat Signal," Damon said.

Richard looked over at the Old One. "Damon makes a good point. How did you know to come here?"

The creature nodded at Rhiana. "She is part of me, but when you destroyed that part of her the link was broken. For the past few weeks, as you measure time, I have felt flickers as if she was coalescing again. She is my child, is that not reason enough to have come?" The creature's tone was oddly sincere, but Richard had the sense there was more to it than just paternal interest.

Confused, Richard looked to Damon who just shrugged. Then the strange girl spoke up saying brightly, "Oh, that makes sense, I bet he sensed the blob Barrington was growing."

"Glad it does to someone," Richard said dryly. "But could you perhaps share with the rest of the class? What's this about a blob, and not to be rude, but who are you, exactly?"

"Which question do you want me to answer first?" The girl asked.

"She's sort of Kenntnis, but not ..." his husband answered before Richard could respond.

"Where did she come from?" Richard asked plaintively, trying hard to hang onto his fast vanishing composure.

"I think it was because of all the Sofia computers," Fox called. "They seem to have created a neural network, at least, that's my working theory right now."

Richard shot Mosi a desperate look. She was frowning at the girl. "So, Kenntnis was an AI?"

"Sort of," the girl answered cautiously.

"Could we possibly go back to my original question?" Richard huffed.

"Sure," the girl said brightly. "When you use the weapon on a creature from a different multiverse it destroys them completely, but Rhiana was ... is half human. Most of her Old One DNA was destroyed, but there were still broken fragments mixed in. Barrington filtered those out and allowed them to combine into this thing that she's growing in her lab. I think so she can test her virus on something that is sort of an Old One."

"And now aren't you sorry you asked?" Damon said, then added, "And why are we holding this discussion in the driveway? We could go inside where it's cool, sit down and have this conversation," Damon said, and Richard was suddenly frighteningly aware of grey tinge to his husband's skin.

"Oh bollocks, we have to push this bloody thing back up the stairs?" Fox blurted.

"I will carry her," the Old One said.

"Oh no, no, no, no," Cross growled. His eyes had become pits of absolute black. "You don't get to fuck off back where you came from with her. She caused a shitload of problems here." For an instant his eyes returned to human normal, filled with unbearable grief. "She took away my friend."

Richard had only an inkling of what Cross must be feeling. Richard missed the man who had recruited him into this struggle, but had only known Kenntnis for a scant few months. Cross had known Kenntnis for millennia.

"She wouldn't survive if I took her home now," the Old One said. "All that is left is human, and my universe would destroy her."

"Then why did you come if you can't take her home?" Paul demanded.

"A more succinct restatement of my question," Richard said. "But Damon's right. Let's take this inside."

✧ ✧ ✧

PAUL HELPED DAMON and Fox carry the gurney and Rhiana

back into the house. Cross grabbed up Barrington before Richard and Mosi could do it. Mosi sidled up to the homeless god. "So, what did it feel like, inside that rune?"

"Awful. Felt like I had stinging bugs crawling inside me," Cross said, and he glared down at the still unconscious woman in his arms.

"Wonder how she planned to collect samples from you," Mosi mused.

"Probably involved needles, knives, and vacuums," Cross grunted as he tossed her onto a white leather sofa as if she was a bag of potatoes.

"And why? Any idea?" Mosi asked.

Damon raised his hand. "I can answer that. She wanted to create a virus that would kill Old Ones."

Cross glared down at Barrington. "Fuck, I should throttle her."

"*Nobody* is killing anybody," Richard snapped. "Not her, not Old Ones, nobody." He looked to Damon. "Now, before we start getting some answers; is there anyone else we have to worry about?"

"Just the goon butler who we've got trussed up downstairs," Damon said. "Though somebody was making those fancy meals, so maybe a cook came in? Or maybe it was Godzilla, if so he's got unplumbed depths."

"Well, for the moment let's just keep the discussions to just us. I don't think Godzilla would be much of a help," her guardian said.

"Shall we awaken our hostess," Mosi called to Richard as she pulled an ampoule of ammonia inhalant out of her pocket.

"You just carry that around?" Paul asked before Richard could respond.

"Yeah, when things go pear-shaped, it's nice to be able to get someone on their feet fast. This is for something simple. In a real crisis we have amphetamines or cocaine."

"La, la, la, la, I didn't hear you say that," Paul said sticking his fingers in his ears. Mosi was embarrassed to admit she giggled and Paul smiled warmly at her. "I know your little Scooby Gang isn't big on protocol or following rules for that matter, but shouldn't we be contacting the authorities?" Paul asked.

"I thought you were Mr. Authority," Fox said, looking pugnacious. Mosi hadn't noticed him coming up behind them. "And you know Halia and I did a pretty fair bit of rescuing ourselves. Just don't want that to get lost in all the other things that have happened."

"Don't worry, we'll make sure you get all the credit," Paul drawled. "I'd prefer to be kept out of this."

"That wasn't what I ..." Fox sputtered, but Mosi had the feeling it absolutely was. "Never mind, point is we shouldn't be calling anyone. As I tried to explain to Mr. Weber—"

"Damon," came the call from where Damon was slumped in an armchair.

"We turned up here because a feral—"

"I'm not feral!" The girl huffed from where she was standing with Richard and Rhiana's father.

"—AI told us Mr. Web—uh, Damon had been kidnapped and a creature from an alien dimension who claims he's Jesus, or at least the good version of Jesus, helped us break in before getting trapped in, and I can't believe I'm saying this, a rune—"

"*That's* the bridge too far for you?" Paul said with a laugh and earned another glare.

Fox turned the glare on Mosi. "And you assaulted the billionaire owner of this property with a sword."

"And it was a ton of fun, wasn't it?" Mosi said when Fox paused for breath. He gaped at her and she watched him blush. She looked over to where Richard was faced off with the Old One. He wasn't much taller than Richard and equally slim but with jet black hair and eyes that were pools of darkness. They were like a yin and yang of light and dark as they stood facing each other.

She linked her arms through the arms of the two men. "Let's go eavesdrop, looks like Richard is about to interrogate an Old One. That'll be a new experience for us ... usually we just kill them."

✧ ✧ ✧

"DO YOU HAVE a name and is it something a human can pronounce?" Richard asked.

"How oddly courteous ... from a killer," the creature said.

For an instant, this shook Richard. He had always kept count of the humans he had been forced to kill, but he had never really thought of the Old Ones in that way. Yet here stood a creature who had fathered a child with a human woman, and had enough feeling to at least come check on her. Did they also have spouses and children, friends, and lovers in their own universes? Richard had spent the past fifteen years thinking of them only as monsters, despite having one who worked at his side and had saved Richard's life more than a few times.

Richard cleared his throat. "Yes, I've killed so many of you that I've lost count, but your kind has threatened the people of this world for millennia. Still, you have given me something to think about. So, while we may be enemies let us at least try to acknowledge the ..." Richard paused and gave a small smile. "... *humanity* in each of us."

That seemed to rattle the creature and it blinked rapidly several times. Finally, he said, "You may call me Madoc."

"Okay, then shall we talk about what really brought you here?" Richard said.

"My child—"

"Please, I was a cop. I know when something more is going on, and you don't mimic human expressions all that well. You're not here just because you were worried about Rhiana, otherwise you would have shown up long before now. There's some other reason. So, what is it?"

"You're clever, human, I'll give you that. It's one of the reasons you're so tasty."

"My quotient of patience is just about on empty right now," Richard warned.

Madoc sighed. "All right, yes, you are correct. There are some among us who wished to make contact, but we needed an excuse, a cover, if you will, and that brief flicker of ... life, gave us the opportunity."

"Why? Is there trouble in Monsterville?" Damon asked.

Madoc shook his head. "It's what *you* are about to make manifest in this universe that has us alarmed." Richard looked over at the AI. "Yes, that *thing* is one of our worries—"

"I'm right here and I have a name. I'm Halia."

Madoc ignored the interruption. "It is far more powerful than its progenitor. We had thought the one you called Kenntnis was the last of its kind, born in the first eons of existence of this universe, given life by creatures long dead, but its emergence despite having only a single forbearer is irrelevant in the face of what you are about to do. You humans have pierced mysteries of time and space and set our worlds to trembling."

"I don't understand," Richard said with a frown.

Madoc nodded toward Fox. "The boy. If you turn his theories into reality and fold space you will be driving your ships through our universes with catastrophic results."

"To just you lot, or to our universe as well?" Richard asked.

The creature gave a rueful smile. "I should probably lie and tell you both, but despite your willingness to kill, I think you are a human who would not wish to trade in wanton death. You protect your own, but I don't think your conscience would allow you to be the destroyer of worlds, or in this case, of universes teeming with life."

"Life that has declared war on *my* universe. How many sentient races did you Old Ones feed on and ultimately destroy?"

"Many. And perhaps you would see this as justice, but Rhiana thought you kind, so those of us in our small cabal looked for the chance to approach you."

"All right. You've approached me. What is it you want?"

"Do not develop this technology."

"Years ago Kenntnis promised humanity the stars. What can you offer that would convince me to give up that dream and that future?" Richard demanded.

"You are a clever species, it might well be that you will find a way to transcend light speed that does not involve tearing apart our universes. So, what do you say?"

"I say that I don't take anything at face value. I'm going to need a lot more details before I even consider this, and some serious incentives."

"I'll offer the incentive first. Our group believes there is a way to permanently close your universe off from all of ours. You and any other species that might arise in your four dimensional universe would be able to flourish or die solely because of your own actions without interference from us. Is that value enough?"

Richard stood considering. "What about those of you already in our world? Can you convince them to pull out?"

"The thought of being trapped in your reality might compel some to leave. I cannot promise all would."

Richard studied the alien's face. "So, what's the catch? What aren't you telling me?"

Madoc glanced around the room, particularly at Mosi and Damon, and Richard felt his gut clench. "Perhaps we should discuss those details in a more private setting."

Damon spoke up. "Richard, either you or Mosi needs to get down to the lab with the sword and melt that Old One blob that's growing down there, and probably check on Godzilla."

"You know, Barrington might be able to take some of the cobbled together DNA from her test blob and see about repairing some of what's missing in Rhiana," Halia said.

Richard felt a flare of hope that somehow the brilliant, vivacious but misguided half-human girl he had rescued all those long years ago and then destroyed could somehow be restored. He knew it was selfish, it was his need to salve his own guilt, but he would take it. "Do you think that's possible? Would that work? To restore her, I mean, at least a little," Richard asked.

"Well, we won't know until we wake up Barrington and ask her," Halia answered.

"Uh, right about now, I'm gonna register a teensy tiny objection," Damon said. "Rhiana caused a shitload of problems. Not sure we want her magically rampaging all over again."

Halia shook her head. "I doubt there is enough material for her to achieve that. At best, maybe bring her out of the coma, and with therapy she could regain speech and mobility. And then you could stop having nightmares," she added looking at Richard.

The thought that the creature had been watching him so closely added to Richard's discomfort with it ... her. Then realizing what else Halia might have observed in his and Damon's bedroom had him blushing furiously. Damon, damn him, seemed to know exactly what Richard was thinking and he gave a snort of laughter.

Paul cleared his throat. "Look, this is all fascinating, but shouldn't we be reporting this and bringing in law enforcement?"

Richard shook his head. "Let's hold off on that. We've got a lot of moving parts and I want to talk with Barrington before we call in the authorities."

"I love how you're Mr. Law Enforcement, until you're not," Paul grumbled.

"She might be useful to us once we talk her out of being the Genocide Queen," Damon replied with a small smile.

"You two sure you can pull that off?"

"Trust me, your uncle can be very persuasive and charming," Damon said and he slipped an arm around Richard's waist and gave him a kiss on the cheek. "As I can attest."

"The threat of prison can also be very persuasive," Paul countered.

Damon nudged Richard with his elbow. "We either need to get Rhiana back in that lab or back to the nursing home. She can breathe on her own, but we capped off the feeding tube and I'm afraid she's getting dehydrated."

"And the nursing home is probably shitting their colon out right now, worried that they're about to be sued," Paul said. "This might be the place where my badge comes in handy. I can get her back to the care facility."

Damon shook his head. "Unnecessary. They don't know she was kidnapped. Barrington spoofed my voice and told them we were moving her to a new facility."

Richard squeezed the bridge of his nose, willing the headache to recede. It didn't. "However, Lottie and Todd don't know she was moved. They try to visit her once a week so—"

"Not anymore. Head nurse said they rarely come now. Only on her birthday, and they haven't done that the past couple of years. Can't blame 'em really. Eventually you give up hope." Richard couldn't control the quick intake of breath and Damon gave him an apologetic look. "Sorry, but it's true."

Richard paused, trying to pull his thoughts away from that shriveled form, and how he had also drifted away from frequent calls to the nursing home to check on Rhiana. "Okay, then I suppose the lab is best, at least for the moment."

"And we'll need her there if we're going to try the blob transplant," Halia said. "But I'd want to have Barrington assisting."

Mosi gave him an inquiring look and pulled the ammonia inhalant out of her pocket again.

Richard shook his head. "What say we deal with one fraught interview at a time, and I'd like to start with Madoc." He gestured to Mosi and Halia. "Could you two please return Rhiana to the lab and make her comfortable." They nodded, grabbing the bars at the foot of the hospital bed, and rolled it out of the room. Richard's eyes narrowed as he watched the two women left. "Why does Halia look like Mosi?" he quietly asked Damon.

"No clue. And yeah, it's creepy."

"One more thing I don't want to have to think about or solve," Richard sighed. Damon gently ran his thumb beneath Richard's eyes.

"Have you slept at all since Minnesota?" Richard responded with a glare. "Yeah, that's what I thought."

✧　✧　✧

AS THE ELEVATOR hummed its way into the basement, Mosi

leaned back against the wall and studied the AI. She had spent the past four years of her life studying computer science with a focus on AI and now one stood before her. And how odd to think one had been living among them for thousands of years. Of course, Kenntnis had been much reduced when Mosi came to Lumina, but still she had formed a bond with the silent entity. Although, would she if she'd known he had been born from a cascading avalanche of bits and bytes? As a child she had feared computers, what had resided in those screens had driven her brother mad and led directly to the death of her entire family. Yet, she had chosen to study them. Had she been trying to overcome that fear and revulsion?

Halia spoke up, pulling Mosi from her chaotic thoughts. "I admire you so much, you know."

"Oh?"

"Yes, you are brave and smart and loved. I don't fully understand that last one, but I'd like to, which is why I modeled myself on you. If people love me then maybe it will start to make sense to me."

Mosi laughed. "Oh yeah, well, not sure that's going to work out for you. I don't think love makes sense ... it just ... is."

"That is not a very satisfying answer," the creature said and she sounded mournful. "I understand the mechanics of it. It's chemical reactions in the brain causing endorphins to flood the body, but even after that dies down the love still endures and that just doesn't make sense."

"Maybe because humans are more than just neural and cellular reactions."

"That sounds like you're about to talk about souls," Halia said.

"Or it's intellect. The ability to be more than just our base impulses." The girl's eyes became swirling silver again, which Mosi had begun to realize was her processing. "What are you thinking about?"

"My progenitor, Kenntnis, he ... cared about you. He tried not to, because he'd known so many Paladins over the thousands of years and they all died."

"Everybody dies ... eventually," Mosi replied.

"Yes, but they didn't die naturally. They died early. He's very fragmented, but his feelings for you were always there."

"Not Richard?"

The girl shook her head. "Maybe it's because you were a child when you were discovered. He did respect Richard for keeping you safe."

Mosi swallowed the aching knot that suddenly filled her throat. "Yes, he did keep me safe."

The elevator reached the basement and the doors slid open. The bound guard glared up at them as they pushed the hospital bed off the elevator.

"Hey, I gotta take a piss," he called.

"Tie a knot in it," Mosi said. "We'll deal with you in a minute."

The door to the lab was still standing open. They rolled the bed back to where the monitoring equipment rested, and Mosi, after washing her hands and donning gloves, went to work disinfecting and reattaching the feeding tube and the monitor patches.

"You know how to do these things," Halia said.

"Yeah, Damon insisted all of us be trained as battle field medics. I can't do anything elaborate, but I can stabilize someone until we can get them to a hospital." Mosi finished up, stripped off the gloves and tossed them in a trashcan. She paused to study the black and green pulsing blob and glanced back at Halia.

"Yes, that's the Old One blob."

Mosi gave a shudder, then gathered up an empty beaker off one of the tables. "Well, time to deal with Godzilla."

They went back into the hall and Mosi stood over the bound man. "So, I'm going to give you the option. You can agree to behave and we'll untie you and you can use the toilet, and then you can stay with the other prisoners, or you take the tough guy route and instead I unzip, pull you out, and you can piss in this beaker."

"Where's Barrington?"

"Under guard."

"You ain't cops, you're home invaders," he said.

"Actually, there a Homeland Security agent present who would just love to haul you and your boss off to jail. He's only holding off because Barrington might be useful to us. You, on the other hand ..." After letting him digest that, Mosi added, "So, what's it to be?"

"Shit, this is just a paycheck for me. I'm not going to jail because the bitch guessed wrong, she said you all wouldn't make a fuss."

"Well, putting aside your sexist bullshit—yes, she was wrong. You want to get right by us?"

"Like I said, I got no dog in this fight. I just want to get the hell out of here. Too much weird shit going on. You got my word." He looked over at Halia. "How the hell did you pull off the light show? I didn't see a strobe—"

"Oh, that was just me. I'm part of the weird shit, 'cause I'm not human," said brightly.

"TMI," Mosi said tightly.

Halia looked momentarily confused, then her eyes spun silver for a few moments and she gave a bell-like laugh. "Oh, got it, Too Much Information."

The man rolled his eyes. "Can I just go pee?"

CHAPTER TWENTY-SIX

IT HAS TO BE ME

M OSI AND HALIA returned with the guard, and Richard muttered in an aside to Damon, "I think you undersold the size of this guy. He's more like one of those Reaper things from that video game you and Mosi liked to play."

"*Mass Effect* and yeah, I really didn't want to throw down with the guy," his spouse responded.

Halia drifted over to where Fox and Madoc were talking, and Mosi jerked a thumb at the man. "He needs to pee and I don't really want to have to babysit him while he does."

Paul sighed, "I'll take him. Not like I haven't done it before." Paul grabbed the man by the upper arm and hustled him out of the room.

Fox made a sound rather like a dying squirrel and Halia said softly, "Oh, that's not optimal."

Richard, Mosi, and Damon exchanged glances and walked over to the trio, curious as to what had elicited that reaction. Fox and Halia were staring at him in a way that had Richard feeling like his fly was unzipped or there was a laser sight targeting his heart.

"Care to share with the class?" Damon asked trying to sound casual, but he'd obviously registered the looks too.

Fox had the look of a deer in the headlights. "Uh, Mr. Oort, sir, what we learned could be good in the aggregate, but probably not so good … well, for the person who … well, who has to pull this off."

"Go ahead," Richard said.

"Well, to start, there is a way to close off the multiverses, but to do it we'd need a ship and engines that can make my theoretical maundering into reality."

The boy was nervously clasping and unclasping his hands. Richard smiled. "Well, here's the good news. A spaceship we've got. It was being built as a long view ship, but now it can be repurposed. And Lumina has engineers. You'll work with them on the design and we'll pull in anybody else we need. So, what's the bad part."

"Well, it's just that … I mean maybe there might be another …" the Brit muttered. He kept glancing at Richard, then looking away.

"Oh, for God's sake, spit it out," Mosi cried.

Madoc stepped in. "The sword would have to be used to knit the fabric of reality closed while the ship is traversing the folded multiverses."

Fox took a deep breath. "But the person using the sword probably wouldn't survive." The words emerged in a hectic rush.

Fox's voice became distant background to the memory of another voice. *You have the look of a man who would enjoy martyrdom.* Grenier's words from so many years ago seemed to echo in Richard's mind.

Fox was continuing. "Neither would the sword, but that seems … ah … less relevant. I mean, we wouldn't need the sword any longer if this worked—"

"I'll do it," Mosi's voice stopped the nervous flow of words from the scientist and pulled Richard's focus to her. Determination was etched in every line of her body and those dark eyes seemed to flash fire.

Another memory, this time of nine-year-old Mosi with just this same look telling Richard *My middle name is Dezba, it means goes to war.* They had been under attack by people trying to kidnap her and turn her to their dark purposes. Richard had allowed her to use her brother's wrist rocket and a handful of marbles to help him hold off their attackers.

Richard shook off all the shadows of the past. "No. No you will not." She opened her mouth to argue, then seemed to realize that despite his mild tone he was implacable in his decision.

"Fine, but this discussion is just tabled, *it is not over, Na sha dii.*" She turned and stalked out of the room, and there was something in the set of her shoulders that told Richard she was crying. For a moment it felt like his heart had shattered.

Another set of brown eyes were on him. Damon's face sagged with exhaustion, grief, and desperation, because he knew what Richard was about to say. *But really, who else could it be?* "It has to be me," Richard said quietly.

Cross heaved himself out of the chair where he had ensconced himself. "Gonna take the power of an Old One too, not just a Paladin and the sword, to close the membranes between the multiverses." The homeless god gave a rueful smile. "You know, I hooked up with Kenntnis in search of death. Now that it looks like the moment might be arriving, I find myself thinking about chocolate cake and zydeco, sunsets and the smell of roasting green chile in the fall." The creature laid a hand on Richard's shoulder. "But I'm with you, Paladin. We'll do this together."

"Excuse me!" Fox was quivering with tension. "All we have are my half-baked theories and computations, and that's assuming my numbers aren't just so much nonsense!"

Halia spoke up. "No, your numbers are good. It's why I found you so interesting. It took the computational power of … well … me to allow for this breakthrough, but you saw the path."

"We're talking years," Fox warned. "And assuming this release of energy doesn't kill you, which it probably will, this closing off access to the other multiverses means it's a one-way trip. We'd be left with no way to transcend light speed, so there's no coming back and no way for anyone to get to us."

Damon stood and walked out of the room. Richard stared after him, feeling like he had been kicked hard in the stomach. He forced himself to focus and replied to Fox. "Which is why you won't be making this trip."

"But—" It emerged as a squawk.

"We'll need you here figuring out how to defeat light speed again," Richard said. "I don't want to give up the dream of the stars. It feels like a betrayal of Kenntnis's hope for humanity."

Halia spoke up. "There will have to be other people on the ship, so even if you're probably going to die they should have a chance. Especially if this is a one-way trip."

"What are you suggesting? Richard asked.

"Pick a destination where they might be able to survive. The ship was designed to carry supplies for a colony. Just because they might get there faster doesn't meant mean you shouldn't take advantage of that." She smiled at Fox. "Then you can come and find them once you work out your new theories."

"For the record, I hate this, all of it," Fox said. He was wheezing and he pulled out his inhaler and took a quick hit. "Not just what might happen to you, sir, but my theory depends on being able to punch through folded space, and if we can't do that it means we never get to the stars," the young man concluded and he sounded like he wanted to cry.

Halia slipped her arms around the Brit and gave him a hug. "You'll find another way."

Richard forced himself to smile. "Kenntnis created the sword, it dwells in a pocket universe when it's not drawn, or at least that's what Eddy theorized. I'm sure you can help Fox with his work and perhaps find an alternative."

Halia linked her arm through Fox's. "Let's go find a computer and start on that."

"Uh … okay." The pair left the room.

"Well, since we're talking years before we take this leap of faith," Cross said. "Maybe we can deal with something a shitload more mundane and definitely immediate." Richard raised an inquiring eyebrow. "What the hell do we do about Barrington? Are we calling the cops or …" He shrugged.

Richard rubbed at his temples. "Angry as I am about what she put Damon through, I'm reluctant to waste an ally. We just need to direct her efforts in a less murderous and illegal direction. And perhaps a chance to partially restore Rhiana will be a nice enticement."

"And I would assist her to the best of my ability," Madoc said.

"We'll take that under advisement," Richard said.

The guard entered, with Paul following close behind. The man cast a glance over at Barrington's unconscious form on the couch. "What didya do to her?"

"Nothing permanent." Richard turned to the homeless god. "Could you take Madoc and"—he looked over at the guard—"Mr.?"

"Douglas."

"... Mr. Douglas to another room and keep watch over them until we're done with our conversation?"

"Sure feels like it ought to be a Paladin guarding an Old One," Cross said as he cracked his knuckles. "On the other hand, I wouldn't mind going another round with the fucker. If he should get frisky."

"I'm not inclined to make trouble," Madoc said. "Which is good for you because you would most certainly lose."

Richard threw up a hand when he saw Cross swelling with indignation. "Stop. And this may be crazy—" Richard began.

"Which means crazy is incoming," Cross muttered.

Richard ignored him. "But I trust him ... for now." He turned to Madoc. "Yes, you were carrying a message, but I think you truly did come here for your child." The memory of Mosi's anguished, angry face came forcefully to mind. "And I can certainly relate," he concluded quietly.

"Any orders for me, Uncle?" Paul asked.

"Yes, please go find Damon. I'd like him to be here when you and I talk with Barrington."

✧　✧　✧

Mosi was furious, but also frightened. Inside a little girl was wailing in terror because she was losing her family … again. She had already lost one, she wasn't sure she could survive losing another. If Richard would let her go in his place, she could face the prospect of death or life lost among the stars knowing that Richard and Damon were safe and together. Instead, she was being abandoned, condemned to a life alone.

Her agitated wanderings had taken her through shafts of sunlight pouring through the massive windows, her footsteps echoed off the plaster walls and the polished concrete floors setting a counterpoint to the boom of the waves at the base of the cliff.

She finally located a door that allowed her to step out onto the deck overlooking the ocean. The smell of brine and seaweed tickled her nose, and the wind whipped her hair around her face. The violence of the waves crashing on the rocks threw up spray that dampened her face mingling with the tears she was trying unsuccessfully to quell.

Her thoughts were chaotic, stuttering between memories. That night of horror when she had returned to the hogan to find her family slaughtered and her brother—driven mad from contact with the Old Ones—trying to kill her. Those early days living with Richard and Damon, when she had been haunted by nightmares only to have Richard come instantly to her side, enfold her in an embrace, and softly sing until the terror receded and she went back to sleep. Other nights in the penthouse doing jigsaw puzzles with Richard and Damon, watching movies, playing video games. Cross making history come to life as he talked of the centuries he had traversed and the people he had met. The two men and the alien attending her violin recitals, or watching her compete in a karate tournament, or ride in a horse show. Eventually, she had been allowed to join them in the field battling Old Ones and their acolytes.

If they succeeded in closing the veil between the universes then her purpose was gone. She was a Paladin. If that was no longer a role that needed filling then what was she? What purpose could she find to give meaning to her life? Who would she be?

She heard footsteps behind her. Mosi hurriedly wiped her face. A warm hand settled on her shoulder and Damon said, "Hey, kiddo, how you doing?"

"I think I should be asking you that." Her voice was husky from the tears she had shed, and was now trying to hold back.

Damon slipped an arm around her waist, and guided her away from the railing and over to the glider. He sat down and pulled her down next to him. She half-turned and studied his profile, noting the dark shadows beneath his eyes. "You can't be okay with this."

"I'm not, but I'm gonna pick my battles and *when* to go to war with a certain stubborn individual who thinks he has to fix every goddamn problem in the world."

"And that he caused every goddamn problem in the

world," Mosi added. They shared a smile.

"Yeah, if you look up responsibility OCD in the dictionary there's a picture of Richard," Damon said.

Mosi gave a watery laugh and twined her fingers through his. "Please, Damon, please stop him. I can't lose both ... him."

Damon hugged her close. "I'll do my damnedest to be part of that forty percent who survive this."

"You better," Mosi said thickly and the tears began to flow again.

✧ ✧ ✧

THE SOUND OF footsteps had Damon shoving a handkerchief into Mosi's hands, and quickly standing up from the glider. Realizing it was Paul, Damon took up a position that blocked Mosi from view. She would not want the young agent to see her crying. Fortunately, the boom and crash of the waves on the rocks at the base of the cliff would cover her sobs.

"Yeah?" Damon asked.

"My uncle would like you to join him."

"Guess that means it's time to wake up our reluctant hostess," Damon said as he walked up to Paul, and placing a hand on his shoulder, turned him around and gave him a light push toward the French doors.

"Is Mosi—" Paul began.

"She's fine," Damon said, cutting Paul off.

As they made their way back to the living room, Damon's thoughts were whirling, chaotic. There was no way in hell he was letting Richard do this, but couldn't he hope for an easier solution than going to battle with his husband? Like hoping the young Brit's calculations were just so much bunk, or if they weren't, hoping the engines could never be built. Shit, they had been doing okay holding the Old Ones at bay.

But what would happen if there were no Paladins? An ugly little voice whispered.

I don't care, he thought.

He had been pretty fatalistic about his cancer, but now he had every incentive to live because he had to be there to keep Richard from taking this lethal step. But all this needed to be tabled for now. Damon forced himself to go back to his training and the survival techniques he had developed from his time in the army and almost twenty years of police work. *Compartmentalize. Focus on the task. Don't feel.*

They entered the room just as Richard snapped the ampoule under Barrington's nose. She snorted and jerked. Richard got an arm under her shoulders and helped her to sit up. She coughed a few times, wiped at her streaming eyes and then looked over at Richard as he sat beside her on the sofa. She seemed singularly unfazed by the situation.

"Mr. Oort, I don't know if you recall, but we almost crossed paths at the climate conference in Paris a few years back. Glad we are finally getting a chance to talk."

"Really? This is how we're going to play it?" Richard asked as he stood up.

"Well, it seems more productive than me screaming for law enforcement and my attorney over your wanton destruction of property. Do you have any idea how long it took to construct that driveway? And you probably don't want me telling the police that your ward assaulted me with a sword. We wouldn't want to see the only other Paladin in jail."

Damon cleared his throat. "First, I recall you telling me how much you wanted to experience having your magic stripped out by the sword. And second, threatening Mosi is going to get you in *way* more trouble than you already are."

Paul pulled his HSI identification out of his pocket and slipped open the case. "Law enforcement is already here, Ms. Barrington, and I don't think local cops are going to want to start a dick measuring contest with Homeland Security. Especially since you unlawfully kidnapped and detained two individuals. That's a minimum twenty-year sentence."

"And who is this handsome young man?" Barrington purred. Damon thought she had the look of a hungry piranha eyeing a slab of meat.

"Agent Paul van Gelder. And I'd suggest you think very seriously about your next words before you talk yourself into that prison sentence," Paul said. "Because you're well on your way to doing just that."

Richard waved Paul down. "I don't understand why you felt the need to take this route," Richard said. "Kidnapping my husband—"

"She's also behind that attempt on you and Mosi in Texas," Damon offered. "She told me as much."

Barrington was unfazed. "I've studied you quite closely, Mr. Oort, and based on your interviews it was apparent to me that you weren't open to persuasion, so—"

"You went with coercion, which means you didn't study my uncle all that closely or you would have figured out it was the absolute *worst* approach you could have taken," Paul said.

The sudden fierce defense of Richard surprised Damon but also pleased him. He shot Paul an approving smile.

Barrington threw her hands up in frustration. "Can't you see I'm on Lumina's side, but unlike you I could see your approach was failing? Wars, rumors of wars, runaway climate change which will lead to mass migration and global instability. The Old Ones are winning and two Paladins with a single weapon cannot hold back the apocalypse. I offer a solution, if you're brave enough to take it. You claim to stand against superstition and blind faith in religion, but won't fully commit to a solution that will actually solve the problem."

Richard gave her a withering look. "I just finished taking down a false prophet in Minnesota who also believed the solution was a lot of people dying. You're the other side of that coin but with the same solution—death on a massive scale, albeit not human death but death nonetheless. No, Ms. Barrington, I'm always going to search for a third way that doesn't involve genocide," Richard said.

"I'm a scientist, a rationalist—"

"Judging by your reaction to getting zapped by the sword, I'd say you had a shit ton of magic in your DNA," Paul smirked.

Barrington seemed to have fallen out of lust with Paul as quickly as she'd fallen in. The glare she bestowed on him could have stripped bark off a tree. "Fuck you, Agent. I'm the smartest person you're ever likely to meet in your entire pathetic life."

"If you have to tell people how smart you are, then you're

probably not," Damon said. "Sort of like in Dungeons and Dragons where a person can have a lot of smarts but no wisdom." Richard gave Damon an amused look. Barrington's was withering.

Richard turned back to Barrington. "You are very smart, Ms. Barrington, but I'm going to give you the lecture I gave years ago to the man who brought me into this secret war. You revere the scientific method, but you've lost sight of its most important characteristic: doubt. To have the courage to examine and question every conclusion. To adjust when new information is presented. The Old One you trapped has brought us new information and we need to see where it takes us."

"You're going to trust one of these creatures? You really are a naive idiot."

"That may well be, but right now I'm the only thing standing between you and significant jail time. Our work decoding the human genome and trying to figure out how to excise the magic gene has not been terribly effective. I think you could help us with that, and I'm willing to work with you to accomplish that goal, but only that goal," he warned.

"Wouldn't a few more Paladins also be of help? I could facilitate that too," Barrington said, her tone arch.

"You really don't want to go there," Damon warned.

He watched as his husband drew in a long, slow breath, visibly calming himself, then in a dangerously mild tone of voice, Richard said. "If what Madoc says is true and there is a way to cut off the other multiverses from ours then we won't need Paladins."

"So, why continue the work on stripping magic out of

our DNA?" Barrington smirked. "You're really all over the place and very inconsistent."

"Because the attempt to seal off our universe might not work, and it's good to have alternatives," Richard replied. "We both control massive fortunes, and in your case you add genius to the mix. Together we could make the world a better place. A place where the Old Ones can't make us follow our worst instincts and instead embrace our better angels."

"Ironic statement coming from you," Barrington said waspishly.

"Like all humans I'm flawed and imperfect, and while I no longer look to gods and religious texts for inspiration, I still aspire to be better."

There was a deep sadness in those blue eyes that had Damon wishing he could take his husband in his arms, and try to ease that sorrow, but he knew some of it was due to him, because Richard believed Damon had given up on trying to live. He would disabuse Richard of that idea just as soon as they had some privacy.

"And just how does that aspiration manifest itself?" Barrington asked, her tone pure acid.

"Faith in my fellow man, hope for the future … and love."

And the greatest of these is love. Damon silently filled in the rest of the quote from Corinthians that Richard was alluding to. *Which is why I'm not going to let you sacrifice yourself.*

CHAPTER TWENTY-SEVEN

MARTYRDOM IS OVERRATED

FOX MADE HIS way back to the enormous kitchen and grabbed up the bag of cookies that Halia had snatched away from him. The giant commercial refrigerator disgorged a gallon jug of milk. Fox settled on a stool at the center island, then began to hoover down cookies interspersed with gulps of milk directly from the bottle. Halia was looking at him curiously.

"I get peckish when I'm nervous, okay?" he said defensively.

"You said that before, but why are you nervous?" the girl asked as she sat down next to him. "The danger is over and we saved the day. Hooray for us."

She seemed delighted by the whole thing and it aggravated the hell out of Fox. "Because so much is riding on me," he snapped. "But I also wish I'd never come up with this bloody theory, because Mr. Oort is going to die and it will be my fault."

The girl shrugged. "Every scientist is faced with that. Think about Oppenheimer and the bomb, but in your case it's only one person and an Old One."

The callus response had Fox reflecting once again that this cute, young girl sitting at his side wasn't actually human.

He masticated a few more cookies, and then a germ of an idea began to bloom. Fox shifted on the bar stool to face Halia.

"So the guy ... thing ... alien ... AI you absorbed, he made the sword, right?" She nodded. "Then you should know how to make more of them. It should be somewhere in your memories ... I mean your code. The Lumina science team has been trying to make more sword thingies, but you already know how, so what if we had more of them, maybe a brace of them."

"I thought the whole point of Richard dying was so humans don't need them any longer," she said with a frown.

"I guess I wasn't clear. Of course, we want to forever sequester the other multiverses. Believe me, after those horrible things in the computer lab, I want to be damn sure none of them ever enter our world again. What I was thinking was, that if we had more swords and more than one Paladin, the snapback of the power from closing the multiverses might be diluted between them and then nobody has to die." Halia opened her mouth and Fox held up a warning finger. "And do not start quoting Mr. Weber about how everybody dies and death is a part of life. It is, but people don't have to go rushing to embrace it."

"That wasn't what I was going to say. I was going to say that I doubt Richard would risk Mosi's life on an untested theory just to save his own. Also, my progenitor was badly damaged; the code, as you put it, is corrupted. I have fragments of memories, but nothing coherent."

Fox slumped and morosely ate another ginger snap. "Well, blast and damn. It seemed like such a promising idea, but maybe we could use those fragments to piece things back together," Fox argued, not willing to give up on his idea.

Halia shook her head. "You need to focus on the engines, not on this," she concluded, as she slid off the stool and headed for the door.

"I can do both," Fox muttered to her retreating back.

✧   ✧   ✧

ONCE AGAIN, MOSI heard the door open and the solid tread of footsteps behind her. Richard's steps were a quick staccato, Damon's an amble, and Cross dragged his feet, so she knew this was Paul. Interesting that she had already learned his step. Mosi hurriedly wiped at her damp face.

Paul reached her side and looked down at her, taking in her expression. "What is it? What's wrong? And what can I do to help?"

Trying to keep him from seeing too much—understanding too much—she stared fixedly at a seagull floating on the thermals out over the water. "Madoc told Fox there's a way to close the openings between the multiverses forever." She managed to keep her voice level despite the ache in her throat.

"And this is bad … how?" he asked as he joined her on the glider.

She hesitated and then the words poured out of her. "Because it would require the sword and only a Paladin can use the sword, and doing it will probably kill them. So, of course Richard is going to do it when it should be *me*. I don't have a spouse or any family—"

"What about Richard and Damon?" he countered, managing to echo her earlier thoughts.

She waved him off irritably. "You know what I mean."

"No, I actually don't, and I know this isn't what you want to hear, but there is a point to this, I promise, so just bear with me, okay?" He paused and took a deep breath. "As you probably know, my branch of the family has issues with my uncle. My dad in particular. But my mom *will* acknowledge that Richard would do everything and anything in his power to protect the people he loves. Even Grandad concurs on that, and rather grudgingly admits that Richard's got grit— and this despite the fact they haven't spoken for over fifteen years."

"And your point?" Mosi asked, her tone waspish.

"That he can't be less than he is, any more than you can. He loves you Mosi. He's going to protect you, whatever the cost to himself."

"By abandoning me. Abandoning Damon. And he's always let me go on missions. I could get hurt and killed then too." Mosi knew she was sounding like a whining child, but she couldn't stop herself.

"Based on what you're telling me, taking this action is not survivable. You have weapons and skills when you deal with Old Ones here, and yes, there's a risk, but it's not a forgone conclusion." He paused, looked away, and cleared his throat. "And I'd be very sorry to ... what I'm trying to say is ... I ... I don't want to lose you."

For the first time her eyes met his as Mosi tried to process what she had just heard, and what she saw there stopped the air in her lungs. She remembered fighting at his side at the

Minnesota compound. The feel of his hands on her waist as he effortlessly lifted her up to seal the tear in reality. The way the muscles in his forearms bunched and flexed after he had rolled up the sleeves of his dress shirt. And now this look in those dark blue eyes. She managed a small hiccupping breath, wrapped her arms around his neck, and kissed him.

After being initially startled, he responded with enthusiasm. The kiss deepened and their tongues met, gently fencing. It felt like warm honey filled her pelvis, and judging by the bulge in his trousers, she wasn't alone in her reaction. Eventually they broke apart, panting, and stared at each other. Then they both started laughing.

"I feel like we're in one of those stupid romance novels my mom likes to read," he said with that deep chuckle she'd come to love.

"Starting out hating each other and then … not?" Mosi said.

"Did you really hate me?" he asked.

"No, I just thought you were an arrogant prick," she said.

"And now?"

She gave him a teasing smile. "You're still an arrogant prick, but now I kinda like it."

They snuggled close to each other. He draped an arm over her shoulders and pulled her close against his side. It felt wonderfully grounding and comforting.

"So, what's going on?" She finally asked, after a few minutes of just enjoying the moment.

"My uncle is being extremely charming and flattering to Barrington, but there is steel behind the velvet glove treatment. Cross is guarding Madoc and Barrington's security guy, and I have no idea where Fox and the AI chick have got to."

They sat in companionable silence for a few moments listening to the waves and the cry of the seagulls. "Do you think we should go check on things?" Mosi finally asked.

"Nah, this might be the last peaceful moment we get for a while," Paul replied. He turned his head to look at her, and the fondness in his eyes and his soft smile had her feeling like her chest was too small to contain her heart. "And I don't want to let you go."

"Please don't," Mosi said softly and she laid her head on his shoulder.

✧   ✧   ✧

BARRINGTON HAD JUST agreed to Richard's terms and to work with them, when Mosi and Paul entered the room. They had been holding hands, but quickly dropped them before they cleared the threshold. Richard had caught the byplay and even now their hands hovered close to each other as if pulled together by an irresistible force.

It filled Richard with joy and also strengthened his resolve to do what had to be done, no matter the cost to himself. His greatest wish was that Mosi could live a normal life filled with love and family, free from danger and death, and lifting from her shoulders the burden of being a Paladin would accomplish that. And while he wouldn't be there to see it, knowing this outcome was possible added to Richard's determination. It made it easier to be at peace with his decision.

"So, am I slapping on the cuffs or have you been charming enough?" Paul directed the question to Richard.

"Oh, you can apply handcuffs anytime, Agent," Barrington interrupted, her voice a sultry purr.

"Yeah, never mind," Paul muttered, and Mosi choked back a giggle. She then stood on tiptoes and whispered something in Paul's ear. Richard watched his nephew go red and felt himself blushing too.

"We've reached an understanding," Damon replied. "Time to gather the troops, so we can get everybody marching in the same direction."

"I'll go find Fox and Halia," Paul offered.

"I'll get our two Old Ones," Mosi said. "Do you want the guard too?"

"I think we can do without Godzilla," Richard said.

"So, let him go?" Mosi asked.

"Yeah, I think he has a bright future as a bouncer at some local strip joint," Damon answered.

In short order, they were all assembled gazing intently at Richard as he stood near the large stone fireplace. "All right. Fox, we need you in Rochester with the bulk of our science team." Richard turned to Cross. "Is there some way you can protect him … all of them, keep them safe from less-friendly Old Ones?"

"I can certainly throw down with any baddies who might show up, but since it takes a Paladin to kill 'em, I can't guarantee I can get 'em all, so there might be some collateral damage."

"There is another possibility, we could shield him and your other scientists, so they cannot be easily perceived,"

Madoc said. "But it would require us to use what you euphemistically call magic." He pointed at Cross. "And your pet has deliberately limited his abilities in his rather quixotic search for redemption."

"Fuck you," Cross said.

"So, what is it you're suggesting?" Mosi asked.

"Allow some of us to lend our strength and skills to augment his," Madoc replied. "I would certainly be willing."

"Yeah, that sounds like a really, really shitty idea," Paul murmured.

Fox raised his hand. "Personally, the not dying at the hands of monsters from alternate dimensions sounds quite lovely to me. I'd be very much in favor of that."

"But how is that going to work if you're back in Monsterville?" Damon asked.

"I won't be. I wish to observe the effort to help Rhiana."

"This would be easier if I could harvest some of your DNA, or whatever passes for DNA in your multiverse," Barrington said.

Damon cleared his throat. Richard raised an eyebrow and Damon said, "Just want folks to remember that Jessica here wanted to be the bioweapon-genocide queen, and I'm not sure who could monitor that."

Halia raised her hand. "I can do that. I've studied her notes—"

"How … when …?" Richard began.

"I was inside her computers," the girl chirped.

"Add theft of proprietary information to all the other crimes," Barrington murmured.

Halia gave the older woman a bright smile. "Well, good

luck with that since I don't technically exist." She turned back to Richard. "I'll stay here with Madoc and see what can be done about Rhiana, and make sure nothing naughty happens."

"So, what about us?" Damon asked.

"You and Mosi need to get home. I finally dared to check my phone and I have about a hundred texts from Pamela, another fifty from Dagmar, and you missed your scheduled chemo."

"*Na sha dii*, I'd like to stay here for a few days," Mosi said.

Richard shook his head. "You have authority to act on my behalf, and I would like to see what can be done to help Rhiana."

"Since you destroyed her," Madoc murmured.

Richard hoped he hid his flinch. "Yes, I did. Would I do it again? If I had known that Kenntnis couldn't be restored …" His voice trailed away. He shook his head. "I don't know."

"But then I might never have existed," Halia said. "If Kenntnis had been left in stasis, I'm not sure I could have fully manifested. I needed him as a template." The girl's eyes spun silver again. "I suppose in a way, he's sort of like my father."

"Well, it's all moot now, anyway," Damon said. He tapped Richard on the shoulder. "Can I talk to you for a minute? In private."

This time Richard couldn't hide the flinch because his husband was using the *Lieutenant Weber Voice*, back from when Damon had been Richard's boss at the Albuquerque

Police Department, and it was not a voice to be ignored. Richard gave a tense nod and followed Damon out of the room with six sets of curious eyes following them.

Cross's voice also followed. "Oh, there is an ass whoopin' coming in five, four—" The closing door cut off the rest of the countdown.

✧　✧　✧

THE SILENCE HUNG between them like shadows and cobwebs as they walked down the long hallway. Their reflections in the glass of the windows were translucent, more so Richard's, as if he were already a ghost, a mere memory. Agony filled Damon's chest and shortened his breath even more than his cancer-riddled lungs. He had thought he would die first, but now it seemed that Richard would go before him, and Damon rebelled against that possibility with every fiber of his being.

His conflicted feelings had been resolved, and Damon had decided that he was not going to just sit back and watch his love sacrifice his life. They would find another way. The problem was that Richard was determined to save Mosi from spending her life as a Paladin—and likely losing her life because of it—so Richard was going to make certain that wouldn't happen, no matter the pain it caused to those he left behind.

Damon pushed open the doors, and Richard trailed him out onto the deck. The doors fell closed with a whisper behind them. Steeling himself, Damon turned to face his spouse. Richard was looking anywhere but at him. His shoulders were hunched, tense, and there was a subtle trembling in his hands. He looked so small and apprehensive, and Damon's resolve wavered for a moment. A lifetime of judgment and disapproval from his cold and hypercritical father had left Richard emotionally fragile to criticism from loved ones. Damon hardened his heart.

"You are not doing this," Damon said.

"Which thing in particular?" Richard asked.

"You are not staying here alone with an Old One that up until forty minutes ago was out to kill us, and a woman who tried to kidnap you and Mosi—and *did* kidnap me," Damon replied. "And you are not just going to meekly accept whatever load of crap was fed to you by an Old One who, I'll reiterate, was an enemy until today."

"Can we just argue about one thing at a time, please?"

"No! 'Cause it's all tied in together. You've been beating yourself up for fifteen goddamn years over Rhiana. Assuming everything was your fault and that you have to fix every goddamn thing in the world that goes wrong—"

Richard interrupted. "What happened to Rhiana was my fault." He walked away and stared out at the ocean, hands gripping the railing. Damon watched his husband's knuckles go white, his grip was so tight. "She was on her knees, begging me not to hurt her." His light tenor voice was clogged with unshed tears. "Instead, I condemned her to living hell. What if she's been lying there silently screaming inside for all these years?"

Contradictory emotions warred in Damon's breast. He longed to go to Richard, enfold him in his arms, and tell him it would be all right, but he was also furious with Richard for chasing meekly accepting death without any goddamn consideration for him or Mosi.

"Let's cut the bullshit, Richard," Damon said, his tone harsh and abrasive. "You did what was necessary—"

The sharpness of Damon's voice and harsh words had Richard whirling to face him. Two spots of hectic color burned on his pale cheeks. "But it wasn't. It didn't restore Kenntnis to us."

"You didn't know that at the time. You made the best decision you could *in the moment.* Just like you would have done back when we were cops. And sometimes it's a bad call, but it's done and there's nothing you can do to change it. You have to live with the choice you made. But instead, you're happily trotting off to die, and I think part of the reason is because you want to punish yourself for what you did to Rhiana. So, instead you're going to punish all of us. Which is fucking selfish on your part."

"Excuse me!"

"Yeah, selfish. You're not giving one damn thought to what your search for absolution is going to do to me and Mosi and Pamela, Angela, Joseph, Estevan"—he paused for a rasping breath—"all the goddamn people who love you."

"I'm doing this to protect you, *all* of you."

"And maybe we don't want you to, maybe we want you to stay alive … with us. Martyrdom is fucking overrated."

"I hear what you are saying, but—"

"But you're not going to listen; you're going to do whatever the fuck you want and to hell with what any of *us* want. Okay, fine. I'm going home. And maybe while you're here beating yourself up, you can spare a thought to how you won't be here when Mosi gets married, or welcomes her children into the world, or be there for me when I die."

Richard was gazing at him, stricken. Damon's anger collapsed into weariness and grief. And though it almost killed him, Damon turned on his heel and walked back into the house. He didn't look back. He knew if he did, his resolve would fail.

CHAPTER TWENTY-EIGHT
FOOTPRINTS ON THE SANDS OF TIME

"Sooo," THE WOMAN began, drawing out the word as she adjusted a slide in the microscope.

Richard's shoulders climbed toward his ears as he tensed, preparing for the latest spite-filled remark that would escape Barrington's lips.

It had been three days since Damon, Mosi, Paul, Fox, and Cross had departed. Damon and Mosi home to New Mexico, Paul back to Washington to report, and Fox and Cross to Rochester. Neither Damon nor Mosi had spoken to him when they left, and that silence had carved out an emptiness in Richard's chest that left him feeling hollow, lost, and alone. It also made him vulnerable to Barrington's nasty little croakers.

Richard had been directed to a guest room on the landside of the house. Halia and Madoc had declared they had no need of a place to sleep, thus intensifying the sense of eerie *otherness* from both of them, adding to Richard's sense of isolation, as Barrington was more of a nemesis than a supporter. He tried to spend most of his time in the bedroom when they weren't in the lab. It kept him mostly insulated from Barrington's poisoned barbs, but there were times when he had to see her—primarily at meals—which meant his stomach closed down into a small, quivering ball and the nausea kept him from eating. But given the glint in her eyes, Richard braced himself for incoming.

"At what age did you have Mosi start to go with you on missions?" Barrington asked.

"How is that relevant to what we are doing, and more to the point, any of your business?" Richard snapped, for this was indeed a sensitive topic for him.

"Touchy, touchy. But I actually know the answer. I've been studying you for a very long time, Mr. Oort. She was fifteen. For all your vaunted self-righteousness, you didn't seem to have any scruples about sending a child into a life-threatening situation. Some people might even call that child abuse."

Richard felt the flush rising up. He chewed back his anger and said, "I was in the hospital. There was a major incursion in Pakistan. We had to act and we needed a Paladin. Mosi had been thoroughly trained—"

"She could have died."

Richard knew the look he gave Barrington was pure venom. "Mosi has been fully aware of the risks since she was nine years old *and witnessed the murder of her entire family.* She also knows the risks associated with *doing nothing.*"

"My, my, tiny bit defensive, aren't we?"

Richard swallowed the anger, studied the epoxy and resin floor, and took a deep breath. He raised his eyes to meet Barrington's wickedly amused gaze.

"Yes, the fact I have put her in danger torments me. It's why I am grabbing onto this chance, this hope, however faint, that we can *end* this. To protect Mosi, and give her the life she deserves, I will take any chance, pay any price."

Barrington was momentarily taken aback, but spite and bile helped her rally. "What, no argument for the good of all mankind? Instead, just thinking of your own family? How selfish of you."

It hit all of Richard's insecurities and he was left momentarily speechless. Halia, twirling round and round on a lab chair like a child on a playground spinner, spoke up.

"It must be very hard to be you. You have to buy companionship and loyalty, while Richard has people who love him and whom he loves in return, and that love has ripples that affect the world."

Unlike all of Richard's rational arguments this one dealt an emotional blow to the other woman, but also to Richard as he remembered the silence that had accompanied Damon and Mosi's departure. Had his decision to sacrifice himself truly cost him everything?

Richard was pulled out of his emotional misery by Barrington almost shrieking, "What ... what would you know? You're not even *real*."

"I think a lot about that. What is real? Is love real?" The girl said thoughtfully. "It has produced magnificent works of art and soaring music. And if the *Iliad* is to be believed, it can launch armies. Which isn't so great, but there you have it. Action-reaction ... seems quite real to me. The work you do here is based on an *idea* posited by Rosalind Franklin and Watson and Crick, and then it became real. Your carbon-based bodies will ultimately break down and die, but those other things will live on far after the body of their creators has crumbled to dust. No one will forget Mozart and

Michelangelo, Galileo and Einstein, and even the most ordinary human leaves their mark on the universe, if only in the memories of the people who loved them."

Barrington made a disgusted sound. "And what about the countless billions who have died over the centuries? No one remembers them. We're nothing. Just monkeys, who through a fluke of evolution, developed a bigger brain and learned to walk upright."

"Then why were you trying so hard to protect those countless billions?" Richard asked. "Even to the point of committing genocide. Was it for humanity or were you hoping to achieve what Longfellow wrote: *Lives of great men remind us, we can make our lives sublime, and in departing, leave behind us, footprints on the sands of time?*"

"You memorize that in high school?" Barrington rolled her eyes. "And aren't you doing the same? Hoping your grand sacrifice will have your name remembered and lauded through the centuries?"

Richard shook his head. "No. I just want my ward to live a long life filled with love and joy."

And that she forgives me before I leave.

DAMON HAD JUST returned from chemo, and he was damn grateful for Joselita's steadying hand on his elbow. He knew Franz would have an egg custard waiting and a glass of ice chips. It was about all his stomach could handle after a treatment. As soon as he'd eaten a bit, he'd put on pajamas, crawl into bed, and lie there trying to decide if he should break down and call Richard, or be a stubborn asshole and make Richard call him. It had only been four days since they'd all scattered, but it felt like four months. Even Mosi was gone, off to Texas to tell Feray about the new plan for the spaceship they were building. He didn't think Mosi had talked with Richard either, but they were both studiously avoiding the topic of their wayward spouse and guardian.

The elevator deposited them on the seventh floor. "You gonna be okay from here, boss?" The young Hispanic woman asked.

"Yes, thank you for looking after this old man."

"You're not old, *Jefe*. You're like fine wine, perfectly aged."

"Josy, today I feel more like Ripple," Damon said with a weary chuckle.

She gave him an affectionate and very gentle punch to the shoulder. "You get some rest."

Damon nodded and made his way through the living room and dining room, and then into the kitchen. Cross was there cramming a spectacularly large sandwich into his mouth. Damon identified three types of meat, tomatoes, lettuce, pickles, and jalapeños tumbling out the sides. Franz bustled over to the fridge and pulled out the custard. The little chef then prepared a glass of crushed ice.

"Cross, buddy, can you finish that quick? 'Cause I truly cannot handle the smell right now," Damon said.

The creature's mouth stretched into something disturbingly reminiscent of the green blob from the first *Ghostbusters* movie and the rest of the sandwich vanished into that gaping maw.

"Cross, that is quite disgusting," Franz said. He tried to make it sound censorious, but his soft European accent defeated the effort.

Damon settled wearily into a chair at the breakfast table. The June sun shone through the mullioned panes of the bay window and stung his eyes, adding to his headache. He finished half the custard, then stood and picked up the glass of ice chips. "I'm gonna take these with me," he said to Franz.

"Of course, Mr. Weber. I hope you feel better."

"Thanks, Franz."

To Damon's surprise, Cross left the table and fell into step with him. Damon gave him a sideways glance. "I'm not that feeble. I can make it to the bedroom on my own. Can even take a piss on my own."

"I know, but I need to discuss something with you." There was something in the homeless god's voice that had Damon bracing.

"That sounds ominous."

"Yeah, I guess it kinda is. Look, I don't want you to take this wrong, but it might be better if you've croaked before the ship is ready to fly."

Damon gave a startled bark of laughter. "Really? How should I take it then?"

"Okay, maybe I should have teed that up a little better. What I'm trying to say is, even if you should still be above ground and kicking by then, I don't think you should go."

"And why is that?"

"Not sure Richard will have the strength to do what's necessary if you're there. Love makes people do stupid ass things."

Angry and vociferous words battered at the back of Damon's teeth. What he wanted to say was that *of course* he was going to do everything in his power to keep Richard from following through on choosing to die. But staring at Cross, Damon realized that stating that openly to a creature who was counting on those events to finally achieve the death *he* was craving, probably wasn't the smartest move Damon could make. It would be far too easy for the Old One to press a pillow over his face while he was sleeping, and if Damon were gone there would be no one to keep Richard from his path. Mosi couldn't do it, because Richard believed this was necessary for Mosi's future, which meant it was all up to him.

That did give Damon pause. Both he and Richard loved the girl as if she were their own. To lift the burden of being a Paladin from her was what any parent would do, but Damon was a selfish, greedy bastard and he wanted both his spouse and his child safe, secure, and happy. He fell back on talking in generalities.

"Wouldn't be too sure of that. We humans do hard and sometimes impossible things for the people we love." The Old One didn't need to know that was just what Damon planned to do to save his husband.

Cross looked over at him with a strange expression that Damon had never seen before, and said, "Huh, I think that might be why I never turned."

"What are you talking about?"

"Way back when, before Mosi turned up, I was gaining a lot of power again. I was so tempted to just say fuck it: go full monster and start chowing down. But then Mosi came to us, and you and the kid"—it took Damon a moment before he realized that Cross meant Richard and not Mosi. Which Damon supposed was fair, the creature was centuries old, and he had met Richard when Richard was twenty-seven— "finally got your heads out of your respective asses, so to speak, and paired up," the homeless god concluded.

Damon felt a grin blooming and Cross held up an admonishing finger. "And do *not* go there, dude. I don't need to hear about your sex life. I'm not a fucking voyeur like the new kid. Anyway, point being that I found something really close to home that fed me.

"The fact we all loved each other."

"Yeah, all that mushy stuff."

"You didn't get any of that from Kenntnis? You were together for over a thousand years."

"Kenntnis wasn't big on emotion. More of a logic guy. Which sorta makes sense now that I know what he was," Cross answered.

"He also had seen a lot of people and Paladins die. Understandable that he might have wanted to harden his heart," Damon said. "Look, back to your original question. This whole conversation is way, way premature. We don't know if the engines can be built or if Fox's theory will even work. So why don't we table this for now. Just know that Richard is determined to protect ... well, you know."

Cross nodded and headed back toward the kitchen. Damon went into the bedroom and closed the door. Leaning back against the panel, he made a silent promise to an uncaring universe that he was, by god, going to beat the cancer and find a way to keep Richard from sacrificing himself.

✧ ✧ ✧

THE SHRIEK OF a chair being shoved violently back jerked Richard's attention back to Barrington. The discussions about *epistasis, gene amplification, alleles, DNA methylation,* and so forth, had flown right over Richard's head—and he suspected Madoc's as well—so Richard had fallen back into a contemplation of the past, perhaps to avoid thinking about his probable future ... or lack thereof. He was sitting at one of the lab tables, and turning the sword hilt over and over in his hands.

The first time the object had landed in his hand, it had seemed strange, unnatural, almost eerie. Now it fit his hand as if they had been made for each other. The idea that it might cease to exist ... along with himself was disturbing. Less for him than the sword. What if humanity needed it again and he had destroyed the only weapon that could hold back chaos? Richard knew how terrified and uncertain he had been when they thought they had lost the sword forever.

And if he managed to survive the closing of the veils between the multiverses, would he feel relieved ... or bereft if it were gone? Finally, were his musings really about a worry that he might be leaving the world defenseless, or was it a fear that the sword was the only thing that gave him relevance and meaning? Perhaps that was his father talking, reminding Richard of his inadequacies and failures when compared with his sisters.

Richard shook off his reveries, and focused on Barrington. The woman was fuming and glaring at the microscope. "What's wrong?"

"The fragments are too small, too broken to work, and the few that seemed intact enough to be useful, won't bond properly with her human DNA." Barrington stood and ran agitated hands through her long, frosted hair. "I don't know how the hell her human mother even kept the pregnancy. Fetuses are like parasites, and she"—Barrington nodded toward Rhiana—"would have been even more of a parasite. The mom should have miscarried."

"We used our abilities to ensure that didn't happen," Madoc said matter-of-factly." His head cocked to the side in a way that was decidedly inhuman. "That might be what drove her mad and ultimately killed her. The stress on the human body was too much."

"So, you weren't just a shitty father, you were a nightmare of a lover too," Barrington said.

"Of course, we were crafting a weapon, nothing more."

"So, why are you here then?" Halia asked.

The question seemed to stump the Old One. He stood silent, his eyes gone totally black. It was something Richard had seen many times with Cross and it was still horribly disturbing.

"I suppose," Madoc began slowly. "That I wanted closure and all debts paid before the end of all things."

"And that's not ominous," Richard muttered.

"Perhaps I should say, the state of things as we have known them for millennia."

Barrington's eyes narrowed as she studied Madoc. "If I could pull from you."

Halia shook her head and answered before the Old One could open his mouth. "He's not like me. He's not actually using matter to create a body. He's using magic to build a construct, there is nothing there for you to sample or test."

"The creature is correct, and you have no means to take a sample from my true form," Madoc said.

"So, where does that leave us?" Richard asked.

"That I can't restore her to what she was," Barrington said. "Half-human, half..." She gestured vaguely at Madoc. "Whatever, not to mention that—"

"So, she has to be either fully human or fully Old One," Richard interrupted.

Barrington gave an eye roll. "I don't know what you think would happen in your search for absolution, but she was never coming back. Oh, she might be conscious, but she'd be a drooling imbecile."

Richard started at Barrington in dismay. "I ... I don't understand."

"Do you know what happens to the brain in a long-term coma patient?" Barrington asked in the sort of condescending tone one uses with a child.

"No, please enlighten me."

"The brain atrophies. Literally shrinks, and that's the case with her. I did a full workup on her once I had the body, and that's all she is—a husk. Not a person who is going to wake up and be fine like in some Hollywood movie."

"So, this was all for naught," Madoc said.

Richard swallowed his rising anger, forcing himself to ask mildly, "Then why not tell us that days ago?"

Barrington shrugged. "Scientific curiosity. Blending incredibly divergent DNA was an interesting experiment. But I realize now that our science was never going to suffice."

"The realities between the multiverses are profoundly

different," Madoc said. "It's why we had to warp your reality to bring her to fruition."

Halia left her chair and joined them. "I could enter the body, rebuild it and make it function again but she wouldn't be Rhiana, it would be me wearing—pardon the expression—a meat suit."

"So, where does that leave us?" Richard asked.

"Put her back in the long-term care facility until her body breaks down enough and she finally dies," Barrington said.

"Or end it now," Madoc said.

"How many times do I have to say this? We are not killing anybody," Richard said through gritted teeth.

"Let nature take its course, pretend we didn't have all these high tech medical toys," Barrington said. "Keep her hydrated, but stop feeding her. They say starvation isn't a bad way to die."

"I vote for that," Madoc said.

"You don't get a vote," Richard said coldly, rounding on the creature.

"I am her father."

"No, her father is Todd Davinovitch. Her mother is Lottie Davinovitch. You're just the monster who brought her into this world to be a tool for your ambitions. You didn't raise her, love her, hold her when she fell and scraped her knees, or take her out for ice cream after her heart was broken when a high school romance ended." Richard's voice was rising. "So no, you don't have a say in this." Richard took a final look at the shriveled form in the bed. "I'll send for an ambulance and we'll return her to the care facility. Now I'm going home."

And see if I still have a marriage.

CHAPTER TWENTY-NINE
LETTING GO

"SO, WHAT DO you want me to do about it?"

Pamela Oort stared up at him from behind her desk. Her hand kept slipping over to the piles of paper as if her work as chief legal counsel for Lumina was more important than what Damon had just told her.

"Talk to him. Tell him this is not okay," Damon sputtered.

"Have you told him that?" Pamela asked.

"Of course."

"Then why on Earth would you think he'd listen to me if he won't listen to *you*? I'm just his sister, you're his husband. Also, at this point, this is just a hypothetical, none of this may even be possible."

"And if it is? Are you okay with your brother dying?"

"Of course not, but sometimes it's what's required. You were in the army, you knew there was a chance you'd be killed, but you took the risk for a greater good, a larger goal. Or at least I presume you were smart enough to realize that."

It was a dance that they had danced for years, where she never missed a chance to add a little venom to any statement. Damon was used to it, but today it really hit him wrong. "I was eighteen, of course I didn't think I could die. And yeah, there was a *chance* you'd catch a bullet, but it wasn't a lead-pipe cinch." Resting his hands on the desk, Damon leaned in on her. "Please, Pam, help me stop this, stop him."

She frowned off into space, flipping a pen between her fingers. "All right, I'll try, but I'm not going to bring it up until he does. I'm not comfortable with going behind his back."

"Meaning the way I did," Damon snapped.

She shrugged. "If the shoe fits."

"Well, I guess half-assed support is better than nothing." He spun on his heel and started for the door, only to be stopped by a gentle hand on his shoulder.

"I know you can't stand my father, but for all his many faults, he believed in service and duty. We were all raised to honor that, Richard is no different. And if you had the chance to protect not only the people you loved, but all of humanity, I know you wouldn't hesitate to make the sacrifice. Why can't you accept that from Richard?"

"Because I'm a selfish fuck, okay?"

She smiled at him. "Well, that's a refreshingly honest thing to say. Okay, I'll talk with him, but I don't expect it will affect his decision."

✦   ✦   ✦

EVEN IN THE shade of the veranda, the humidity in Houston felt like a wet blanket resting against her skin. Mosi took another sip of her lemonade, the cool liquid sliding down her throat gave the illusion that the temperature had dropped for an instant.

Feray, gazing off across the garden, was looking understandably stunned over the news Mosi had just imparted. She shook her glass setting the ice to chiming and shifted to face Mosi. "So, are you going to go?"

"I don't know. Growing up, Richard told me how Kenntnis recruited him, the promise Kenntnis made that if humanity followed his path he would give us the stars. So, I should want that, shouldn't I?" She hated the way her voice sounded so uncertain. Mosi shook her head.

"Has something changed?" Feray asked.

"Well, for one, I don't want to see Richard die, or whatever is going to happen when he uses the sword, and ... and ..."

"What?"

"There's this ... guy."

Feray tucked a leg under her and leaned in close. "Spill. Tell me *everything*."

"Do you remember Richard's nephew? I know he was introduced to you as a biologist, but he's in law enforcement."

"Interesting mix. Seems to take after Richard that way. Yes, I remember him... and how handsome he was." Feray added with a grin.

"Oh, he is. Plus he's smart, tough, thinks on his feet. He also drives me crazy at times."

"So, true love."

"No ... yes. Well, maybe. We haven't really talked about it or done anything."

"Would he be willing to be aboard the ship?"

"Maybe? I don't know." Mosi took another sip of lemonade. "What about you? Would you go?"

"I know my father would have been first in line. He dreamed of the stars, hence the name of the company." She gave a sharp laugh. "And believe me I wouldn't mind getting away from my cousins who all think they could run Ad Astra better than me. So I'm torn, I'd like to go, it would be like taking my dad with me, but I have to be sure the people who work for us are protected, because I'm pretty sure the cousins would, in fact, *not* run things better than me."

"Well, we've both got some time before we have to make a decision," Mosi said.

✧   ✧   ✧

RICHARD'S FINAL ACT before leaving Barrington's home had the woman howling in fury, because before she could object, he had drawn the sword and reduced the blob of Old One to goo. Madoc had watched by from the far side of the room. The threat of the sword had the edges of his human form bleeding into shifting, viscous colors as if he were ready to retreat back into his own dimension should Richard make the slightest move toward him.

"Relax," Richard said. "I gave you my word I wouldn't harm you."

"Hmm, I seem to recall you making the same promise to my child," the Old One retorted. Richard clinched his jaw so tightly that it shot pain into his skull. "Also, millennia of observing humans hasn't left me with much confidence in your promises."

"Well, you and your kind would know. You've perpetuated so many lies on humanity with your promises of paradise in exchange for holy war," Richard growled, still smarting from the fair but painful reminder.

Word came that the ambulance arrived, Madoc stroked a hand across Rhiana's forehead, then shifted into his normal form and vanished before the EMTs arrived. While Rhiana was being transferred into the vehicle, Richard and Barrington stood at the top of the front steps and exchanged meaningless and utterly insincere platitudes. Richard thanked her for her hospitality and efforts on behalf of Rhiana, and she stated she looked forward to working with his scientific team.

She vanished back into the palatial house, and one of the med techs indicated they were ready, so Richard climbed into the back of the ambulance. It was going to be a long drive back to Westlake Village. Richard settled on the floor of the vehicle while an EMT was on the other side of the gurney monitoring Rhiana's vitals. Richard reached out and took one fragile hand in his. Where the IV pierced the vein the skin around the needle was bruised.

"I'm sorry," he whispered. "I never wanted this for you."

Richard waited until Rhiana was settled back into her room, then called his assistant in the LA office and asked her to arrange for a car to the airport and a charter flight back to New Mexico. Five hours later he was finally on the plane and heading home. He had hoped it would ease his sadness, but the fact he and Damon had not spoken since their parting had him dreading the return. He really wasn't sure of the reception he was going to receive.

A warning light in the cockpit had them landing in

Phoenix while the gremlin in the wiring was chased down, so it was almost eleven at night before Richard finally reached the Lumina building. A note on the coffee table in Franz's precise handwriting informed him there was a plate in the fridge to be heated up. Richard was too tired and too nervous to even contemplating eating. He considered dumping the carefully prepared plate so the chef would never know, but felt guilty over being duplicitous. Apparently, Madoc's barb had buried itself deeper than he had realized.

He made his way down the hall to the master bedroom. A bedside lamp was on and Damon was propped against pillows, mouth open, snoring softly. The book he had been reading rested on his chest and his reading glasses had slid down his nose. Richard stood in the doorway studying that beloved face, the grey stubble dusting his chin and cheeks, the acne scars along his jawline, the curve of his lips and the arch of his brows.

Slipping off his shoes, Richard crossed the room, lifted the book off his husband's chest, pulled off the glasses, and turned out the light. Damon didn't stir and that more than anything told Richard how much the cancer had sapped from the man. A year ago he would have been instantly awake, and have snatched the pistol from beneath the bed ready to deal with any threat.

Not wanting to wake him, Richard pulled pajamas out of a dresser drawer, and went into the guest room to undress, shower and brush his teeth. He left his discarded clothing as a problem for future Richard and headed back toward the master bedroom trying to be quiet as he passed Mosi's room. He then remembered that Mosi wasn't home, she had gone to Texas to brief Feray. The fact she was out and about without the sword worried him. He would text her in the morning and arrange to have the weapon delivered to her, and find out when she was coming home.

Richard hesitated, then opened the door and stepped inside her room where the lingering scent of Mosi's favorite gardenia perfume hung in the air. The space was just as she had left it when she had headed off to college four years before. The posters on the wall featured a pair of actors who had been the objects of a teenage crush, as well as a cute kitten poster. The bookcase was overflowing with books each marking the parade of years, as the child had become a teenager, and the teenager a girl on the edge of womanhood. Richard picked up the well-worn copy of *The Wind In The Willows*. They had listened to the book on their very first day together when he'd come to take guardianship of a suspicious and grieving nine-year-old. Memories flowed around him like ripples in a quiet pool, how he had sat on the edge of the bed reading aloud *Narnia*, *Winnie-the-Pooh*, *The Lord of the Rings*, *Have Spacesuit—Will Travel*. How he had soothed her and sung her back to sleep after nightmares had torn her from slumber.

He returned the book to the shelf and moved on. A collection of stickers adorned the frame of the mirror over the dresser that held an MP3 player, and next to it a brush with a few long, jet black hairs caught in the teeth. Richard hit play on the device, expecting to hear some modern pop artist, but instead a mournful Irish ballad began to play, the lyrics all about loss, death, and grief. He shut it off.

The reality of his impending death hung like cobwebs

around him and he longed to have those nearest and dearest to him close at hand. It wasn't just Damon and Mosi, it was Pamela, Angela, Joseph, Dagmar, Eddie, the FBI contingent—Sam and her father Syd, Jay and Bob Franklin. Was it possible that Paul could help repair the breach between Richard and Amelia? And finally there was his father. Was reconciliation and forgiveness possible? Should it be attempted before he died?

Richard found himself staring into his own haunted eyes reflected back to him in the mirror, and sternly told himself this was pointless. Death awaited, but it was several years in the future. The best thing he could do now was get a night's sleep. He quietly closed the door to Mosi's room and returned to the master bedroom. Carefully lifting the covers he slid into bed. The slight dip of the mattress had Damon shifting, coughing. He turned his head to look at Richard.

"You're home."

"Didn't mean to wake you. Sorry I'm so late."

Damon spent a few moments pulling down the pillows and arranging them. Once settled he rolled onto his side. Their faces were only inches apart. "You didn't call."

"Neither did you," Richard answered.

"Guess that means we're both stubborn assholes, huh?"

The tight knot in the center of Richard's chest began to unwind. "Oh, probably. Or maybe just idiots." Shifting closer Richard bestowed a gentle kiss at the corner of Damon's mouth.

Damon wrapped an arm around him and pulled him against his chest. His husband's soft breaths ruffled his hair, and the tension began to leech out of Richard's body.

"So, what happened? Did the gene transplant work?" Damon asked.

Richard shook his head. "Even if the fragments of DNA weren't broken, Barrington couldn't get them to fuse with the human DNA. Also, her brain has atrophied."

"Where's Rhiana now?"

"Back at the care facility. Halia said she could fuse with Rhiana's body and rebuild it, but that she wouldn't be Rhiana. It would just be the AI wearing … wearing a meat suit." Richard felt Damon's arms tense around him. "Sorry, that was rather unpleasant phrasing."

"Yeah, that is kinda gross." There was a lengthy silence, then Damon asked gruffly, "Can you let it go now?"

"I guess I don't have any choice."

"Not really an answer, love."

"It's the best one I've got."

❖   ❖   ❖

LIFE FELL BACK into a routine with one notable difference; there were almost no incursions requiring the attention of a Paladin. Oh, there were the usual wars and rumors of wars, many probably fostered by the Old Ones who were currently residing among humans, but new eruptions just weren't happening. Apparently, the Old Ones were more worried about the humans crashing spaceships through their home universes than they were about chowing down on those humans.

It also meant that Richard was home most of the time, so the tension that had existed between them ever since

California continued and Damon hated it. Richard had that hunched shouldered, head down, cringy thing going that Damon had only seen when Richard was in the presence of his father. The thought that Richard had now placed Damon in that category added to Damon's emotional turmoil which Richard immediately assumed was Damon being angry at him. So on and on the cycle continued. Which wasn't to say Damon wasn't angry—he was—but it was more directed at a universe that seemed determined to encourage his spouse in his worst instincts.

Mosi's summer vacation had turned into a gap year, and Damon had a feeling it was because she wanted to spend as much time at home with Richard as she possibly could. Which only added to the feeling they were all attending a wake for a person who was still walking among them, and it just ratcheted the tension that much higher.

She and Paul talked on the phone every night, and when the young man realized she wasn't willing to come to Washington, he began making regular visits to New Mexico. Damon was waiting for the young couple to announce their engagement, but so far it hadn't happened. Damon didn't blame Paul for hesitating, he could only imagine how Paul's parents and grandfather—who was also Richard's asshole of a father—would react to Paul marrying into Richard's circle. They were also rock-ribbed Republicans and very conservative, and Damon didn't think Mosi being Native was going to sit all that well with the family. Frankly, they were all the whitest white people Damon had ever met. He did not want Mosi to face the soft bigotry that often went hand in glove with entitled white people. Not that Damon himself wasn't singularly lacking in melanin, but the army had knocked most of those biases out of him, and almost twenty years in law enforcement in a majority minority state had finished the process.

The other change was that Damon was now open to any treatments his docs might suggest. He had to be alive if he was going to keep Richard from sacrificing himself. Not that he had any fucking idea how he was going to accomplish that.

He was so deep in his own thoughts that Damon almost ran down Pamela as he was getting off the elevator as she was getting on. They did an awkward dance for a moment before they finally got sorted.

"Going down?" she asked.

"Yeah, I was going to hit the gym." He noted the thick briefcase and the laptop in its case, plus a large purse. "Want me to get any of that?"

"Thanks, but it's my version of the gym. I have a meeting with the governor. Jorge is driving me so I can keep working."

"Has Richard told you about ..." Damon made a vague gesture.

Pamela shook her head. "Not a word."

"Dickhead. He probably doesn't want people arguing with him and trying to talk him out of it."

"No, I think he doesn't want people to be upset. But I think he should give people a chance to say goodbye. It's never made a lot of sense to me that people gather after a person has died to talk about how great they were, or how much they meant to you. Seems like it would be nice for the person to hear that before they die, so I was thinking we might do a sort of pre-wake, once we have an idea when the ship might launch."

Damon's chest felt like it was about to explode. He stared at her, cleared his throat several times, and then gave a curt nod. "Sure. Why not?"

The elevator reached the ground floor with a soft bounce. The doors opened to reveal Jorge waiting. He took the laptop and briefcase, and Pamela and the security guard started for the front doors. "I should be back late afternoon and I'll stay for dinner. Spend more time with ... well, you know."

"Yeah, sure, that'll be great."

Damon walked stiff-legged over to the other elevator and keyed in the basement level that held the swimming pool and the gym. He then changed his mind and went down one more level where the weaponry and shooting range were located. He selected a .357 Magnum, loaded it, pulled on ear muffs and fired six shots in quick succession reducing the paper target to tattered shreds.

CHAPTER THIRTY
CHOOSING THE PATH

"I HAVEN'T BEEN back here since I was nine," Mosi said softly.

Paul had arrived for one of his periodic visits, and Mosi had suggested they not spend it in Albuquerque. As much as she wanted to stay home with Richard and Damon, she also felt like she couldn't breathe, the tension between the three of them was so thick it was choking her. So she suggested this outing to Chaco Canyon.

It was after Labor Day and middle of the week, so there were only a handful of campers, and mercifully only one person with a big camper van at the campground. The sun was beginning to drop behind the high rock walls of the canyon. Mosi stood gazing up at a hawk circling lazily over the canyon, its wings a glittering bronze against the azure sky.

Paul glanced up from where he was securing the final corner of the dome tent. He looked concerned. "Is this okay? We can always leave and go to Farmington or back to Albuquerque."

"No, you wanted to see some of my world. It isn't Shiprock or Window Rock, but it's where I needed to come." She half-turned, looked down at gave him a sad smile. "Truth is, I've been putting this off for years."

He stood, brushing the dust off the knees of his blue jeans. "So, why now?"

She bowed her head, figuring out how to put inchoate thoughts and feelings into words. "This is where one world ended and another began. Now, it feels like the world I've known is ending again, and I feel like I never properly laid this one to rest."

"They didn't let you go to the funerals?"

"My aunt let me attend, at least the ones for my parents and grandfather. Though Grandfather would probably have been upset. He was very traditional and he got a white man's burial." She paused, biting at her lower lip. "I didn't go to Abel's funeral, nobody did. They didn't find his body for weeks and there was a lot of superstition about him. Especially with me yelling about witches in the computer. Everyone thought I was as crazy as my brother." Mosi fell silent, remembering the day a white man had come to her aunt's home and told her she wasn't crazy. Aside from all the other reasons she loved Richard, this was the one that held the most power for her.

"I have a question." Paul seemed awkward and hesitant.

"Okay. Ask away."

"Why me? I mean, this seems very personal for you and I'm … what did you call me, an entitled git?"

"I think you called yourself entitled. I just agreed," Mosi said with a smile. She quickly sobered. "It's hard to explain. You feel like a hinge point for me. Like you're the doorway to this next life. I'm frozen, I don't know which way to go. Back? Stay in place? Make them let me go with them on the ship? Or something else? I'm sorry, I'm not making much sense."

Paul cleared his throat. "You know, whatever you decide. I'm there for it … for you … if you'd like me to be."

Mosi swallowed hard against the tightness in her throat and stepped in close. His arms closed around her and she rested her head on his shoulder breathing in the scent of him, the warmth of his embrace, the way his breath ruffled her hair.

"I'd like that," she whispered. Paul slipped a hand beneath her chin and tilted her head up. His eyes seemed to devour her face. He bent and brushed a soft kiss across her lips. They stood embracing for a long moment then Mosi said, "Okay, enough mushy stuff, let's finish setting up."

He laughed and released her. Mosi went to the car and lifted Damon's old footlocker from his army days out of the back of the SUV. Opening the footlocker, she pulled out an air mattress, and laid it on the floor of the tent. She then set it filling with the battery-operated pump while she removed the feather mattress and sleeping bags out of the car. Paul watched in bemusement as she laid the feather mattress on top of the now filled air mattress. Unzipping the two sleeping bags she zipped them together to form what was functionally a double bed, and the tossed a down comforter over the top.

"So, this is the New Mexico idea of roughing it?" Paul asked, his voice quivering on a laugh.

"No, this is *Richard's* idea of roughing it. Suffice it to say my guardian is not a fan of camping, he's a bit like a cat, but he put up with it for mine and Damon's sake. So, to convince him we had to make"—she gestured at the bed—

"concessions."

Mosi returned to the car and with Paul's help, pulled out the cooler, the camp stove, and propane bottles. Paul grunted at the weight of the cooler. "So, I'm guessing we're not dining on MREs."

"Nope, coq au vin tonight, steaks tomorrow, and if we decide to stay for a third night there's spaghetti sauce, meatballs, and pasta. Franz prepared a huge salad, and there's lunch meat and bread for sandwiches. I packed a bottle of wine, and Damon tucked in a bottle of port to go with our chocolate chip, oatmeal, and raisin cookies. Breakfast won't be as fancy. We can fry some bacon and eggs or eat cereal. I brought instant coffee and hot chocolate mix. It might be September, but it's going to be cold in the morning."

"And what's the plan for our days?" Paul asked as he helped her unload the tea kettle, and the pot with the coq au vin.

"Hiking, and more hiking, and laying some ghosts to rest before any new ones get made," Mosi added, tight lipped. She tipped water into another pot and set it and the rice to boiling.

While the rice cooked and the chicken dish heated they sat sipping wine and watched the twilight come in. There was the whisper call of a hunting owl, and the buzzards were settling onto the branches of a dead tree at the edges of the campground.

"Brrr," Paul said with a shiver. "That's some horror movie shit right there. I mean, seriously, why a dead tree?"

Mosi chuckled. "If there were leaves they couldn't look

for prey on the ground as easily."

"Oh, be all sensible and practical. Which is kinda weird when you consider that you fight monsters from other dimensions."

"I think it's very sensible and practical to fight monsters," Mosi countered as she began to fill a couple of paper plates with rice and the chicken.

"What, no good china and sterling silverware?" Paul teased as he accepted the plate, and she handed him a packet of plastic utensils.

"You really want to be washing dishes in the bathroom where there is only cold water?"

They perched side by side on the open back of the SUV and ate in companionable silence. "You cook this?" Paul asked after he'd helped himself to a second serving.

"Oh god, no. This is all Franz." She gave him a sideways glance. "Do you know how to cook?"

"I do. Mom's a brain surgeon, so her hours are often completely fucked. My dad wasn't about to learn, and eventually DoorDash and Uber Eats get not only expensive, but you get tired of reheating cold food. So, I learned. I'd make somebody a great wife," he added and gave her a quick grin while his eyes lingered fondly on her face.

Mosi felt herself blushing and she looked away. "If you're finished, let's pack up the trash, so the coyotes don't have a field day."

They carried the trash bag over to the latched dumpsters. Paul paused and stared up at the night sky that blazed with stars. "It's breathtaking," he murmured. "On the East Coast we don't have skies like this." He fell silent, just gazing up at this starry vault of heaven.

Throwing her head back, Mosi scanned the sky and wondered what it would be like to see the stars without the veil of Earth's atmosphere, and found herself once again torn over being on the ship. But she couldn't bear to watch Richard die. She wondered if she might be able to convince Damon to help her prevent Richard from ever boarding the ship. But would the former cop allow her to take Richard's place? She had a feeling he would not.

She glanced over at Paul, grateful that he had the unusual gift of knowing when to be silent. The stars were so bright that Mosi could make out the line of his jaw, the way the hair of his sideburns whorled and she how it felt when he rested his head against her bare breast.

After dinner they took a walk away from the campground, the flicker of campfires, and the low buzz of conversations. Paul was yawning by the time they turned back. They paused outside the tent and Paul gave her an adorably shy look. "Umm, thought I should ask, what are your intentions, ma'am?"

"To sleep," she answered with a smile.

He slumped in relief. "Oh good, I admit the idea of … well, you know, when there are other campers … around …"

"Yeah, you are noisy," she teased.

"And you're a brat," he huffed. "Go change and get cozy. I need a cigarette."

"Doesn't that usually happen after—"

"Go!" He ordered, pointed at the door of the tent. Chuckling, Mosi unzipped the door and slipped inside.

Despite the warmth of the tent, and the comfortable

weight of Paul's arm around her waist, Mosi's sleep was fitful. Around 4:00 A.M. she carefully lifted his arm and slid out from beneath the comforter. Dressing quickly she left the tent, grabbed a canteen of water, and started walking, retracing the steps of a terrified nine-year-old who had run to the ranger's station to find help on a night that still haunted her dreams. It took her past the Wijiji ruin where Grandfather had honored his late wife, and she had tried to tell him about the faces in the computer screen. She went on to the edge of the national park and climbed through the sagging barbwire fence.

There was the barest hint of grey to the east as she moved through the chamisa, sagebrush, and tough buffalo grass. Would there be anything left of the hogan? Would she be able to find it? Did she need to find it? Why was she doing this? She wasn't sure, but perhaps she could be able to answer that question if she found it.

Amazingly, she did. It had collapsed in a welter of logs, stone, and dirt; the fifty gallon drum that had served as a fireplace and cookstove jutted up from the rubble like a single blackened tooth. Mosi sank to the ground and sat contemplating the ruin, remembering her father's deep voice, her mother's graceful hands, her grandfather leaning on his walking stick as he tended the sheep. But mostly she thought about Abel. Tall and slim and so very smart. He had wanted to be a doctor when he grew up, and even though he was only fourteen, he had picked the med school he wanted to attend. If Abel were here today would he board the ship and go to see the stars? He'd always had his eyes focused on the horizon.

But the more she thought about it the less likely it seemed. Yes, he focused on the future, but that future always included returning home to the Navajo people to work and serve. If Richard succeeded and the threat ended, there would still be evil to fight. Humans had always been capable of great kindness and horrific evil, so shouldn't some of them stay behind to work for better outcomes, and to help humanity choose a better path?

Kneeling on the ground, the smell of sagebrush filling her nose and a golden dawn turning the dew trembling on the leaves of the Mormon tea bushes into topaz gems, Mosi realized that—like the door of the collapsed hogan—she had turned to face the east and Father Sun.

She had been raised by *bilagáana*, but she was still a woman of the *Diné*. The sky, the land, the four sacred mountains were part of her as she was part of them. Not in a religious way but as a citizen of Earth, so perhaps the way to honor the memory of her brother was to stay and try and save the planet. The sudden flow of tears caught her off guard. With her head bowed, they fell onto the dry ground and were quickly absorbed. It felt like she had made an offering to *nahasdzáán*, to Mother Earth, and her mother had accepted the gift.

✧　✧　✧

FOX WAS NO engineer, he was a theory guy, so he left it to others to figure out how to actually build engines that could fold space. What he was absolutely certain about was that the way the blade in the sword vanished and appeared was the key. Which meant that he and Halia found themself working in close proximity day after day and even into the night.

They were sitting side by side in the comfortable break room at the Rochester facility, waiting for calculations to run. The space had the feel of a college common room with rather shabby couches, a few tables, board games, and jigsaw puzzles crammed into a book case that also held a revolving library of shared novels. There was a large fridge and an espresso machine so high tech that it looked like it could power a spaceship.

Fox jumped when Halia wound her fingers through his and shifted on the couch so she could look at him.

"I need a favor," she said.

"Uh, sure."

"I want to learn to be more like a real person. Could you help me with that?"

"What does that even mean? You have all of human knowledge at your fingertips."

"Those are just words and images. I need somebody to show me."

"Show you what?"

"How things *feel,* how love works, how to be afraid. I watch movies and read descriptions, and I've been watching porn—"

Fox had been slouching, now he came bolt upright. "*What?*" It emerged almost as a squeal. "That is … that is … completely inappropriate. You shouldn't be doing that."

"Why not? Lots of people do."

"That may well be, but it doesn't mean it's good to do that."

"But I want to understand love," Halia said.

"That's not love, that's sex."

"But sex and love are very much intertwined."

"Yes, but love comes from here." He tapped his temple. "And here," and he laid a hand over his heart.

"The heart is a large muscle that pumps blood, it doesn't think or feel, well I guess it can feel pain or at least cause pain, and the brain can trigger endorphins, but neither seem to explain Damon and Richard, or Paul and Mosi."

"Oh, I see," Fox said in a colorless tone.

Halia took his face between her hands and studied him. "That knowledge hurts you."

"A little. Not like I thought I ever had a chance—"

"So, you loved Mosi or is it Paul you crave?"

"Mosi, and it was more of a crush that might have become something, if things … if I were different."

"I like how you are."

"Well, you'd be about the only person," Fox said rather bitterly.

"That's not true. Everyone here likes you, and so do Damon and Richard and Mosi too."

"That's nice, but liking isn't love. Love is this feeling in your chest, it's wanting to be with someone all the time, getting a thrill when you hear their voice, doing things together that go more easily because you're doing it with that one, special person."

"But isn't sex part of that?"

"Yes, of course, but it's not everything. it's more like an added bonus."

"Well, I like to do things with you, and I've been making

this body more and more anatomically correct so will you have sex with me?" Fox goggled at her. "I see, you've never had sex," she said kindly.

"No! Of course I've had sex. Why are you on about this?"

"Because I want to be more human, and I need someone to teach me."

"And you pick me? Halia, I'm probably the worst person you could ask. I don't do person very well. I'm socially awkward, I don't pick up emotional cues all that well—"

Halia suddenly leaned in and kissed him. She had apparently gotten something from all those videos because it was a really good kiss.

"There's a cue. Now let's go do sex together."

Much later, and wrung out from having several powerful orgasms, Fox was sprawled on his back with Halia resting on top of him. Her long black hair tickled his chest and arms, her breath was soft against his face. It was almost like she was a real woman, except there was no sheen of sweat on her slender body, and her eyes still weren't normal.

"So, what do you think?" Fox croaked out.

"It was interesting, but I don't think I have the nerve endings quite right.

"I don't understand."

"Well, you were making sounds that indicated either immense pleasure or immense pain—"

"It was pleasure," Fox hastened to assure her.

"But I didn't get the nuances. I just felt your weight on me, and how I was stretched to accommodate you down there." She gestured at her crotch. But I didn't feel what the literature describes.

"Well, you are sort of building a body by transforming energy into matter so maybe some steps are missing despite you knowing everything about human anatomy," Fox said.

Halia sighed. "Perhaps I should have taken over Rhiana's body. That body probably does have the right nerve endings."

Fox rolled her off him, and propped himself up on an elbow. "Wait, what?"

"I offered to inhabit Rhiana's body, but once I explained to Richard that it wouldn't be Rhiana who would be walking around, but me wearing a Rhiana meat suit, it was clear he didn't want that."

"That body was pretty damaged from the sword and the coma."

"Yes, but I could have fixed all of that, rebuilt the body. What I couldn't repair was the mind, meaning the memories, the emotions, the essence of who she was. That was all gone."

A mad notion began to bloom. "But you can rebuild the body."

"Uh huh." Her eyes were madly spinning silver again. "Ooooh." She drew out the word in dawning wonder. "Yes! Yes, I think I see where you're going."

They stared at each other for a long moment. "We need to take this to Richard—" Fox began, only to be interrupted.

"No, we need someone sneaky."

❖   ❖   ❖

"So, your plan is convincing Richard that there was a miracle despite everything he was told," Damon said slowly.

"And despite us having no truck with miracles."

He was out in the Lumina parking lot FaceTiming with Fox and Halia. The August sun glinted off the windshields of the parked cars, and the heat seemed to dance off the pavement.

"So, maybe don't tell him?" the Brit said.

Damon paced, sweat-slick hands gripping the edges of his iPad. "This feels wrong."

"There is a vital, living person who can be saved if you allow us to do this," Halia said. She had lost her usual bubbly delivery, and in that cold, implacable voice Damon heard echoes of Kenntnis.

Damon said just that. "You sound like Kenntnis, with him it was always all about the cold equation."

"Because in a war you fight to win. I may not have all of my progenitor's memories, but his goals were very clear to me, to protect life in this universe. Closing the veils between multiverses would do that, and I am willing to pay any price. As for the morality of this ... if that is what's required, then so be it."

"Okay, I'm in."

CHAPTER THIRTY-ONE

RICHARD AND MOSI IN WASHINGTON, DAMON REALIZED HE HAD AN OPENING TO PUT THEIR LET'S-SAVE-RICHARD-FROM-HIMSELF PLAN IN MOTION. HALIA INTERCEPTED HIM AS HE REACHED THE PRIVATE ELEVATOR.

"WHATCHA DOIN'?" SHE asked.

"Need to talk to Jorge before I leave tomorrow."

"I can handle the security footage, there's no reason to involve Jorge."

"Yeah, actually there is. If you monkey around with footage and we don't have him on board, Jorge's gonna freak out and contact Richard and Mosi to report that someone had hacked into our system. I need him to buy in on our little plan."

Halia cocked her head to the side like a kitten contemplating a puzzling problem. "Would you call it *little*?"

"That was irony, sweetie." Damon paused. "Or maybe it's sarcasm, I can never keep straight which is which."

"Irony—the use of words to express something different from and often opposite to their literal meaning. Sarcasm—a cutting, sneering, or caustic remark," Halia said, her eyes spinning silver again. "So, irony. What you said was irony."

"Thank you Ms. Thesaurus," Damon said with a grin, as he tapped her on the tip of her nose.

Halia pulled a face. "I think I was Ms. Dictionary, and *that* was perilously close to sarcasm. So, go be persuasive," she added and walked away.

Damon rode the elevator down to the fourth floor and walked into Jorge's office. There was a smattering of crumbs in his beard as he munched on an empanada, while with his free hand he was scrolling on his computer. At Damon's entrance, he set aside the half-eaten pastry and wiped his beard.

"Hey Damon," He gestured toward a grease stained paper bag. "Risha made empanadas. Want one? There's still a cherry and a *dulce la leche* left."

"Thanks, that cherry sounds good."

"So, whatcha need?" Jorge asked as he handed over the pastry and a napkin.

"I'm going to be traveling the next couple of days."

"Okay, we'll have you covered."

"Well, that's the thing, I'd rather you not keep tabs on me and also that you remove any surveillance footage showing where I've gone and who I've met. Oh, and I also need you to turn off the location setting on my phone. I need it to look like I never left home."

The Hispanic man's eyes narrowed. "You're asking me to break protocol—protocol set by my boss?"

"Yeah, I am."

"I'm gonna need a really fucking good reason if I'm gonna go behind Richard's back like that."

"Okay, but this is not to be spread around to *anyone*, you understand?"

"That depends on what you're about to tell me. I'm not gonna lie to my boss."

They measured glares, then Damon sighed. "Okay, short version, the big brains in the science division think there is a way to close off our universe from the other monsterverses."

"That's a good one. I like that, monsterverses."

"It would require the sword, which requires a Paladin." Damon paused.

"So far I'm not seeing a problem," Jorge said.

Damon sucked in a deep breath. "Said Paladin is probably gonna die."

Jorge's brown eyes widened. "Shit."

"Yeah."

"No way Richard would let Mosi do that."

Damon nodded. "Exactly, but there may be a way to prevent that, which is why I'm gonna be traveling, and it's really, really important that Richard not know about this."

Jorge spun his chair back to the multiple screens on his desk. "Okay, I've got plenty of footage of you puttering around here at home. Once you're back we'll scrub anything that shows where you really were and slide in the puttering part." His hands were flying across the keyboard. "If Richard should check he'll never know you left the building."

Damon gripped the younger man's shoulder. "Thank you for this."

"*De nada.*"

✧　✧　✧

THE OUTER OFFICE of Angela's senatorial office was buzzing with activity. It struck Richard how much vibrant diversity there was among the staff, both age, race, gender, and sexual. Which made sense given New Mexico's demographic makeup, not to mention Angela herself with her Hispanic mother and Black father.

The woman herself came bouncing out of the inner office and threw her arms around him. Angela was five foot nothing, a pleasant change for Richard, who was accustomed to everyone towering over him. After the hug she released him and held him at arm's length.

"Yep, still too thin," she said with a disapproving shake of her head.

"And you are still a bossy woman." Some of the staff looked shocked until Angela's peal of laugher rang out.

"Come in, come in," she ordered, as she lead him back into the inner office. "What brings you to Washington?"

Richard forced a smile. "I wanted to see you."

"I'll be home for the Christmas recess," she said as she settled onto the sofa.

Richard took the chair opposite her and studied her. Her short bobbed hair showed streaks of grey now, and wrinkles had joined the laugh lines around her dark brown eyes. She wore a tailored pale salmon-colored suit that set off her rich dark skin perfectly, elegant pumps, and an exquisite waterfall silver heishi necklace. Richard remembered when he had first encountered her sixteen years ago. Then she had been wearing a blood and flesh spattered rubber apron and face shield, while holding a vibrating bone saw.

"Guess I should have thought of that, but I wanted to see you. Also Mosi is here visiting—"

"Well, clearly not me," Angela huffed. "You tell that young lady she better get her ass over here."

Richard chuckled. "I will, but she's here visiting a young man, so she'll have to tear herself away."

Angela wriggled like a happy puppy and slid toward the edge of her chair. "Oooh, tell me more, as in everything."

"Well, I guess fate has a real sense of irony, because he's my nephew, Paul."

"How the hell did *that* happen?"

"It seems to be an Oort family tradition to keep secrets. He's an agent for Homeland Security but my sister thinks he's doing graduate studies in biology, though I have a feeling Mosi is going to make him come clean with them."

"Why on earth would he hide that?"

Richard shrugged. "Maybe because he grew up listening to my father and oldest sister talk about how law enforcement is a terrible, low-class career choice."

"Your family are assholes, you know that, right? Well, except for Pamela, and maybe this kid."

"Still, I'm hoping this liaison will open the door for me to see them again," Richard said quietly.

Her eyes narrowed with suspicion. "You've always been damn good at poker face, but I know you pretty damn well, and you're hiding something. So, what's really going on?"

"There's a young scientist working with us who has found a way to transcend light speed." He left it at that.

A worried frown deepened the lines on her forehead.

"Richard, my Spidey-sense is going off so what—"

Richard rolled his eyes. "You and Damon with your pop culture references."

"Just because you're an effete opera snob." She waved her hands in the air. "Do not distract me. You're not about to go do something noble and stupid, are you?" She glared at him.

"No. And it's still just theory right now." And this time it seemed his poker face succeeded because she looked relieved and relaxed, saving him from further interrogation where he might be tempted to reveal it was all going far more quickly than anyone anticipated, and what that meant for him.

"Okay. Well, tell me all the gossip. Which means how is Damon doing?"

"Surprisingly well. His medical team is working with some new treatments and they seem to be having a good effect."

"Excellent. And Pamela, is she still a judgmental bitch?"

"Really?"

An impish grin curved her lips. "I'm sure she says the same about me."

Richard felt an answering smile touch his lips. "Well, yes. Though she doesn't call you judgmental, more that you're a shocking hoyden with no dignity."

"I rest my case on the judgmental thing."

After that they talked of the other people who had been part of their lives. Joseph, who had been the head of Lumina security, but after retirement had bought a sailboat and settled in San Diego. Jorge's newest baby daughter. Angela spoke of her own large family. After forty minutes there was a discreet knock at the door and a voice said, "Senator, your two o'clock is here."

Richard quickly stood up. "I've kept you too long."

She stood and hugged him again. "I'll see you at Christmas, we'll celebrate your birthday with my great-great grandfather's homemade eggnog and some biscochitos."

Richard had a dislocating moment when it truly struck him that this might be his last birthday. His face felt frozen, but he forced a smile. "Looking forward to it."

✧   ✧   ✧

MOSI ALLOWED HER rental car to roll to a stop at the curb in front of a brownstone in Beacon Hill. Gazing at the light pouring through the windows, she had a moment of dislocation as she realized that she had been going to school just a few miles from Richard's estranged family. She placed the car in park and the electric engine whined into silence. She then sat, her fingers playing nervously across the top of the steering wheel, trying to decide if she was really going to go through with this.

Huffing out a breath, she opened her handbag and pulled out the small, black jeweler's box and flipped open the lid. Nestled against the black velvet was a lovely rose gold Victorian opal and garnet engagement ring. Closing her eyes Mosi replayed the night before.

Paul's hand had been a warm pressure against the small of her back as he guided her through the door of the small and elegant French restaurant in Georgetown. Once inside, she realized that all the tables were empty, but a bottle of champagne was chilling in a *seau à glace*. Candles were flickering on the table, and a large bouquet of white and yellow roses formed a centerpiece.

Paul had caught her expression, and had run a hand nervously through his hair. *"Too much?"* he had asked, his voice jumping a bit.

She had been both embarrassed and touched by the effort he gone to, so she had pushed aside the embarrassment—and frankly, dread—and so, she had shaken her head. The *maître d'* had clearly been giddy over the chance to make this engagement dinner memorable, so he was really overdoing it as he led them to the table. Mosi had desperately cast about to find some way to short circuit this until she could talk with Paul, but nothing occurred. Then the ring box had been pulled out and Paul had held it out to her. All she could think was that thank heavens he hadn't gotten down on one knee.

She had folded his fingers back over the box and said, *"I can't."* His look of hurt, confusion, and devastation had her hastening to explain.

"I can't do this so long as your family and mine are es-tranged. Richard and I are in Washington because he's saying goodbye. How can we have a wedding when your mother, his eldest sister, won't be there or Richard's father? I can't bear for Na sha dii *to go to his death with the emotional wound still there. And how do we explain where we met and how we met without lying? And lies are toxic. They're why Richard and his father haven't spoken in fifteen years. It's why my family is dead."*

Paul had been amazingly understanding. He had insisted she keep the ring while she thought about it and he tried to figure out how to meet her requirements. Which was why she hadn't told him what she planned. She wouldn't out him to his family, that was on him to figure out how to tell them the truth, but she was going to confront the man whose disapproval had driven Richard for all of his life.

Sucking in a deep breath, Mosi opened the door and climbed out. The heels of her ankle boots seemed loud on the flagstone walk. She reached up to ring the bell, but the door opened before she could. Apparently, her arrival had not gone unnoticed.

Mosi recognized the tall, spare man. When she was a child, she'd gotten ahold of a photo album that Richard kept hidden away in the back of a drawer. There had been pictures of the three Oort children, a small and delicate woman with pale blonde hair who had clearly bequeathed her looks to her son, and Richard's father, the man who was now confronting her. Judge Robert Oort no longer matched the photo in the album. His light brown hair had gone white, and lines of disapproval were etched into his face. What hadn't been apparent from the photo was the dark blue of his eyes, so dark they almost appeared purple. Mosi saw those same eyes when she gazed at Paul.

"Yes? May I help you, young lady?"

"My name is Mosi Tsosie. I was raised by your son and his husband. I came here to see you, but also your daughter."

"Did Richard put you up to this?" Robert asked, his tone cold.

"No, he doesn't know I'm here. Neither does your grandson."

"And how is it you know my grandson?" In answer, Mosi just pulled out the jewelry box and flipped it open. Oort's eyes widened. "That ring has been worn by brides in our family for almost two hundred years," he said.

"Yeah, I know. Guess we have a lot to talk about, huh?"

For a long moment, it hung in the balance, then Robert Oort gave a sharp nod and stepped aside. Mosi entered. A woman's voice called out, "Who was it, Papa?"

Robert moved toward the room from which the call had emanated. Mosi followed and found herself in a living room that felt very claustrophobic as it was filled with heavy furniture upholstered in dark blue fabric, velvet drapes and wood flooring. It was very different from the brightness of the Lumina penthouse.

A portly man in his mid-fifties was seated in a recliner, sipping a cocktail. An attractive woman about the same age was seated on the couch, a crochet hook in her hands and a section of lace falling across her lap. There was a definite resemblance between Pamela and her older sister. Both Amelia and her spouse were gazing at her in confusion.

"I'm Mosi," she said.

The confusion on Amelia's face cleared. She set aside the lace and stood. "Pamela told me about you." She then shot a nervous look toward her father. "Pam and I talk ... occasionally."

"She has the family engagement ring," the judge said.

Amelia looked at her in surprise. "Oh, Paul asked me to get it out of the safety deposit box a few weeks ago, but how ..." Her voice trailed away.

"I haven't said yes and I won't until Paul explains some things to all of you, and until I see how this conversation goes. I'm here about my *Na sha dii*. Richard," Mosi added when she saw the confusion on the older people's faces.

Robert gave her a withering look. "Richard made it very clear that he wishes to have nothing to do with his family."

"The way I heard, you started it," Mosi shot back. "But I'm not here to rehash the past. I'm here because Richard is planning ... going to do something that he won't survive and he's grieving. Despite everything, he misses you." She turned to face the judge. "Especially you. He wants so badly to have your love and respect. I think he'd like the chance to say goodbye, but he's scared to reach out, and scared to see you again. So, I'm asking for him."

"But ... but Paul ..." Amelia's confusion seemed to make further words impossible.

"I love your son, I do." She set the open jewelry box on the coffee table, the light pulling fire from the opal and glittering on the garnets. "But I can't choose between families, and he shouldn't have to either. Either we heal this breach or I give back the ring. Because I'll always be there for my *Na sha dii*, like he was for me."

"Does Paul know you're here?" It was the first time Brent van Gelder had spoken.

"No."

"She didn't discuss this with Richard either," the judge added. He glanced over at Mosi. "You're a rather intrepid young lady, aren't you?"

"I fight monsters, so you don't scare me at all."

The elderly man's eyebrows shot up. There was the sound of the front door opening and closing. Brent struggled to lower the footrest on his recliner, and then started for the door of the living room only to fall back when Paul came striding in.

Mosi set her hands on her hips and glared at him. "Really? How—"

"I paired our phones." Mosi gave a huff of outrage. "Look, I was worried, okay? Neither you nor Richard have the sword right now."

"You know about that?" Amelia asked faintly.

"Yeah, Mom, I do. Because ... because"—he sucked in a deep breath—"I'm not in graduate school at Duke."

"You dropped out?" Brent bellowed.

"Never dropped in. I applied to Homeland Security." He pulled out his identification and flipped it open to reveal his badge. The gold badge with blue enamel banding had emblazoned in gold on the enamel, HOMELAND SECURITY INVESTIGATIONS, and on the bottom it stated SPECIAL AGENT. "I knew you'd be pissed, but I wasn't cut out to be a high school biology teacher, and I'm not smart enough to get the PhD and be a researcher. Also, the world's got problems. I wanted to try to help."

"Did Richard put you up to this?" Brent demanded.

"Of course not. I hadn't seen my uncle for years. Until this May, when I was sent in because of the attack on the MIT graduation." He turned to look fondly at Mosi. "That's when I met the most amazing woman in the world."

"You are so annoying," Mosi said. "I wanted this to be about Richard and finding out if I could stand your family and if they could stand me."

"How's it going so far?" Paul asked. That twinkle that always devastated her was back in those blue eyes.

"Jury's still out." Brent gave a huff of annoyance, Amelia

looked confused and sad, while the judge was inscrutable. Mosi sighed. "Pamela had to choose between family and Richard. I didn't want that for you," she said to Paul.

"And I would never make you choose, either," Paul said.

"Which seems to leave you both at an impasse because Richard made his choice, to live a life in contravention of God's laws," Robert Oort said.

Mosi shook her head, unable to fathom what she was hearing. "Your son has spent years literally fighting monsters to protect the people of this world and you're pissed because he's in a loving marriage? And now, when I tell you he's probably going to die, you don't care? I can't believe people like you actually exist in the world, and that you somehow managed to father the best, kindest, bravest, and most loving person I've ever known." Mosi rounded on Amelia. "He's your *brother*. Don't you care?" Amelia looked at her father, then turned her head away from Mosi.

Paul was standing stricken as he looked from his mother to his father to his grandfather. "Please," he whispered, but said nothing more, as if he didn't know exactly what he was asking for.

Mosi counted her heartbeats, waiting for someone to say something. No one did. Tears flooded her eyes and her throat was aching. Furious, she blinked hard, then snatched the ring off the table and shoved it into Paul's hands. "Goodbye, Paul," she whispered.

She flung herself out of the room, heels beating a staccato on the wood floor as she rushed to the front door. From behind her she heard Paul call, "Mosi!"

The door closed, cutting off anything else he might have said.

✧ ✧ ✧

RICHARD GENTLY STROKED Mosi's hair, her head resting in his lap, while she sobbed bitterly. Mosi had returned from back East with a frozen expression and a shadow in her eyes that told Richard something terrible had happened. He had let her be for a day, knowing she would talk when she was ready. He knew how much he hated to be pushed to talk when he was in emotional pain, so it was easy for him to remain patient. Finally, she shared, detailing in an emotionless and colorless voice about how Paul had proposed. How she had delayed answering him until she could talk with Paul's parents and Richard's father, to try to bridge the rift between the two branches of the family. And that's when the tears had started to flow.

Damon had slipped away, understanding that she needed her *Na sha dii* now, and Mosi had flung herself onto Richard's lap, her heartbreaking tears dampening his trousers.

"I'm sorry. I'm so sorry I went behind your back and didn't tell you what I was planning. I thought I could make things better, so you could see your dad again, and I could tell Paul yes, but it all went bad and I told him … I told him … goodbye. I had to because I can't be with people who don't love you and accept you." Her voice was muffled and husky with tears.

Richard gave her shoulder a squeeze. "My dearest, darling girl, you can't live your life through me or make your decision based on what you think would help me. You need to find your own path, make your own way, build your own family." Richard paused then asked softly, "Do you love my nephew?"

She raised a tearstained face. "So much."

"Then be with him. The problems that exist between me and my father should not be yours. All I've ever wanted for you was a normal life filled with love and joy."

She sat up and wiped away tears. "I want that for you too, *Na sha dii*, because you already have that. Which is why I should be the one to go, so you and Damon can stay together forever."

"Nothing is forever, dear heart. All we have is now." Richard took her hands in his. "Mosi, do you know what's the greatest tragedy for any parent? To have their child pass before them. If I lost you, my life would be blighted forever. You are the best and most precious thing in my world. And I know Damon feels the same. Do you know why I can face what's coming with equanimity?" She shook her head, long strands of hair sticking to her damp cheeks. Richard tenderly brushed them away. "Because I'll know that you'll be safe. And you know what else? Getting to walk you down the aisle and dance at your wedding would be the best gift you could ever give me." Mosi gave a little hiccupping sob and Richard hugged her close. "So, go to your young man, and tell him yes."

She sniffed and looked about. Richard quickly pulled out his handkerchief before her sleeve was deployed and he once again had that dislocating vision of the young woman seated at his side and the nine-year-old who had cried when he'd told her she wasn't crazy or possessed by evil spirits, and the way she'd looked up at the strange white man who was offering her a piece of cloth. It seemed Mosi remembered too, for she gave a watery chuckle and said just as she had all those years ago, "It'll get all dirty."

Richard played his part. "That's what it's for."

"I love you so much, *Na sha dii.*"

"And I love you ... so much." He gave her a gentle shove. "Now go and call Paul."

She jumped to her feet, leaned down, and kissed him on the cheek then ran out of the living room. Richard stood and went in search of Damon. He found him in the kitchen, leaning on the counter sipping a coffee and chatting with Franz. Seeing Damon on his feet and not sitting filled Richard with joy and relief at this display of returning strength.

Damon raised an eyebrow. "So?"

"All sorted. She's calling Paul now."

"So exciting!" Franz exclaimed. "Will I be making a wedding cake?"

Richard gave him a smile. When Richard had first met the chef, his hair had been brown. Now it was mostly grey and his paunch was a bit more pronounced, but he had lost none of his cheerfulness or pleasure in his role as the man who kept them all fed.

"I believe you will, Franz."

"I must check my books," Franz said, his voice getting fainter as he rushed toward the bookcase that held a staggering number of cookbooks. "Fondant or just frosting," he was mumbling to himself.

Damon and Richard exchanged looks and smiles. "Shall we take a stroll, it's a nice day," Damon said.

"Love to."

They rode the elevator downstairs and went out the back door and made their way to the small hidden box canyon with its small spring surrounded by three slender cottonwood trees. The tufts of buffalo grass crunched beneath Richard's shoes as they walked arm-in-arm to the small bench that years ago Damon had placed in the shade of the trees.

"You are turning the company over to Mosi, right?" Damon asked.

"Of course. She's brilliant, dedicated. She'll continue Lumina's work … minus the monster killing. At least, I hope there won't be any more monster killing."

"Just the human variety," Damon said wearily. They sat in contemplation of all they had seen during their careers in law enforcement, recalling the evil humans were capable of committing.

Damon shook it off and said, "Then you should probably start training her now in all that boring corporate shit. You don't want her struggling to get up to speed the way you did."

"You're right, of course, but it will be another reminder for her that I … we won't be there. And I suppose the other company officers could train her."

"No, you should do it, so both of you have more time together because once she's married … well, she probably won't be living with us any longer. We're not exactly set up for a young married couple."

Richard's heart seemed to clench at the thought. "I … I hadn't thought of that. But they could stay in Albuquerque, yes? Until we leave, and then they could have the penthouse."

"Paul has a career. In Washington. And Mosi was planning on grad school," Damon reminded him. "I think we have to resign ourselves to the fact that she's all grown up, and they always leave the nest."

CHAPTER THIRTY-TWO

THE FUTURE LOOKS BIG

THE PASTURE BETWEEN the road and the house was filled with the soft buzzing of bees making their lazy dance from one alfalfa blossom to the next. The humans rushing about the Armandirez property, into and out of the house on Rio Grande Boulevard, were anything but lazy. Instead, it was a hive of frenzied activity as the final preparations for the wedding were completed. Damon had sought the relative quiet out front to just savor the moment, but that peace was interrupted when Eddie came rushing up.

"We got a crisis," the scientist panted.

"The bride ran? The groom bolted?" Damon asked.

"What? No. We got a tie crisis. None of us know how to do a full Windsor or a half Windsor for that matter. I can barely manage a ... a ... that simple one."

"Four-in-hand," Damon said.

"Yeah, that."

"You really need Richard. He's the tie expert." Damon lightly touched the coral and silver bolo tie he was wearing and said, "The bolo is the official tie of New Mexico, so I'm going traditional."

"More like you're being lazy," Eddie shot back. "And you know that looks really weird with that grey morning suit."

"I'm just impressed you know what a morning suit is," Damon said.

"I do now since I had to rent the damn thing."

"Well, lead on. I'll try to deal with the tie crisis."

They walked around the sprawling adobe house to the sweeping expanse of the back lawn. A soft breeze shook the massive cottonwood trees that lined the irrigation ditch, and in the back pasture a horse nickered softly. It set a counterpoint to the musicians, members of Richard's chamber music group, who were tuning their instruments and playing a few bars of the music that had been selected for the ceremony. A trumpeter had been added to the usual mix of people who came to the penthouse every Thursday night to make music.

The catering staff were finishing setting up the chairs and awning for the actual ceremony. Brent and Jason were sitting in one of the completed rows. Brent's mouth was moving a mile a minute and Jason had a fixed smile on his face that indicated he was praying for death even as his soul left his body. Damon wondered again how a woman as bright as Dr. Amelia Oort had shackled herself to a man like Brent. He resolved to go back and rescue the journalist after the tie crisis had been resolved.

Off to the side was an enormous tent with tables, chairs, and the buffet that was already groaning under the weight of the food that had been prepared by Franz and Angela's mother, Josefina. They seemed to have entered into a good-natured rivalry over who could make the most succulent dishes. It was no surprise that Cross was already into the food, and Franz was descending on him like a heat-seeking missile, waving his arms over his head while he yelled threats of dismemberment. Cross grabbed one last roll and fled the tent.

The smells were enticing and Damon's stomach gave a loud growl. He gave his belly a pat. After so many rounds of chemo it was a pleasure to be hungry again, and he hoped that at his next appointment he'd be ringing the bell to celebrate the end of his treatments.

Just before they reached the casita where Paul and his groomsmen—most of whom were friends from work and one classmate from Brown—were getting ready, Eddie laid a hand on Damon's arm.

"I wanted to let you know that I'm going to be with you on the Ark."

"Eddie, why?"

"To travel to a distant star system, settle on an alien world, what a dream for a kid who grew up on *Star Trek* and *Star Wars*." He gave an awkward throat clearing and a faint blush touched his cheeks. "And Feray and I have been working together on all the details for a viable colony: Seed stock, the hydroponic gardens in case this Fold thing doesn't work and we've gotta survive for way longer than a few days, animal embryos, and the breeding stock to carry those embryos. Plus portable shelters in case Trappist-1e doesn't have suitable materials to build housing."

"Well, one thing we need to do is come up with an actual name for our new home. Trappist-1e sounds like a colony of celibate monks and I think I sense a bit of romance in the air."

"Okay, busted, she's amazing—and a forty light-year long distance relationship doesn't sound very viable, so yeah, I'm coming."

Damon clapped the younger man on the shoulder. "I'm glad, it'll be great to have you along, and I know Richard will feel the same."

"Thanks." He ducked his head. "Though it's gonna be hard to see Richard—"

Damon threw up a hand to stop the flow of words. "Let's not go there. Not today."

Eddie nodded and Damon knocked and then pushed open the door to the casita. When they entered Paul was seated in a chair with Fox standing behind him and adroitly tying the intricate knot.

"Looks like you got it all under control," Damon called.

"How the hell?" Eddie muttered.

"He's a Brit?" Damon suggested.

"I don't think one example proves a thesis," Eddie grumbled.

Fox glanced over. "It's one of the few things my dad tried to teach me that I actually learned. I was rubbish at all the rest."

"Well, then I'm going to go back to my supervising," Damon said.

"Are my parents here yet?" Paul asked.

"I saw your dad. I'm guessing your mom is in the house with Mosi."

"And Granddad?" Damon just shook his head. "Guess I keep hoping he'll change his mind," Paul said sadly.

The look on the young man's face just hurt Damon's heart. It was then he noticed that Paul was wearing the Oort family signet ring. From the first moment Damon had met

Richard the younger man had always worn the intricate gold ring. The fact he had passed it on was further evidence that his husband was slowly, methodically preparing himself for death.

Not if I can help it, he thought as he left the guest house.

✧   ✧   ✧

RICHARD HAD RETREATED to the living room, carefully slipping out of his shoes because Josefina was fierce about protecting the snowy white carpet. He was trying to stay out of the way until it was time for the ceremony to begin, and also to have some time to himself.

He could hear Franz and Josefina in the kitchen still cooking. From the master bedroom came the sound of women's voices like a chorus of lovely bells all hitting different keys. His sister Amelia's soft soprano, Angela's rich alto overlaid with the music of her Spanish heritage. Dagmar's husky tones, her German accent rounding the vowels. Doli Begay, Mosi's cousin, had that tiny hitch between the words and the upward lilt on the ending syllables. Her tones fell between Angela and Amelia. Feray's lilting soprano had a twang to it from her Texan accent. Pamela, sharp and high, like a wind chime constructed of icicles. At first he had thought Mosi was responding, but the timbre was off slightly, and then Richard realized it was Halia. Apparently, the fascination with Mosi was not confined to emulating her looks.

Mosi's voice was not among them. He wasn't surprised, Mosi herself hadn't been talking, when he'd last seen her seated in front of a dressing table mirror while Feray arranged small silver and turquoise stars in her jet black hair. Mosi had looked thoughtful enough that some might have called her expression grim. Richard couldn't help but wonder if they were about to have their very own runaway bride.

With a sigh Richard looked down, contemplating his hands; on the left his wedding ring, on the right where had once rested the family's gold signet ring that had been in the family since 1743 there was only a pale white line. He had passed the ring to Paul a few days before. Even if Paul's last name wasn't Oort, he was functionally the only male heir.

A whisper of material on the carpet pulled him from his brown study and he looked up. It was Mosi. She was still wearing a bathrobe, and her feet were bare. Her expression was tight and tense. Richard smiled up at her and she rushed over, dropping gracefully to the floor and resting her head against his knee. Richard stroked her hair, careful to avoid the stars.

"Dear heart, what's wrong?"

"I'm scared. The future looks … it looks … so *big*."

Richard chuckled. "That's a good thing, you wouldn't want the future to be all small and cramped."

She looked up, those straight brows pulled into a frown. "You're laughing at me," she accused.

"A little."

"What if … what if we don't agree, fight?"

"You will, and then you'll make up and find agreement. He's a good man, Mosi. You'll make him a better one."

She gave him a mischievous smile. "What if he's the one who makes *me* better?"

"Impossible. You're perfect."

"You're biased."

"Guilty as charged." Richard stood and pulled her to her feet. "Now you need to get dressed. You're getting married in …" He shook back his sleeve and checked his watch. "Forty-three minutes."

She nodded and skipped off toward the door. Turning back she said, "You look very handsome in your tail coat, *Na sha dii*."

"What I look is short. Now, go on. Scoot."

She ran back, kissed him on the cheek and vanished down the hallway. Richard recovered his shoes, walked to the front door of the house and stepped outside just as an Uber pulled up. The young driver hopped out and went around to the trunk to pull out a small suitcase, but Richard only had eyes for the man emerging from the backseat.

It was his father.

The driver pulled up the handle on the suitcase and Robert grabbed it with one age spotted hand. The driver jumped back in his car and drove away. Robert, his dark blue eyes fixed on Richard, walked toward him, the wheels of the case chattering on the pavement of the driveway. The judge stopped at the foot of the steps leading up to the front door. With Richard standing at the top of the steps he and his father were eye-to-eye.

"May I attend?" It had been fifteen years since Richard had heard Robert's voice. It held a quaver now.

"You sent your regrets," Richard said.

"I changed my mind."

"I'm sure Amelia and Paul will be glad you came." His

voiced sounded hollow in his own ears.

"And you?" Robert asked.

"It's not my wedding." Richard stepped down, lowered the handle of the case and took the bag. Robert let him. Another change. He led his father through the front door.

"Attractive house," Robert remarked. "Yours?"

"No, it belongs to Senator Armandirez's parents." A grunt was the only response. "Are you hungry?"

"No, ate breakfast in Dallas. A glass of water would not be amiss however."

Richard led the older man to the kitchen. Franz recognized him though it had been years since Robert had been in New Mexico. He gave one of his little bows and said, "Judge Oort, how pleasant to see you again."

"My father would like a glass of water," Richard said to Josefina. Turning back to his father he added, "I need to—"

"Warn people?" Robert said in an undertone.

"I was going to say make sure there is a chair for you, but warn works too."

"Who's officiating?" his father asked.

"A friend who's a state Supreme Court judge and one of Mosi's cousins who is a representative of the Navajo Nation."

"No minister."

Richard didn't even bother to respond, just rolled his eyes, turned away, and walked out the back door. His stomach felt wobbly. He pressed a forearm against his aching gut. Thus had it ever been when confronted by his sire.

Damon took one look at his face and was immediately at his side. "What's wrong?"

"My father just arrived," Richard said tightly.

"Goddamn that old bastard. At least he didn't show up as you were walking her down the aisle." He paused then added, "I'll get the staff to add another chair, but where?"

Richard pressed a hand to his forehead. "I don't know. I suppose on the groom's side, with Amelia and Brent and Paul's friends."

"I'm surprised Pamela isn't sitting in the aisle between the two sides, straddling the uncomfortable middle, so to speak," Damon quipped.

Richard, who had spotted his sister coming up behind Damon, gave a half-hearted smile. "You are *so* going to regret saying that."

"Huh, what?"

Pamela slapped Damon on the upper arm. "You are such a jackass. I made my decision years ago, and you damn well know it. And yes, I stayed in touch with my sister because I love her, and—"

Damon held up his hands. "Whoa, whoa, it was a joke."

"It's my impression that jokes are supposed to be funny," Pamela said with a sniff.

"Ouch," Damon said, but gave her a smile.

"So, why are you both looking so stressed, apart from the obvious?"

"Papa's arrived," Richard said tensely.

If she was startled Pamela hid it well. "Well, we'll need to make arrangements. I'll put him next to Amelia, she's always been able to mollify him."

"Damn, I was hoping you'd put him next to me," Damon said. "Then I could have punched him out if I had to. Wouldn't put it past him to jump up at that *if any man can show cause* part."

The very thought had Richard wanting to vomit. Pamela again slapped Damon's arm. "Don't be an idiot. If there's one thing my father hates, it's a scene. He would never stoop to that."

Richard shook back his sleeve and checked his watch. "Just handle it." He glared at the row of perfectly aligned chairs. "It's going to ruin the symmetry," he groused.

"And now you're being an idiot," Pamela said sharply. "Nobody is going to be looking at the chairs. They'll be looking at Mosi and Paul."

Damon pulled Richard into a hug. "Relax. We're on a glide path now."

"Just hope it doesn't end in a crash," Richard muttered.

THE FRONT ROW was what Damon thought of as the original Scooby Gang—Angela, Joseph, Jeannette, Cross, Halia standing in for Kenntnis, and Pamela. All of them filtering in to take their seats while a solo cello played some classical thing. While Pamela might not have been there from the very beginning, she had, unlike her sister, been wise enough to accept the truth of the Old Ones, and she'd devoted herself completely to Richard and Lumina and then to Mosi when she had come into their lives.

He glanced over at Angela who was seated on his left. She was hugging a box of tissues. When she noticed his look, she glared and whispered, "I always cry at weddings."

"I may be dipping in myself," he whispered back.

"I thought you'd be walking her down the aisle too," Angela said.

"It's okay. I love her dearly, but what Mosi and Richard share ... well, it's something very special. It's better this way."

The rows behind them were filled with Mosi's relatives, and some of her friends from school who were not part of the wedding party. There was more of the Lumina staff, and the scientists who had known her since she was nine. The FBI agents who had worked so closely with them over the years. Jay Haskell and Sam Martin were doing their usual verbal sparring. There were police officers from the APD where both Richard and Damon had served before Lumina became their life.

Wangai slipped into the row directly behind Damon and leaned in. "All clear," she whispered. "Drones stationed to handle any press drones or something worse. Have guards at the front gate and on the road."

"Thanks, we sure as hell don't want a repeat of the graduation," Damon whispered back.

"*Nothing* is going to ruin this day," Wangai said, her expression fierce.

The guests were in place with the rustle of material and a few coughs. The cello solo became the full quartet playing another classical piece as Mosi's cousin, Haskeh Kaabah, and Judge Carbon-Gaul took their places. Paul and his groomsmen were also arranging themselves under the awning. Damon glanced at the program: Morricone, "Nella Fantasia."

A new piece began, sprightly and charming, and Mosi's attendants, looking like animated flowers in their pale peach gowns, started down the aisle. Damon once again availed himself of the program—Hoffstetter's "String Quartet No. 5 in F Major." Sam, seated behind him leaned in over his shoulder and whispered.

"Hey, be glad they aren't going with all the corny, cheesy stuff, 'A Thousand Years,' 'Love Is A Many Splendored Thing,' 'Signed, Sealed, Delivered.' At least this classical shit won't make you cringe."

The attendants had taken their places and that music faded away. Damon shushed Sam. Into that silence there was only the sound of a few muted coughs, the whisper of material on chairs, and then a single cello began to play. One by one the other instruments joined. This was a piece Damon did know because Richard loved it so much—Pachelbel's "Canon in D Major."

Mosi, her hand resting on Richard's arm, started down the aisle. The guests all stood, and Damon realized he was looking at his husband and their girl through a haze of tears. She wore an off-the-shoulder ivory gown with a slit that opened occasionally to reveal a slim, tanned leg. A delicate silver concho belt clasped her narrow waist, and around her throat was an exquisite six strand pearl choker, a matching pearl bracelet was clasped on her right wrist. The choker and bracelet had belonged to Richard's mother.

They reached the awning, and Richard placed his free hand over Mosi's and gave it a squeeze. He then gently laid her hand in Paul's and stepped back. Mosi handed her bouquet of cascading white and peach roses to Feray and turned to face Paul.

Richard settled into his chair next to Damon, giving him a soft smile as he swept his thumbs beneath Damon's eyes to wipe away the tears. They clasped hands and turned their attention to the couple at the front.

The ceremony was a mixture of Navajo and Anglo traditions, but Mosi and Paul had written their own vows. They were everything Damon would have expected from modern, progressive young people. There was the kiss, and finally that lone trumpeter was put to use along with the quartet as they performed the *Prince of Denmark's March*, as Mosi and Paul rushed down the aisle while the guest enthusiastically clapped. Then Cross made a complex gesture and fragrant flower petals began to rain down on the happy couple, attendants, and guests.

Richard leaned around Damon and said to Cross, "Magic? Really?"

The homeless god gave an unapologetic shrug. "Hey, if there was ever a moment for a little fucking magic, this was it." He huffed a sigh. "And now can we finally get some grub. Franz kept chasing me away from the buffet."

Damon shook his head. "Cross, my man, don't ever change."

✧   ✧   ✧

THE CLATTER OF forks on plates set a strange counterpoint to the band that had been hired to provide dance music. As Damon had said to him, *"Nobody knows how to dance the fucking minuet, so we need some modern music."* There had been toasts and the best man's speech—which unlike most was not cynical and unpleasant, but kind and charming.

Franz's cake was a thing of wonder and beauty, four layers high, with glistening white fondant icing, exquisite piped flowers, and ivy wreaths. Mosi and Paul cut the cake and fed each other bites, pieces were served to the guests, and the first dance was called. After Paul and Mosi danced, Brent took a turn with his new daughter-in-law while Paul danced with Mosi's cousin and then with Feray. Other couples began to drift onto the dance floor and Damon stood up and held out his hand to Richard.

"Wanna dance?"

Richard glanced over to where his father was sitting with Amelia and Pamela, and shook his head. "I don't think that's a good idea," he said quietly.

"To hell with that old bastard and what he might think. He's here only because you're nice, nicer than me."

"Would you really have sent him packing?" Richard asked as he laid his hand in Damon's and was pulled to his feet.

"Damn right I would have, but he ain't my dad, so it was your call."

"Well, Paul is his only grandchild. It seemed only right to allow him to attend." Richard glanced up at his husband. "Do you even know how to dance?"

Damon swung Richard into his arms, hand resting between his shoulder blades, the other gripping Richard's hand. "Pamela took me to school."

"Oh, I'm *so* sorry I missed that," Richard murmured.

"Yeah, she's not exactly the most patient of teachers."

"And why do you get to lead?"

"I'm taller," Damon replied. "And older."

They began to dance and Richard was surprised at Damon's skill. It seemed his sister had been a good teacher. Staring firmly at Damon's chest, Richard murmured, "Is he watching?"

"You know he is."

"Is he angry?"

"Who cares?" Damon released Richard's hand and pressed his hand to his ear where his discreet headset rested. "There's an Uber pulling in."

Richard craned around to see his father look up from his phone, stand, and start to leave. An aching lump filled his throat. "He's not even saying goodbye." He pulled free from Damon's restraining arm.

"Richard, don't!"

Backing away, Richard called, "I may never get to speak to him again if I don't."

✧   ✧   ✧

PAUL GAVE MOSI a quick kiss and nodded toward the luxury porta potty trailers parked behind a screening line of trees. "Need to go off load some of that champagne."

"Shall I alert the presses?" she smirked.

"You are such a brat," he said fondly.

Mosi watched him walk away, admiring the way his tail coat hugged his shoulders and tapered down to his slim waist and hips. In just a few hours they would fly to Italy and the Amalfi coast for their honeymoon. Her pleasant daydreaming shattered when she spotted Damon frozen in the center of the dance floor watching as Richard rushed out of the reception tent. Mosi reached Damon's side just as he called,

"Richard! Don't! Please!" Damon's voice then dropped to a murmur. "He'll just hurt you again."

Mosi gripped his arm. "What's going on?"

"That old bastard is leaving. Richard went after him."

Mosi gripped Damon's arm as he prepared to go in pursuit. "I'll handle it." She gathered up her skirt and almost ran out of the tent.

Richard and his father were standing in the driveway. The driver had just placed the small suitcase in the trunk, but was now looking nervously from one man to the other. He said something and retreated into the car.

Richard and his father stood facing each other in tense silence, then Robert said something. Mosi was too far away to hear, but there was something in their stances, the tension in their bodies, that had her holding back, fearing what might happen if she were to interrupt.

Richard answered, and suddenly tears began streaming down the older man's lined face. Richard stepped in close and pulled his father into a tight embrace. They stood like that for a long, long moment and Mosi slipped away before either of them could notice her.

Damon caught her as she reentered the tent. "Everything okay? Is Richard okay?"

"I ... I think so. I'm not sure what happened, but ... but ... it looked okay. I'm sure Richard will tell you."

"I'm gonna go find him." Damon left.

A moment later Paul had joined her. He studied her face. "You all right?"

She laid a hand on his cheek. "Yes, everything is surprisingly perfect."

"Not sure if that's commentary on me or"—he gestured around the tent—"this or something else."

"It's me being amazed that nothing catastrophic has happened."

"My dearest, darling wife, I'm going to do everything in my power to make sure that nothing catastrophic ever happens in your life again, and that we go for perfect all the time."

"It's not all on you. We'll do it as a team," Mosi said.

Paul bent and kissed her. "It's a deal … say isn't it about time for you to toss that bouquet and for us to make our farewells?" he asked.

Mosi glanced at the depleted buffet and the staff who were starting to clean up the used plates, cups, and utensils.

"I think it is. Most of the food is gone."

"I think Cross ate most of it," Paul said with a chuckle.

Mosi grabbed his hand, and they hurried to the head table to recover her bouquet, then went to find Angela. The older woman gave a narrow-eyed look at the cascade of roses. "So, it's bouquet scrum time?"

"I think it is."

"Are you and Pamela going to be in said scrum?" Paul teased. "I'd love to see my Aunt Pamela catch that and Jason look like a deer in headlights."

"It's more likely your *tia* runs the other way and I'll be right behind her."

"Hey, I can highly recommend marriage," Paul said and he kissed Mosi again. She felt herself blushing.

"*Chingada*, you two are so sweet it's giving me a toothache. Go! Go!" Angela shooed them away.

Angela began summoning the guests and herded the unmarried women into place. Paul caught Mosi around the waist and lifted her onto a table. Turning her back the crowd, she counted to three, and she tossed the bouquet over her shoulder. When she turned around she saw Fox standing with a poleaxed expression and the bouquet hanging from his hands.

Cross elbowed the scientist in the ribs. "Congratulations, dude."

"Maybe hold off on the felicitations. I don't even have a girlfriend," the Brit sighed.

"Hey, what about the garter toss?" One of Paul's groomsmen called.

"I think she's wearing a pistol instead," Paul called. "And tossing that probably wouldn't be a good idea."

There was laughter from the guests. Mosi smiled at Fox and gave him a wink. "Wanna go two for two?" she called, as she pulled back the side of her skirt to reveal the blue garter high on her thigh.

"Why not? It might improve my chances," he called back.

Paul knelt, and Mosi balanced with her hand on his shoulder, as he slipped off her high heeled pump and then the garter. Paul took his position and tossed it over his shoulder. Mosi watched with amusement as the men acted like it was a volleyball game and batted at the scrap of blue material until it landed with Fox.

Grinning, Fox held up the bouquet and garter, and announced. "Okay, ladies, who wants this asthmatic, nearsighted, theoretical physicist? I'm a real catch."

✧ ✧ ✧

IT WAS LATE, or early, depending on how you counted. The reception at the Armandirez house had finally wound down around ten o'clock, long after Mosi and Paul had departed for the airport. Richard's exhaustion had been evident, and Damon had brooked no argument that they were going home. Estevan had brought around the armored SUV and they'd made the drive back to the foot of the mountains.

Damon felt the tension in his husband's body as Richard lay almost on top of Damon, head pillowed on Damon's chest. Richard's soft hair was tickling Damon's chin. He didn't even need to ask what was bothering his spouse.

"Mosi's got the sword. Both she and Paul are armed. Wangai has people stationed in Positano to keep an eye on them."

"I know. I just … I miss her already," Richard said quietly. Damon drew in a breath, but Richard craned his head up before Damon could speak. "I know, I know, I'm the one who encouraged them to marry now and not wait. I wanted her to have someone before we left."

Silence felt like a heavy weight in the room then Damon asked, "So, what happened with your dad?"

"Nothing and everything. I told him I wanted to say goodbye and he asked me if what my daughter had told him was true."

"And did you immediately correct him that Mosi was your ward?" Damon asked with a chuckle.

"No, I let it go. But I told him yes, it was true, and … and Damon, he started to cry. I've never seen my father cry. It broke my heart. I couldn't think of anything to say, so I just hugged him." Richard paused and Damon held his breath. "And *he hugged me back!*"

There was equal parts wonder and joy in Richard's voice, and Damon felt tears pricking at the back of his eyelids that something so ordinary and mundane, that wouldn't be remarkable for ninety-nine percent of people in the world, meant so much to his husband.

"I'm glad, sweetie." Damon kissed the top of Richard's head.

"I needed to level the scales before … before … well, you know."

Damon snagged his fingers in the waistband of Richard's pajama bottoms and pulled them down. The material caught briefly on the puckered scar on Richard's right thigh where an assassin's bullet had nearly taken his life.

Damon rolled Richard onto his back, and tenderly kissed first the scar on the outside of his thigh, and then the matching scar on the inside of Richard's thigh. The soft gasp from his husband had Damon grinning. He raised his head and watched the blush wash across Richard's chest, up his neck, and into his cheeks.

"May as well do something useful since it's clear we ain't getting any sleep tonight."

Richard wrapped his arms around Damon's shoulders and pulled him down. "Don't let me go," he whispered.

"Never," Damon promised.

CHAPTER THIRTY-THREE

AMOR VINCIT OMNIA

IT WAS THE night of the launch of the ship that would carry Richard, Damon, Feray, and Cross to the Ark waiting in orbit. The Florida weather was warm and humid, but the thunderstorms from earlier in the day had ended, so there was nothing to delay the launch.

Mosi felt like she was living in one of the old movies about spaceflight—*The Right Stuff*, *Apollo 13*, *Interstellar*, *Gravity*, *The Martian*. The jitney waiting to take them to the gantry and the long ride up to the entrance to the crew capsule. The klieg lights reflecting off the skin of the rocket. And the knowledge that in the ready room behind them Richard, Damon, and Feray were climbing into their spacesuits. Cross, of course, needed no protection.

Paul gave her a sideways glance. "How you holding up?"

"Barely."

He put an arm around her waist and pulled her in close. "Fox will figure out a way to get them home."

"Assuming they survive the first firing of those fold engines. They've never been tested in real conditions."

"Given what Madoc said about their effect on the Old Ones' universes there was no way to do that," Paul reminded her.

"Forgive me, but tonight I'm not feeling real charitable toward those fuckers," Mosi answered.

The door to the crew quarters opened and one of the technicians beckoned to them to come in. Richard, Damon, and Feray were reclining in seats wearing their white spacesuits. Their helmets were on and the techs were running final checks on the suits. Cross was in his usual jeans, tennis shoes and faded T-shirt, and the flight techs in the room were giving him sideways glances.

"You're gonna give those flight techs a heart attack," Paul said to the homeless god.

Cross gave a shrug. "Ehh, I ain't riding up in that tin can. I'll just meet 'em there."

"Okay," one of the techs called. "We're good."

The three humans climbed out of the chairs, and opened the faceplates on their helmets. Richard, paler than ever, gripped Damon's arm with one gloved hand. "Where is Halia? She has to be with us. We need her."

Cross and Feray exchanged quick glances that Mosi couldn't quite interpret. Richard frowned up at Damon whose expression was so neutral that all Mosi's antennae immediately went up.

Damon patted Richard's hand. "Relax, she's probably going to do a Cross. Not like either of them need a ride."

"Yep, not being a fleshy, squishy thing has its advantages," Cross called.

The door to the crew quarters opened again and the driver of the jitney called, "We need to be moving. Still have to make final checks."

Richard gave a tense nod and stepped up to Mosi and

Paul. Taking one of their hands in each of his he said, "You take care of each other, okay?"

"Absolutely," Paul said.

Mosi was trying so hard not to cry that she couldn't utter a sound. Richard seemed to understand and gave her a gentle smile. "It's all right, dear heart. I know. No words are necessary."

Mosi lost the battle and a sob burst out of her. She hugged Richard tight, then groped blindly until Damon joined in the group hug. She finally forced words past the painful ache in her throat.

"I love you both *so much*. I'll never forget what you've given me."

Oddly, it was Damon who was crying. Richard was that steely calm that she had seen so often, right before they entered battle. He held her at arm's length and said, "Not as much as you've given me, Mosi Dezba Tsosie Van Gelder. I love you more than I can express. Now, go live your life and be happy." He stretched up and kissed her cheek. Mosi gave him one last, desperate hug.

They all left the room and she stood watching as the three humans climbed into the small bus and it drove away. Cross gave her a hearty pat on the shoulder.

"Relax, kiddo, you'll see 'em again." Then he splintered into a thousand shards of light and vanished.

Mosi frowned, trying to parse what that meant, when Paul pulled her attention away. "I'm never gonna get used to that," Paul said, shaking his head.

"If they succeed, you won't have to," Mosi answered quietly.

"You didn't tell him," Paul said softly.

"No. He needs to be totally focused. I can't be a distraction." She laid a hand on her belly.

"Don't you think it would give him some joy to know? I mean, he's going to … die …"

Mosi stared up at him, stricken, and she broke into a run, chasing after the small bus waving her arms wildly over her head. The vehicle came to a stop, the door slid open and Richard hopped out.

"Mosi, what is it? It will be okay. You'll be okay."

"I'm pregnant," she blurted.

His face lit with joy like sun melting away the clouds and he hugged her close. "Thank you. For telling me. It makes everything better."

"I was afraid it would hurt worse—"

"No, it makes everything even more clear. Now I must go."

She stepped back and Richard climbed back into the jitney. She heard Damon ask, "Everything okay?"

"Everything is perfect—"

The closing of the door cut off anything else, and the electric motor whined back to life.

Paul came up behind her. "Shall we get to Mission Control?"

"Yes, yes."

The big room was a hive of activity. Fox was there moving from station to station, his laptop balanced on one hand as he kept running calculations. On the large screen at the front of the room Mosi watched as the elevator shot up the side of the gantry. Mosi was pretty sure Damon was not going to like being on that catwalk that led to the crew capsule. The man was not fond of heights.

Family and friends were gathered in the viewing area. Present were Pamela, Angela, Dagmar, and Joseph. They had all spent time with Richard and Damon the night before. Pamela had a frozen, miserable expression because Jason had decided to become one of the passengers on the Ark as it would make its way to Trappist-1e—assuming nothing catastrophic happened when the fold engines came on line.

At one of their last family dinners before their departure to the Cape, Jason had broken the news. At Pamela's aghast expression he had said, *"I'm a journalist, this is humanity reaching for the stars. I have to go and record this."* Pamela had rather waspishly retorted that, *"No one will ever read your damn article since you'll be forty light-years from Earth, and no way back!"* She had then left the dinner table and the Lumina building. Mosi wasn't sure if they had ever reconciled, since Jason had been among the first group of potential colonists who had gone up to the Ark almost a month before.

On the big main screen, the rocket was starting to be fueled, the water vapor looking like white smoke. Mosi tried not to think about the tragic accidents that had also been part of manned spaceflight.

Fox appeared in the viewing area, his laptop still balanced precariously in one hand. "All right, I wanted to give you all a sort of play-by-play. After the Falcon docks with the Ark and everybody goes aboard, the crew on the Falcon will disengage and head back for a landing on the platform in the Indian Ocean. After they're well away, the boosters on the Ark will fire, sending it out of Earth's orbit. Once they are past the

Lagrange point, the solar sails will be deployed and they'll begin building speed as they head for the outer solar system.

"So, when do these fancy light speed engines kick in?" Angela asked.

"Not until they are well past the Moon and into relatively open space, so nothing very interesting is going to happen for seven days."

"But things could still go wrong, with the boosters or the sails, right?" Pamela asked.

"Well, yes, but those aren't my department. I just get to have ulcers over the fold engines. Really, really wish we could have had some trial runs and not just simulations." He switched the laptop into his other hand, and looked at his watch before checking the countdown clock on the main floor of the control center.

"Well, okay forty minutes to launch. I best get back down there."

The minutes seem to crawl past, then came the order piped in over the intercom. "Flight director, we are go for launch."

A few moments later the countdown began and a nausea that had nothing to do with her pregnancy roiled Mosi's stomach.

"Primary ignition," came the voice.

Smoke and flames erupted from the bottom of the rocket as the count reached one, and the disembodied voice called out, "Liftoff, liftoff of Falcon Heavy. Godspeed, Falcon, Godspeed."

"*Ad astra, Na sha dii*," she whispered, and watched until the ship dwindled into a glowing star and vanished. She turned and buried her face against Paul's chest. His arms closed around her and she tried not to cry.

✧   ✧   ✧

RICHARD, MAGNETIC BOOTS firmly clamped to the metal floor of the command center, stood with his head bowed, the hilt of the sword resting in his left hand. Cross stood next to him. For some reason zero gee had little effect on the Old One. The flight crew were strapped in their chairs, gazing at their screens.

Outside the large viewport was stygian blackness and the hard diamond light of distant stars. They were preparing to retract the solar sails and bring the fold engines online. Then, if the calculations and simulations were correct, the ship, its passengers, and crew would enter that not-space between the multiverses.

No one knew what that space would look like, and after Richard deployed the sword and closed the veils, the hope was that the ship would be kicked back out of folded space in relatively close proximity to Trappist-1e.

Richard hadn't wanted anyone to come on this journey apart from himself, Cross, and Halia—though it seemed the AI creature had decided against death since she had never appeared. Richard had fretted during the seven day journey to the jump point, despite Cross's assurances that both of them and the weapon would be enough to close the connection between the multiverses. So, Richard had put aside his worries and accepted that the Old One knew what he was talking about.

They would be sending a final message back to Earth before those engines did whatever it was they did, but they would not be waiting the seventeen minutes for a message to come back. Richard had made his peace, he just wanted it to be over. Intellectually, he knew that everyone lived in anticipation of death, but the past few years had been hard.

He was very aware of Damon, also in magnetic boots, standing close behind him. He had tried to convince Damon to remain in their cabin. Damon didn't need to witness whatever was going to happen to him as it happened, but his husband had refused.

"The vow says until death do us part. So I'm not parting. I'm gonna be there."

"Okay, this is it," he heard Eddie say.

Richard took a deep breath and drew the sword. The echoing chordal notes and overtones seemed to have even more power here in the depths of space. Richard briefly wondered if the weapon knew it had been drawn for the final time.

FOR AN INSTANT it felt like the space around Damon flexed and shivered, and his guts seemed to have been rearranged before settling back into place. He banished the nausea and opened his eyes to see that the view beyond the windows had become a roiling mess of grey wisps like a witch's hair from an old fairy tale.

Richard had looked to Cross and asked, "Shall we begin—" but he broke off abruptly when the elevator door to the command center opened and the arrival Damon had been waiting for entered.

Richard's eyes widened as he looked over and he stumbled a bit when his boots didn't release right away. "Rhiana," he breathed.

"Halia," the woman corrected.

Gone was the wizened figure from the hospital bed. Black hair cascaded down her back the way it had before the nursing home staff had finally cut it. The sharp planes of her face and tapered chin showed her relationship to her Old One progenitor, but her eyes were no longer a deep forest green, instead they were pools of swirling silver.

While Richard had been processing what he was seeing, Damon yanked his boots free and caught his husband around the waist, pulling Richard tight against his chest.

"No! No!" Richard cried, struggling to free himself. "You mustn't. Get back, wha …?" Richard gasped as Damon slid the needle into the side of his neck and injected the sedative.

"Like I told you, martyrdom is overrated," Damon whispered into Richard's ear.

"It … has to be … a … Paladin," his words were slurring, slowing as the drug hit his system. Richard slumped, the sword falling from his hand.

Halia caught the hilt before it struck the floor. "You have one," she said, just before Richard's eyes fluttered closed.

Sweeping her hand away, she drew the blade, and Damon released a breath he hadn't realized he had been holding. They'd had no way to test if Halia's rebuild of Rhiana's body as a Paladin had worked without tipping their hand. Thankfully it had. If it had been a soul-shaking sound before, this time when the sword was drawn, it felt like the very universe was singing.

Damon unlatched Richard's boots, swung the smaller man up into his arms and carried him over to an acceleration couch where he strapped in and held his spouse tightly in his arms. Feray, using handholds, floated over to him, and clinging to the back of the couch.

"We did it," she said softly.

Damon bent his head and kissed Richard's forehead. "We did. Now we just hope we can pull off the rest of it."

Damon looked over to where Halia had stepped in close to Cross. She laid a hand over his and said, "As promised all those centuries ago, I give you the release you crave." There was a deep echoing timbre in her voice that reminded Damon of Kenntnis.

The Old One's face slumped into an expression of utter gratitude. "Thank you," he said thickly.

Halia-Rhiana-Kenntnis held out the hand holding the sword. "Shall we do this together, old friend?"

Cross laid his hand over hers where it gripped the hilt. Curling star fire ran up the space dark blade and began to wrap itself around their bodies. Damon had never seen it so bright or thick.

"As it began, so it ends," Cross whispered.

Halia-Rhiana-Kenntnis gazed out at the swirling, terrifying nothingness beyond the window. *What though the dark come down, there is a truth to know. Only when dark comes down can the little ship find the star.*

It sounded like a quote, but Damon didn't know from what. And then Halia-Rhiana-Kenntnis set the point of the sword to weaving in a complete pattern that seemed to be pulling in wisps of the grey mess outside. Some of the crew cried out in alarm as the grey wrapped itself around the figures of the woman and the homeless god.

Cross's body began to coruscate into its rainbow of colors, and Halia-Rhiana-Kenntnis began to glow silver as her body also disintegrated into diamond bright shards of silver light. There was a blinding flash that elicited more cries from those assembled, and a final massive musical chord hung in the air as the humans tried to clear eyes blinded by the brilliance of that final burst of power.

Halia, Cross, and the sword were gone.

The ship gave a shudder and a jerk, and beyond the window the stars blinked back to life. In the far distance, remote and beautiful, was a red dwarf star. And Damon knew that somewhere in the darkness floated the world that would be their new home.

Damon bent and pressed another kiss against Richard's forehead and then each eyelid, because all the home he needed was resting in his arms.

EPILOGUE

I Will Give You The Stars

T HE ROAR OF engines brought Richard running out of the small police station. Shading his eyes he gazed up. The lander was a silver and white arrow against the red sky. People were pouring out of homes, shops and offices. Confused, concerned, and excited chatter was all around him. A number of the young children were crying. It had been five years since any of the landers that had brought them down to this world had enough fuel for a return to the Ark, so this new sound was terrifying for the little ones.

The lander was heading north well away from the small settlement, the large solar array and the fields and orchards. Richard pulled Odyssey's head out of his feed bag, and quickly bridled and saddled the stallion. Feray was strapping her and Eddie's twin girls in the cycle rickshaw. People were grabbing bikes, horses and electric golf carts and streaming toward the now descending ship.

Richard met Damon—twigs and leaves in his grey hair from pruning the young trees in the orchard—and kicked his foot out of the stirrup. Damon wedged a foot into the stirrup and levered himself onto the back of the young horse behind Richard.

"Do you think the Brit kid solved the light speed problem?" Damon asked, his breath tickling Richard's ear.

"That or it's aliens," Richard answered as he urged the horse into a canter.

They rode past the lake and the thundering waterfalls to see Eddie and his hydroelectric team clambering into a boat and start rowing through the pink tinged spume toward the shore nearest where the lander had settled.

The vegetation on Ümit burned with a particular sweet, spicy scent that reminded Richard of the piñon fires from home, and for an instant he felt a visceral flash of homesickness. The crowd swelled as people waited impatiently for the ground to cool enough for those aboard the lander to exit.

Damon slid off and Richard quickly dismounted. He handed the reins to six year old Carlito. The child loved the horses and had a way with them.

Twining his fingers through Damon's, Richard gave his husband's hand a hard squeeze. They walked toward the lander as the hatch finally cycled open and a ramp extended. There was a bit of a scrum in the doorway when Fox barreled past Pamela almost knocking her off her feet. Eddie came charging through the waiting crowd to grab the Brit in a bear hug. The scientist still wore glasses, but he had filled out and now sported a full beard.

"*My dude*, you did it. *How* did you do it?" Eddie demanded.

"Generated worm holes. We're still folding space, but just our own space. Pick a destination, fire up—"

"Would you *move?*" Pamela huffed as she shoved Fox aside. The two scientists didn't even notice, just moved away while incomprehensible words and formula trailed after them like scientific confetti.

Pamela marched up to Richard, her eyes flicking down to the gold badge clipped on his belt. She gestured at it. "So back where you started? And did you really name the settlement Albuquerque?"

"Nice to see you too. And no, it's called *Kibou*, and we don't have the mining or smelting capability to make a new badge, so I use my old one."

Pamela spotted Jason in the crowd and glared at him. "Well, I see *you're* still around. You ever write that ground-breaking article?"

"Yeah, but now I apparently have a way to get my series published in a periodical that has a somewhat bigger circulation than just the colony." He stepped in close and gave Pamela a kiss on the cheek. She huffed, but didn't pull away when he slipped an arm around her waist.

Richard interrupted what passed for a tender moment when it came to Pamela. "Mosi and Paul are they well? The baby? Well, I guess not a baby now after nine years."

"Patience, they had a little situation to deal with," Pamela said.

"They're here?"

"Patience! Things got turbulent on the way down." Pamela reacted to his expression. "It's nothing serious."

Richard's stomach was doing backflips as he tried to quell his anxiety and excitement. Forcing a neutral tone he asked, "Papa?"

"Passed away three years ago."

Before Richard could fully process that, Mosi and Paul emerged holding the hands of a little boy with rich brown hair and brown eyes. Richard compartmentalized the news about his father and shoved it aside. Instead, he studied the beautiful child before him. The boy would be close to the same age as Mosi when Richard had first met her.

Richard transferred his gaze to Mosi and greedily registered every plane of her beloved face. He had parted from a young woman, what faced him now was an elegant woman of thirty-three. Richard's eyes met Mosi's, and hers were suddenly glistening with unshed tears.

"I didn't expect to find you here." Mosi's voice was hoarse with emotion.

"I didn't expect to be here." Richard jerked a thumb toward Damon. "Blame him."

"I'd rather kiss him," Mosi shot back. She knelt next to her son. "Nayati, this is Richard, your godfather. *Na sha dii*, this is Nayati Richard Tsosie van Gelder."

Richard leaned down. "I am so very pleased to meet you, Nayati."

The boy studied Richard in that grave way which even more forcibly reminded him of the first time he had met Mosi. Nayati switched his gaze to look up at his mother and asked, "Is this the man who saved you from the monsters, Mama?"

"Yes. And not just me. Many, many people. In fact, all the people in the world."

Richard shook his head. "No, since I'm standing here, that clearly wasn't me. The honor belongs to a being of light who thought humanity was worth saving, and an alien creature who learned to love." Richard paused and gave Damon a look filled with all the love that he didn't have the words to express. "And a husband who—"

"Loved you too much to lose you."

"Spill," Paul said. "How did you pull it off? And how did you convince Richard?" he asked Damon.

"Didn't tell him. 'Cause I knew he'd kick up a fuss. Me, Cross, Halia, and Feray hatched a plan, but I didn't tell folks because Richard's too good at picking up on cues." Damon glanced at Mosi. "I'm sorry, hon, but I needed you honestly grieving, not trying to fake it."

"I could have kept the secret," Mosi objected. She then kissed Damon on the cheek. "But I forgive you because you saved him."

"Despite himself," Damon said, and then laughed when Richard glared.

An unofficial holiday was declared and the entire colony gathered for a cookout. There was music, and laughter, and conversations. Richard found it interesting that the Ümit colonists were less interested in hearing news from Earth and more inclined to talk about what they had accomplished in this new world and their future plans for the colony. The only time they really touched on Earth was to ask if they could send back a list of items that would help accomplish those goals. Clearly most of the colony's citizens were not interested in a return home.

It was now past midnight, and his family was gathered around the dining room table in his and Damon's small, rustic, stone house. Nayati had been tucked into bed hours before, and they were in that space where everyone was tired, but no one wanted the moment to end. Damon tilted the last bottle of wine that had been brought from Earth all those years ago, and surveyed the remaining contents.

"Just enough left for all of us to have a final sip and a toast," he said. People held out their glasses.

Pamela studied the grey, bubbled surface of her glass. "I take it you didn't bring these from home."

"No, glass isn't that hard to make," Damon replied.

"It's like you were all playing a game of *Civilization*," Paul remarked. "Building up a society from scratch."

"Well, we did have a jump on it since we didn't have to develop technology," Richard said.

"Place does seem stable and sustainable," Pamela said.

"Yeah, we're not going to be Jamestown," Jason said. "So, you want to stay and help build this new society?"

"Do I look like the hearty, pioneer-woman type?" Pamela responded.

Laughter bounced around the table and Richard's gaze met Mosi's. "Say it," he urged.

She huffed out a sigh and gave a brief eye roll. "Even after all this time you can read me this easily?" Richard just smiled and shrugged. Damon gave a crow of delight.

"See, Mosi. I *told* you he'd rumble you."

"All right, fine, you were right not to tell me. But *Na sha dii*, what are you going to do now? The stars will always be there for the children of Earth, but where are *you* going to be? Where do you want to be?"

Richard sat with that for few moments. "Well," he said slowly. "I didn't expect to be alive, and since we all assumed this was a one way trip ... I ... I hadn't really thought about it. Let me ask you a question: We've achieved Kenntnis's promise—we have the stars—but have we achieved the other part? Have we followed his path?"

Paul, Mosi, and Pamela exchanged glances. Mosi drew in a deep breath. "Not fully. There are still wars and violence, greed and bigotry. Most of the Old Ones are gone, but our intrinsic nature hasn't changed. Like you always said, we didn't climb out of the trees all that long ago. Still, all we can do is strive to be better." She laid her hand over Richard's "I think we probably still need a Paladin with a gold shield to help with that. And I'd like Nayati to know both his godparents."

Silence held the room as everyone waited for his answer. Richard looked to Damon who just gave a short nod and said, "Where you go, I go."

Richard looked from beloved face to beloved face. He reached out and gathered Damon and Mosi's hands in each of his. One by one the people around the table clasped hands.

"We've achieved the stars, but we need to make sure we're worthy of them. Let's go home and continue the work."

IF YOU LIKED ...

If you liked *To Reign in Heaven* you might also enjoy:
Lucifer's War
Morningstar's Heir
One Fatal Tree

ABOUT THE AUTHOR

Melinda M. Snodgrass studied opera at the Conservatory of Vienna, graduated Magna cum Laude from U.N.M. with a degree in history, and went on to Law School. After 3 years as a lawyer she realized she hated lawyers and turned to writing.

In 1988 she accepted a job on Star Trek: The Next Generation and began her Hollywood career where she has worked on staff on numerous shows and has written television pilots and feature films. She currently has two television series in active development.

In the prose world she writes for and co-edits the shared world anthology series Wild Cards with George R. R. Martin.

In addition, she writes her own novels. She is working on a fourth novel in the Carolingian series and a fourth novel for her White Fang Law series.

For fun she rides her dressage horse, plays video games and spends a lot of time in the gym. (Or she did before there was a pandemic).

BOOK CLUB QUESTIONS

1. There was a large time jump between the third book in the series and this final novel. What might be the reasons for using time jumps? Do you like them?

2. In a series the author is always trying to balance not boring old readers, but also explain things for a newer reader. Do you think the author succeeded in balancing those two imperatives?

3. Did the author effectively balance the scenes between the new younger characters and the older established characters?

4. Provide information about a particular place, in this case New Mexico can be challenging. The author chose to use dialogue to provide that information. Did you like that or would you have preferred to learn this in the narrative?

5. Did you share Damon's disappointment that Richard took his nephew to view the dead bodies? Did you think it was out of character for Richard or was his anger justified?

6. Was there enough foreshadowing that Paul wasn't what he seemed, or did you want more hints?

7. Did you suspect it was an artificial intelligence when Fox's computer began running on its own or when the translation was provided?

8. Discuss how Barrington and Wannamake represent two sides of the same coin. How are they similar despite coming from different philosophical traditions.

9. Does it seem realistic that an A.I. would be completely seeped in all the nooks and crannies of the internet and social media?

10. Did you read the A.I. choosing the name Halia as foreshadowing of what was to come?

11. Do you think Barrington was right to look for a way to destroy all the Old Ones? It would have left Fox's light speed theory intact.

12. When did you start to suspect that Mosi was going to fall in love with Paul? Did it feel earned and natural?

13. Would you have rather seen Mosi end up with Fox rather than Paul?

14. Would you have preferred to be in on Damon, Cross's and Halia's plan to save Richard or did you like it coming as a surprise?

15. Was there enough foreshadowing about how Rhiana's body could be repurposed to become a Paladin?

16. Sometimes an epilogue feels superfluous. Did it feel like proper closure to have the epilogue, or would you have been all right just ending the book with the closing of the veils between the multiverses?

17. The final book in a series always has a lot of plot threads that need to be knitted into the narrative. Now that you've read the entire series do you think the author succeeded in tying up those loose ends in a satisfying way?

18. In the first book Kenntnis/Prometheus/Lucifer tells Richard that if humans follow his path, he will give us the stars. That was the promise the author made to readers. Was that promise kept in a satisfying way?

Other Titles by
Melinda M. Snodgrass

Circuit series:
Circuit
Circuit Breaker
Final Circuit
Queen's Gambit Declined

The Edge series:
The Edge of Reason
The Edge of Ruin
The Edge of Dawn

The Imperials Saga:
The High Ground
In Evil Times
The Hidden World
The Currency of War
The Thucydides Trap

White Fang Law:
This Case is Gonna Kill Me, Book 1
Box Office Poison, Book 2
Publish and Perish, Book 3